DEAD DOCKET

FORGE BOOKS BY MITCHELL GRAHAM

Majestic Descending
Dead Docket

DEAD DOCKET

MITCHELL GRAHAM

A TOM DOHERTY ASSOCIATES BOOK
NEW YORK

This is a work of fiction. All of the characters, organizations, and events portrayed in this novel are either products of the author's imagination or are used fictitiously.

DEAD DOCKET

A Forge Book
Published by Tom Doherty Associates, LLC
175 Fifth Avenue
New York, NY 10010

www.tor-forge.com

Forge® is a registered trademark of Tom Doherty Associates, LLC.

Library of Congress Cataloging-in-Publication Data

Graham, Mitchell.
Dead docket / Mitchell Graham. — 1st hardcover ed.
  p. cm.
"A Tom Doherty Associates book."
ISBN-13: 978-0-7653-2245-6
ISBN-10: 0-7653-2245-5
I. Title.
PS3607.R346D43 2009
813'.6—dc22

2009003159

First Edition: July 2009

Printed in the United States of America

0 9 8 7 6 5 4 3 2 1

ACKNOWLEDGMENTS

WHILE writers take all the credit for what they publish, the real truth, being honest with one's self, is that the crafting of a novel is a team effort. It's as simple as that. Being more fortunate than most, I have had the good fortune to have in my corner, my editor and friend, Claire Eddy, and the wonderful team at Forge. A big tip of the hat goes to Kristin Sevick, who has always been there when I needed her. Also, a big note of thanks to Jack Dann, a brilliant author in his own right and my good friend, who made the whole venture possible.

DEAD DOCKET

PROLOGUE

Cloudland Canyon, Georgia

They were coming.

He could see their flashlight beams moving in the darkness as they searched the lower trail for him. He was nearly blind from exhaustion, but had been lucky so far. What he had to do might take another hour at most, but there was still enough time—barely. The searchers were getting closer, calling their names in the night.

Thirty minutes earlier, he had opened the trunk of his car and carefully lifted the girl out. Oddly, she put up no resistance or struggle. She simply stared at him. The task was harder than he thought . . . infinitely harder. For the first hundred yards he carried her along a rough trail cut into the mountain's side. Even in daylight it would have been difficult to negotiate, but in the dark it was far worse. The higher up they went, the more difficult it became as the incline steepened. Moisture from the cool night air clung to the ground, making the rocks slippery and the footing treacherous.

Andre Rostov stopped to drag some air into his lungs. He needed to think. To his left was a single dirt track that split off from the main trail and angled sharply up the canyon wall. That had to be it. In fifteen minutes they would be at the canyon rim.

His plan had been hastily put together and its timing was hurried, but there was little choice in the matter. They were coming.

"*Sarah . . . Andre?*" the voices called in the darkness.

Andre froze. The people looking for them were a hundred feet below. If he pushed himself a little harder, he could definitely reach the spot. Tree roots reached out, threatening to snag his ankles as he fought his way up the slope. Still the girl made no sound. Her eyes remained fixed on him in silent accusation. Thorns tore at his clothing.

His shoulders were aching so badly the pain was nearly unbearable, yet he forced his feet to move, one step at a time. His breath was coming in ragged gasps now.

Love could make a person do strange things. It was funny how his mind worked at a time like this. He was in love with Sarah; there was no question about it. When they were apart he felt empty and alone. Being with her made him feel alive. Soon they would be together . . . forever.

"Just a little more," he whispered.

The girl made no response, though he could feel her eyes on him.

When his feet finally touched the packed dirt that marked the upper trail, he stopped to rest again. His lungs were burning.

"*Sarah . . . Andre?*" the voices called once more.

They were closer now.

Nearby, an owl hooted in a gnarled tree and caused him to jump. For one brief moment, a pair of luminous gold eyes shone back at him in the darkness. They were gone a second later.

Hurry! His mind shouted.

Lifting her up again, Andre staggered forward, constantly checking over his shoulder for the searchers. Through a spiderweb of branches he could see their flashlights sweeping the ground as they moved up the path. The place he wanted was less than fifty yards away. He would make it; he was sure of that now.

"*Sarah . . . Andre?*"

On the verge of exhaustion, Andre forced himself to drag her the last twenty yards to the canyon's rim. Far below, a waterfall cascaded over slate and sandstone into an ink-black pool. A friend once mentioned that it had a name, but he couldn't remember what it was now. His arms were so heavy he could barely move them. Inch by inch he drew closer to the ledge.

"Everything will be all right," he whispered

Those were the last words he spoke to her.

She made no sound or cry for help as her body tumbled through the air, turning over and over in slow motion. After what seemed like an eternity, a dull thud reached his ears when she struck the rocks below.

"Dear God, what have I done?" he whispered to himself.

Andre squeezed his eyes shut and stood there for almost a full minute, his heart pounding rapidly in his chest. Then he turned and started walking toward the lights.

PART I

THE MISSING FILE

ONE

DELANEY

THE telephone startled me when it rang. I was in the process of rereading a student's answer to my evidence exam and it still made no sense. I tossed the paper down and pressed the intercom button.

"Yes?"

"Professor Delaney, there's a police officer and another gentleman here to see you," my secretary said.

"Really?"

"Yes, sir," Maria continued. "They'd like to know if you have a moment. I explained we're in the middle of exams week and that you're very busy."

The underlying message was that neither had an appointment. *Subtlety* and *Maria* do not often appear in the same sentence together. She's a good secretary, very good as a matter of fact, but she tends to be overprotective, at least where I'm concerned. One of her talents is deflecting unannounced visitors, which she was trying to do now. My lioness at the gate.

Dropping by without an appointment isn't kosher in Maria's view. Somehow it offends her sense of propriety. This is all the more true when exams roll around and our faculty is under pressure to get their grades in on time. The last thing we'd want is to delay dumping another batch of lawyers on the world.

I could have asked whoever was outside to come back later, but being a former cop, I tend to make allowances. There's no law that says I have to, but the fraternity is a small one and I'm not that far removed from it.

"No problem," I replied. "I'll be right out."

A number of colleagues have jumped on me for doing this. In

their view it's more dignified to have your secretary show people in, as opposed to a professor going out to get them. It's a needless pretense, but to each his own.

The police officer and his companion were sitting side by side on our reception room couch when I came through the door. They both stood up at the same time. I recognized them immediately.

Frank O'Connor shook my hand and following it with a hug. So did his brother, Nick. Twenty years earlier, Frank had been my father's partner—that is, until a drunk driver on the Cross Bronx Expressway ended their relationship. The driver crossed the centerline and slammed into my dad's car, killing him.

I hadn't seen much of the O'Connors over the past year. Every now and then we would run into each other, but our relationship wasn't what you'd call close anymore. From the street clothes and the chest holster peeking out from under his suit jacket, I guessed that Frank still carried a detective's shield. Nick, the man in uniform, held the rank of deputy chief with the department and presided over Manhattan South.

"Well, this is an unexpected surprise. What's up, fellas?"

"We just stopped by to talk if you have a minute," Frank said.

I didn't, but I told them it was no problem.

I noted their expressions were uncharacteristically somber, indicating the visit was something more than just social. At the same time I also noticed that Frank hadn't shaved. He looked about a half day beyond a five o'clock shadow, which was unusual from what I remembered of the man.

"Maria . . . this is Frank and Nick O'Connor. Frank and my dad were partners."

"Oh, pleased to meet you," Maria said, warming a little. "You should have told me you knew Professor Delaney."

"Sorry," Frank said. "Pleased to meet you, too, ma'am."

Nick responded in a similar manner. Since everyone was pleased to meet each other, I motioned for them to follow me into my office.

"How about some coffee?" I asked before we left the reception area.

"Sure, Johnny, if it wouldn't be too much trouble," Frank said.

Nick passed. Maria was out of her chair in a flash and beat me to the pot before I could reach it. "*I'll* bring it in, Professor," she said. "How do you take it, Officer?"

"A little milk and sugar, please."

"She probably saved your life," I told Frank. "I'm not known for my coffee skills around here."

By professorial standards, my office isn't large. This is because I'm relatively new to John Jay's faculty, having only taught at the law college for the past eight years. We have an unwritten rule that says the longer you stay, the bigger your office. It's pretty much the same in most places: you pay your dues and move up the pecking order. My room is about twelve feet square and contains a desk and two wooden chairs for guests. I also have a leather couch, which was unusable at the moment since it was piled high with ungraded exam papers. I pointed Frank and Nick to the chairs.

Opposite the couch is a bookshelf lined with copies of the United States Code and the New York State Statutes. If you look closely, you'll also see a number of texts on evidence and forensic studies, the subjects I teach.

I sat on the front edge of my desk rather than behind it, and we made small talk until Maria showed up with the coffee. After handing Frank his cup, she gave me a knowing sort of look and said she would hold my calls. Apparently I wasn't the only one blessed with intuition.

"So, how can I help you?" I asked when the door closed.

Frank took a deep breath and let it out. "John, Sarah was killed in a camping accident last week."

My stomach dropped several inches at the words. Sarah was Frank's daughter and had been in my evidence class the preceding year. She was a bright, decent kid with a bubbly personality. When the term ended, she had transferred to Emory University's law school in Atlanta.

"Jesus Christ, Frank. I'm so sorry. How did it happen?"

"She, uh . . ."

Frank's voice faltered and he looked out the window. His brother placed a consoling hand on his back and finished the sentence for him.

"Sarah and some friends were camping at a place called Cloudland

Canyon. It's somewhere in north Georgia. The sheriff's department told us that she was out walking at night and went over a cliff."

I was taken aback by the news and shook my head in disbelief. What do you say in a situation like that? What does anyone say? A lawyer's stock-in-trade are his words and I searched for the right ones, but all I could manage was to repeat how sorry I was. It wasn't much, but it was true. I'd always liked Sarah.

"Look, if there's anything I can do . . ."

"Yeah," Frank said. His eyes were red-rimmed when he turned back to me. "Lucille would have come too," he explained, "but she's still pretty broken up. You understand."

"Sure, sure," I said quickly. "She wouldn't be human if she wasn't." Lucille was Frank's wife. "The last I heard, Sarah got some sort of scholarship, isn't that right?"

It was small talk and I was just trying to relieve the awkwardness of the moment.

Frank nodded. He was a big man in his late fifties, still hard and fit, the old school pull-yourself-up-by-your-bootstraps type.

"It's called the Hoch-Halpern Endowment. Sarah applied for it the end of last term. We wanted her to stay in New York of course, but law school tuition can get pretty steep. I guess you know that."

"I meant what I said, Frank. If there's anything I can do for you or the family, just ask."

The brothers looked at each other and I saw a silent communication pass between them.

"Johnny, we haven't had a lot of contact with lawyers over the years," Nick said. "Mike Franklin at the Forty-third suggested we give you a call. He said you'd know what to do as far as the legal stuff is concerned. We don't have a clue where to start. Sarah was a real fan of yours. It was always Professor Delaney this and Professor Delaney that. She . . . she was so excited about studying law."

Like his brother, Nick broke off what he was saying and stared down at his feet until he composed himself. I could see they were both having a rough time and my heart went out to them. The reason for their visit was now obvious. It wasn't that I was close to the O'Connors. I wasn't. After I retired from the force and went over to the dark side, as they say, we'd only seen each other sporadically. The word *retired* is being used tongue in cheek here. Truth is, my *retirement* was hastened by three bullets I took to the chest, but that's another story. The bottom line is that cops stick with cops. It's pretty much like having an extended family.

"No problem," I heard myself say. "I'll be happy to look into it, though you need to understand I'm not an expert in this area of the law. We might need to retain an estate attorney if it's over my head. You said Sarah died in Georgia?"

"Right," Frank said. "Does that make a difference?"

"It could, particularly if she established residence there. I'll check and find out. Do either of you know if she had a will?"

Frank shrugged. "I'm not sure. Isn't that something all law students do?"

"Not quite." I smiled. "It's a fifty-fifty shot at best. Maybe not even that good. A lot depends on whether she did or didn't. I have a friend who practices law in Atlanta. Is it all right if I give her a call and get some advice on the best way to proceed?"

"No problem," Frank said. "We'll put the whole thing in your hands. Just keep us informed." He paused for a moment and looked as if he were searching for the right words. "Listen Johnny, I don't have a lot of money, but if you tell me what this'll cost, I'll write out a check."

I waved him off when he took out his checkbook. Unwritten rule one: You don't charge partners when they ask for help. Unwritten rule two: Rule one applies to your father's partners.

"We can talk about that later. Right now, I don't even know if I can help. Like I said, this isn't my area of expertise. If the situation's good I'll tell you and if it's bad I'll tell you. Either way you'll have the truth, okay?"

"Okay," Frank replied.

I moved a pile of test papers on my desk aside and grabbed a yellow legal pad. "I'd better take down some basic information."

I asked the brothers to provide me with Sarah's social security number, copies of her birth certificate, and her driver's license.

To be honest, I wasn't happy about having the problem dumped in my lap. I'm not proud to say that. It was a headache I didn't need just then, plus I was out of my depth. As a general rule, I don't jump into a situation unless I know what I'm letting myself in for. But I'd made the offer and we had history together. After twenty minutes I exhausted most of what I remembered regarding wills and estates, which wasn't all that extensive. Good-byes were said and I promised to get in touch with them as soon as I had more information.

TWO

DELANEY

WHEN they were gone, my thoughts turned to Sarah O'Connor. She had been a standout in our school—a girl with brains, looks, and a decent personality. I remembered how hard she had worked in my class, never once playing the old-friend-of-the-family card. I respected her for that, and the A she made was strictly on her own. For her to die so young and so senselessly was a shock.

I sat back in my chair and rubbed my face with my hands, then picked up the phone and punched a button on the intercom. I have one of those twenty-button sets. Somewhere along the line, the insert that listed the numbers for the other teachers in my department had disappeared from the base unit and maintenance had never gotten around to replacing it. I held my breath as the phone rang.

"Yes?" a voice answered.

"Irwin, it's John. Do you have a minute?"

"Of course. What can I do for you?"

"I need to see you about a problem. Is now a good time?"

"Absolutely."

Irwin Zeller is a slightly built man with a head of curly brown hair. He had recently turned fifty and he was six years my senior. He had been teaching law at John Jay for the past two decades. The owlish appearance he projected was accentuated by a pair of thick glasses and a tendency to blink when he was considering a problem. Several years earlier, when my predecessor unexpectedly died of a heart attack, Irwin was the one who recommended me for the teaching position I now hold.

His office was more opulent than mine. A pair of oriental rugs divided the room into a work area and a visitor's area. A burgundy

leather couch with rolled arms sat along the left wall and looked dignified against the wood paneling.

"It's open," Irwin called out when I knocked.

I came in and we shook hands.

"Am I catching you at a bad time?"

"Not at all. I'm just working on an appellate brief for Maybery,
Halter, and Troutman, but it's not due until later this week. What's
the problem?"

My eyes traveled to a pile of papers stacked on an old-fashioned
rolltop desk, roughly twice the size of mine. Irwin's window faces the
school's quadrangle. Mine faces a brick wall.

I took a few minutes to bring my friend up to speed on the situation with Sarah O'Connor. While I was speaking, Irwin got up and
walked over to a bookcase with a glass enclosure, removed a copy of
our school's yearbook, and began flipping through it. He located the
part that contained photographs of last year's freshman class and ran
his finger down the page until he came to Sarah's picture.

"Awful," he said, shaking his head. "Just awful. I don't think she
was in any of my classes. She was certainly an attractive girl."

He turned the book around so I could see. Sarah's large brown
eyes stared back at me. It was the kind of face the camera loved, as
photographers say.

I nodded my agreement. "Her family's pretty broken up."

Irwin shook his head again in sympathy. "What a shame. So . . .
I'm guessing they've asked you to probate her will?"

"Assuming she has one. The problem is, I've never done a will
probate before. That's why I'm here. I need to see what I've let myself in for."

"It's all pretty boilerplate. I've got everything you'll need."

Irwin went to a filing cabinet at the corner of the room and retrieved three eight-by-ten manila envelopes.

"This is to probate a will with assets under five thousand dollars,"
he said, handing me the first envelope. "You'll find all the forms there."

I hefted it a couple of times and looked at him.

"Each one has a set of instructions," he continued. "I don't know
how much money the girl had, but I can't imagine a law student's
estate being very large."

He handed me the second envelope.

"On the chance that it's over five thousand dollars, you'll use these forms. They're for standard estates. This last package contains an application for Letters of Administration, if she died without a will."

"Pretty impressive, Irwin. I have trouble finding my car keys."

"Part of the advantage of doing this for twenty years," he said with a smile. "I'll be tied up on this brief until Thursday. If you get bogged down, call me and I'll try to guide you through the maze."

"I will. Looks like I've got my homework for the evening."

"It's not that hard, John. Why don't you stop by for dinner and we'll spend a little time going through everything? Charlotte's cooking a pot roast and she always makes more than we can eat."

Irwin was a good man, but I'd already imposed enough; plus there was still that pile of test papers waiting for me back in my office.

"Thanks, I'll take a rain check. If I don't get my exams in by Monday, Babs Ramsey will have my head on a platter. Now I have this to deal with," I said, indicating the envelopes he had just given me.

"Well, it's nice of you to help," he said, patting me on the arm. "Not to add to your workload, but here's something else you might want to glance over."

Irwin pulled a paperbound book off one of his shelves and handed it to me.

"I put this together two years ago, for one of the Bar's continuing education seminars. The law hasn't changed. It will take you through the steps one by one."

"Probate for Dummies," I said, pretending to read the title.

Irwin smiled and adjusted his glasses. "The first thing you should do is inventory the girl's possessions and secure them."

I glanced at the book again. It was about three inches thick. The spine was held together by a plastic fastener.

"Thanks, buddy. I'll give you a call after I get lost."

"Unlikely. You're much too methodical a fellow, John. I wish more of our colleagues were."

WITH a little help from Maria, I scrounged up a cardboard box and piled my exams into it. Irwin's book went on top along with the three packages he had given me. My agenda for the weekend was now set, so I said good-bye and headed for the teacher's parking lot on Twelfth Avenue.

The white 1960 Jaguar XK-150S was still where I'd left it. Considering the neighborhood this always comes as a mild surprise. One day I half expected to find the spot empty or the car sitting up on crates. Hell's Kitchen isn't what it used to be in the old days. The area is making a comeback, but it's not there yet. On the street side of the fence was a girl in a hot pink miniskirt, fishnet stockings, and impossibly high heels. Her shoes were made of clear plastic. She was leaning into a car, talking with the driver. A short distance away, a tall black man lounged against a Cadillac Escalade with chrome spinner wheels, watching the transaction. The gold chains and other jewelry he was wearing nearly caused me to squint. He looked like a poster child for Pimps R Us.

The girl couldn't have been more than sixteen. It just breaks your heart to see someone that young being swallowed up by the streets. Maybe I was reading too much into the scene, profiling as they say. It's not politically correct, but living in the real world helps. I shook my head and turned away.

To my surprise, I saw two coeds walking toward me.

"Hi, Professor Delaney," Alexis Carter said, flashing me a big smile.

"Hey, Professor," her companion echoed, a bit less enthusiastically.

"Ladies . . . to what do I owe the honor of this visit?" I asked, opening my trunk and putting the box inside.

"I wanted to show Melissa your car," Alexis said. "It's awesome."

"Thank you."

"A bunch of students are getting together at Winston's tonight and we wanted to invite you. Some of the other teachers will be there."

Alexis is a pretty blonde with what one of my colleagues once described as a very healthy figure. She was wearing a pair of tight-fitting jeans that rode low on her hips and a top that left her midriff bare. The pants were stylishly ripped at the knees.

"That's sweet of you to ask," I said. "Unfortunately, I'll have to beg off. I've got a lot of work to do."

"Oh, what a shame," Alexis said. She moved a little closer and touched the lapel of my jacket. "I . . . that is, *we*, were hoping you could come."

The other girl responded with a weak smile and quickly broke eye contact. To my mind, she looked distinctly uncomfortable with the situation. Her name was Melissa Sorrensen and she was one of the editors on our school's law review.

"Maybe another time," I said, stepping around Alexis and opening the driver's door. "If I don't get my test papers finished, a lot of students will be upset."

Her face took on a pouting expression. "Oh," she said, drawing out the word. "Professor Shaffer told us you live at the Dakota. Is that true?"

I made a mental note to kick Paul Shaffer the next time I saw him. "That's right."

"Is it as great as they say?"

"Not really. It's just an old building."

I reached inside the car, released the roof's latches, then went around to the other side to put down the top.

"I'd love to see it sometime," Alexis said, lowering her voice a notch.

What she was doing didn't surprise me—only its obviousness did. When lawyers get together they talk as much as anyone, and rumor had it that she had earned her Contracts grade the old-fashioned way. I'll spare you the details.

"Maybe I'll have a group of you up one day," I told them.

"Have you gotten to our papers yet?" Alexis asked.

"I, uh . . . don't recall," I lied. "It's possible." Fact is, I was reading her paper when the O'Connor brothers had shown up.

"Professor, I'd like to make an appointment to talk to you about my grade next week. I'm up for a summer clerk's position with the Cahill firm."

Her companion finally had enough. "Alexis, I'll wait for you in the student lounge," she said. "Have a nice weekend, Professor Delaney."

We both watched her walk away. Since I didn't want to squeeze past Alexis again, I swung my leg over the passenger door and, with some minor acrobatics, shifted myself behind the steering wheel.

Alexis remained undeterred. She rested her elbows on the door and leaned forward until her cleavage showed. Young Ms. Carter was definitely healthy and she definitely wasn't wearing a bra.

"Will you be in your office tomorrow?" she asked softly.

"I doubt it," I said, making a pretense of adjusting the rearview mirror.

"Would it be okay if I call you over the weekend?"

I counted to five mentally. It's not that I'm big on moral absolutes, but there are some roads you don't go down and this was one of them.

"Probably not the best idea," I said. I tapped her on the elbows to move and started the Jag's engine. "Give Maria a buzz on Monday and she'll set up an appointment for you."

The pouting expression returned to Alexis's face, but she stepped back.

"Bye," she said softly, wiggling her fingers at me.

THREE

DELANEY

WHEN I finally put Irwin's book down, it was dark outside my window. The clock on the mantel read eight thirty. I rubbed the bridge of my nose and leaned back in the chair. Irwin was right. The first thing I had to do was gather Sarah's possessions and make an inventory of them. If she had a will I assumed it would turn up during that process. If not, I would ask a local judge to appoint me as interim administrator of her estate. Since Frank and Lucille were her next of kin, I jotted down a note on my legal pad to get their consent, along with the keys to Sarah's apartment and her car.

Despite my colleagues' urgings, I haven't bought a PDA yet. The letters stand for "personal data assistant" and I'm sure they can do all sorts of wonderful things, but frankly I don't have that much to remember and I'm a pretty organized fellow. A legal pad works just as well and you never need batteries.

The question in my mind was how best to handle the situation. It had been three weeks since I'd seen Katherine and she was due to fly up to New York the following weekend. For the past year we'd been doing the long-distance thing, which hadn't been easy. We really care for each other, a lot as a matter of fact, but the separations were getting tougher and tougher to deal with. We both knew commuting between Atlanta and New York couldn't go on forever, but we were still in that gee-life's-wonderful-and-it's-great-to-be-in-love state.

The last time we got together she raised the possibility of my relocating. It was the second time the subject had come up, and while she didn't push very hard, I took it as a warning shot across my bow.

Neither of us has mentioned the word *marriage* yet, but it's reasonably certain we were headed in that direction. We'd met on a cruise nearly a year ago and had been going hot and heavy since. It's not that I'm opposed to relocating. My son had started his second year at Penn State, and my mother recently announced that she was planning to move to Florida for the warmer weather and to be near her brother. The good news is she likes Katherine and they get along well, so I asked myself what I was waiting for.

Great question.

Other than the job, there was nothing holding me in New York except for the fact that I like the city. I know all about the prices, the cost of living, the traffic, and the general level of insanity you encounter, but it's still an amazing place.

My personal goal where New York is concerned is to get everyone who walks around talking to themselves together and pair them up. At least that way it will look like they're having conversations.

One argument I usually muster against leaving is that my friends are here. They're mostly cops and lawyers, but to be completely honest, I could probably make friends in Atlanta as well. Still, marriage and moving to the South are big decisions, so I've been taking matters slowly. I was born and raised in New York, and living anywhere else is tantamount to camping out. I weighed these facts as I sat there and came up with several legitimate reasons for me to stay. In the end, I wasn't sure who I was trying to convince. I took another sip of coffee.

After several minutes, no lightbulbs went on in my mind, and my thoughts returned to Sarah's case. As I saw it, my choices were fairly straightforward. I could travel to Atlanta and try to handle the situation myself, or I could call Katherine for help. Being a local, she could probably do this faster and more efficiently than I could. From personal experience, I knew how much a detective on the New York police force made. Frank O'Connor wasn't rolling in money and I had no desire to add to his problems. Another minute or two mulling the situation over brought me to a decision. If they would cover my airfare, I'd save them the money on legal fees. It was a fair trade and my good deed for the day.

I phoned Frank and told him I'd be flying down to Atlanta the following morning. He was more than grateful. The students' exams would have to come with me, but I figured I could work on them on the plane. A call to Delta Airlines revealed there were plenty of seats available, so I made a reservation. The next step was to let Katherine know. She answered her phone on the second ring.

"Hi, honey," she said.

Her use of the expression caught me off guard. "Hey, that's the first time you called me honey."

"I thought I'd try it out. What's up?"

"How would you like some company this weekend?"

"Are you serious?"

I took a few minutes to explain about Sarah O'Connor.

"Gee, I got all excited for nothing," Katherine said. "I thought you were coming because you wanted my body and couldn't stand being away from me."

"I can't. But I had to level with Sarah's family. I told Frank the trip might be part social and he was fine with it."

"That's what I love about you, John. I wonder if Alley knew her; Emory's not a very big school."

Alley is Katherine's daughter and is short for Allison. "Maybe you can give her a call and ask."

"I won't have to, she's downstairs."

"I thought she had her own apartment now."

"She does, but the food is free here," Katherine explained. "Plus, I have a washer and dryer, which makes coming home doubly attractive. She showed up earlier with a bag of clothes it took both of us to carry in. At the moment, she and her roommate are devouring an apple pie I bought at Costco yesterday."

"Sounds irresistible."

"They also wanted some advice on how to handle their moot court project. You remember what the first year of law school was like."

I did remember.

"So what do we have to do?" Katherine asked.

This was typical of her. Katherine is one of the most giving and supportive women I've ever met. Her question made me feel like a rat for trying to come up with reasons to stay in New York. Score one for her.

"The first thing is to make an inventory of Sarah's possessions and apply to the court for ancillary administration," I said, reading a paragraph in Irwin's book.

"Wow. Do you just know this stuff off the top of your head? I haven't handled an estate case in years."

I glanced at my reflection in the mirror and allowed myself a smug smile. "I guess I have a good memory. Whatcha doin' now?"

"Shopping."

"I thought you said you were home."

"I am. I'm on eBay. I just bought the most amazing Lacroix suit."

"Lacroix? Did you give up on that Miriam Haskell stuff?"

"No, I still buy it, but I discovered they have designer suits, too. It's so much fun to shop this way."

Katherine went on to describe her suit in some detail and I pretended to listen as she explained how eBay worked. Personally, I can't see buying designer suits online or anything you have to try on, but a lot of women seem to be into that lately. I knew of two in my department who were hooked. They talk about eBay and the bargains they find all the time.

"Sounds great," I said. "I can't wait to see you."

"Me, too."

"So . . . what are you wearing right now?"

"That sexy nightgown and the matching lingerie set you bought for me," she answered, lowering her voice.

An image of the last time we were together flashed into my mind in some detail and I sat up a little straighter in the chair.

"Uh . . . I guess I should get back to grading these papers. After that I think I'll take a cold shower—a long one."

Katherine giggled.

I gave her my flight information and she promised to meet me at the airport. With the vision of her in a see-through nightie now firmly lodged in my brain, I decided to add a set of push-ups to my regimen before the shower.

AFTER she hung up, Katherine straightened her sweatshirt and went into the kitchen to fix herself a cup of peppermint tea. She was still smiling when the water began to boil.

FOUR

THURMAN

HORACE Womack picked up the memo lying on his desk and read through it one more time. It was a routine single-paragraph request from the Records Department at the U.S. Attorney's office in New York regarding a girl named Sarah O'Connor and a file that had turned up missing. Nothing in the wording appeared urgent. It wasn't even marked priority.

According to the administrator who had forwarded it, O'Connor was now a law student at Emory University and had worked with the U.S. Attorney's office the previous summer as a clerk. She was supposedly the last one to have seen the file. They wanted someone to contact her and check if she knew anything about it.

Womack shook his head. The request was over a month old and had filtered down to the Georgia Bureau of Investigation's field office. That weekend, he was the Duty Agent, so the problem was now his. Not exactly an earth-shaking law enforcement issue.

Womack yawned and ran a hand through his hair. Pattern baldness ran in his family. He glanced at a mirror on the wall and tilted his head downward for a better look at his scalp, grimacing. There was definitely less hair than last week, he decided. He had just turned forty. His wife didn't seem to mind. She told him it made him look mature. Maturity wasn't what he needed; he needed more hair.

Womack returned to the memo. Under normal circumstances he would have waited until Monday to get in touch with Sarah O'Connor, but a phone call he received earlier had changed all that. Phillip Thurman, the FBI's Senior Agent in Charge wanted to meet with him about the very memo he was now holding. The fact that the feds were interested wasn't unusual; that it had come from Phillip Thurman was. Thurman wasn't your run-of-the-mill agent. Being Senior Agent in Charge meant he held a position equivalent to that of a regional director in the Bureau, and regional directors didn't get involved in requests as mundane as this one.

Something was up. He supposed he would find out what that was when Thurman arrived. In their phone call, Thurman had been deferential but quite insistent. He made it clear he didn't want to wait until Monday; he wanted to meet that very afternoon.

Womack pushed himself back from the desk, got up, and wandered down the hall to the sandwich machine. He studied the selections for a few seconds before making his choice. A tuna sandwich dropped from its holder into an opening at the bottom of the machine. He took it out, removed the cellophane wrapper, and took a bite.

"Horace Womack?" a voice behind him said.

Womack turned. "Mm-hmm," he said, trying to swallow and answer at the same time.

"I'm Phil Thurman," Thurman said, holding out his hand. "Didn't mean to startle you."

Womack motioned for Thurman to wait as the food worked its way down his esophagus. "It's okay," he said, shaking the other man's hand. "You got here pretty fast."

"How about if we talk in your office?"

Womack shrugged. "Sure. You want something to eat?" he asked, gesturing toward the vending machines.

"No thanks. I have two meetings later and I'm already behind schedule."

Womack nodded and headed down the hall with Thurman following. Once they were seated, Womack asked, "So, what can I do for you?"

"Have you made any progress on New York's request yet?"

"Progress? Central dispatch just sent it up this morning. I was going to run out to Emory and talk to this, uh . . ."

Womack paused and picked up the memo, looking for the name he wanted.

"Sarah O'Connor," Thurman said, filling in the blank.

"Right, Sarah O'Connor. I thought I would get with her on Monday . . . unless that's a problem."

"You'd be a little late. Ms. O'Connor was killed in a camping accident about two weeks ago at Cloudland Canyon. How long has your office been sitting on this?"

"We haven't been sitting at all," Womack said defensively. "Like I told you, I just got the memo. It wasn't even addressed to me. New York marked it 'Attention: Duty Officer.' The attorney general's office sent it through the departmental mail to our downtown office and they forwarded it here."

Womack slid the memo across his desk for Thurman to see. The FBI agent looked at it for a moment then massaged the back of his neck with his fingers.

"Wonderful," he said. "The incompetence of some people never fails to amaze me."

"How come the Bureau is so interested in this? It looks pretty routine."

"In the first place, the missing file is the property of the United States government, so we have jurisdiction. On my way here I placed a call to your section chief. You'll be getting a formal memo from him later this afternoon. As of right now you and I are working together. My office is taking over this case and I was assured I'd receive full cooperation from your department."

"*What* case? All I can see is you're hunting for a file that's been dead docketed for more than fifteen years. I don't get it. What's so important about it?"

"That's part of the problem," Thurman replied. "We don't know. What we do know is that it involves a man named Warren Blendel, who is about as dangerous and dirty as they come. His operation is based in New York, but he has business interests, some legitimate and some not, in eight major cities across the country."

"That's it?"

"I'll level with you, Womack . . . twenty years ago, Blendel killed two of my men in the most brutal way imaginable. Parts of them were found in different boroughs throughout New York City. We were never able to prove he was involved, but there's no question in my mind that he was behind the killings. The Bureau wants Blendel. . . . *I* want Blendel."

"And you think this O'Connor girl took the file?"

Thurman leaned forward in his seat, his eyes suddenly intense. "I don't know, but if she did, you and I are going to find out why."

For a moment it appeared that Thurman was going to say something else but then he changed his mind.

"We're going to find out," he repeated quietly, only this time it was more to himself than to Womack.

FIVE

DELANEY

I SPOTTED Katherine at the top of the escalator. As soon as we saw each other, she slipped under the security rope and ran to meet me. The moment we kissed, I grew conscious of her perfume and the pressure of her breasts against my chest. Living in Atlanta gained a little more ground in my mind. Every time I see her, it gives my heart a tug. Goofy, I know, but I can look at her for hours, and I don't mean in a sexual context. For all I care, she can be lying on the bed in a T-shirt and sweatpants reading a book. It's the little things, as they say.

That day, she was dressed in a black wool suit with understated rhinestone buttons. The jacket showed off her slender waist and the skirt ended about six inches above her knees.

"You look great," I said as we headed toward the baggage claim area.

"So do you."

She slipped an arm around my waist and gave me an affectionate squeeze. "After we get your bag, I need to make a quick stop at my office before we go to the girl's house."

"No problem."

"By the way, I talked with Alley and it turns out she did know Sarah O'Connor. They met at her roommate's party a few months ago."

"Really?"

Frank hadn't mentioned that Sarah had a roommate and I wondered whether he knew.

Katherine continued. "She and Alley were only acquaintances, but Alley said Sarah and the roommate both seemed nice. Most of the school's already heard about the accident."

I nodded. "Do you know how to get to her house?"

"I'm pretty sure. We can always use the navigation system if we get lost."

"You bought a navigation system for the Mercedes?"

"Uh-uh, I got a new car last week. I thought I'd surprise you. It's a silver Lexus. You'll love it."

I stopped walking and looked at her. "I guess the law firm's doing pretty well. You pick that up on eBay, too?"

Katherine poked me in the ribs with her knuckle. "We're doing very well, thank you. In fact, we're thinking of adding a new associate. Do you know anyone who might be interested in the position?"

"Only if it involves working closely under the senior partner."

She giggled. "It might . . . for the right candidate."

My suitcase chose that moment to make an appearance, giving me an excuse to change topics. Katherine responded with a flat look, but didn't push the subject further.

As we pulled out of the parking lot, she checked her voice messages by pressing a button on her steering wheel. Somehow the car connected to her cell phone and a voice came on over the speaker system. It was all very high tech. The third message was from her mother.

"Hi, sweetheart. It's me. I know you've got a lot going on, but I wanted to let you know that I was talking with my friend Sylvia Kaufman. She lives about a mile from you. Anyway, she went to the Department of Transportation today to renew her driver's license, and would you believe it, their whole computer system was down? It took her three hours to get through the line. The poor thing nearly plotzed because she had to go to the bathroom.

"So I was thinking, if you need to go there, maybe plan ahead a little and empty your bladder before you leave.

"Okay, that's it. So give me a call when you get a chance. Oh, this is your mother."

Katherine's shoulders slumped and she put her head on the steering wheel.

"Good advice," I said.

"She treats me like I'm nine years old."

I rubbed the back of her neck affectionately. "You don't look nine to me."

"I'm glad you think so. The last time she came to visit, I took her to see my new office and she started rearranging our lobby furniture into cozy conversation groups. I love her to death, but she drives me nuts."

I suppressed a smile and nodded sympathetically. I'd finally broken my mother and aunts of the same habit several years ago. Apparently they're convinced men are genetically incapable of placing chairs and sofas where they want them to be. They also think I won't notice any changes they make.

As it turned out, the law firm of Katherine Adams & Associates was doing better than all right. It was formed eleven months earlier, following the *Ocean Majestic* disaster, and all but one of Katherine's clients had gone with her when she left her old firm. Unlike her former partners, who tried to save their own necks after a lawsuit was filed, Katherine's clients showed a good deal more courage, if not character, in sticking by her. Since the split, she had picked up a dozen new divorce cases—all high profile. This is what she does for a living, which is slightly scary when you think about it. It's a field I stay far away from, professionally and personally.

Jimmy d'Taglia, one of Katherine's associates, had been nearly as productive. Recently, he'd won a large product-liability case that drew national attention and, according to Katherine, was on the verge of settling two other suits in the mid-seven-figure range. Ilene Starkey, another lawyer who chose to leave Boyd, Stevenson, Levitt, and Adams when Katherine did, was also going great guns. In short, the office was flourishing.

They were located on the fifty-first floor of a modern high-rise just off I-285. Though the building is officially in Cobb County, Katherine had somehow managed to convince the post office they really were in Atlanta, thus wrangling a big-city address out of them rather than a suburban one. I wasn't sure how she had accomplished this.

On our way up to her office, a woman in the elevator remarked how much she liked the suit Katherine won on eBay. I made a mental note to check the site out when I got a chance.

The lobby had changed since my last visit. They now had a reception desk and a smiling young lady who greeted us as we came through a set of double glass doors. She was blond, perky, and reminded me a bit of Alexis Carter . . . without the excess cleavage or affectation. I kept these observations to myself.

As a rule I'm usually straightforward with Katherine about most things. However, the last time I mentioned that a student had tried to flirt with me, the response I got was distinctly cool rather than amused. Certain subjects are best avoided.

Katherine's office is conservative, well decorated, and more feminine than the rest of the firm. The walls are painted sea foam green. The chairs and couch all have gold fringe. A French needlepoint of a Renaissance scene hangs on the wall opposite her diplomas.

The moment the door was closed, an impulse seized me and I kissed Ms. Adams as she turned around. Perhaps it was a little shallow on my part, but her skirt was really tight across her hips, and seeing her again reminded me of how much I had missed her. The push-ups I'd been doing to get my mind off sex had helped, but not that much.

My impulse turned into an urge as passion and other things rose. Katherine responded by pressing her thighs against mine. In seconds my hands started to roam, first across her back and then down to the curve of her buttocks. But for the intercom's beep, we might have shattered the Commandments on the spot.

Katherine took a deep breath. "Yes?"

"I'm sorry to interrupt, K.J.," her secretary said, "but your conference call is ready."

"Right," she answered, tucking a strand of hair behind her ear and giving me a mischievous smile.

"You want me to wait outside?" I whispered.

She shook her head no and pointed me toward the couch. "I'll pick up," she told the intercom.

Katherine put the call on speakerphone. The other participants were one Darrell Kingsley, a Superior Court Judge, and a very Southern-sounding lawyer named Palmer Wainwright. From what I was able to gather, there seemed to be a dispute over some discovery requests in one of her cases.

Wainwright's position was that his client had complied with the law by producing his financial records. Katherine, however, argued

the compliance was a sham designed to put her client to unnecessary trouble and expense.

Wainwright immediately jumped to the offensive. "Your Honor,
when I read over counsel's motion, I was, quite frankly, dismayed by it.
We delivered each and every document she asked for two weeks ago."

"Ms. Adams?" the judge queried.

"What they delivered, Your Honor, were twenty-eight separate
boxes filled with papers that were in no particular order. Cell phone
records were mixed in with checking account statements. The stock
brokerage records of Mr. Wainwright's client were in at least seven different places and many documents had pages missing. Some of the
properties the parties own contained files with warranty deeds and
some didn't. It would take us the better part of a month to make any
sense out of what they've given us."

"But Ms. Adams, if he's produced the records—"

"He *may* have produced the records," Katherine countered. "Unfortunately, I have no way of knowing if he did, since Mr. Wainwright failed to make any formal response as the law requires. He
simply dumped the boxes on us. My client shouldn't have to pay for
my time trying to unscramble them."

"Well, I'm sorry if Ms. Adams is too busy to do a little organization," Wainwright cut in. "This is a big case, Judge, and I can assure
the court everything is there. The fact is, my client's every bit as busy
as she is."

The argument went back and forth like that for maybe ten minutes.

I listened to the way Katherine conducted herself and was impressed. She was professional and practical without being aggressive. At one point she looked at me and winked. Unfortunately, the
judge didn't share my view, and from the comments he was making,
it appeared she was going to lose her motion.

Then there was a light tap on the door. It was followed by Alley
Adams, who poked her head into the room. When she saw me, she
mouthed the word *hi,* and wiggled her fingers in a greeting. Katherine placed a finger over her lips and motioned for her daughter to
join us.

Wainwright was in the process of telling Judge Kingsley how much attorney's fees his side had incurred in having to defend the motion. He argued that it was frivolous and had only been brought to harass his client, a prominent and well-respected physician.

While this was going on, Alley placed a photocopy of a case on Katherine's desk and jabbed her finger at a portion that was highlighted in yellow. She glanced over her shoulder and flashed me a big smile. Not for the first time I was struck by how much alike mother and daughter were.

"Ms. Adams," the judge said, "if I understand you correctly, you're not disagreeing that opposing counsel produced the records you subpoenaed. He's an officer of the court just as you are, and if he states he's given you everything, I don't see what else the man can do. I think he even said he sent you a letter referencing his compliance."

There was a sound of papers being rustled.

"Yes, here it is in my notes. Unless you have something else you'd like me to consider, I'm going to deny your motion."

"Actually there is one more thing, Your Honor," Katherine told him. "There's a Supreme Court decision that says our discovery statutes were created to take the surprise out of litigation. The opinion further states, and I'm quoting, 'a lawyer should not have to guess as to what is, and what is not, being produced by his opponent.' "

"I understand that, ma'am," the judge replied.

Katherine ignored the interruption. "The case goes on to state, 'This requires the party served to make a formal response to those things asked for.' Now, Mr. Wainwright hasn't objected to our requests, so I think it's clear we're entitled to the documents. The important part of the opinion says, 'producing an unorganized batch of papers in a thinly veiled attempt to comply with discovery constitutes no response at all.'

"I have the case in front of me, if the court needs it, Your Honor."

There was a silence.

"No, no," Judge Kingsley finally said. "Actually, I do recall that case. Thank you for refreshing my memory. Mr. Wainwright, I'm going to give you ten days to resubmit the documents Ms. Adams has asked for. You're to do it in some logical form that she and her client will be able to read and review. In addition, I'm granting the plaintiff's motion and awarding them the sum of one thousand five hundred dollars in attorney's fees. I'll have my clerk prepare an order and send it to each of you. Are there any other questions?"

"No, Your Honor," said Katherine.

"Uh . . . no," Wainwright responded.

As soon as the call was over, I got up and gave Alley a hug and a quick kiss on the cheek. Then I looked down at the case she had found. The name at the top of the page read, *Kingsley v. Kingsley*. It was a copy of the judge's own divorce eight years earlier.

SIX

DELANEY

SARAH O'Connor's house was located in Morningside Heights, one of Atlanta's older residential neighborhoods. It was a one-story brick structure that looked about forty or fifty years old. There was little to distinguish it from the other homes along the street. According to Alley, a lot of Emory students lived in this part of town. Her own apartment was five blocks away.

Thanks to Katherine's foresight, we now had a digital camera with us to make a record of Sarah's furniture and her personal effects. She'd also located a nearby storage facility where the furniture could be kept until I obtained a final order from the court. My contribution was to look up a moving company in the yellow pages. I made arrangements with them to meet us there the following day.

When we entered the house, it had a stale smell to it. I identified a plastic bag filled with garbage as the source and carried it out to the trash can. Sarah's car, a late-model Toyota, was parked in a one-car garage next to the house.

My son's apartment at Penn State had a similar look and feel. Though Sarah's place was slightly neater, it seemed to contain the same collection of pizza boxes and beer cans. The furniture was eclectic, and I use that term advisedly. My guess was that most of it had come from Sarah's parents and secondhand stores. As we walked around, I studied some of the posters on the wall. Two of them were of café scenes with French slogans at the bottom. I didn't know what they said. The others were a Van Gogh reproduction and a cover of the Beatles' *Rubber Soul* album.

Katherine opened the windows to let some fresh air in and we began the depressing task of going through the rooms one by one and listing their contents. It took me a minute or two to figure out how to work the digital camera. Instant gratification, those things. You press a button and a picture shows up.

The house contained three small bedrooms, only one of which had a bed in it. One was being used for storage, and the other had two desks, his and hers from the look of the contents on top. I'd been wondering about the roommate since Katherine had mentioned it.

Frank O'Connor was a detail kind of guy and he hadn't said anything about Sarah living with someone. It was possible he knew and was just too shaken up by recent events to mention it but the odds were it was going to come as a shock. In today's society this isn't such a big deal anymore and I'm not one to judge. But I wasn't looking forward to breaking the news to him.

The roommate was a complication I hadn't counted on. Of course, we didn't want to take any furniture out of the house that wasn't Sarah's. I also wasn't ready to broach the roommate issue with Frank until I gave the matter more thought. In the end, I eased around the problem by placing a call to Nick and asking him for a list of Sarah's furniture. He had no clue, but phoned Sarah's mother and got back to us in fifteen minutes.

After that, it took us about an hour to complete our inventory. I made notes on my legal pad while Katherine used a shiny new PDA to jot things down. Unfortunately, no Last Will and Testament turned up during our search.

We did find a number of photos of the O'Connor family. One was Sarah and her brother; two were of Frank and Lucille. On the nightstand next to the bed was a framed picture of Sarah and a good-looking kid with heavy eyebrows taken at a beach somewhere. From the unopened mail on the kitchen counter we determined the boy's name was Andre Rostov. I made a note of that and continued sorting through the rest of the mail. It was just the usual stuff: magazines, bills, and a couple of pieces from Emory's Registrar's Office. Katherine separated Andre's mail and placed Sarah's in a box she had brought from the office. The woman thought of everything.

While we were making our inventory, a feeling that something wasn't quite right began to creep up on me. It was nothing I identified immediately, but the longer we stayed there the stronger it got.

"Anything strike you as unusual?" I finally asked.

"Yep," Katherine answered. "Where's old Andre?"

Despite the facetious tone, I recognized the expression on her face. When Katherine gets down to business you can almost feel the neurons in her brain firing. It was obvious no one had been in the home for quite some time.

I glanced through the mail again. The most recent postmark was ten days old. Out of curiosity, I went out to the mailbox and checked inside. It was nearly full. I retrieved whatever was there and brought it back, leaving Andre's share on the counter. If they were living together, why hadn't he returned?

"That's Sarah's car outside, isn't it?" Katherine asked.

"Right."

"Well, then she obviously didn't use it to drive to Cloudland Canyon."

"She probably went with her boyfriend."

Katherine pursed her lips. "Odd."

"What is?"

"That they decided to go at all. When did you say she died?"

I consulted my notes. "May twenty-fifth."

Katherine punched a few buttons on her PDA. "The twenty-fifth was a Tuesday and according to Alley, they were in the middle of exams that week."

We stared at each other for several seconds.

From past experience, I knew how anal law students could be when it comes to studying for their exams. It was possible Sarah didn't have any tests the following day and was simply taking a break. For the moment, I simply filed the information away. It might mean something and it might not. The easiest thing would be to talk with Andre and ask him. I tore a piece of paper off my legal pad and left a note on the counter asking him to call me when he got a chance. When I was through, Katherine and I went to the garage for a closer look at Sarah's car. Frank had given me a spare set of keys and one of them fit the door. We swung it open and looked inside.

There were a couple of law books on the front seat. Technically they're called hornbooks. Don't ask me why. I found a loose-leaf that had been neatly divided into separate sections for torts, contracts, criminal procedure, and corporations. Sarah's name and phone number were on the inside cover. Her handwriting was neat and precise.

Katherine and I had already decided to bring the car back to her place. With both James and Alley away at school, she had more than enough room. Her youngest son, Zach, was still living at home and was a year away from getting his own car.

The nagging feeling that something was wrong continued to peck at me as we walked back inside. Maybe it was instinct that prompted me to take another look at Sarah's bedroom. For the first time I began to examine the scene critically. That was when I noticed the carpet had recently been vacuumed. By itself this was no big deal. Sarah might have done a quick cleanup before she left on her trip.

"What are you looking at?" Katherine asked.

I pointed to the carpet. She put a hand on my shoulder and entered the room to stand alongside me.

"The bed's been moved," she said.

At the base of the floor you could see indentations in the carpeting. Again, no big deal, except the bed was a four-poster and I doubted that a woman, even a strong one, could have lifted it.

During my years as a detective, I'd run across a number of situations where crime scenes had been swept. People do this to remove evidence or sometimes to conceal it. Sarah's room had a similar feel. Gradually, I began to notice details I had overlooked earlier. There was a layer of dust on the dresser and nightstands, but the only marks were the ones Katherine and I had made. I walked across to the bathroom and examined it from the doorway. The mirror and faucets were all spotless, as were the tub and sink.

While Katherine watched, I went over the room inch by inch.

It took five minutes to find the hidden cameras. The first was a pinhole model concealed in an overhead air-conditioning vent. The other was located behind the dresser mirror. I motioned Katherine over and showed her where the silver backing had been scraped away.

"What the hell is this?" she asked.

I shook my head slowly.

We found the box of tapes stashed in a corner of the attic under some insulation. There were four of them. Our suspicions were now

aroused. I put the first one in the VCR and pressed PLAY. When it began I half expected to see some kind of home sex video. As far as I'm
concerned, what couples do behind closed doors is their own business. A second later, the feeling in my stomach worsened. Katherine
sat next to me on the couch.

There was sex all right, only it was hardcore porn. The tape depicted a lesbian scene between Sarah and a tall blond girl. Katherine
left the room after a few minutes. Not wanting to be written off as
pervert or a voyeur, I fast-forwarded to the end. That's the way it is
with pornography. You watch it for fifteen minutes and you want to
go home and have sex. You watch it for another fifteen minutes and
you never want to have sex again.

The production was about bad as it gets. I won't bore you with
details, unless whipping, hot candle wax, and being beaten with a
ruler are your thing. They're not mine. Basically, I'm a dull guy. I
watched the other tapes long enough to identify that Sarah was in
each one of them. The whole experience was depressing. It was like
looking at an entirely different person from the girl in my class a
year ago. That Sarah was funny, intelligent, and a hard worker. In
fact, she was one of the brightest, most personable kids I've met. So
why this?

My first inclination was to start a fire and pitch the tapes in. My
earlier concern about telling Frank O'Connor his little girl was
shacking up with a guy suddenly took a backseat to what I had just
seen.

"What are you going to do, John?" Katherine asked from the next
room.

It was a great question because I didn't have a clue. "I don't
know. I need some time to think. What's your opinion?"

"There's such a thing as having too much information. If Alley
ever got mixed up with garbage like that I wouldn't want to know
the details. It's your call, though."

"Yeah, it's my call," I repeated to myself.

I flipped off the television and stacked the tapes in Katherine's
cardboard box, along with Sarah's mail. As far as I was concerned
we were done. Since there was no sign of a will, the only option

open to me was to apply for Letters of Administration with the local court. I wasn't sure how the process worked in Georgia, but I
suspected it would involve furnishing the clerk with a death certificate.

I also wanted to talk to Andre and find out his story, particularly
since he was one of the stars in the last tape. The reason I had gone
through all four of them had nothing to do with lascivious motives or
even morbid curiosity. From my standpoint, as I viewed the final
tape, I got the impression it had been made without Sarah O'Connor's knowledge. In other words, she appeared to be on drugs. Her
demeanor was distinctly compliant and her movements had a ro-
botic feel them. At least that's how I rationalized it. Denial can be a
wonderful thing. The reason I say this is because while it was running, boyfriend Andre kept glancing at the mirror and overhead
cameras. Unlike the others, which had a more professional, you'll
pardon the expression, appearance, the last tape was strictly amateur
night.

I glanced at the photograph of Sarah and her family on the coffee
table and thought of the woman I had just seen. I couldn't put the two
together. My contact with her had been when she was little and then
later as a student, but how well did I really know her? I came up with
ten different reasons why she might turn to this kind of sleaze. Each
one was more creative than the last and none of them played well.
With a start I realized Katherine had been watching me from the
doorway.

"The family doesn't need to know about this," I said, shaking my
head.

"Okay."

"It wouldn't do anything but hurt them and they've been through
enough."

Katherine just stared at me with those big blue eyes of hers.

"Do you see what I'm saying?"

"I see it, John."

"Good, then I guess we're done."

"Right," she said quietly.

"I'll drive Sarah's car and follow you back to your place. Then we can head down to the court. I also need to stop by the bank and let them know about Sarah's death."

Katherine came forward and put her arms around my neck. "Honey, I'm really sorry."

This time I wasn't surprised when she used the word *honey*. In fact, I kind of liked it.

SEVEN

DELANEY

KATHERINE'S home is a big, sprawling Tudor mansion set on four wooded acres. It's at least five hundred feet off the main road and you have to drive through a pair of ten-foot-high iron gates to get in, so there's not much chance of anyone stopping by for a cup of sugar.

I've stayed at her house several times over the last year and it never fails to impress. There are a number of statues around the property—Greek or Roman, I can never tell which, and a tall four-tiered fountain on her back patio where she spends a lot of time sketching with charcoal. It's like being in a private park. The house was part of her divorce settlement from the heart surgeon, as she referred to him. I'd heard his name once or twice from the kids, but I couldn't recall ever hearing her speak it. Their breakup was not what you'd call amicable. These days, they only talked to one another when necessity dictated.

After we locked Sarah's car, I placed the keys in an envelope, labeled it, and stuck it in my file. Katherine lent me one of those expandable folders that comes with a flap because all I'd brought from New York was Irwin's book, my legal pad, a suitcase, and a pile of test papers. During the plane ride I made a dent in them, but there was still a long way to go. Every year it seems my student's answers get longer and more creative as opposed to more accurate. "Professor Delaney, I'm not sure what you're looking for in this fact pattern, but I want to say how much I enjoyed your course. . . ." You get the picture.

Until Katherine asked if I wanted something to eat, I hadn't realized how hungry I was. I took a seat at her kitchen table and watched as she prepared a couple of sandwiches for us. She went about the job without any fuss, which is pretty much the way she does most things. The sandwich she made for herself was half the height of mine and her beverage of choice was cold water from a pitcher in the fridge. She brought out a beer for me.

"I didn't know you drank beer," I said.

"I don't. I got them for you."

Score another point for Atlanta and long-term relationships.

"Thanks. That was really thoughtful."

"I also bought you a robe, a pair of slippers, and a toothbrush."

"Jeez. How come I rate all that?"

"I just want you to be comfortable here, John. Besides, if Zach's home I can't have you running around in your boxers."

"Point taken. But thanks again. The next time you come up to New York I'll surprise you with something. What would you like?"

Katherine eyes met mine over the top of her sandwich, but she didn't respond. Her expression was one I couldn't interpret and I decided to change the topic.

"The last tape I saw looked like it was made without Sarah knowing it."

Katherine stopped chewing. "Seriously?"

"I'm pretty sure."

Katherine put down her sandwich and took a sip of water. "Is it possible you're reading something into it?"

"Maybe. I'll show you if you like."

"I'll take your word. It would be pretty scummy if her boyfriend did that without her knowledge. Even if you're right, what difference does it make, John? There were four tapes. Was it the same with all of them?"

"No, only the last one I looked at."

"So . . ."

I shook my head and paused for a few seconds. "I just hate the thought of showing that crap to Sarah's family."

"I know."

"And I'd be breaking the law if I destroyed them."

Katherine shrugged. "I didn't see anything."

"Right. Do you know how I can obtain a death certificate for her?"

"I imagine the sheriff's office in the county where she died will have it. We can give them a call, but you might not need one at all. I

spoke to Jimmy D and he said all we'll have to do is fill out the application and make a suggestion of death into the record."

"*A suggestion of death?* Excuse me, Your Honor, I'd like to suggest
that my client is dead?"

"It's a term of art, John," she explained. "But yes, that's pretty
much it. What do they call it in New York?"

"I honestly don't know. God, you people are so polite down here.
How long will it take us to get to the court?"

"A half hour, depending on traffic. If everything goes quickly,
we might have enough time to drop by the school and pick up
her records. Maybe we can get a line on the boyfriend while we're
there."

I sat back in the chair. "Am I that obvious?"

Katherine leaned forward and kissed my cheek. "It's written all
over your face, honey. You're probably a lousy poker player."

Several responses occurred to me but none seemed terribly pro-
found, so I maintained my dignity and let it go. We finished eating
and headed out to the car. Without being asked, Katherine handed
me her keys and got in on the passenger side. I'd never driven a Lexus
before and had to agree it was a classy ride . . . nearly as classy as its
owner.

Ten minutes later we turned onto I-75 and headed toward downtown Atlanta.

Along the way Katherine pointed out some local sights for me,
one of which was the Richard Russell Federal Building where she
had worked as an Assistant U.S. Attorney for eight years before going into private practice. When we got to the courthouse she told me
where to find the lawyers' lounge and the restrooms. Apparently,
this is basic information Atlanta lawyers pass on to each other. She
said it was one of the first things her former boss had taught her. I
kept waiting for a secret handshake.

Despite a new multimillion-dollar judicial-government complex
directly across the street, Fulton County's Probate Court continues
to languish in the old courthouse. According to a dedication plaque
at the entrance, the building was opened for business in 1911. Eight
broad marble steps lead visitors up to a massive portico and four heavy
bronze doors. The lobby is directly behind them. From Katherine's

comments I gathered we were to count ourselves lucky the Probate Court was on the first floor. According to her, the elevators were notoriously erratic, which could sometimes make getting to the upper floors an adventure. I spotted another brass plaque on the way to the clerk's office informing me that Fulton County had been named to honor Robert Fulton, the fellow who invented the steamboat. Interestingly, he never set foot in Georgia.

A clerk at the reception desk put down a novel she was reading and looked through my papers with a frown. "Was someone from your office here earlier about this?"

"No," I said, surprised.

She lifted her shoulders. "Maybe I'm confused. We get a lot of similar names. Do you have a death certificate?"

"Actually, I don't. We haven't had a chance to pick it up yet."

"You'll need a death certificate to complete probate."

"I understand."

"You can mail it in if you like. That'll save you a trip."

"Thanks, I appreciate that. I'm sure the family will, too."

"All right, if you'll raise your right hand. Do you solemnly swear that you will faithfully discharge your duties as interim administrator according to the laws of the State of Georgia and that everything contained in this petition is true and correct?"

"I do."

"Okay," she said, placing an official-looking stamp on the corner of the papers, with an impressive thump. "Since you don't have a death certificate you'll have to see Judge Fraser and make a Suggestion of Death to the court. He's just down the hall on the left."

Katherine and I found his chambers without difficulty and handed the secretary our petition.

"You caught us at a good time," she said, "but you'll have to speak up. The judge is a little hard of hearing." She motioned toward the door behind her with her head.

As it turned out, Judge Compton Fraser was not only hard of hearing, he was also partially blind. Retired from the bench twenty years earlier, he was now what is known as a Senior Judge, which means he fills in for whoever is on vacation. After looking at him I guessed that he was somewhere in his early eighties.

The secretary's knock probably woke him up. She stuck her head into his office.

"Your Honor, there are two people here to see you," she said, practically shouting.

"Come in. Come in," the judge said. "Good to see you all again. What can I do for you?"

Katherine and I glanced over our shoulders to see if anyone had come in behind us.

"This is their petition, Your Honor," the secretary explained, placing our papers in front of him. She gave me a you're-on-your-own smile and went back to her desk.

"Have a seat, young fella, and let me look this over," Judge Fraser said. "Your client can sit down, too, if she likes."

Katherine rolled her eyes and took a seat.

When the judge finished reading, he nodded to me. "All right, Counselor, make out your case."

That threw me, but I decided to improvise. "We're here to get temporary Letters of Administration, Your Honor."

Judge Fraser's brows came together and he scowled at me; then he put his nose about a half inch from the petition and scowled at it. "I thought this was a divorce."

"Uh . . . no, Judge. It's a petition for—"

"I usually handle the uncontested divorce cases on Thursdays."

"Yes, I'm sorry, Your Honor. I guess I should have been clearer. This is Katherine Adams, by the way. She's an attorney."

"Is that so?" he said, leaning back in his seat. "That's good. She's much too pretty to be getting divorced." He smiled at Katherine. "If I were twenty years younger, I'd give you a run for your money, son. He treats you well, does he?"

"Oh, very well," Katherine said.

"Well, that's the way it should be. A man needs to show respect for women. A lot of men don't these days, you know. You remember that, Colonel, and you'll be all right." The last part was directed toward me.

I had no clue as to why he had just called me Colonel, but I decided not to compound my ignorance by asking. "I will, Your Honor."

"Fine, fine. Well, it's been nice to see you both. Stop by anytime."

I looked at Katherine and got only a blank stare in return. Underneath, I had no doubt she was laughing her head off.

"Uh, Your Honor, I do need to get these Letters of Administration signed," I prompted.

"Letters of Administration? Why didn't you say so?" He looked at the papers again. "Is your death certificate attached?"

"No, Judge, we're going to mail it in. I can make a Suggestion of Death to the court," I said, hoping that would do the trick.

The judge nodded and leaned back in his chair again. "All right, go ahead."

Once again I drew an absolute blank. "I guess I'd like to suggest that my client is deceased and that probate of her estate is necessary." It was the only thing I could come up with.

"That's a shame. How'd it happen, Colonel?"

I made a mental note to ask Katherine how I'd managed to get drafted once we were alone.

"Terrible," Judge Fraser said when I finished. "I knew some O'Connors up in Cherokee County. Are they related?"

"I don't think so, Judge."

"Elaine and I used to go camping there, but that was years ago. Not much fish in the streams anymore."

For the next ten minutes Judge Fraser told us camping stories and I did my best to appear interested. Katherine smiled and listened politely. When he finally ran out of steam, the judge said, "Well, sir, it appears that you've made out a *prima facie* case as required. So here you are."

He scrawled his signature across the bottom of the page and pushed it back toward me. "Make sure you get your inventory in as soon as possible."

"I will. Thanks for seeing us, Your Honor."

"My pleasure. Just make sure you treat this pretty lady right, now, hear? Problems can always be worked out if two people try hard enough."

"Yes, sir, I will."

We managed to keep our faces straight until we got outside. Then we both cracked up.

"He was really bright when he was on the bench," Katherine told me. "At least he still has an eye for beauty."

"Absolutely."

I didn't want to ask how long ago Judge Fraser had been on the bench and I supposed his being available did more good than harm. But I shuddered to think what might happen if they ever let him handle a real case. In all likelihood they only funneled the harmless tasks to him now.

"By the way," I asked, "what was all that stuff about my being a colonel?"

Katherine giggled. "During the Civil War all the lawyers were made colonels in the Army and Navy of Georgia. The law's still on the books. You can write to the governor's office and they'll send you your commission."

"Are you serious? *The Army and Navy of Georgia?*"

"It's a joke, of course, but I know a number of attorneys who have them as souvenirs. It's not done much anymore, but when I first moved here, some of the older judges used to refer to lawyers that way. I probably had the same look the first time I heard the expression."

"Women lawyers are colonels, too?"

"Generals," she answered.

I shook my head and we trudged back down the hall to file our papers with the clerk.

EIGHT

NICK O'CONNOR

THE house was the largest Nick O'Connor had ever been in, with the possible exception of Hearst Castle, which he'd visited years ago during a family vacation. A pair of massive front gates and an impossibly long driveway were meant to discourage visitors and intimidate anyone who might be there for legitimate reasons.

O'Connor shifted in his seat and looked around the circular library, taking in its details. It was paneled in African mahogany and had a ceiling that was at least forty feet high. There was a second floor of sorts, though it was little more than a catwalk that ran around the room. It was there to give access to a series of shelves lined with leather-bound books. O'Connor guessed most of them were original editions. Whether Warren Blendel had actually read any was questionable. They were simply part of the show. It was Blendel's technique to make you wait. O'Connor had seen him do this a dozen times over the years, and it didn't surprise him now.

Warren Blendel was a wealthy man, a very wealthy one, who possessed a peculiar talent for spotting weaknesses in others and exploiting them to his own ends. Their relationship had been symbiotic from the beginning. Thanks to Blendel, O'Connor had been able to afford a home in Westchester and put two boys through college, something he might never have accomplished on a civil servant's salary, deputy chief or not. In return, O'Connor kept his people away from Blendel's businesses, deflecting certain investigations, and burying others.

A number of those businesses were perfectly legitimate. In this sense, Blendel had been a visionary. When things started to heat up for organized crime, he simply adapted and changed with the times.

O'Connor had long since abandoned any concern over accepting

money from someone like Warren Blendel. Graft was a fact of life
and Blendel's fingers reached into a dozen different places.

Rationalization could be a very useful tool if one employed it correctly.

O'Connor didn't get up when the door opened. A shelf of books
at the far end of the room swung outward on a hinge and Blendel
entered. He was followed by two men and a woman he recognized
as Blendel's wife, Linda. She was a former photographer's model.
Mrs. Blendel had begun attending their "business meetings" several
years earlier. She was tall, elegant, and her hair contained only a few
strands of gray.

The man behind Blendel was his head of security, Hans Schiller, a
large fellow who wore his hair in a military crew cut. O'Connor esti-
mated he was at least six foot seven. Schiller's job was to take care of
problems whenever they arose, which wasn't often. Mr. Blendel was
not a man to suffer difficulty lightly despite the refined image he projected to the world.

The last man in the room made O'Connor uncomfortable. Joshua
Silver had appeared on the scene about five years earlier and his relationship with Blendel was curious to say the least. What little O'Connor knew about him wasn't good.

Silver hardly spoke and had a tendency to stare at people in the
same unblinking way that a snake might when observing its prey. He
spent hours talking privately with Blendel and about what O'Connor
could only guess. When they weren't immersed in conversation, the
majority of Silver's time was spent reading or going through a complex martial arts routine. From conversations with Schiller, O'Connor knew that Silver was adept with electronic gadgetry. He was also
adept at hurting people. This became evident with two prostitutes
who had visited his quarters and came away from the experience injured. O'Connor had been called in to get the women medical attention and out of town as quickly as possible. Silver's most notable
features were his skin, eyes, and the color of his hair, which was nearly
white. He was a partial albino.

Out of curiosity O'Connor once did a background check on him.
He came up with very little of substance. The NCIC showed Silver

had two arrests for assault ten years earlier, both of which had been dropped. The international records produced similar results.

The following day, however, he was surprised to receive a visit from not only the Central Intelligence Agency, but from two Interpol agents who wanted to know why he was interested in Joshua Silver. O'Connor played it off, saying he had heard the name from one of his street sources in connection with a Harlem drug killing and was simply checking it out. He was still working as detective at the time.

The agents told him that Silver was wanted for questioning in at least five countries in connection with pay-for-hire murders and was to be considered extremely dangerous. The CIA agent revealed that Silver had once been a member of the U.S. Army Special Ops division in Bosnia, but went AWOL after killing another man in his unit. According to the reports, he cut the man's liver out while he was still alive.

O'Connor wanted as little to do with Joshua Silver as possible.

"My apologies for keeping you waiting, Nick," Blendel said, taking a seat behind his desk. "Thank you for coming. May I offer you something to drink?"

"A glass of water would be nice, Mr. B."

Blendel smiled and pressed a button on his intercom. "Please bring Chief O'Connor a glass of water."

"Ice?"

"Sure."

Schiller acknowledged him with a nod and sat down on a couch near the window. Linda Blendel took a chair next to her husband and crossed her legs. Joshua leaned against the wall at the rear of the room and remained standing. O'Connor twisted around in his seat and looked at him for a second before he turned back to Blendel. He didn't like having Silver behind him. A moment later, a servant entered through the regular door with the water and left again.

"I trust everything's all right with the family?" Blendel asked.

"They're fine, Mr. B. Thank you."

"My condolences about your niece."

"I appreciate that."

"The reason I asked you here tonight, Nick, is because I need to know that things are progressing where the girl is concerned."

"Everything is under control, Mr. B. There's nothing to worry about."

"That's excellent."

Linda Blendel lit a cigarette and expelled a long stream of smoke into the air. Her husband eyed it with a look of distaste, but said nothing.

"Exactly what are you doing, Chief?" she asked.

"We hired a family friend to settle Sarah's estate. He's a lawyer. It was Frankie's idea, so I went along with him. The guy doesn't practice law very much. He teaches at City College, though I think they changed the law school's name to John Jay College of Criminal Justice now."

Schiller picked up a file resting on his lap and read from it. He had a faint but noticeable German accent. "John Delaney is an ex–New York police detective first grade, previously assigned to the homicide division. Thirteen years ago he was injured in the line of duty after being shot in the chest three times. He took early retirement on a medical disability. Prior to entering the police force Mr. Delaney attended City College as a night student, where he earned his undergraduate degree in criminal justice. During his convalescence, he went on to acquire a Juris Doctorate in the law and passed the New York bar exam on his first attempt. Herr Delaney was later hired to replace Bernard Streck, a professor at John Jay who died of a heart attack some eight years ago. Presently, he teaches evidence and a course on forensic science there."

Oddly, when Schiller finished speaking, he closed the file and handed it not to Warren Blendel but to his wife.

She asked, "Is there a reason why you picked Mr. Delaney, Nick?"

O'Connor was surprised at her taking the lead, which was out of character for the Blendels. In all of their previous meetings Linda had merely been an observer. From time to time they had exchanged pleasantries with one another, but that was about it. This was the first instance he could recall her questioning him on a business matter. He glanced at Blendel before he answered and got nothing from the man's face. If anything, Blendel seemed slightly uninterested and was arranging and rearranging paper clips on his desk.

"Like I said, he's a friend of the family. It was Frankie's idea to go to him. I figured if I tried to talk him out of using Delaney it would only raise suspicions."

"Of course," Linda said.

"There won't be any trouble," O'Connor insisted. "Delaney has a girlfriend down in Atlanta, so I'm guessing the trip won't be strictly business, if you know what I mean."

Blendel finally pushed the paper clips aside and considered O'Connor for a moment.

"In retrospect, Nick, I fear Mr. Delaney may not have been the best choice given the circumstances." He reached out and took the file from Linda, then ran his finger down one of the pages, taking a moment to read what was there before he continued. "He is an intelligent and resourceful man, albeit removed from police work for several years. I hope you'll understand why I've asked Hans to monitor the situation."

"Sure," O'Connor said. "That's your choice." Then he jerked his thumb in Joshua's direction. "And where does he come in?"

Joshua pushed himself off the wall and came to sit on the corner of Blendel's desk.

Linda Blendel explained. "Joshua is additional insurance."

"For what?"

"To see that everything goes smoothly," she said. "Your niece's accident was a terrible tragedy, but the truth is, it really saved us a great deal of trouble. We simply want to make sure the situation remains stable."

"And you have some reason to think it won't?"

"Anything is possible. How much do you know about John Delaney's lady friend?" Linda asked.

O'Connor shrugged. "Not a heck of a lot except she's a lawyer and her name is Katherine something. Delaney met her on a ship last year. They've had a thing going ever since, but that's about it."

Warren Blendel glanced at Schiller, who opened a second file, slightly thicker than the first one, and began to read.

"Katherine Adams was a partner in the law firm of Boyd, Stevenson, Levitt, and Adams in Atlanta. Following the much-publicized sinking of the *Ocean Majestic* last year, she left her employment there and formed her own firm. They are said to be doing quite well.

She has three children and was previously married to a prominent heart surgeon. The marriage, however, ended in a bitter divorce. She was awarded custody of the children along with the family home, a twenty-eight-room mansion on four acres in Atlanta's suburbs. Interestingly, she is missing the ring finger of her left hand."

"And why is that interesting?" O'Connor asked.

"Because Ms. Adams's maiden name is Naismith," Schiller replied, "and she did not lose the finger as a result of an accident or an illness. It was cut off by a man named Richard Jenks, twenty-five years ago in Columbus, Ohio. She was a college student at the time."

O'Connor's brows came together as he searched his memory. "I remember that name," he said. "Jenks killed a bunch of coeds at Ohio State before the cops got him. He set himself and his cabin on fire. The guy was certifiable. He actually decapitated some of the girls and mounted their heads on his wall. The others he mutilated. He was a fuckin' lunatic."

"But one girl got away," Linda Blendel said.

"Adams?"

"She was Naismith then, but yes, Ms. Adams was the one who survived. Since that time she has suffered a type of post-traumatic stress disorder that subjects her to violent flashbacks. These attacks are held in check by medication."

Joshua frowned and took the file from Linda, then walked over to a chair in the corner, sat down, and started reading.

O'Connor watched him for a moment, and shook his head. He then returned his attention to the Blendels. "So what does all this have to do with the price of tea in China?"

"Ordinarily not much," Blendel said. "We're sharing this information with you because it pays to know who you're dealing with. You're our point man here, Nick. Our people in Atlanta tell us Ms. Adams is an intuitive and highly skilled lawyer. She's said to be quite tenacious in court. Some of that tenacity came to the surface when the *Majestic* went down last year and everyone was trying to make her the scapegoat. You may recall she initially identified the wrong man as being responsible. That character trait also appeared when she was a young girl and her survival was at stake."

"But we're not going to court, unless I'm missing something."

Blendel opened his mouth to speak, but his wife took the lead once again. "No, we're not going to court, Chief. What Warren is saying is that we don't want you to take this matter lightly. Judging by what Mr. Delaney and Ms. Adams have been able to accomplish in the past, they should be considered serious opponents. We're at a juncture where we can't afford any mistakes. You have a job to do, so let's get it done quickly, quietly, and with as little outside involvement as possible."

Blendel's sudden preoccupation with John Delaney and his girlfriend was confusing and didn't make any sense in the big picture, but this wasn't the time or place to pursue the subject, O'Connor concluded. He simply filed the information away and resolved to speak with Warren privately when he got the chance. The old man was acting strangely. He tried to catch his eye, but Blendel was looking elsewhere. Specifically, he was watching Joshua as he continued to pore over the file on Katherine Adams.

NINE

JOSHUA

WHEN the others were gone, Blendel shifted his attention back to Joshua Silver, who was still reading in the corner of the library. He had been staring at a news photo of Katherine for several minutes. Every once in a while the tip of his tongue flicked out to touch his upper lip.

Blendel pushed himself up from his desk and went to stand by his young protégé. He gently massaged Joshua's neck.

"What do you find so interesting, my boy?"

Joshua's response was to raise his shoulders slightly, but he offered nothing beyond that. After several seconds, he turned to stare out the patio window.

Blendel wasn't surprised by this behavior. He'd seen it before. He inclined his head sideways and looked down at the photograph. "She has an interesting face, this woman. Quite pretty. Her eyes are vaguely almond-shaped, wouldn't you say?"

Joshua nodded absently. It was Katherine's expression that had initially caught his attention. From the caption at the bottom of the photo he could see that it had been taken about a year earlier. It showed her in front of a courthouse speaking to the media after a trial. She looked very cool, very calm, and in control of the situation. The more he studied it, the more he could feel the pressure building inside him.

They always looked calm in the beginning, particularly the beautiful ones, until they found out who was really in charge. He was the master of life and death. That was how he thought of himself. Sex wasn't necessary. It was merely a tool to be used when the situation called for it. The ability to exercise complete control over another was a true aphrodisiac. Sometimes his victims, though he never thought of them that way, would beg and sometimes they would cry. He liked it when they begged. The pressure inside him went up another notch. He fantasized for several moments about how the Adams woman would react when he had her all to himself. Then he realized Blendel was saying something.

"What?"

"I said, you know how much I rely on you. Joshua. Getting the file is important to me. But no matter what, I don't want you to endanger yourself. Nothing is worth that. You've been like a son to me. . . ."

Joshua looked up at Warren Blendel and patted him on the hand with a smile. The man was a great deal different from his own father, a Bible-thumping hypocrite who worked religious revival shows throughout the Midwest. Blendel cared for him, truly cared. As a result, he now had a home and was treated like part of the family. It had almost been too easy.

When they first met by chance in a park five years earlier, they had talked for hours. He came to learn the old man's son had died of rheumatic fever as a child. It left a void in his life, one Joshua was more than willing to fill, particularly since it suited his own ends at the time. He saw the opening when Blendel told him how important a family was to him. Except for the army, he hadn't had a real family since he was fifteen. It was the year his father had hospitalized him during an alcoholic rage. The attack wasn't the first one.

Blendel understood. To his surprise, he found out that he and the old man had something in common. Blendel's father was a dockworker, with hands the size of hams, who beat him unmercifully when he was a child.

Living with Warren and Linda had been mutually beneficial for them all. Every now and then, he would do "favors" for his surrogate father. If they involved hurting someone, well, that couldn't be helped. A safe haven from the world was important to Joshua, so important he would kill if the situation warranted. Blendel had promised the house would be his one day. If the old man was aware of his oddities he said nothing about them. He never asked where Joshua went at night or about the girls he brought back to his room. His own father had once split his lip for looking at a neighbor girl in a "dirty" way.

Joshua's thoughts regarding his father produced an inward sigh. Despite the old bastard's shortcomings, he could absolutely weave magic in his sermons. People sat on long wooden benches mesmerized by his words. It was as if he were speaking to their very souls. Out of curiosity Joshua once looked up *mesmerized* in the dictionary and found that Mesmer was a real person—a hypnotist, in fact. That appealed to him, because a hypnotist was someone in charge. Unfortunately, he had not inherited his father's ability to charm the masses. His talent had surfaced on a different plane—the ability to exercise control. Early on he found that he could get friends to lie for him. Occasionally, he would convince them to steal something insignificant from the corner store. It wasn't that he wanted what they brought back. That wasn't the point. Just having someone do it was the real rush.

The night he beat his father to death with a baseball bat, the little town of Brenton, Kansas, had been shocked. For the umpteenth time the old drunk came to him smelling of sour whiskey and touching him where no parent should ever touch a child.

The sheriff's deputies, when they heard how he had suffered, shook their heads in sympathy and called in a social worker. His story made her want to comfort him. But what to do? A murder had been committed and that wasn't something you could sweep under the rug.

Even the state prosecutor, a man of long experience, wasn't immune after reading the physician's report on Joshua. The boy had scars around his anus, a sure sign of penetration and evidence of the preacher's perversions. He met with the county judge in his chambers along with Joshua's attorney, and a deal was worked out. None of them were quite certain of Joshua's real age, but he certainly looked old enough. If the Marines would take him, the solution to the problem was at hand. During the interview the boy explained that he was all alone in the world and how much he wanted a family of his own. And didn't the Marines advertise themselves as a band of brothers? Or maybe it was the Army.

The charge of second-degree murder was reduced to justifiable homicide and Joshua was shipped off to Parris Island.

He felt Blendel massaging the muscles of his shoulder and reached up to put his hand over the old man's.

"I'll always be here for you," he said with a smile. "You have nothing to worry about . . . Dad."

He thought the last part was a nice touch.

TEN

DELANEY

EMORY University is a mixture of old Southern architecture and modern buildings. The campus is lined with trees and walking paths. According to Katherine, the school had nearly doubled in size in the seventies and eighties, thanks to the generosity of an "anonymous benefactor." It now boasts one of the finest medical and law schools in the nation. The "anonymity" of the benefactor is an inside joke in Atlanta, because nearly everyone knows who he was—one of the heirs to the Coca-Cola fortune.

Once we located the Registrar's Office, I explained our situation regarding Sarah to a pleasant-looking woman at the reception desk. She examined the court documents, expressed her condolences, and pointed us toward the law school.

The dean was waiting for us in the lobby when we arrived.

Ben Chambers was a well-dressed man in his late fifties with an affable manner. I was surprised to find that he and Katherine knew each other. He kissed her on the cheek and shook my hand.

"Professor Delaney," he said, "I'm sorry to meet you under these circumstances. I've heard a lot about you from Katherine. Why don't we go up to my office where we can talk?"

On the way I glanced at Katherine and only got an unreadable smile in return. Chambers's office was large and decorated with cherry wood paneling, crown molding, and a pair of oriental rugs. The furniture was comfortable and of good quality; pretty much what you'd expect for the dean of a major law school. His desk was a French writing table with brass scrollwork down the legs. Overall, the room made a very dignified and proper impression.

"It's a terrible tragedy to lose one of our students," Chambers said, "particularly one as bright and personable as Sarah O'Connor was. I want to express my heartfelt sympathies to you and her family."

"Did you know her well?" I asked.

"Not as well as I would have liked. I try to meet all our students, but we have over eight hundred in the law school, so it's sometimes difficult. We did speak a few times and she seemed like a lovely young woman to me. She was on scholarship here, I believe."

"That's what her father told me," I said. "He mentioned the name, though I can't recall it at the moment. I'll have to notify them about her death next week."

"Maybe I can help," Chambers said. He reached behind him and punched a few keys on his computer. A page appeared on the screen. "Let's see . . . it's called the Hoch-Halpern Endowment. This is a new one for us. May I ask how Sarah's family is holding up?"

The wooden expression on Frank O'Connor's face surfaced in my mind. It was the look of a man drained of energy and spirit. "Not great," I said, "but they're dealing with it."

Chambers nodded his understanding. "My secretary will be back in a moment. I've asked her to make a copy of Sarah's records for you."

"I appreciate that."

"So . . . Katherine tells me you teach evidence and forensics at John Jay in New York. How do you like it?"

"It's a change from what I used to do, but so far it's been fun. You have to stay on your toes all the time. If you don't, the kids will eat you alive."

Chambers chuckled. "Babs Ramsey used to say the same thing when she was teaching. She's still dean up there, isn't she?"

"Sure is. You know each other?"

"It's a small community. I think you'll find Emory is a lot different from New York's City College system, John. Of course, we're highly competitive salary-wise—you have to be in this market—but our atmosphere is more laid back. One thing we ask of our teachers is that they make a serious commitment to the profession by keeping up with current legal trends and publishing their work."

"Oh, sure," I said, remembering the old "publish or perish" maxim that came with most university teaching positions.

For some reason Chambers went on to tell me about the school's health care plan, their tenure rules, and the retirement benefits they offered. I wasn't sure why he was doing this, but as long as he was being cooperative I figured I ought to listen out of courtesy. It wasn't like I had a lot of choice since his secretary wasn't back yet.

"Next month we're having a little get-together at my house. Most of the faculty and our board of directors will be there. Perhaps you and Katherine can join us?"

"Really?" Katherine said, "What day is it, Ben?"

Chambers took a PDA from the inside pocket of his jacket and consulted it. "Let's see," he said. "It's on Saturday, June twelfth, at two o'clock. I hope you can both make it."

"We'll try," I said. "Thanks for the invitation." I was still confused about why we were being invited, though the reason was beginning to dawn on me.

"That's great. Wally Djrenjsky is retiring at the end of next year. This will give you a good chance to meet the rest of our crew."

"Wally Djrenjsky?"

"Our evidence teacher."

I shot a quick glance at Katherine, but all I got was that pleasant smile again. She was right; I wasn't in her league when it came to playing poker. The secretary's arrival stopped me from sticking my other foot in my mouth and gave me a chance to recover from the realization that my girlfriend had set up this "chance meeting."

"I appreciate the copies, Dean," I said.

"Call me Ben."

"I'd like to ask another favor, if I may. Are you familiar with a student named Andre Rostov?"

Chambers's brows furrowed and he thought for a second. "That name doesn't ring a bell. Is he in our law school?"

"I really don't know. It's possible. We saw some mail addressed to him from Emory at Sarah's house, so I'm assuming he's a student."

Chambers turned to his secretary. "Martha, would you check the name for us? By the way, Martha Keller—this is Professor John De-

laney from New York. Martha actually runs the place," he added
with a wink. "I think you already know Ms. Adams."

"I do indeed," Martha said, shaking our hands in turn. "Just give
me a moment. Oh, Ms. Adams, I want to tell you that Alley is such
a nice girl. We're delighted to have her here."

"Thank you," Katherine said.

Martha disappeared through the door and we heard her typing at
her keyboard.

"Got him," she called through the doorway. "Andre's not in the
law school. He's enrolled in the medical school—second year. He
works at the hospital three nights a week and the clinic every other
Saturday. I'm printing his contact information for you now."

"The miracles of modern technology," Ben Chambers said. Then
he lowered his voice. "Martha could probably tell you his shoe size
and blood type if you asked her."

"Let's stick with the phone number for the time being," I said.

"Wonderful. I'll send Katherine directions to my house. I look forward to seeing you both again."

We said our good-byes and headed for the door. As promised,
Martha had a file waiting for us. She said she was looking forward
to seeing me again, too. It was amazing what a popular fellow I was
becoming.

"What?" Katherine said when we were alone in the hall.

"What was that all about?"

"I ran into Ben at a conference a few months ago and he mentioned that Djrenjsky was retiring. Naturally, your name came up."

"Naturally."

"It *did*," she insisted. "I'm proud of you, John, and I thought you
might want to keep your options open, in case, well . . . you know."

I knew. Katherine and her friend Beth once did a high five and
said, "Behind every great man, there's an even greater woman." Now
that I thought about it, I seemed to remember seeing a pillow in her
house with the same expression. The sad thing is any guy who thinks
men are in control doesn't have a clue.

We could have gotten into an argument, but having been married
and divorced myself, I tried to learn something from the experience.

If you have half a brain you don't let the little things bother you. If they do, you'd stay bothered all the time.

I leaned over and kissed Katherine on the forehead. "It might be a good idea," I told her. "Thanks, honey."

She responded with a smile that lit up the corridor, then squeezed my arm. We walked hand in hand toward the medical college like a couple of school kids.

MARTHA Keller had paved the way for us. Her counterpart, a diminutive woman named Susan Ash, came out to greet us in the lobby. She told us that Andre was attending a neurology lecture at the moment. We followed Susan down a long hall as she gave us a mini-tour of the school with pretty much the same it's-wonderful-to-work-here speech that Ben Chambers had used. I caught the look that passed between her and Katherine and decided that I was definitely outmanned . . . out-womanned, in this case.

Eventually, we came to the auditorium where a lecture was in progress. The room was an amphitheater. Fifteen students and a professor were gathered around a cadaver on the stage. The students were taking notes while the teacher spoke. On the wall behind them was an anatomical chart of the human body. Susan gave Katherine's hand a quick squeeze and departed. We sat down in the top row to wait.

The professor's voice drifted up to us. "The two major nerves we're studying today have their origin in the upper spinal column. They emerge from the scapula and continue down the length of the arm into the hand. Now if you will all move a bit closer, once we peel back this gentleman's skin, you'll have a better look at them."

Generally, I'm not squeamish, but I suddenly became conscious that the lunch Katherine had fixed for us was still in my stomach. The smell of formaldehyde wasn't helping matters either. As a kid I'd always associated it with a visit to the doctor's office and it usually wound up with me getting a needle. Funny how the mind works. I decided to look out the window and count leaves on the nearest tree.

Katherine, on the other hand, appeared fascinated by what was going on. She leaned forward in her seat and watched intently. If she had a legal pad, she would probably be taking notes.

When I ran out of leaves on the first branch I started on the next one. I don't recall what number I reached, but I was glad when the professor pulled the sheet back over his cold friend and declared the lecture over. We caught up with Andre in the lobby.

"Mr. Rostov, can I have a word with you?" I said.

Andre turned around and looked from Katherine to me. He was a little shorter than I was, maybe six feet. His face was reasonably handsome and his hair was black.

"Sure."

"I'm John Delaney and this is Katherine Adams," I said, introducing ourselves. "We're both attorneys. I've been hired by Sarah O'Connor's family to settle her estate. I understand you two were acquainted?"

There was a slight hesitation before he replied, "What can I do for you?"

"Do you want to talk out here or would you prefer somewhere more private?" I asked.

Andre looked around and spotted an empty classroom. "We can use this room."

"How long did you and Sarah know each other?" I asked once we got inside.

"About six months. We met at a party."

"And you were with her the night she died?"

He stared down at his feet for several seconds, then nodded. "Yeah. Going camping was a pretty bad idea. We had an argument and Sarah decided to take a walk. She never came back."

"Can you tell me what prompted you to go to Cloudland Canyon?"

"What do you mean?"

"Wasn't it exam week? I understand that's about a two-hour ride from here."

"Not for the medical school. I knew Sarah was under a lot of pressure and I thought a break would be good for her. She wasn't doing that well in her corporations class, so I suggested we forget about the books for a night and camp out. I don't even remember what the fight was about. Something stupid."

"Most of them are," I agreed. "How long were you both living together?"

Andre's eyes came up to meet mine. "Two months," he replied. Beyond that, he didn't show a reaction, though his expression grew cautious. Over the years, I've learned when interrogating subjects, it's often the little things that make a difference, like jaw muscles tightening, hands clenching, or an increase in the volume of their voice. Reactions of this type are largely involuntary and are good indicators of deception.

As I waited for him to continue, the silence grew heavy.

"Look, she didn't want her dad to know," he finally said. "He's some big-time cop up in New York. Sarah said he'd go through the roof if he found out. Are you going to tell him?"

I shrugged. "Probably not. I don't see what good it would do."

Andre nodded and appeared to relax. He sat on one of the desks and crossed his ankles. I thought the gesture was forced.

"Sarah meant a lot to me," he said. "If I hadn't asked her to go . . ."

"Were you at the funeral?" Katherine asked.

"I flew up for it and met her mom and dad. They were both really nice. This whole business hit me pretty hard. I was in love with her."

"Yeah, we could tell that from the tapes," I said.

That did it.

Andre's head snapped around toward me. "Those are private property, man."

"Funny, I didn't see your name on them."

"They're private," he repeated. "Sarah and I made them for each other. You have no right to them."

"Actually, I do. The courts say I'm responsible for gathering her property. Tell me I'm wrong, Andre, but I got the impression one of them was taken without her knowledge."

Mr. Rostov's eyes moved from me to Katherine then back to me again. His surprise gradually faded and was replaced by another expression—something harder and more calculating. He laughed once to himself. "We were both over twenty-one and consenting adults. There's nothing you can do, so piss off."

"You're wrong," Katherine said. "There's a great deal we can do, like letting the Fitness Committee know about your little hidden cameras and speaking to the dean of this college. Then there's the American Medical Association, who I'm sure would be really interested."

"You do and I'll sue your ass for invasion of privacy."

Andre took a step toward Katherine, but that was as far as he got. I moved in front of him and put a hand on his chest.

"You got a problem?" he asked.

It took a good deal of self-control on my part not to dump him on his ass. I wanted to—in fact, I wanted to very much, but that wouldn't have been particularly lawyerlike.

"Cool off, sonny," I said. "You want to know if I've got a problem? The answer's yes. Only I haven't decided what to do about it yet. Sarah's family's been hurt enough and I don't want to toss your film exploits in their lap. Her father would probably come after you with a gun and I wouldn't blame him. Now why don't you back up, unless you want to see how fast I can put you in your own hospital?"

For a second I thought he was going to swing at me, which would have been fine. But he thought about it and settled for a sneer.

Then, without another word, our new friend picked up his books and left the room.

ELEVEN

DELANEY

ON our way home, Katherine and I discussed what happened. Andre's reaction had surprised me. I don't know what I was expecting, but that definitely wasn't it. In one second he went from grieving lover to something closer to a pimp. It didn't make sense. I know couples make films like that all the time. Maybe it was just a case of runaway hormones, but something wasn't adding up. I couldn't get the vacant look I saw in Sarah's eyes on the last tape out of my head.

KATHERINE'S youngest child, Zach, met us at the front door, all smiles. He seemed to have grown two inches since the last time I'd seen him, which was only a month earlier. We'd hit it off from the start. He's one of the more together sixteen-year-olds I've met, an even-tempered kid with a good nature. According to Katherine, Zach had handled her divorce as well as could be expected, shuttling back and forth between her home and her ex's without any major problems. After saying hello, he asked permission to sleep at a friend's house for the weekend. Apparently, there was a paintball tournament on Saturday and his team was playing.

Katherine hates the sport as only a mother can. Not unusual where your son gets shot up with paint pellets and comes home with purple bruises. Nevertheless, she gave in and said it was okay on the condition all his homework was finished before he left. Zach gave her a kiss and disappeared up the stairs. A second later, his stereo came on. Whatever song he was listening to might have contained words. I couldn't be sure. I shook my head and looked at the nearest wall for a moment. It was actually shaking. My son had gone through a similar phase, as most teenagers do. All you can do is make sure there's enough aspirin around and wait it out.

That evening we ordered Chinese in and watched an old Spencer Tracy movie on the television. We were joined by her cat, Peeka, who insisted on wedging himself between us on the couch. Katherine likes cats more than dogs. I'm the opposite. I have to admit Peeka is different—a regular nutcase. If he were a person, the cops would have arrested him for stalking. Every time you turn around, he's there staring at you.

When the movie ended, I pulled Sarah's student file out and began leafing through it. It contained the usual documents: a transcript of her grades, her law school application, complete with letters of recommendation, records from the school's health clinic, and several pieces of correspondence from the law firm of Sheppard & Rainey. The letters caught my eye and I began reading.

Turns out they were the attorneys who administered the Hoch-Halpern Endowment, Sarah's scholarship. I jotted down the name and made a note to call them and let them know of her death when I got back to New York. The last item I examined was a "personal statement" Sarah had filled out for the admissions committee about why she wanted to study law. I'd done the same thing when I applied to law school.

As I began reading it, a sense of intruding on something private descended on me. I'd seen personal statements before, but there was a poignancy to this one that grabbed my insides. Sarah wrote about learning to respect the law from her father and how much it meant to her to be doing something that would make a difference in the world. She thought the law was a noble, decent profession. Maybe it was.

My contact with the O'Connor family had drifted since my father's death, but we were close once. I could still remember Sunday outings and pickup softball games. A picture emerged in my mind of Sarah as a skinny twelve-year-old playing soccer, red cheeked and laughing her head off as she ran for a ball. Then I saw here her in my evidence class. She was older and more serious, but basically the same person. I couldn't reconcile those images with what was on the tapes.

Eventually, guilt set in and I closed the file. I retrieved my stack of exams and started grading them again.

Three hours later, Katherine entered the room and gently began massaging my neck and shoulders.

"I didn't know you wore glasses," she said.

"They're just for reading. I got them a few months ago."

"Cute."

"Cute?"

"Mm-hmm. How are the papers going?"

"Slowly." I said, stretching. "What time is it?"

"One in the morning."

"Oh, for chrissake, I'm sorry, honey. I didn't realize the time."

Her hands moved from my neck to my chest. "I was getting a little lonely and thought I'd come check on you."

The message came through loud and clear. I set the papers aside and pulled her onto my lap. "We wouldn't want that, now, would we?"

Katherine's eyes met mine and she shook her head slightly.

"Uh . . . right. Let me jump in the shower and I'll join you in a minute," I said. "Do you think Zach's asleep?"

"Mm-hmm."

That was when I noticed what she was wearing under her robe—nothing.

For a moment I considered vaulting the couch and sprinting into the bathroom, but as a professor of law, one has to maintain a certain degree of decorum. Regardless, I got there in record time and would have been out just as quickly, but halfway through I found that I had company. I nearly drowned trying to be creative.

In the morning we ate breakfast on the patio. Orange juice and a bagel for me; sliced cantaloupe and coffee for her. Zach apparently woke on his own and caught the school bus. He left us a note saying he'd be back on Saturday after the tournament. All was well in the world.

I sat there listening to the splash of Katherine's fountain and trying to convince myself that Atlanta really was a great place to live. This wasn't much of a stretch. It's somewhat cliché these days to say you've found a soul mate, the expression's been used to death, but that's how I was feeling and I was pretty sure Katherine was on the same page.

We could have stayed in bed the whole morning or played footsie under the table with each other, but there was work to do. I needed a copy of Sarah's death certificate and I needed to move the case along before any more surprises popped up. During the night—I couldn't say exactly when—I reached the decision to trash the tapes. There isn't much I'm certain of, but there was no question on this one. Frank and Lucille O'Connor were better off not knowing they existed.

I informed Katherine about wanting to pick up Sarah's death certificate rather than wait for it to arrive in the mail. She responded by picking up the telephone and placing a call to the Dade County sheriff's office.

UNLIKE its Florida counterpart, Georgia's Dade County uses English as its principal language. The sheriff's office is located in the little town of Trenton, a pleasant community in the extreme northwest corner of the state.

We arrived around 11 a.m., parked in the town square, and asked directions from an elderly fellow sitting in front of the local barber shop.

He watched us approach and said, "Morning, folks."

Katherine said good morning back and nudged me in the ribs when I didn't respond. New Yorkers don't do that.

"Uh . . . good morning," I said.

"Beautiful day. Y'all visiting?"

"We are," I told him. "We're trying to find the sheriff's office. Can you tell me how to get there?"

"Something the matter, son?"

"No, nothing's wrong. We just need to pick up some papers."

"If you're going to court today, Lucas could clean you up in no time," he said, gesturing at the barbershop with his head. "He ain't real busy at the moment and Judge Jackson's a stickler for lawyers making a good appearance in his courtroom."

I glanced at my reflection in the window. I might have been overdue for a haircut, but I thought I looked reasonably presentable.

"What makes you think we're going to court?" I asked.

"Well, you're lawyers, ain't you?"

Katherine laughed. "Does it show that much?"

He hiked his shoulders. "On the whole, little lady, I'd say you're too good-looking to be a lawyer, but that attaché case of yours is a dead giveaway. So's the file the young feller's carrying."

Katherine and I managed to keep straight faces.

"I'll pass on the haircut," I said. "We're just here to see the sheriff. You're right about the lawyer part, though."

"Knew it," he said, snapping his fingers.

"Can you give us directions?" Katherine prompted.

"Sure can. Go to the end of this street, just past where the Delacort Inn used to be, then turn left. It'll be the second house on the right. There's a sign up top. Didn't used to have one, but they do now."

We thanked him and started off. I didn't know the first thing about a Delacort Inn or how to find something that wasn't there anymore, but the end-of-the-street part made sense. While we were walking I glanced at Katherine. "Do you think I need cleaning up?"

"Nope, can't say as I do," she said, doing a reasonable imitation of our new acquaintance. "You seem like a nice clean-cut young feller to me . . . for a Yankee, that is." For emphasis, she spat on the sidewalk, something I'd rarely, if ever, seen a woman do. I wasn't even sure they *could* spit.

Ms. Adams's act caught me completely off guard and I started laughing. We'd been with each other for over a year and it was the first time I'd ever seen this side of her. Live and learn.

It was a warm spring day and strolling along together felt good in a way that's hard to describe. Despite the circumstances that had brought us to Trenton, I was enjoying myself.

THE sheriff turned out to be a woman named Sophie Clark. We walked in on her while she was in the process of painting the lobby. She was on top of a stepladder, holding roller in one hand.

"Hi," she called down. "Give me a second and I'll be right with you. My desk is buried somewhere under this drop cloth. I've already got your file out."

I frowned and glanced at a mirror on the wall to see if someone had hung a sign on my back that said LAWYER.

"I like the color," Katherine told her.

Sophie's face lit up. "I've been trying to add a woman's touch to this place for years. The guys don't care much for it, but I'm hoping it'll grow on them."

"What do they know?" Katherine said. "I think it looks nice."

"Exactly," Sophie agreed with an emphatic nod.

The sheriff clambered down off the ladder and wiped her hands on a cloth in her back pocket. She looked to be about five foot nine and maybe thirty pounds overweight. Her grip was stronger than most men I knew.

Sophie said, "After I took office last September, the Town Council promptly cut my budget. I guess they weren't crazy about having a woman in this position. It took me a month of lobbying and yelling my head off before I got them to buy this house for us. We won't enough have money for repairs until the next budget. Until then I'm the chief cook and bottle washer."

"Well, I think it's great," Katherine said, surveying the rest of the office. "There's a lot of potential, and the flowers are a nice touch."

Sophie smiled at the compliment. "I take it you're Katherine Adams and Professor Delaney."

"John," I replied.

"Sounds good. Katherine tells me you used to be a detective."

"That's right. I was with NYPD homicide for twelve years."

"Is that how you got this case?"

"No, I'm a friend of the family. Sarah's dad and my dad were partners."

Sophie stuck out her lower lip and nodded her approval. "Well . . . it's real decent of you to come all this way to help them, John. Keep us in mind if you ever decide to get back into law enforcement. I'll wring some money out of those tightwads for a third deputy next year."

I smiled. "Sure will."

"Give me a second," Sophie said. She located the edge of the drop cloth, disappeared under it, and reemerged a few seconds later with an eight-by-ten yellow envelope that she handed to me.

I removed the death certificate and read through the coroner's conclusions at the bottom of the page. "Accidental death due to a fall."

"Pity about that young girl. We've had three deaths at the canyon this year."

"Really?" said Katherine.

"There are signs posted all along the upper trail warning hikers to exercise caution, but some people just don't pay attention, and . . ." Sophie finished the sentence by making a diving motion with her hand.

"Was an autopsy done?" I asked.

The question seemed to surprise her. "Sure. It's standard procedure."

"Do you suppose I could have a copy of it?"

"Why in the world would you want the autopsy report? The girl was positively identified by two people and there's no question about her cause of death."

"I know. It turns out all the students at Sarah's law school have a benefits package as part of the annual fees they pay. A small amount goes to life insurance. My guess is the insurance company will eventually ask for it, so I'm trying to cover my bases."

Sophie stared at me for a moment and then went into the next room, where a filing cabinet was located. She returned with a manila folder, shaking her head. "I hope you both have strong stomachs," she said.

"Why?" Katherine asked.

"First, Sarah fell a long way down a rocky canyon. Second, she was out there for two days before our search team found her body. By that time the animals had gotten to her. What you're going to see isn't pretty," she added, handing me the folder.

Her point became clear a second later. I could have lived my life just as happily had I not opened that folder, but people have a morbid fascination with accidents and gruesome pictures. It's sort of like watching the *Jerry Springer* show. Over the years I'd viewed my share of crime scene victims; more than my share, actually. Katherine immediately gasped and turned away. I felt like I'd just gotten blindsided.

Sarah's body was bloated and swollen. Her left arm and leg were bent at impossible angles, as was her neck. Sophie's comment about the animals getting to her hit home with full force. Most of Sarah's face was gone. It was barely recognizable as human.

My stomach started doing flips and I shut the file.

Sophie patted me on the back sympathetically and fished a bottle of scotch out of her desk. She poured two drinks and handed them to Katherine and me. Then she poured one for herself.

"I reacted the same way when Clyde sent them over."

"Clyde?" I asked.

"Clyde Broome, our county medical examiner."

I downed my drink in a single gulp. Some of the color returned to Katherine's face as she finished hers.

"Sorry. I tried to warn you," Sophie said. "This is one of the worst cases we've had in a long while, and let me tell you, I've seen a bunch."

"Why did it take so long to find her?" Katherine asked.

"We searched the wrong area the first day. According to the witnesses, the night it happened Sarah and her boyfriend got into an argument and she stalked off. We figure she got lost and wandered around for a while. At some point she missed her footing and took the plunge. Her friends stayed out looking for her until noon the next day before they called us. The search team didn't get organized until that afternoon, and Cloudland Canyon's a pretty big place."

"Damn," Katherine said, sitting on the edge of the desk.

"You can have copies of their statements if you want 'em."

We spent ten more minutes with Sophie before we said good-bye. It was a long ride back to Atlanta.

TWELVE

SCHILLER

ACROSS the street from the sheriff's office, two men in a black SUV watched Delaney and Katherine go in. The SUV's windows were heavily tinted to prevent anyone from seeing inside. The men were still there when they came out. Twenty minutes earlier, Hans Schiller had trained a small parabolic dish with an eighteen-inch microphone at the house. Its common name was a Super Ear, and with it you could listen to conversations a block away. Only a few government agencies had access to them. The man next to him also watched the couple intently through a pair of binoculars. After a few minutes he set the binoculars down, picked up the file on Katherine Adams, and began reading it—again.

Joshua Silver was not an easy person to be around, Schiller decided. His skin was largely devoid of color and his eyes were so pale you could practically see through them. The physical abnormalities aside, this was not what disturbed him. It was Silver's personality . . . or the lack of it. Hours might pass without him uttering a word. He would sit immobile, lost in his own world, alone with whatever thoughts were going around in his head. What those thoughts were, Schiller had no desire to speculate. For the last three days his companion had read and reread the files on Delaney and Katherine Adams so many times, he had lost count. He seemed to have fixated on the woman's background. Before leaving New York, Joshua downloaded all the newspaper accounts he could find on the Ohio serial killer, Richard Jenks. Jenks had set fire to his cabin, burning himself and the three girls he had kidnapped to death before the authorities could reach him. Adams was the only one to have escaped.

"What are you whistling?" Schiller asked.

"Just some tune I heard."

"Well, stop it. It's getting on my nerves."

Joshua eyes moved to Schiller for a moment, but he stopped the whistling and picked up the binoculars again, training them on Katherine.

"She really is missing a finger. Do you want to see?" he asked, offering the binoculars to Schiller.

"Who cares about her goddamn finger, Joshua? It has nothing to do with why we are here. Our concern is the file—nothing more."

Joshua tilted his head slightly to one side and stared at him for a long moment, then went back to watching.

The decision to bring Joshua on this mission was a mistake. Schiller knew that. The man might be incredibly efficient, but he was a time bomb waiting to go off. When they returned to New York, he intended to speak to Blendel about it, or Linda Blendel, which would be more useful. The husband still made the decisions—at least on the surface—but it was now his wife who called the shots. He wasn't sure when Blendel had lost his nerve. The man still could make a good show of it, but something had definitely changed in his personality. Perhaps it was advancing age.

To look at Warren and Linda Blendel, you'd never know anything was wrong. They continued to attend charity functions in Manhattan and the Hamptons when necessity dictated just as they always had. Blendel, he knew, was once considered the boy wonder of organized crime, full of spit and fire. Now the man tended to avoid arguments, of which there were plenty, particularly with Madam Blendel, who was eighteen years his junior.

Schiller couldn't recall how many men had passed through Linda Blendel's bedroom since he arrived on the scene. There was the tennis instructor, the pool boy (despite the cliché), and her personal fitness trainer, not to mention himself in recent years. He harbored no illusions where she was concerned. The woman was like a democratic drawbridge, going up and down for anyone who caught her eye. His role, as he viewed it, was just part of the services he performed as a loyal employee. If her husband was aware of these dalliances, he never let on.

THE truth was that Blendel caught a lucky break with the girl's accident, but then he had always been lucky. The man was a survivor.

Smarter than most of his contemporaries, he had seen the handwriting on the wall and moved his operations from the city to the suburbs years earlier. The police were becoming increasingly sophisticated, employing more and more modern techniques, so he adapted as well. There might not be as much money from drugs and pornography on the city's outskirts, but it was certainly enough to go around. It wasn't that Blendel even needed it anymore.

Ego, Schiller thought morosely. *This is what it always comes down to.*

Blendel once told him that a man must never give up what he had fought for. "To do so, shows weakness, Hans. There are people were out there waiting for the first crack in the armor."

That made sense. The important thing now was to put this matter to rest—quickly. Schiller's sources in the Justice Department told him the FBI was also moving to recover the file. Loose ends were dangerous and his employers were not people who liked such things.

"What do you think?" he asked Joshua.

"They know nothing. Their questions were all routine."

"Yah, but the file wasn't in the girl's house or we'd have found it."

"Perhaps. . . ."

Both men stopped speaking as Katherine and Delaney passed their car. Joshua reached up and adjusted the rearview to watch them. He licked his lips.

"She has a fine body," he said.

Schiller took a mental breath. "We could have done a more thorough job in our search," he replied.

"Not without tearing the place apart."

"They'll move the girl's furniture to storage tomorrow. Once that's done, I say we go back to the house and do it correctly. Afterwards, we can check the storage area."

"And if we still come up with zero?"

Joshua shrugged. "Then we'll look elsewhere," he answered, his eyes never leaving Katherine's retreating form.

THIRTEEN

DELANEY

KATHERINE and I changed clothes and went for a run at a nearby park that winds along the Chattahoochee River. After being cooped up in a car for several hours, it felt good to move. We had the death certificate and all the legal papers were filed, so there was no harm in taking a break. The moving company wasn't scheduled to pick up Sarah's furniture until the following day. As a cautionary matter, I called to confirm our appointment and they assured me they would be there by 10 a.m. The tapes Sarah had made were still unsettling, but I decided not to dwell on them any longer. Let the dead keep their secrets.

Ms. Adams, as I mentioned before, is in excellent shape. She moved along the running path easily somehow managing to keep up a steady stream of conversation. I did my best to stay with her, but after a mile it was obvious she could run rings around me. Having to talk and jog without sounding like I was having a heart attack wasn't easy, and I made it to the finish line mostly on male pride.

The next morning I got in touch with Frank O'Connor.

"Frank, it's John Delaney. I'm here in Atlanta and wanted to update you on our progress."

"Hey, Johnny. Great to hear from you. I appreciate the call." He sounded genuinely pleased.

"I filed papers with the Fulton County Probate Court yesterday. Since we haven't located Sarah's will, we're assuming she didn't have one and we're proceeding with a statutory administration. The judge appointed me temporary administrator."

"That's fine," Frank said.

"Katherine and I also secured the car when we were at her house.

We went through the place pretty thoroughly and made a photographic inventory of all her furniture, clothes, and personal property. I've hired a moving company that is coming out later today to pack everything up. Once that's done we'll put it all in storage."

"Right, right. It sounds good."

"Listen, Frank, I know this is painful, but you and Lucille really need to sit down and discuss what you want me to do. Once I hand in my inventory to the court and get a final order, I'm supposed to turn over all of Sarah's property to you. Our other choice would be to liquidate everything. Do you get what I'm saying?"

The silence on the end of the line was followed by a long breath.

"I understand. It's just a little tough dealing with this now. You try to think about other things and keep busy—but it stays with you, you know?"

"I know," I said quietly.

Another breath. "All right, I'll talk with Lucille tonight. Do you want me to call you at the office or your home?"

"Either one will be fine."

I also gave him Katherine's number.

"Johnny . . . thanks for everything you're doing. I just can't deal with this now."

"No problem, pal. By the way, Katherine and I ran into a young man named Andre Rostov, who sends his condolences. He was a friend of Sarah's."

Frank thought for a minute. "I remember him. He and Sarah were dating. He's a nice kid, a medical student. He came up here for her funeral with a couple of his friends."

I asked, "Were they dating long?"

"A couple of months. Why?"

"Just curious, that's all. I wanted to let you know we ran into him. Ben Chambers, the dean of the law school, also sent his condolences."

"Chambers, right. I spoke with him on the phone. If you see him, tell him we appreciated the flowers and the card. The whole faculty signed it."

We said our good-byes and hung up. If Frank knew Sarah and Andre had been living together he gave no indication of it. My guess was that he didn't and I decided to leave the matter where it was.

Katherine and I spent a quiet evening together and took in a movie. I was in favor of something where people and cars get blown up; she wanted a chick flick. In the end we compromised and went to a comedy. It was a good decision, because we both came out of the theater feeling a little better. I needed to get those autopsy images out of my head.

On the way home we stopped at a local supermarket and picked up a platter of shrimp, a box of pricey crackers, and some fancy spread from the gourmet section. Then we located a wine store. Katherine elected to wait in the car and sent me in to pick out whatever I liked.

To put it mildly, my knowledge on the subject of wine is sorely limited. When you buy wine you have to have some idea what you're talking about or you end up sounding like the village idiot. Over the years, I've tried assimilating the basics, but they've never stuck, so I did the next best thing—I found the manager and asked him for a recommendation. Of course, he wanted to know what kind of wine I was partial to. I really didn't care. To me, they all taste the same and I only drink it when someone hands me a glass at a party. However, I could see Katherine through the store window patiently waiting. She wiggled her fingers at me and I wiggled mine back. In view of the pricey crackers and fancy spread we had just bought, I thought champagne would be overkill. Romantic maybe, but definitely overkill. In the back of my mind I remembered that white wine was supposed to go well with fish.

"White, I suppose," I told the man.

"Domestic or foreign?"

"Uh . . . foreign."

"Are you looking for something full-bodied or fruity?"

"Aren't they all fruity? I mean they come from grapes."

"Sure, but there are other fruits the vintners can blend. For example, many wines have a noticeable citrus quality and many—"

"Look buddy, let me level with you. I have a tough time telling one wine from another. I just want one that tastes good. How about if you surprise me?"

He gave me a knowing smile. "All right, what price range shall we start?"

I shrugged. "I don't know. What's reasonable?"

"Oh, you could go from six dollars to over ninety."

See what I mean? It's like being stuck in a goddamn maze.

"Does twenty dollars sound right?" I asked.

"Oh my, yes. You could get a nice chardonnay. They're always a safe bet. We also have some German Rieslings in that range which are a lot of fun. In my opinion, they're every bit as good as some of the French labels." He picked up a bottle and handed it to me. "This one is racy and it has a fruity bouquet with a highly refined nose."

"Right, that clears it up. Uh, aren't they supposed to come with corks?"

"Some do and some don't."

"I thought the better ones have corks. I'll look pretty stupid sniffing a cap."

A long-suffering expression appeared on the manager's face. He picked another bottle off the shelf and handed it to me. "Try this one, pal. Just stick it in the fridge for about thirty minutes before you drink it."

I thanked him and headed back to the car.

"What did you get?" Katherine asked.

"A nice Riesling."

"Good. I like German wines. It'll go great with the shrimp."

"That's what I thought. A lot of that French stuff is overrated."

Katherine smiled and slipped her arm through mine as we drove. Once we got to her place she brought out a pair of long-stemmed glasses and I put the wine in the refrigerator as instructed. Throughout the day, the temperature had dropped considerably and it was now somewhere in the mid-fifties. I joined Ms. Adams in the family room. She already had a fire going in the fireplace and had lit a number of scented candles.

"I thought this would be romantic," she said, snuggling next to me on the couch.

"How about we get naked and do it right here in front of the fire?"

"Sex isn't the same as romance, John."

I could have argued this point, but I had the feeling if I did, romance was the only thing I would get that evening. The fact is, the fire was nice and the candles didn't smell all that bad. I found a Norah Jones CD that I knew Katherine liked and put it on. We sat there holding hands and watched the fire. After a half hour I figured the wine was ready, so I got it out of the fridge and poured a glass for each of us, commenting on its fruity taste. That was as far as I could push it. I simply couldn't bring myself to say anything about its "refined nose" without my own growing larger. So much for sophistication.

Katherine moved closer and rested her head on my chest. Her fingers gently trailed up the inside of my thigh which caused some other things to grow. The wine might have been partly responsible, but most of the credit went to Katherine's fingers. I responded by kissing the nape of her neck. Then I kissed her on the ears and along her jawline. Eventually, she got up and stretched in front of the firelight, her figure a silhouette. She took her time removing her blouse and bra. Her skirt and panties followed a moment later. My own clothes came off at a much faster rate. What was left of my wine disappeared in a single gulp and I went to her. In the end it was a spectacular evening. Maybe those Germans are on to something after all.

The next morning I rolled over to find I was the only one in bed. The clock read 7:30 a.m. I was aware Katherine liked to exercise early, so I put on the new robe she'd bought me and went in search of my girlfriend.

I found her in the family room standing in front of a full-length mirror. One leg was up on a brass ballet bar fully extended; the other one was straight. I stood in the doorway and watched as she bent from the waist, nearly touching her knee with her nose. Nothing lascivious here. She was wearing gray sweatpants and a dancer's top. Her hair was pulled back in a ponytail. I just like looking at her. On the stereo an old Donna Summer song was playing.

It took a moment before I realized that she was reading Sarah's file.

Katherine became aware I was standing there and glanced at me from under her arm. "Morning, honey. Did you sleep well?"

"I don't recall sleeping much, but what there was was great. How about you?"

I got a mischievous smile for a reply. "I'll fix us breakfast in a few minutes," she said.

"No hurry."

She blew me a kiss and continued to stretch as she read, one arm extended above her head and the other was out in front of her. Ballerinas have a name for this position, I think, except they don't use files.

I was about to head into the kitchen and start the coffee going when her voice stopped me.

"John, how tall was Sarah O'Connor?"

"I have no idea. Middle height. Why?"

Katherine slowly took her leg off the bar, picked up a towel, and draped it around her neck. Frowning, she looked first at one page of Sarah's file and then flipped to another.

"What's up?" I prompted.

"Take a look at this."

I came over, kissed her on the cheek, and took the file from her. She had marked two pages with paper clips. One was the coroner's report; the other was a photocopy of Sarah's medical records from Emory's student health center. At the top of the coroner's report, the vital statistics listed her height as five feet seven inches and her weight at 131 pounds. I turned to the second page and had to read what I saw there twice. Sometime in early February, Sarah had stopped by the clinic complaining of a cold. Whoever did the intake on her listed her weight as 119 pounds and her height as five feet five inches.

I blinked in surprise and looked at Katherine. "Do you think they made a mistake?"

"Someone sure did," she replied. "I can see gaining a few pounds, but not growing two inches. What do you make of it?"

"I don't know. There could be any number of explanations. Most likely, someone got the numbers mixed up."

"Sure, I guess."

"Not everyone's as smart or as beautiful as you," I said, giving her another kiss. "In all likelihood, no one will ever notice the discrepancy, but I suppose we should check it out."

"How?"

"Law students are fingerprinted when they enter school, so I'm guessing the correct information will be on the card she filled out."

"Sounds good. What would you like for breakfast?"

"How about some of your famous French toast and a little bacon?"

"John, you should really eat more fruit. It's a lot healthier."

"Okay, put some fruit on top of the toast. It'll cancel out the bacon."

My witty remark earned me a flat look and a jab in the ribs.

"I'm serious. I want you to take better care of yourself. It sets a good example for the children."

I could have pointed out that Zach ate more junk food than any kid I'd ever met, and that her other "children" were grown. But this wasn't a fulcrum on which the universe rested, and giving in was no big deal. You stay ahead of the game that way.

Being a conciliatory type, I said, "Well, maybe a plate of pineapple or melon would be a good idea. I'll try it with some of that granola you eat."

Katherine wrapped her arms around my neck and gave me a hug, then went into the kitchen. When she was gone I sat down on the couch and started reading Sarah's file again.

WE arrived at Sarah's house ahead of the movers. There was some time to kill, so I decided to check the rooms again to make sure we hadn't missed anything. I wasn't particularly bothered by the discrepancies in her file, but I needed to clear the matter up before it became a problem.

Everything in the house appeared quite normal . . . until I got to Sarah's bedroom. Not only had the four-poster bed been moved so that the feet were now back in their original indentations, the dresser was also missing the layer of dust I had seen a day ago. Instinct took over and I began to examine the room more closely. There were other changes, not a lot, but changes nonetheless. I wasn't sure what to make of this, but I decided not to mention it to Katherine. There was no point in alarming her. For all I knew they could have been Andre's doing. What disturbed me was that there was no reason for them.

While Katherine was busy labeling boxes and supervising the movers, I placed a phone call to Ben Chambers. I was going to leave a message because it was a Saturday, but was surprised to find him in. I mentioned that to his secretary, Martha. Before putting me through, she explained they were working a six-day week because of a trustee meeting later in the day.

"John, what a nice surprise. Are you enjoying your stay?"

"Sure am, Ben. I need a favor, though, if you can mange it."

"Shoot."

"Can I get a copy of Sarah's fingerprint card?"

There was a pause at the other end of the line. "That's an odd request. Do you mind if I ask why?"

I told him.

This time the pause was longer. "I understand. It's probably human error as you say, but it can't hurt to check. To be honest, I don't even know if we keep fingerprint cards here at the school. I suspect they're all sent to the Georgia Bureau of Investigation."

"That makes sense. If you do locate them, could you give me a call back?"

"No problem. I'll be in a planning meeting until noon. But I'll have Martha get in touch with you."

I debated whether to share my suspicions with Ben about someone going through Sarah's house, but again decided to keep this to myself. As a rule I don't like making statements I can't back up. Fifteen minutes later my cell phone rang.

"Good morning, Professor Delaney. This is Martha Keller. Dean Chambers asked me to check if we maintain copies of student fingerprint cards here. Unfortunately, we don't. They're all sent to the GBI for a background check and that sort of thing. I have the contact information about who to call if you still want it."

"Wonderful, Martha. Tell Ben I said it's okay for him to give you that raise."

She giggled. "I will. You mention it, too."

My phone call to the Georgia Bureau of Investigation got me exactly nowhere. After I conveyed my request to the receptionist, she promptly placed me on hold. Three minutes passed and I was about to hang up when a fellow named Horace Womack came on the line.

"This is Special Agent Womack. I understand you're interested in obtaining a copy of a deceased person's fingerprint card?"

"That's right."

"Do you suspect foul play was involved in her death?"

"No, no, nothing like that. I just think someone at the Emory student clinic made a mistake regarding her height and weight and I'm trying to clear it up."

"Understood. What is your name, sir?"

"John Delaney."

"May I ask what your relationship is to the deceased, Mr. Delaney?"

"I'm a friend of the family as well as their attorney. I was recently appointed administrator of Ms. O'Connor's estate. The reason I need the fingerprint card is because—"

"Right, you told the secretary something about a possible insurance claim. Do I have that correct?"

"Yes, you do."

"And where are you calling from, Mr. Delaney."

"I'm at Sarah O'Connor's house with another lawyer and the moving company. We're in the midst of transferring her property to storage at the moment. What difference does it make where I'm calling from?"

"I see. May I have the name of the other party with you?"

I frowned. "Why is that important?"

"Just basic information. I'm completing my notes."

"You need notes for this? Look, this isn't a big deal. A simple yes or no will do."

"Understood, John. Do you mind if I call you John?"

I took a deep breath. "No, Horace, I don't."

"Okay, let's see; where were we?"

"You were asking who else is here with me. The other attorney's name is Katherine Adams. There are also three guys from the moving company with us. One of them is named Oswaldo. I didn't catch the others' names."

"Thanks. Is that Katherine with a *K* or a *C*?"

"*K.*"

"All right. I'll need to get your social security number and date of birth, if you don't mind."

"Actually, I do. I was a homicide detective for twelve years with the NYPD. What's with the full-court press?"

I could practically hear Womack thinking as he repeated to himself, "Homicide detective . . . New York Police Department." He was typing on a keyboard.

"Bear with me, John. You know how it is. You say you're at the O'Connor house now?"

"That's what I said."

"Is there a contact number where I can reach you?"

"Sure." I gave him my number.

"That sounds like a cell phone. Are you staying here in town?"

"I am."

"And the address?"

"All right, *Horace*, listen up. We're though playing twenty questions. You can check me out if you want. I teach law at John Jay College of Criminal Justice in New York and my former boss is still with the NYPD. His name is Dave Varley. If you want to cut through the rest of this bullshit, I'll be happy to fax you a copy of the probate court's order. Now do I get the fingerprint card or not?"

"Unfortunately, we have a departmental policy against giving those out. They're government property and we can't have the information falling into the wrong hands—identity theft and all that. I'm sure you understand. It's also a matter of homeland security."

"Her height and weight are matters of homeland security?"

Womack's chuckle sounded about as forced as you can get. "Bureaucracy, right?" he said. "But them's the rules. Now let me ask you—"

"Why the hell didn't you just say this at the beginning of our call?"

"I don't mean to upset you. Perhaps you'd like to speak to a supervisor?"

I pulled the phone away from my ear and stared at the receiver. I couldn't believe what I was hearing.

"Let me try this again. I can't see any way a dead girl's height and weight qualify as state secrets. How about if you just hang on to the card and tell me what it says?"

Another chuckle. "Sorry, no can do. We're not permitted to reveal the contents of any official government documents without proper authorization."

"Such as?"

"Such as a court order."

"You're kidding?"

"I wish I were, John, you being a former detective and all. Is there anything else I can do for you?"

I resisted the urge to tell him what he could do and disconnected. Katherine came out of the house, took one look at my face, and raised her eyebrows in a silent question.

"I just called your Georgia Bureau of Investigation to ask for a copy of Sarah's fingerprint card. The guy who answered completely stonewalled me. What ever happened to Southern hospitality?"

"Why wouldn't they give it to you?"

"The duty agent or whoever the hell he was told me I had to apply for a court order."

"*What?*"

"I'm serious."

"That's weird."

LESS than a half hour after my phone conversation with the GBI, the movers informed me they had finished loading the boxes on to the truck. I was in the middle of giving them directions to the storage place when a black Mercury Marquis pulled up to the curb and two men in gray suits got out. Neither buttoned their jackets.

I made them as law enforcement immediately. Cops are taught to leave their jackets open in case they have to go for their gun. The man on the left was middle height and somewhere in his early forties. He looked reasonably fit. His companion was at least ten years older and maybe twenty pounds overweight. He wore his hair in a crew cut and reminded me of what a master sergeant might look like if you stuck him in civilian clothes.

"Professor Delaney," the man on the left said, extending his hand to me. "I'm Horace Womack and this is Special Agent Phillip Thurman with the FBI. We'd like to talk with you if you have a moment."

I have to admit the suddenness of their appearance surprised me. For the last hour I'd been expecting the other shoe to fall, and this was it.

"Sure."

"And you must be Katherine Adams," Womack said, turning to Katherine. "I'm Horace Womack."

Katherine shook his hand. "Pleased to meet you."

Thurman introduced himself.

I offered to take them back inside, but they declined.

"You want to talk out here?" I asked.

"Not really," Thurman replied. "I was hoping you'd both come down to my office. It's a little quieter and we can chat in private."

"It's probably not the best time," I told him. "We have to make sure my client's possessions are secured, then I have to go to the court and apply for an order so I can get her fingerprint card."

"Listen, I'm sorry about that," Womack said. "You caught me off guard earlier. If you'll tell me where you're moving Ms. O'Connor's things to, we can follow you. Then we can head over to Phil's office."

I looked at Katherine and she raised her shoulders, indicating it was my call.

"We're putting them at the Store-All facility on Briarcliff Road," I said. "But we're not going anywhere until I get some straight answers."

"Technically we could take you in for questioning," Womack said, "but I'm hoping we won't have to do that."

Katherine's pleasant demeanor promptly evaporated. "Technically, you can do squat, Agent Womack. I was with the U.S. Attorney's office for eight years and I don't like being bullied. If you take us in for questioning, you'd damn well better have a good reason for it, or I'm going to eat your lunch. Now let's see some ID."

It was neat watching her shift gears like that. I didn't even have to act macho. If I ever get into a fight I'm definitely calling Katherine to defend me. Both agents reached for their wallets and produced their badges and identification cards, complete with photos.

Thurman was nonplussed, but he decided to backtrack. "Let me apologize. Maybe we're coming on a little strong. How about if I ask if you would *please* come with us? I assure you my request is a legitimate one."

"And it has something to do with Sarah's death?" I asked.

"It might," Thurman answered. "The problem is we don't know yet. You threw us a curve a while ago, and we're trying to assess if the height and weight discrepancy you found means anything."

That the United States government and the Georgia Bureau of Investigation were interested at all was sufficient to pique my interest. I looked at Katherine for confirmation and got her silent assent. Couples do that. It's a great way to communicate.

"All right," I said. "Let me get Sarah's property secured and we'll follow you. What's the address in case we get lost?"

"It's located at—"

"I know where it is," Katherine said.

IT took Oswaldo and his men about an hour to finish unloading everything. We all watched as Sarah's furniture and her possessions were piled into the little cubicle. It was a depressing experience and I tried not to think about her. I did, of course. Like Frank said—it stays with you. I had no clue as to why both the FBI and the GBI were interested in Sarah, but I figured it wouldn't be long before I found out.

The most obvious reason was that her death hadn't been an accident, but even that made no sense. The feds don't get involved in a case unless it involves kidnapping or the crime crosses state lines. Homicides are generally handled by local police and sheriff's departments. I glanced at Womack and Thurman and got unreadable cop faces in return.

FOURTEEN

DELANEY

Phil Thurman's office was about a fifteen-minute drive from the Store-All facility. It was located on the fourth floor of a building off I-85. We quickly found out Mr. Thurman was more than your run-of-the-mill federal agent; he was the Agent in Charge of Atlanta's field office, which meant fourteen satellite offices scattered across the state reported to him. What I'm saying is Phillip Thurman was no lightweight. Once we entered the room, he immediately took control of the conversation.

"Horace tells me you're ex-law enforcement, John."

"That's right."

"According to your captain, you were injured in the line of duty and retired on a medical pension at three-quarters pay."

"Right again." I recognized he was just going through the preliminaries. Clearly, he and Womack had done their homework.

"And you, Ms. Adams," he said turning to Katherine, "indicated you were previously with the U.S. Attorney's office. Was that here in Atlanta?"

"Yes, it was."

"Who was your boss, if you don't mind my asking?"

"I don't mind. His name was Ray Rosen."

"I know Ray quite well. Any objection if I give him a call?"

"Suit yourself. If you'd like to talk in private, John and I can step outside."

"That won't be necessary. I've heard your name before. I just can't place where."

"I've worked with your office in the past, but that was several years ago."

"No, it was something else."

"You're probably thinking of the cruise ship that sank last year."

Thurman snapped his fingers and leaned back in his seat. "Now I remember. You fingered the wrong perpetrator or something like that."

"Or something like that."

Womack scribbled a note on a piece of paper and passed it to Thurman, who read it and raised his eyebrows. "Right," Womack said. "That story was pretty big news for a while. If memory serves, you had it out with the real villain later on. Am I correct?"

"You're on a roll," Katherine said. "Out of curiosity, do these questions have anything to do with Sarah O'Connor's death or are we just making idle chitchat?"

"Idle chitchat," Thurman said. "I was trying to build rapport. Actually, I'm quite personable once you get to know me."

"I'll take your word for it."

Thurman gave her a tight-lipped smile as he reached for the phone. He dialed a number and waited, keeping his eyes fixed on Katherine. "Ray Rosen, please. This is Special Agent Phillip Thurman with the FBI."

A pause.

"Ray . . . Phil Thurman. How are you doing? Swell. Listen, I've got a young lady with me named Katherine Adams. She says she used to work for you."

I couldn't hear what was being said on the other end of the line and Thurman's face gave no clue. He merely nodded and scratched a few more notes on his pad.

"All right, that's great. Yeah, I'll be sure to tell her. Give my regards to Suzy."

Thurman tossed his pen on the desk and looked at Katherine. "Ray says if you're ready to come back to work, your old job's still waiting. According to him, you're quite a trial lawyer, Ms. Adams."

"Thank you."

"Do you mind my asking what your connection to Sarah O'Connor is?"

"None; I'm connected to him," Katherine said, motioning toward me with her head.

Thurman and Womack both turned to me for an explanation.

"I told Horace earlier that I'm a friend of the O'Connor family. They approached me a few days ago and asked if I would help with Sarah's estate. I called Katherine in because she's local."

"Who approached you?" Thurman asked.

"My clients."

"And they would be?"

"The people who hired me."

The color rose slightly in Thurman's face, but he kept his composure, which was good because I can be very annoying.

"Don't jerk me around, Delaney," he said quietly. "You guys aren't as tough as you think."

I got to my feet and Katherine followed suit. "Fellas, I don't see this conversation going anywhere. You asked us here on the pretext of talking about Sarah O'Connor and so far all I've heard is bullshit. It's been nice speaking with you, gentlemen."

Thurman's voice stopped me before I got to the door. "How much do you really know about Sarah O'Connor, Professor?"

"Like I told your partner, I'm a friend of the family. But to answer your question, I knew her since she was a kid. She was also a student in my evidence class."

"And that's it?"

"Yeah, that's it. The only reason I took the case was to help her family out. This isn't even my field. I may be wrong, but my guess is you're about to tell us there's something in the discrepancy between the coroner's report, the hospital records, and what Sarah's fingerprint card says."

Thurman's eyes shifted between Katherine and me. Several seconds ticked by before he made up his mind.

"You happen to be correct. Ms. O'Connor's ID card lists her height as five feet five inches. That matches up with her health records and what she put down on her law school application. Her undergraduate record at Boston College indicates the same data."

"So you think the coroner made a mistake?" I asked.

"It's possible. The problem is, we spoke with him earlier and *he* doesn't think so. In fact, he was pretty damn adamant about it."

"What about exhuming the body?" Katherine asked.

"We were going to talk to you about that, because logically that would have been our next step. Unfortunately, Sarah O'Connor was cremated."

"I had no idea," I said.

"I thought you were a friend of the family," Womack said.

"I am, but we haven't been close for a while. Her father was my dad's partner. He and his brother came to my office in New York a couple of days ago and broke the news of Sarah's death to me. The funeral was already over by then."

Womack nodded and made a note on his pad.

"As you've probably guessed," Thurman went on, "our interest in Sarah O'Connor is more than just a passing one. Last year Ms. O'Connor did an internship with the U.S. Attorney's office in Manhattan. Apparently you and she had something in common after all, Ms. Adams.

"After she was accepted to Emory she tendered her notice and left the job. The departure was a little sudden, but those things happen. About a month later they discovered one of their files was missing. We think she took it."

"What kind of file was it?"

"An excellent question, Professor. And the answer is we don't know. We only know it was a closed case and we don't have the first notion as to why she would have taken it. We were hoping the file would turn up among her possessions and make matters easy for everyone. Did either of you happen to run across it?"

"Before I answer your question, I'd like to ask one of my own. Have any of your people entered Sarah's home to have, shall we say, an informal look around in the last few days?"

Thurman and Womack both appeared surprised and exchanged a glance with each other.

"No," said Thurman. "Not to my knowledge."

"Same here," Womack replied. "Why do you ask?"

"Because I'm pretty sure someone went through Sarah's house."

"And you base that on what?" Thurman asked.

"Observation. Katherine and I both noticed something wasn't kosher when we got there. There were no prints on the bedroom furniture and someone had recently cleaned the place with a vacuum. Sarah had one of those plush carpets that show footprints easily and there weren't any. Also, a four-poster bed had been moved."

"Maybe it was the maid," Womack said.

"I don't think so. Particularly in light of what you just told me," I replied.

"I can assure you it wasn't anyone connected with this office, but I'll certainly check into it," Thurman said.

I continued, "And here's something else. Katherine and I were first at the house this past Thursday and we locked up when we left. When I checked today, I noticed the bed had been moved so as to put the legs back in their original position."

To Katherine's credit, she kept a poker face and showed no reaction to my statement.

"Are you positive about that?" Thurman asked.

"Pretty positive."

Again, there was a pause before he spoke. "Professor, would you be willing to let our people take a look at the items you placed in storage? We'd also like to examine the house, if you'll agree."

His request was a formality and we both knew it. Assuming they could tie Sarah to the file, they'd have no trouble procuring a search warrant for her home and personal effects. I had no choice but to tell Frank and Lucille of this development, and I wasn't looking forward to that. However, until push came to shove, I figured the best way to handle the situation would be to say yes and keep things as amicable as possible.

"No problem," I told him. "Do you know *anything* about the file you can share with us?"

Thurman replied, "Not a great deal. To begin with, it was over twenty years old. When the U.S. Attorney's office discovered it missing, they did an audit and came up with a case number. We contacted the lawyer who originally handled it, but he only had the vaguest recollection about what kind of case it was. He retired to Florida five years ago and has the beginnings of Alzheimer's. He's still pretty sharp, but there are large gaps in his memory."

I let out a breath and leaned back in my chair. "Not much help there."

"No, not much," Thurman agreed. "We did catch one break. The departmental supervisor is still with the Attorney General's office and she was more helpful. Her name is Eleanor Crisp. It seems Ms. Crisp had a habit of keeping her own filing system and she came up with a name for us—Landmark Productions. We cross-checked and found the company is owned by a man named Warren Blendel."

"Was it a prosecution case?" Katherine asked.

"No, it never got that far. Unfortunately, Blendel's still around. There's no record of any grand jury proceedings against him or against Landmark, so our best guess is the investigation was closed."

"Why is it unfortunate?" I asked.

"Because Blendel's a bad guy—a *very* bad guy. He has ties to organized crime and he's suspected in a half-dozen murders, two of which involved federal agents in New York some years back. He's into drugs, Internet porn . . . you name it. We've never been able to get anything on him. The man's made of Teflon. Obviously, we'd like to know what was in that file and we were hoping to enlist your cooperation."

"Sure," I said. "But there's also the little matter of Sarah O'Connor. I'd hate for her to get lost in the shuffle."

"She won't. You have my word on that," Thurman said. He opened his drawer, pulled out a copy of Sarah's fingerprint card, and slid it across the desk to me. "What you stumbled across adds a new wrinkle to the case nobody was counting on. Probably it's just a clerical error as you've said. We're checking that now. I'll share whatever we come up with and I hope I can count on you to do the same."

I looked at Katherine and she raised her eyebrows. We both knew there was a good chance Thurman wasn't giving us the whole story. I'd dealt with the FBI before, and their idea of sharing information hardly ever matches up with my own. But this wasn't the time or the place to start butting heads. Despite my misgivings I agreed to meet his people at the storage facility. Katherine went to Sarah's house with Womack and his men.

FIFTEEN

BLENDEL

FROM his office window Warren Blendel watched four workmen carrying a large mirror into his home. The mirror was originally part of an English pub on the east side of London and covered nearly an entire wall. Two years earlier, his wife and their decorator, Fredrick, saw it during one of her buying trips. She had the mirror taken apart and shipped to the United States in crates. Linda thought it would make a "whimsical statement" and go perfectly with the replica pub she had installed in their home. He almost never drank.

From Blendel's standpoint, the situation with Sarah O'Connor was going from bad to worse. Now the FBI had entered the picture, according to his sources. Schiller assured him everything was under control, but he could hear uncertainty in the man's voice during their last phone call. Phillip Thurman was one of higher-ups in the Bureau's Organized Crime Division and they had run into each other before. This was a complication he didn't need. His instructions to Schiller had been clear—pull out all the stops, get the file, and get out.

Blendel stopped at the sight of his own reflection in the mirror over his credenza. He looked tired.

According to the listening device Joshua had planted in the Adams woman's car, the feds were still fishing for information. They had no idea what the file contained or why it was so important. The key now was to prevent the damage from spreading further. So far his men had come up empty at the Store-All. Of course, finding the file there would have been too much to hope for. The girl had been too smart. It was all quite depressing.

The sound of raised voices in the courtyard below attracted his attention. Fredrick was shouting something at the Mexican workmen. He saw Blendel and waved. Blendel turned away without responding.

If the file wasn't at Sarah O'Connor's home and it wasn't among her personal effects, he reasoned, then her car had to be the next place to look. He picked up his cell phone and dialed a number.

Hans Schiller answered on the first ring in his precise German accent.

"Yah, we are going to check it tonight. They moved the car to the woman's home. We were there earlier. She has several cameras around her property. Joshua is trying to determine if he can disable them now. We need to make sure they're not tied into a central security system."

Blendel opened his mouth and closed it again. "How long, Hans?"

"A few hours. I don't think Joshua will encounter a problem. He's quite good with electronics. I will contact you the moment we are in."

"And if we don't find the file in her car?"

"Then I think Joshua must have a talk with Andre to make sure he hasn't *forgotten* anything. I was hoping to avoid this because . . . well, you know Joshua. Unfortunately, it's the only way to be certain."

Blendel considered that for a moment. "I want this to go smoothly, Hans."

"Understood completely, *mein herr*."

After they hung up, Blendel's thoughts turned to Joshua. Privately, he agreed with Schiller—the man wasn't all there. You could see that in his eyes. The lights were on, but no one was home. In his business, he had learned a long time ago that results were what counted, and Joshua was an expert at getting results. It would be a shame to hurt young Rostov.

Blendel let out a sigh and sat down at his desk. Good employees were notoriously hard to come by. Still, it was a matter of economies, a balancing act . . . and the fewer loose ends the better. He and his wife were in agreement on this point. He made a mental note to discuss it with her after lunch.

SIXTEEN

JOSHUA

EIGHT years of army specialist training had served Joshua Silver
well. An expert with a wide variety of electronic surveillance devices, he located the four security cameras on Katherine's property
in under twenty minutes. The equipment was of decent quality, but
commercial grade and would present no problem for him. He spent
approximately a half hour filming the woods surrounding Katherine's home along with the front and back doors to her house. Two of
the cameras were trained there. When he was through, he placed the
images on a DVD, then spliced it into the cameras' wires. The DVD
would replay its photos of the doors over and over again in a loop so
that everything appeared normal. It would work well enough until
darkness fell. By then, he and Schiller would be long gone before
anyone noticed there was a problem. Most home-based systems, he
knew, were monitored only from inside the house and provided al-
ternating views of the property. They were fine if you happened to
be standing in front of them.

An hour earlier he had watched as Katherine's car pulled up her
long driveway and out into the street. The main gate automatically
closed after her. From his hiding place in the woods, he caught a
glimpse of her profile as she passed and felt the pressure inside him
tick up a notch.

Now alone, Joshua sauntered down the driveway and up to the
front door. The lock was probably seventy years old and he doubted
they even made them anymore. It was stout enough to prevent honest people from getting in, but simple to open for anyone who had
sufficient skill. He entered the big Tudor house in less than five minutes. The girl's car had yielded nothing, not that he'd expected it to.
All his interest was now focused on Katherine Adams.

Joshua stood in the entry hall and looked around. The floor was constructed of wide wooden planks. They were dark and pitted. He liked that. The walls were covered in a complicated grass cloth. Not really his taste, though he had to admit it had a certain charm. Nearby was a table with a yellow marble top and curved gold legs. On it were several photographs. One was of Katherine and Delaney standing on a curved staircase at a formal party of some sort. He was dressed in a tux and she wore a black evening gown. Her hair was long and slightly teased in the front to give it some height. He would have to talk with her about that. Teased hair made women look cheap. There were other photos on the table displayed in silver frames. They showed Katherine's children and an older couple he assumed were her parents. The resemblance to her mother was obvious in the high cheekbones and blue eyes. Katherine's daughter was also quite attractive despite a small tattoo on her ankle. As a rule he didn't care for tattoos or piercings, but they were useful because they could tell a great deal about a person. Knowledge was power.

One thing about the photos jumped out at him. In each of them Katherine kept her hand out of sight, the one from which Richard Jenks had cut her finger off. He shook his head. So vain.

Joshua wandered into the family room and sat down on a chair with a high carved wooden back. The room was large and the ceiling was at least thirty feet high. It was paneled in reddish oak. Over the fireplace was an oil portrait of a woman with an odd expression. It looked to be of museum quality and was probably two hundred years old judging from her style of dress. For some reason the woman was holding a single large pearl above a golden wine goblet as though she were about to drop it in. That made no sense. He examined her expression for several seconds trying to determine what she was thinking and couldn't. Uncertainty made him uncomfortable and he turned away.

Through a large picture window he could see a brick patio outside and a four-tiered fountain that bubbled water into a retaining pool. Cut into the side of a hill directly behind it were four rows of stone benches in the style of a small amphitheater. What interesting tastes his Katherine had.

As he wandered through the rest of the home, Joshua was aware the pressure inside him was growing. It would have to be released before long. Eventually, he came to Katherine's bedroom. The room contained two master closets. One was filled with her clothes. The other held only a few items of men's clothing, which he guessed belonged to the professor. He took that to be a good sign because it meant their relationship still wasn't permanent. He could tolerate his woman being with another man physically, so long as she remained loyal to him.

In Katherine's closet he slowly breathed in the scent that lingered on some of her blouses. Then he opened her lingerie drawers and examined their contents. Also interesting. On the dresser was a bottle of Joy perfume and another tiny yellow bottle from Capri, Italy, which had a vague floral smell.

Joshua lay down on Katherine's bed and stared up at the ceiling. In between the coffers that crossed the room was brown-gray Venetian plaster. It added an elegant touch without being overstated. The bed's comforter, he thought, was made of Scalamandré fabric and probably cost eight hundred dollars a yard. He smiled to himself because Scalamandré was one of his favorites. Knowing someone's tastes was always a bonus. They would have to discuss this, too, when they met.

SEVENTEEN

DELANEY

SARAH O'Connor's personal effects yielded nothing; nor did the search of her home. I stood at the entrance to the storage bin and watched as the FBI agents went through the boxes one by one. What Katherine and I had rented was about the size of a one-car garage with a metal roll-up door. On impulse, I decided to take Sarah's law books with me rather than lock them away. I set the box off to one side after the agents were finished with it. The men were efficient and went about their business without any fuss or unnecessary conversation. It took them a little over two hours to complete their search.

There was no question in my mind now about someone having gone through Sarah's house, and it definitely wasn't the maid, as Womack had suggested. Unless he and Thurman were better actors than I gave them credit for, I didn't think their people were involved. For the moment, I simply stored these facts away until I had more information to go on. Though the medical examiner might have put down the wrong figures for Sarah's height and weight, I now doubted this as well. I was willing to give odds that Thurman and Womack weren't buying this explanation either. I have good instincts in such matters and there were suddenly too many unanswered questions floating around. Some were connected and others seemed completely random: Sarah's working for the Attorney General; her taking a file, assuming she did; her *accidental* death; and finally, her house being tossed. Add to that the height-weight discrepancy and you had—something.

For the first time an irrational ray of hope that she might still be alive began to creep into my mind and I promptly dismissed it. The sheriff's search party had found *someone* at the bottom of Cloudland

Canyon, but if it wasn't Sarah, then who she? If Sarah was alive, was she hurt? In hiding? And for what reason? At the moment I had more questions than answers. I placed a call to Trenton, Georgia, and asked for Clyde Maddox, the ME that sheriff Sophie Clark had mentioned.

This time I remembered to say good afternoon to the switchboard operator, which would have made Katherine proud. New Yorker I may be, but I'm educable. I've also learned not to mess with secretaries. They run the world.

"Dr. Maddox speaking."

"Doctor, this is John Delaney calling from Atlanta. If you have a moment, I'd like to ask you a couple of questions about a young lady named Sarah O'Connor. I'm the administrator of her estate."

"That'll be fine, son, but all I can tell you is what I told your friend a little while ago."

"My friend?"

"Agent Thurman. I think that was his name. If you give me a moment, I have his card here somewhere."

"That won't be necessary. I'll catch up with Phil later. Just tell me what you told him."

Apparently Mr. Thurman wasn't a man to let the grass grow under his feet.

Dr. Maddox began, "In the first place, I've been coroner here for twenty-six years and I don't make a lot of mistakes. I'm not saying I'm perfect, but I know my business. You understand?"

"Of course."

"Because of the body's condition, I anticipated establishing a positive ID might present a problem, so I took *extra* care with her measurements. They can tell you a lot. In fact, we did them twice just to be sure. My nurse assisted me and we recorded our findings as we went. If I wrote down the decedent was five feet seven inches, that's exactly what she was. The same goes for her weight. In case you're interested, when we do a subject, we don't just load the bodies onto a scale. We weigh them in a saltwater tank. This gives us a fat measurement, as well."

"I see."

"I hope so. We may not have the facilities Atlanta does, but we're every bit as sophisticated."

"Doc, I'm just calling from Atlanta. I don't actually live here. By the way, I appreciate your being so helpful. Did you happen to take a blood sample?"

"It's in the report, son . . . type O negative."

"Sorry, I don't have it in front of me at the moment. That's why I asked." I bent down and picked up a box Katherine had labeled TOILETRIES and pulled the lid back. It contained an assortment of items from Sarah's bathroom.

"Was there anything else?" Maddox asked. "I'm in the middle of a procedure at the moment."

To me, it sounded like he was in the middle of lunch. An image of the good doctor standing over an autopsy victim holding a baloney sandwich flashed into my mind and sent a shudder up my spine.

"I read somewhere that you can conduct a DNA test on hair samples, is that true?" I asked.

"Certainly."

"Would it be possible for you to do it?"

"Me? No. All the DNA tests are done at the University of Georgia or the GBI's crime lab. I don't understand . . . why would you want a DNA test? In addition to what we found, two different people identified her body."

I moved away from the storage bin where both agents were trying very hard to give the impression they weren't listening to our conversation.

"Two people," I repeated. "I know her boyfriend, Andre Rostov, was one. Who was the other?"

Some rustling of papers in the background. "Just a moment. Ah, here it is. Her uncle Nicholas O'Connor was the other man. He took the girl's personal effects back to New York with him and made arrangements to transport her body home for burial. If I'm remembering correctly, he's a high-ranking police officer up there."

"I see. How much of a sample would you need to run a DNA test?"

"Oh, nothing very large. A few hairs or skin cells would suffice, but why go to all that trouble? There doesn't seem to be much question—"

"Phil probably didn't mention it, but I'm dealing with an accidental death claim, and you know how insurance companies can be. How long will it take to get the test?" I asked, looking at Sarah's hairbrush lying in the box.

"Generally a couple of weeks. DNA tests are run in layers—that's the best way I can explain it to a layman. If you're in a hurry, we could probably obtain some preliminary findings in a few days. They wouldn't be anything that would hold up in court, but they might satisfy your insurance company. I don't like those bastards any more than you do."

"Thanks, Doc. How about if I stop by on Monday?"

Katherine's Lexus pulled into the storage company's lot as I was disconnecting. She got out of the car and came to join me. A shake of her head told me the police had turned up nothing at Sarah's house. We waited until the agents had finished their search, then locked up and headed home. Along the way I filled her in on my conversation with Clyde Maddox. She wasn't surprised when I told her Thurman had already made contact with him.

"Do you think he was leveling with us?" she asked.

"Do you?"

She frowned. "No . . . at least, not completely. Thurman glossed over the inconsistencies about Sarah's height and weight as if they weren't important, and I think they are, or at least I do now. My guess is he does, too. It might come down to a mistake, but I suspect he told you just enough so we would agree to let him look through her personal effects without a warrant."

"We'd have done that eventually."

"I know—the problem is he *needed* our cooperation. If we forced him to go for a warrant, we could have tied him up in court for several days—maybe more. Mr. Thurman strikes me as a man in a hurry."

Katherine and I were thinking along the same lines. Our suspicions came to rest on Andre Rostov, whom we both thought was dirty and covering something up. Neither of us bought his grief-stricken lover act. Murderer and porn pimp maybe, but not a grieving lover. Ms. Adams's theory was that he had killed the girl they found at the bottom of Cloudland Canyon, kidnapped Sarah, and was hiding her someplace. Considering her own past, I knew where this idea came from. Richard Jenks had done the same to her when she was a coed at Ohio State. Possibly she was right, but it was lot to assume. Nevertheless the possibility sent a chill down my spine. When confronted with a problem, the simplest explanation usually tends to be the one that works. An old professor of mine once called this the principle of Occam's Razor. I didn't hold out much hope that Sarah was still alive, but Katherine's theory *was* intriguing. The hole in it was that Nick O'Connor's identification of his niece's body tilted the scales the other way. Sarah was dead, and intriguing theories weren't going to bring her back.

"We still have most of the afternoon," Katherine said, interrupting my thoughts. "Do you want to run over to Emory and have another talk with Andre?"

"Good idea. Maybe he can tell us what's going on, because I sure as hell don't have a clue."

"You said both he and her uncle identified the body, right?"

"Right."

"What's the uncle's name?"

"Nick . . . Nick O'Connor."

"Could he have made a legitimate mistake?" Katherine asked. "I mean, her face was pretty smashed up and men aren't all that observant."

I swiveled in my seat and gave her an indignant look.

Katherine ignored it and went on. "I'm just saying that women tend to notice more details than men do. To begin with, this Nick was her uncle, not her father, and—"

"He's a cop, K.J." Katherine has been K.J. to all her friends since she was a kid, and I adopted the nickname. The *J* stands for Jane, her middle name.

"I know. But still . . . he was probably upset at the time." She reached out and rubbed the back of my neck. "Maybe you should speak with him again."

"I will."

I knew where Katherine was going with this. It was like looking at a jigsaw puzzle that someone had dropped on the floor. You knew there was a picture because you could see bits and parts of it. You just couldn't tell what the end result would be.

ANDRE wasn't happy to see us. As soon as he came out of the health clinic he spotted us and his face turned to stone. He promptly did a one-eighty and started back up the steps.

"Mr. Rostov, I'd like to have a word with you."

"My lawyer says I don't have to talk with you, so piss off," he said over his shoulder. "If I see you around here again I'll call campus security."

"I think that's a great idea," I called out. "Then we can all go back to the FBI's office and have a nice little chat."

"Fuck you. It wasn't illegal to make those pictures. I told you before we were both over eighteen."

"We're not interested in your little films. What we'd really like is for you to tell us who was really killed at Cloudland Canyon."

My speech was a pure gamble, but it stopped him cold in his tracks and he turned around.

"I don't know what you're talking about. I've already given my statement to the police."

"I know, I've read it. 'Sarah and I had a fight and she stalked off. When she didn't come back I went to look for her. The next morning we called the sheriff's office for help.' That sound about right?"

"Yeah, that's right," Andre said in a less aggressive tone. His eyes darted between Katherine and me, as though he was looking for a way out.

I waited a long beat to see if more would be forthcoming. Most people are uncomfortable with extended silence. When I worked cases in the past, I've found some subjects would begin volunteering information on the weak points of their story to shore it up. Andre was one of these.

He continued, "I loved her. It happened just like I said."

I nodded and stared at him without responding. After several seconds I put a hand on his shoulder and said, "We're not here to hurt you. We just want the truth. Talk to us, Andre."

"I didn't kill Sarah."

"Nobody said you did. Help us out, though. According to the

coroner, whoever went over that cliff was two inches taller and about thirteen pounds heavier than Sarah was. You can imagine how confusing that is."

Andre shrugged. "I don't have a clue. It's probably a mistake of some kind."

"Now that's exactly what I said to Ms. Adams. Mistakes happen all the time."

"All the time," Katherine echoed.

"Which is why I ordered a DNA test."

"Sarah's body was cremated. There's nothing for you to do a test on."

"Do you know, that's what I thought, too. But it's amazing what they can do these days. I read in *Newsweek* where scientists were able to link Thomas Jefferson's body to one of the slaves he owned. Apparently they had an ongoing love affair or something and they've been dead for what—two hundred years?

"Anyway, the medical examiner told me all I'd need were a few of Sarah's hairs. Turns out I was lucky enough to find them in her hairbrush. So why don't we quit dancing around and you tell us the truth?"

Some of the color had drained out of Andre's face. Suddenly he didn't seem quite so sure of himself. It was like watching a tire go flat. As the seconds ticked by, I was fairly sure we had him. He finally opened his mouth to speak, but oddly closed it again when he noticed something over my shoulder. Katherine and I both turned to look at the same time. Across the street two men were walking together. One was wearing a sports jacket and looked to be in his late forties. He was a large guy with thickset shoulders. I couldn't see his face. The other's hair was nearly as white as his skin. He was dressed in jeans and a T-shirt. Maybe they were looking at us and maybe they weren't. But it was impossible to tell because they both had sunglasses on. They continued down the street and turned the corner.

"I can't talk to you right now," Andre said. "Meet me at our house at eleven o'clock tonight. It'll take me about fifteen minutes to get there after I leave work."

"*Our* house, as in where you and Sarah were living?" I asked.

"Yes."

"Where do you work?" Katherine asked.

Andre motioned with his thumb. "At the clinic. I'm covering for a friend. My shift ends at ten thirty. I've got to go now."

Without another word he hoisted his book bag on to his shoulders and walked rapidly down the street toward the campus library. We watched until he disappeared through its double doors.

"What the hell was that about?" Katherine asked.

"No idea," I said, shaking my head. "Either something spooked him or he's stalling for time."

"Do you think we should let Thurman and Womack know?" Katherine asked as we started back to her car.

"Normally, I'd say yes, but I'd like to play this close for a little while. In the first place we really don't know anything for sure yet, so there's nothing to share. And in the second—"

"You're angry and you want the truth," she said, finishing the sentence for me.

"Yeah . . . something like that."

EIGHTEEN

DELANEY

W E had time to kill until our meeting, so we stopped by Katherine's house to pick up Zach and take him to dinner. It was a pleasant surprise to find her daughter Alley was also home. Katherine's earlier comment about having a free washer and dryer was right on the mark. Alley had brought home another pile of laundry.

The girls wanted rabbit food, while I was in the mood for something a bit more substantial, like a steak. Zach didn't care. In the end, we compromised and settled on a place called Dave & Buster's, largely on Zach's recommendation. He assured us that it was *awesome*. Alley sided with her brother, so I gave in.

Any thoughts of a quiet dinner and good conversation vanished as soon as we walked through the front door. Dave & Buster's is about the size of a football field and has over a hundred video games complete with bells, sirens, and flashing lights that go off every few minutes. It also has eight pool tables and a murder mystery theater where the audience participates with the actors in solving the crime. The decibel rating there is roughly equivalent to New York's Grand Central Station around rush hour.

Off the main lobby they were holding a beach volleyball tournament complete with sand and a lifeguard in a tall chair, who was acting as referee. Zach wolfed down his dinner and promptly disappeared into the arcade. I gave him ten dollars for the games, but he was back after a few minutes saying that he had run out of money. I took a deep breath and forked over a twenty. Alley received the same amount. She rewarded me with a kiss on the cheek and went off to join her brother. Katherine gave my arm an affectionate squeeze and smiled at me. I'm willing to concede my generosity might have been affected by her bare foot creeping up my pant leg and rubbing my calf under the table.

It had been a long time since I played any video games. As a matter of fact, I don't think they even had them when I was growing up. The closest I came was bowling with some buddies a few years back, so I wasn't prepared for the inflationary spiral that had hit the gaming industry. The last time I checked, pinball machines were a quarter. Some of the games at Dave & Buster's cost three dollars a pop. Zach returned again and stood there looking like a lost puppy. I gave him another twenty and he disappeared into the arcade once more.

"The kids may be a while," Katherine said. "Do you want to watch the volleyball match?"

"I think I'll pass. How about if I get us some coffee?"

"That sounds nice." She then glanced toward the volleyball court where there was a good deal of shouting and yelling going on. "My girlfriends and I used to play volleyball at Jones Beach when we were in high school. Have you ever been there? They have a great boardwalk."

"Actually, I used to work there."

"You're kidding!" Katherine exclaimed. "Maybe we saw each other and didn't know it."

"I guess that's possible, but I only worked for three days."

"Three days? Why so short?"

"I really don't want to talk about it, K.J."

Katherine leaned forward and put her elbows on the table. "C'mon, Delaney, give. You can't just say you worked there and then drop it. What did you do?"

I made a motion toward the fellow on the lifeguard stand.

Katherine's mouth opened in shock. "Omigod, you were a lifeguard? That's great. But why did you only work for three days?"

"K.J., it really wasn't all that interesting—"

"*John.*"

"Fine. I'll tell you. On my second day there, some guy swam out too far and got in trouble. Another guard and I went in after him. He was in a state of panic by the time I reached him and he lunged at me. Drowning people do that. The problem was, I was too close and he grabbed me in a bear hug around the head. I couldn't break it so I took him underwater. Unfortunately, when that didn't work either, I kneed him in the balls.

"We came up together and he lunged at me again. He was desperate for anything to keep him up. This time I reacted instinctively and slugged him on the chin. The punch broke his jaw in the process."

"Eewh," Katherine said.

"Yeah, exactly."

"Anyway, my friend and I managed to get him to shore and were doing our best to calm him down, because he was pretty upset. By then a small crowd had gathered. The EMTs and two cops arrived a few minutes later. The guy was lying on the sand moaning. He couldn't decide whether to hold his nuts or his jaw, if you know what I'm saying. One of the cops started asking around if anyone had gotten a look at the fellow who mugged him.

" 'It was him,' the man said, pointing at me.

" 'Huh?' the first cop asked.

" 'I was drowning and calling for help and he swam out and beat the shit out of me.' "

Katherine's coffee chose that moment to go down the wrong way and she started coughing. Nevertheless, she hand-motioned for me to continue.

"Both cops wanted an explanation, so I told them what happened, about it being an accident and all."

Tears were now forming in the corners of Katherine's eyes, but she nodded sympathetically.

"While the EMTs were putting the man on a stretcher, one the cops pulled me aside and said, 'Jesus Christ, kid, you're supposed to save them, not beat the crap out of 'em.'

"His partner put a hand on my shoulder and added, 'Listen, if you ever see me out here and I'm dying or something, I'll handle it myself, okay?'

"I caught all kinds of shit from my friends after that."

"So what happened?" Katherine asked, dabbing a napkin to the corner of her eye.

"The man hired a lawyer and sued the city of New York for a million bucks. I never learned how it turned out 'cause the parks manager called my home the next day and suggested that I try a different line of work."

Ms. Adams's eyeliner was now running down her cheeks thanks to the tears, so she excused herself to go to the ladies' room, still giggling as she went. I sat there and finished my coffee.

When she returned we made our way to the arcade to find the kids. I half expected to see a bunch of children running back and forth with parents watching them from the sidelines.

Not the case.

The place was packed with both adults and teenagers and there were lines everywhere. We spotted Zach near a series of motorcycles that had video screens above them showing an animated race course. His sister was with him. When their turn came, they fed their coin cards into a machine slot and jumped on the bikes. Apparently, money is now obsolete.

The good people at Dave & Buster's don't want their customers burdened with lugging heavy change around, so they give them computerized plastic. It's like having a personal ATM card. Every time you put it in one of the machines, it deducts the correct amount for you. The four cashier windows at the far end of the room reminded me of casinos in Atlantic City. Smiling employees are only too happy to replenish your card with more game credits for as long as your funds hold out.

Katherine and I strolled over to watch the kids in action. Motors revved through overhead speakers and a disembodied computer voice announced, "Bikers ready. Three, two, one—go!" On the video screens cartoon scenery shot by at an incredible pace as Alley and Zach negotiated the turns. Another screen showed their position on the course. The race lasted less than a minute and they finished second and third respectively. Of course, they wanted to try again. Katherine and I dutifully stood there and cheered them on. They were still laughing when they climbed off the bikes.

After some combined family urging, led mostly by Katherine, I gave in and got on one of the motorcycles. This time Zach finished first and won a bunch of little pink tickets that could be redeemed later for "spectacular prizes." Alley was third again and Katherine was sixth. I managed to come in last behind a two-hundred-pound woman whose butt was spilling over the sides of her bike. So much for male ego.

My luck was better with the Skee-Ball machines. Don't ask me where they got the name from. When I was growing up in Queens, our family used to vacation in Far Rockaway during the summers, and my friends and I played them at the boardwalk arcade. Skee-Ball is a game where you get ten wooden balls and roll them along a ramp into holes marked zero through fifty. I impressed everyone with my skill and wound up with a handful of those pink prize tickets, which I turned over to Alley. She had already accumulated four cups of her own, thanks to three young men who were flirting with her and donating their winnings freely. I guess they figured pink tickets are the fastest way to a woman's heart. As if.

Around nine thirty Katherine pointed to her watch and reminded me of the time, so we all trudged up to the redemption counter to claim our prizes. According to Zach, who did a quick count of our winnings, we had a total of 357 tickets. This qualified us for one of three fabulous prizes: a plastic back scratcher, a Chinese finger puzzle made of "the highest quality Taiwanese straw," or a yo-yo. Zach went with the yo-yo.

AFTER dropping Alley and Zach off at the house, we headed across town for our meeting with Andre. Traffic was light, a rarity in Atlanta, and we arrived about twenty minutes early. At that hour of the night the neighborhood was quiet. We found a parking spot a short distance away and walked back to Sarah's house. Here and there you could see couples watching television together through the front windows of the homes. Yellow light spilled onto the lawns. As we approached the house I noticed two things: the first was a late-model green Honda parked in the driveway; the second was that all the lights were off.

I came to a stop and studied the house closely for any sign of movement inside. There was nothing.

"Wait here," I told Katherine

"John, maybe you shouldn't go in," she said, taking my sleeve. "He could be waiting to jump you."

"I don't think so. It would be pretty dumb to leave his car outside and advertise he's there, then turn all the lights off."

"I think we should call the police." I could hear the worry in her voice.

"Just wait here," I said, giving her a quick kiss. "If I'm not out in two minutes, go ahead and call them. This doesn't feel right."

Katherine muttered something under her breath I was probably better off not hearing and I continued up the path. Ten feet from the front door I knew my instincts were right. You could see it wasn't completely closed. I pushed the door open a crack and moved to one side.

"Andre, it's John Delaney. Are you in there?"

No answer.

I waited a few more seconds and called out again.

Silence.

Cautiously, I opened the door all the way, reached inside, and flicked on the lights. The place was as bare as when we had left it and there was no sign of Andre. I looked over my shoulder at Katherine and shook my head. She shook hers back more emphatically, but I suspect we meant different things by it.

I found Andre's body in the bathroom. He had hung himself using two wire hangers. One was wrapped around his throat; the other looped through a pipe running across the ceiling. His face was dark purple and his eyes were open, staring at nothing. Seeing him like that caught me off guard and I took an involuntary step backwards. Once I recovered from the shock, I automatically began to catalogue the scene. First impressions are often the ones that matter most. Andre's hands were free, which meant he could have saved himself had he wanted to. Obviously, he didn't. There was no sign of blood or a struggle of any kind that I could see. The stepladder that was in the garage the day before now lay on its side underneath him. On the counter was a handwritten note. I walked over and starting reading.

Sarah is dead and it's my fault. If I hadn't asked her to go to Cloudland Canyon she would still be alive today. We loved each other. Now, people are trying to turn it into something ugly and I can't live with that. I also can't live without her. I was going to be a doctor

*because I wanted to help children. That will never happen. John
Delaney is responsible for this. My blood is on his hands.*

I heard a floorboard creak behind me followed by a gasp. Katherine's reflection appeared in the mirror. Her hand was over her mouth.

"I think it's time to call the police," I said.

IT took the Atlanta cops fifteen minutes to arrive. Phil Thurman and Horace Womack were right behind them. To say Thurman wasn't happy would have been an understatement. His pleasant demeanor was gone and he was all business now. He walked past us into the house without a word. Katherine and I had just finished giving our statements to one of the uniforms when he came out again and flashed his badge to the officer.

He said, "I'll take it from here. You can talk to them later."

The officer replied, "CID is on the way. I need to stick around."

"Fine," Thurman said. "If you'll excuse us, I'd like a moment alone with these witnesses."

The officer frowned. Uncertain what to do, he looked from me to Katherine to Thurman and then to Womack. After a few seconds he shrugged and went back to his squad car to finish writing up his report. As soon as he was out of earshot, Thurman swung around to face us.

"You want to tell me what you and your playmate are doing here at this time of night, Delaney?"

So much for the professor part.

"Katherine and I met with Rostov earlier this afternoon. We wanted to see if he had any more information about Sarah O'Connor."

"And?"

"And he didn't want to talk. He started to, but something spooked him and he changed his mind. He asked us to meet him here when he got off work. We found him this way, or rather I did."

"You both walked in and found him like that?"

"I didn't say that. All the lights were off, so I asked Katherine to wait outside. She came in afterwards."

"That's correct," Katherine said. "And I don't appreciate being referred to as someone's playmate."

Thurman ignored her remark. "How long did you wait before you entered the house, Ms. Adams?"

"A few minutes, no more."

"So all you have is Delaney's word that Rostov was dead when he got there?"

"Are you kidding?" I said.

"No, Mr. Delaney, I'm not kidding. This is an active investigation and you're sticking your nose in where it's not wanted." He turned back to Katherine. "I asked you a question, Ms. Adams."

"I didn't see Andre hang himself," Katherine said, "nor did I see John strangle him, if that's what you're getting at. The question is inane. We both know the medical examiner can easily fix a time of death."

"And rest assured that's exactly what he'll do," Thurman told her. "Right now I could charge you both with obstructing justice, or hold you on suspicion of murder, do you understand that?"

"I understand you're acting like a horse's ass," I said. "All we did was speak with him—"

"And reveal confidential information about an ongoing investigation," Thurman snapped. "What part of that don't you two understand? This is *official police business*, not amateur night at the Fox."

I felt my face grow hot and had to make an effort to control myself. "First of all, *I'm* the one who brought you the information about the discrepancy in Sarah O'Connor's height and weight. Second, I didn't kill anybody and neither did Katherine. You know it, I know it, and anyone with half a brain knows it. So why don't you tell me where you're going with this?"

The FBI agent and I locked eyes and he brought his face closer me. "I don't like people who say one thing and do another."

"Ah, bullshit."

"We had an agreement to share information, Delaney, and you went behind my back the first chance you got."

"There was nothing *to* share. I told you Rostov didn't want to talk to us at the school."

Horace Womack finally decided to add his bit to the conversation.

"So you set up this midnight rendezvous, right? What do you think we are?"

"You don't want an answer to that, Horace."

Womack's jaw clenched and he took a step toward me but Thurman put a hand on his shoulder, restraining him. "What else did you and Rostov talk about?"

"Just what I told you," I said.

"Then how do you explain the suicide note?" Womack asked. "*John Delaney's responsible. My blood is on his hands. . . .*"

"I don't know where Andre got that from," I said, "unless he killed Sarah and figured we were on to him."

"You told him about the coroner's report?" Womack asked.

"That's right."

"And he just agreed to meet with you?" Thurman asked.

"He only agreed to meet us *after* I told him that we'd ordered a DNA test. It shook him."

"So you say. Who did you ask to do the test?"

"Clyde Maddox, the Dade County ME."

"I'll check that out. In the mean time, I want you both in my office Monday morning at ten a.m. Do I make myself clear? If you're not there, I will absolutely have you arrested."

"You do what you have to," Katherine said. "John and I told you we were going to cooperate and we meant it. And for your information, I don't like having my integrity questioned any more than you do. I've been practicing law in Atlanta for a long time. If I give someone my word, it means something."

"I'm happy for you. Ten o'clock Monday morning."

Thurman spun on his heel and went to speak with the officer sitting in his patrol car. We hung around until the homicide detectives arrived and repeated our story for them. While they were taking notes, I watched the police stretch yellow tape across the driveway and in front of Andre's car. The techs wheeled his body out on a gurney and loaded it into an ambulance. An image of his face flashed into my mind. I kept trying to decide what the expression in his eyes meant and couldn't.

It was well after midnight by the time we got home. There was a note taped to the refrigerator from Alley thanking us for the dinner and saying that she was heading back to her apartment to study for her Agency and Partnerships exam. She also wrote that Zach wanted to be woken up at six forty-five so he could get to school early.

There was another message from Katherine's mother on the answering machine. She played it while pouring a glass of wine for each of us. This time the subject was headphones, specifically the headphones that Katherine wore when she was running. According to her mother, the tiny earpieces were prime sites for bacteria. She wanted Katherine to take an antibiotic if she continued using them. Katherine downed her drink in a single gulp, then poured a second glass for herself and we headed for the bedroom.

While she was soaking in the tub, I found a Bill Allen CD with some quiet jazz and put it on. The album was from a live recording at the Village Vanguard a few years earlier. I was there the night he made it. Katherine joined me a few minutes later smelling clean and fresh.

"Mmm, I like this music," she said, slipping under the covers.

I propped two pillows up behind me and leaned back against the headboard. Ms. Adams snuggled closer and I kissed the nape of her neck. After that, I went quiet and stared up at the ceiling, reflecting on the day's events.

"Are you okay?" she asked.

"Sure, I'm fine," I said, coming back to the present.

Katherine didn't buy my answer. She looked at me and waited.

"What?"

"You just seem distracted. On the ride home you didn't say two words."

I slid an arm around her shoulders and hugged her. "Sorry. This business with the Rostov kid threw me."

Katherine sat up in the bed, the sheet falling away from her breasts. "John, you can't possibly think you're responsible—"

"No, no, no. It's just that what happened doesn't make any sense. Andre didn't seem suicidal to me. And if he was so in love with Sarah, like he said, those videos are a goddamn funny way to show it."

Katherine inched closer and took a nip at my earlobe. "There are all kinds of weirdos out there. You know that better than most. For a moment I thought you and Womack were going to get into it."

"I'm much too dignified a person to engage in something so vulgar as wiping the street with him."

I got an eye roll for a reply.

"How do you see it?" I asked.

"I agree with you. I didn't know Andre from a hole in the ground, but he didn't seem suicidal to me either. Neither of us pushed him very hard, so his reaction was totally out of place. I mean, you can't tell what's going on in someone's head, but I'd really like to have a handwriting expert take a close look at that note."

"You think it was faked?"

"I don't know. I suppose we'll find out when they do an analysis. Do you mind if ask you a question?"

"Sure."

"You told me you haven't had a lot of contact with the O'Connor family over the last year or so, right?"

"Yes, I did."

"But Andre's suicide and Sarah's death have both hit you pretty hard. Is there something I'm missing?"

I picked my wineglass up from the nightstand and swirled the contents around for a moment before I took a sip. "When I was still on the force a social worker came to us about a young boy named Stanley Malassi. He had bruises up and down his legs and across his lower back. Some were old, but several were clearly new. We checked his school records and found out he had shown up twice that year with black eyes. He told his teachers he got them falling off his bike.

"My partner and I started looking at the parents, which is pretty much SOP in abuse cases. After that, we made a visit to their home. The wife was a meek little thing, who had come to the United States from Kosovo a few years earlier to get married. Right away I could tell something wasn't right with her. She had that hundred-yard stare you see in war victims. The husband was a big guy with hands the size of catcher's mitts—a truck driver."

Katherine nodded.

"They both gave us the same story about Stanley. . . . He fell off his bike. I thought it was bullshit and so did my partner, so we ran their records. The wife was clean, but we got a hit on the husband. It turned out he had put a gay guy in the hospital fifteen years earlier for making a pass at him. He did nine months on Rikers Island as a result.

"We dug deeper by asking around the neighborhood and found out Mr. Malassi was your quintessential homophobe. I was convinced the guy was dirty, so I went back to the school to speak with a few of the teachers. Two of them told me they had begun to notice certain affectations in Stanley since the beginning of the term. The bottom line was they both thought he was gay."

"And?"

"My theory was that the father was trying to beat it out of the boy, so I went to him and leaned hard. I told him if he didn't come clean, I would see the story about his arrest got around . . . about how he had been linked with a homosexual."

"What happened?" Katherine asked.

"That night he stuck a shotgun in his mouth and blew his brains out."

Katherine's eyes opened wide in surprise.

"Yeah, exactly," I continued. "It's not smart to play God, K.J. I was so sure I was doing the right thing. It just it didn't turn out that way. Stanley got his bruises because he had been getting into fights with another kid at school."

"Oh, John," Katherine said, touching my face with her fingertips. "This isn't the same thing."

"Isn't it?"

"Not at all. You were hired by Sarah's family to settle her estate. Something weird happened tonight. Fine. Nobody could have predicted it. As an attorney, it's your job to investigate. It would have been unethical if you didn't."

"Maybe," I said, not really convinced. "It's just tough getting those images out of my head."

Katherine shifted positions so that her back was to me and she rested her head on the pillow. Neither of us spoke for several minutes.

"Is there anything I can do to help?" she asked quietly.

I was about to reply when her hips pressed against my genitals and she looked at me over her shoulder.

Oh, boy.

NINETEEN

DELANEY

On Sunday Katherine arranged a brunch date with a couple of her friends, Fran and Marc Silverman. Both had worked with her when she was with the U.S. Attorney's office. Fran was still a prosecutor in the white-collar crimes division, while Marc had moved on and was now part of Coca-Cola's legal department. He was in his early forties, slender, and well dressed.

Atlanta, I've learned, is one of the most brunch-crazy cities in the country. It's definitely the thing to do there. Normally I'm not a big eater and neither is Katherine, but I knew she enjoyed sipping mimosas and having a pleasant conversation with friends, so I went along with the program. Regardless of where you eat, the brunches have way too much food and far too many desserts. I made a mental note to renew my gym membership when I got back to New York.

The Hyatt Regency, where we were meeting Fran and Marc, is an Atlanta landmark. Sitting atop the building is the Polaris Lounge, a big blue dome that looks like a flying saucer. The main attraction, apart from the mimosas, is that the restaurant revolves. Every twenty minutes or so, the dining room completes a 360-degree turn, giving you a tour of Atlanta's skyline and the surrounding countryside. Waiters and locals are only too happy to point out some the more distinctive sights. On our first pass, Marc showed me Coke's headquarters.

"If you count eleven down from the top and six in, that's my office," he said.

"Right."

I tried counting, got mixed up, and figured I'd catch it on the next pass.

"Franny's building is three over from that tall one on the left," he added.

I twisted in my seat and followed where he was pointing. "Impressive."

Marc continued, "Now if you look out there in the distance you can just about make out Stone Mountain. On a clear day you can see it really well."

I lifted a hand to my eyes, shielding them from the glare, and squinted. There might have been an outline, but I couldn't tell with all the haze. Each time I'd been to the Hyatt, one of the waiters had pointed out the mountain to me, so I had a pretty good idea what it looked like.

"Katherine's been promising to take me there, but we haven't made it yet."

"Oh, you'll love it," Fran said. "We used to take the kids to visit all the time. They have a bucket ride that goes to the top, a petting zoo, and a beach."

"A beach?"

"Well, it's not a real beach," she explained. "They brought a bunch of sand in and put it around the lake. People really like it. You and Katherine should definitely go."

"Before or after the petting zoo?"

Fran gave me a light slap on the arm. "The petting zoo's for children. You can walk the nature paths or even climb the mountain. It's not hard. They used to hand out certificates for doing it. I'm not sure it if they still do." She glanced at her husband for confirmation but he only shrugged. "Anyway, it's a nice way to spend the day."

"I'll keep it in mind. Unfortunately, my plane leaves tomorrow night. We'll have to save it for my next trip."

"Katherine says you teach law at Columbia," Marc said.

"No, it's John Jay College of Criminal Justice."

"Sorry. Have you ever done any corporate work, John?"

"Not much. I'm sure it's interesting, though."

"You bet. The hours are long, but there's always something new . . . mergers, acquisitions, contracts, you name it."

"Sounds fascinating."

"Absolutely. Coke has its own litigation team now. The next time you're in town, give me a call and I'll introduce you to Bill Ketchum. He heads up our department. I'm sure you'd hit it off."

I glanced at Katherine out of the corner of my eye. But she seemed to be concentrating on her omelet with more attention than was strictly necessary.

"Sure will, Marc," I said. "That's really nice of you."

"We also have one of the best health care and retirement packages in the industry."

Before Marc could launch into more details about their corporate benefits, I excused myself to go to the restroom. Katherine finally looked up from her omelet and made eye contact with me. She gave me one of her sweet smiles. It didn't take a genius to figure out the conspiracy to get me to relocate to Atlanta was spreading.

After I finished with the restroom, I started back to our group, but stopped in my tracks. The table was gone. Confused, I paused for a second, until I remembered the restaurant was revolving. As I saw it, I had two choices: I could try to chase it down, or I could wait where I was until I spotted a friendly face on the next pass. Frankly, it's a bit disorienting to come out of a bathroom and find that your table has vanished. I went with the first option and began making my way around the dining room's perimeter.

I'd only taken a few steps when something I saw froze me. A young woman was just getting on the elevator that went to the hotel lobby. Our eye contact lasted only a moment before the doors shut, but I could have sworn I'd just seen Sarah O'Connor. My stop was so abrupt, a waiter nearly collided with me. The expression on my face must have registered with him because he asked, "Is everything all right, sir?"

"What?"

"Are you okay?"

"Yeah," I said, recovering from the shock. "Just a little disoriented."

He smiled. "That happens a lot. Do you remember where you were sitting?"

I glanced at the indicator lights above the elevator and saw that it had reached street level. "Our table was opposite Stone Mountain, but that's gone, too."

"No problem, sir. It takes twenty minutes for the restaurant to

make a complete turn. Just follow the outside catwalk around until
you find your party."

"Thanks."

My pulse was beating a mile a minute by the time I returned to
the table. I sat down, trying to decide whether I had actually seen
Sarah or had just imagined it. The mind is a funny thing. You get an
idea in your head, and the brain can make you believe what you
think you saw is real. Psychiatrists have a fancy name for this, but in
lay terms it's called a self-fulfilling prophecy.

I once had a partner who caught two slugs in the chest trying to
bring down a seventeen-year-old boy who was running from her. It
was her first month in robbery/homicide and she was a rookie. The
bullets killed her instantly and there was nothing I could have done to
prevent it. For the next six months I kept seeing her face in crowds
and on bus ads. What I'm saying is, you want to believe someone's not
dead and the next thing you know you start filling in the blanks.
Eventually, I went to our department shrink to talk about what happened and he explained how the process worked. I saw him a few
more times and we talked about stuff I had never talked about with
anyone else. Maybe it released some of my inner demons. Or maybe it
was inner bullshit, your choice, but the bottom line is that I stopped
seeing her. Nevertheless, it was a long time before I worked with a
partner again.

After brunch we headed up Piedmont Avenue past Colony Square
to Atlanta's Botanical Garden. The women wanted to see a special ex-
hibition they were holding. Marc started to make a suggestion about
going home to catch a golf tournament on television, but one look
from Fran settled that. She and Katherine walked in front of us, discussing all the bargains they were finding on eBay, while Marc and I
trailed behind.

The exhibit turned out to be the work of an artist who specializes
in glass sculptures. His flowers were stuck here and there among the
real ones. Most were nice and maybe even interesting, but after the
first dozen or so pieces, even Marc's golf tournament began sounding good to me. I've tried golf a few times and have never gotten the
hang of it. There are too many rules and the ball sits there too long
looking back at you. All the while, Marc kept up a steady stream of

conversation. I tried to participate out of politeness, and most likely did a poor job. I was still off balance from the incident at the hotel and kept glancing around the gardens, half-expecting to see Sarah again.

"Golf's a wonderful game, John," Marc said, his voice cutting into my thoughts.

"What? Oh yeah, definitely."

"If you'd like to give it a try, I've got a spare set of clubs I can let you borrow. The next time you're in town you can meet a few of our members. I have a group that plays every Saturday . . . great guys. We go out around eight a.m. That way we have the rest of the day free for family and stuff. Covington's has a pool and fifteen tennis courts if you're into tennis."

"Covington?"

"Our country club," he explained. "It's about a fifteen minutes' drive past the perimeter on Georgia 400. Definitely a class act."

"I'm sure it is."

"We have a full social calendar and a great youth program."

I put a hand on Marc's arm and slowed down, letting the women proceed on without us. They continued along the path to the next group of stained-glass flowers. "Listen, I appreciate all the information," I said. "But what's going on here?"

Marc glanced at his wife's back and took a deep breath. "What do you think?" he asked out of the corner of his mouth.

Katherine and Fran glanced over their shoulders to see where we were and wiggled their fingers at us. We wiggled back and started walking again.

I told him, "It's not that I don't love her. I just don't see the need to rush things."

"How long have you two been dating?"

"About a year now."

He raised his eyebrows and gave me a look.

"All right, point taken," I said. "I suppose I'll need to get off the pot pretty soon."

"Might not be a bad idea."

"I mean, Katherine's a wonderful girl and about the best partner a man could ask for."

"She cooks, too, right?"

I laughed to myself. "Yeah, she cooks, too."

"Not to mention she's rich, good looking, and smart as a whip."

"You just did."

"Look, my orders come directly from the top," he said, making a small motion with his head in Fran's direction. "You're playing in the big leagues here, pal."

"It's a fucking conspiracy," I muttered.

"Yep. And for the record, I only heard my wife's end of the telephone conversation."

"Got it."

This time it was Marc's turn to stop. "I hope you do, because Katherine's good people. I'm not trying to get into your business . . . well, not too much, but don't be a schmuck, okay? Long-distance relationships have a way of ending badly. That's all I'm saying."

The women were waiting for us and Marc was a decent guy. Maybe his wife had put him up to the sales pitch or maybe he had come up with it all by himself . . . and maybe golf wasn't such a tough sport to learn after all.

TWENTY

DELANEY

ON Monday morning we arrived at Katherine's office early. She had to get ready for a deposition and I didn't feel like hanging around the house alone. Plus, we had to meet with Phil Thurman later that day.

I'd been giving a lot of thought to the Sarah O'Connor situation as well as to my relationship with Katherine. As far as Sarah went, the DNA tests would ultimately settle if it was her at the bottom of Cloudland Canyon. Katherine was another story. No test was going to resolve that issue. It's not that I'm reluctant to set up shop with a woman again. I'm not. I've never been what you'd call a player, unless having a few dates now and then qualifies. The subject of former lovers came up when we first started dating and Katherine denied seeing anyone at the time, but then again so did I. Living together doesn't scare me, or even marriage for that matter. The fact is, you simply get used to your life being a certain way, and change involves risk. I don't remember who said that, but it's true. Maybe it was the psychiatrist.

While Katherine went to check that everything in the conference room was in order for her deposition, I settled into a chair in her office and opened a book I had borrowed from Zach. I hadn't read a fantasy novel in a long time and was pleasantly surprised by this one. It was about a seventeen-year-old boy who finds a ring that his ancestors had created three thousand years earlier. It was supposed to let them turn thought into matter. The only problem was the whole race disappeared in a single night and the boy had no idea what he was holding. Fun stuff.

"Johnny D—what's the good word?" a voice from the doorway asked, pulling me away from the book.

"Jimmy D, how ya doin?" I responded.

Jimmy d'Taglia and I had been working the same schtick for the last year since we discovered that we were both from the Bronx. Jimmy is one of the lawyers who works for Katherine. I pushed myself up from the chair and we shook hands.

"Where's the boss lady?" Jimmy asked.

"In the conference room getting ready for a deposition."

"Cool. Whatcha up to?"

"Not much. Just sitting here reading one of Zach's books." I showed him.

Jimmy's face lit up. "Hey, I read that a couple of years ago. You're gonna love it."

"I'm just killing time. We have an appointment with the FBI in a couple of hours."

"How come? You forget to pay a parking ticket?"

"Not exactly." I told him about Rostov's suicide and about what had happened to Sarah O'Connor. I even mentioned the part about seeing her at the Hyatt.

Jimmy sat on the edge of Katherine's desk and listened without interrupting. I knew from my talks with her that he was something of an oddity on the Atlanta scene. I also knew he was intelligent and a solid trial lawyer. Jimmy was just above middle height and had a head of jet-black hair that he combed straight back. Every time I'd seen him he was immaculately dressed. He favored sharkskin suits and pocket handkerchiefs. Lest I be accused of profiling again, I don't mean the shiny kind movie Mafiosos wore back in the fifties. Jimmy's suits were top quality and tailored by Hugo Boss. Still, the image doesn't take you too far from the stereotype.

Jimmy asked, "Are you thinking the girl might still be alive?"

"I doubt it. If the height and weight discrepancy turns out to be a clerical error, my next appointment will be with a head doctor. Seeing dead people isn't a good thing."

"Yeah, yeah," he agreed, "but if it doesn't, you've got a hell of a weird situation on your hands."

"To put it mildly."

"What strikes me as odd is why would anyone go through the

girl's house? I mean, you're the detective, could you have been wrong about that?"

"Former detective," I corrected, "and no, I don't think so."

"So what were they looking for? That file the FBI man told you about?"

"That would be my guess."

Jimmy frowned and thought for a second, then commented, "Okay, what have we got? A girl who's supposed to be dead, but might not be. A guy who's definitely dead and who either killed her and set it up to make it look like she fell off a cliff . . . or maybe he was working with her—"

My head came up sharply. "What did you just say?"

"I said, maybe they were working together—otherwise she would have come forward by now, unless . . ."

"*She doesn't want to be found*," we both said at the same time.

"But why? I don't get it," Jimmy said.

"Neither do I. None of this makes sense. Let's stay with your theory for a moment. If Sarah and Andre *were* working together, for whatever reason, they probably maintained some form of communication with each other. Plus, you need money to stay underground."

"How so?"

"I mean, she couldn't go back to her parents, and she couldn't go back to her house; therefore, she was living someplace else."

"Like in a hotel?"

"Unlikely," I said. "The days of paying cash are pretty much over. Everyone wants a credit card now for security, and Sarah was no dummy. She'd know credit cards could be traced."

"How about her cell phone and home telephone records?"

I shook my head. "They're just as easy. I'm sure she wouldn't have . . ."

"What?"

An image of Sarah's home flashed into my mind and of her second bedroom in particular—the one she and Andre had used as an office. I remembered seeing two desks, but only one computer.

"I've got an idea. How good are you with computers, Jimmy?"

He shrugged. "Better than the average bear."

I started to respond and then stopped. "Yogi Bear was before your time. How do you know about him?"

"Nickelodeon, man."

Katherine was already in with her client and I didn't want to disturb her, so I left a message with her secretary saying that Jimmy and I were going to check something out at Sarah's storage place and that I'd be back in time for our meeting with Thurman. I suddenly had a burning urge to see what was on Sarah's computer.

IT was Monday and the roads were crowded. Dealing with New York's traffic is no picnic, but Atlanta isn't far behind. This time, our trip took nearly an hour. Once we retrieved Sarah's computer from the Store-All, we headed back to Katherine's house to set it up.

True to his word, Jimmy knew a lot more about computers than the average bear did. We set the CPU and monitor on the kitchen table and plugged it in. Once it booted up, Jimmy punched a few keys and bought up a page on the screen that showed the computer's hardware configuration. As he studied it, his brows came together.

"Hey, John, check the box and see if there's a little camera in there."

I looked. "No, it's clean. Just a bunch of Styrofoam peanuts."

"Dump 'em out on the dining room table, would you? The camera's easy to miss. They're only about so big," he said, illustrating with his fingers.

I spilled half the Styrofoam peanuts on the table and accidentally spilled the other half on the floor, with a curse.

"Nothing."

"That's odd. Do you recall seeing a camera when the movers were packing? According to the configuration profile, it's supposed to be here."

I searched my memory and couldn't remember if Sarah had a camera or not. "Maybe she had one and got rid of it," I suggested.

"I don't think so. The last time her video card was accessed was five days ago."

Five days? My pulse began to quicken. "How can you tell?"

"The computer keeps a history of what sites it visited. When did you say Sarah died?"

"Two weeks ago."

"Then someone's fucking with you, John," he said.

I let that seep in . . . someone *was* fucking with me. But who? I checked my watch. We still had a little over three hours before our meeting with Thurman. Fortunately, Katherine's secretary had reset it because of her deposition, thus buying us a little extra time.

"Are you up for some more exploring?" I asked.

"I'm clear the rest of the day. What do you have in mind?"

I explained to Jimmy about my having seen only one computer at Sarah's house. Then I told him that Andre, who also lived there, had apparently been gone for several days. This raised the obvious question . . . if Sarah was alive and they were communicating with each other, where was Andre's computer?

Our next stop was Emory University. With a little help from the secretary and some asking around, we located a student named George Sachus. He was one of the people Sarah and Andre had gone camping with that night. I was hoping the news of Andre's suicide hadn't circulated around the college yet, because I needed to learn where he had been staying. We caught up with Sachus on his way to the Student Union and introduced ourselves. Like Andre, he was in his third year of medical school.

"Do you mind if we talk while we walk?" he asked. "I'm between classes and I don't get a break again until five o'clock."

"No problem," I said. "Did you know Sarah well?"

"Not really. We only met a few times. She and Andre had just started going out. He was head over heels in love with her, I can tell you that. Her death really hit him hard."

"Of course," I agreed. "Do you have any idea where I can find him? I'm trying to make an inventory of Sarah's personal possessions for the court. I know they were living together, but he wasn't at the house."

"That's because he moved in with Naresh Patel after Sarah died."

"How come he moved out?" Jimmy asked.

"I guess he had to get away from their place for a while. Everything reminded him of her. You can't blame the guy."

Jimmy and I nodded sympathetically.

I inquired, "Do you know how I can get in touch with this Naresh?"

"Sure, hold this for a second," Sachus said, handing me his backpack. It felt like someone had loaded rocks in it. "Sorry, man . . . medical books weigh a ton," he added, noticing my grimace.

He reached into his one of the pockets and produced, what else— a cell phone with a built-in PDA. He poked the gizmo a few times with a plastic stylus.

"Here we go . . . Naresh lives at 4430 Post Oak Tritt in Marietta. He's also doing an internship at Grady Hospital, if that helps."

He supplemented that information with two phone numbers: one for Naresh's home and one for his beeper.

"Did you just say *Tritt*?" Jimmy asked.

"Yeah."

"What's a Tritt?"

"A street, I guess," Sachus said.

"What's it mean?"

Sachus lifted his shoulders. "No idea. Maybe Naresh'll know. Listen, I've got to run. It's been nice meeting you."

For some reason the notion of a street, or any geographic feature for that matter, being named a *Tritt* didn't sit well with Jimmy. He talked about it all the way to the car and eventually phoned Galena Olivares, the secretary he and Katherine shared. He asked her to look the word up in the dictionary.

"See? I told you it was nuts," he said, when she couldn't find it. "Why would anyone call a street a Tritt?"

"Beats me," I replied as we got in the car. "Forget about it, would you? I want to see if I can get a hold of this Naresh at the hospital."

"What for? If he lives on Post Oak *Tritt*, he probably doesn't know squat about anything. I bet no one who lives on that block has the first idea what a Tritt is."

I rolled my eyes.

"All right, fine, but it's still a bullshit name," Jimmy muttered. He punctuated his statement with a curt nod and then looked out the window while I dialed Grady Hospital.

"Hi, this is John Delaney. I'm trying to get a hold of Dr. Naresh Patel. I believe he's a resident there."

"Just a moment," said the operator. "Let's see . . . unfortunately, Dr. Patel is on vacation in India until August third. Would you like to leave a message?"

"No. Thanks very much. I'll give him a call when he returns."

"What's up?" Jimmy asked.

"Patel is in India for the next ten days. Let's head back to the office so I can drop you off."

"And do what?"

"Oh, I might just take a ride out to his house and look around. You've got a lot of work today."

"You're kidding me, right?"

I gave him a flat look.

"You're actually thinking of breaking into the guy's house?"

"That would be a crime. Of course, if I just happen to be in the neighborhood and notice the front door is open . . ."

"Fuckin' Johnny D—you are something else, man. I think I'll tag along."

"Not a good idea, Jimmy. This isn't cops and robbers. You could get in a lot of trouble. This isn't a game."

Jimmy stuck his lower lip out and considered what I had just said. When he spoke again, much of his New York accent seemed to have vanished.

"I know that," he said quietly. "You want to find out if this Andre had a computer there, right?"

"Something like that."

"As I see it, we have two choices: I go back to the office and tell Katherine I let you go alone, or I go with you and watch your back. Frankly, knowing Katherine, the latter is preferable, if you get my meaning. Besides, you might need some help with the computer."

"Are you sure?"

"No problem. Can I ask you a question?"

"Shoot."

"Why aren't you letting the police handle it?"

I stared at my hands for a few seconds and surprised myself by saying, "I don't know, Jimmy. I guess it's a character flaw. I don't like loose ends and I don't like being played for a sucker."

Jimmy shook his head. "Man, you and Katherine are gonna make some pair. I can't wait to see how your kids turn out."

TWENTY-ONE

DELANEY

It didn't take us long to get to Marietta. Thanks to the global positioning system in the Katherine's Lexus, we found Post Oak Tritt without difficulty. I drove past the house slowly to the annoyance of a computerized female voice in the console telling me, "*You have arrived at your destination.*" She sounded annoyed when I didn't stop. What's up with all the voices being female?

Yes, there really is a Post Oak Tritt. It's a long winding street with homes in the $300,000 range. From what I could see, property values appeared to be on the rise. My guess was that most of the houses were worth more for their tear-down value than as places to live. Naresh Patel's home was a modest one-story brick dwelling with a large front yard and lots of trees. The first thing I noticed was that Patel's grass needed cutting, a good indication no one was there. Still, you can't make assumptions. As a cautionary measure, Jimmy and I walked up and knocked on the front door.

When there was no answer, we went around to the back. Whoever tells you cops can open doors using a credit card has been watching too many movies. In the end, Jimmy displayed more of his talents by picking the lock—clear evidence of a misspent youth in the Bronx.

We quickly determined which bedroom was Andre's, thanks to a photo of himself and Sarah on the desk. The computer was there as I'd hoped and it had a tiny camera atop the monitor. A screensaver showing a pendulum making lines in a dish of sand disappeared as soon as Jimmy moved the mouse. Within seconds he managed to bring up a record of the Web sites Andre had visited over the last few weeks.

"Got it," Jimmy said.

"What?" I asked, peering at the monitor.

"If you see here, this address is a video feed. It shows up on the log six different times."

"How can you tell it's video?"

"Watch."

Jimmy hit the ENTER key and a progress bar appeared at the bottom of the screen. When it stopped moving halfway through, I knew something was wrong. The following message popped up a second later:

PAGE CANNOT BE DISPLAYED

"Shit," Jimmy said. "The link's not active anymore."

"Meaning?"

"It could be a couple of things. Either the server is down or the feed has been cut. Sorry, man."

"That's all right. It was worth a shot. Do you have any way of determining the last time Andre connected to this site?"

"Sure."

Jimmy pointed at the screen. "See this column? It represents the date and time."

I stared at the entries on the monitor and did some quick calculations in my head. Andre had used the computer the same day Katherine and I spoke to him at school. That didn't surprise me. More interesting was the last entry. It was made six hours after he was dead.

"Can you make a copy of what's on the screen?"

"No problem," Jimmy said. He pressed the CONTROL and PRINT SCREEN buttons at the same time.

There was a brief delay before the printer started to hum. A moment later it pushed out a page. We also made copies of the computer's history log before we left.

KATHERINE'S deposition was winding up by the time we got back. She saw us through the conference room window and threw a questioning look in my direction. Jimmy waved to her and returned a weak smile.

"You're on your own from here on, buddy," he said out of the corner of his mouth.

"Jimmy, thanks for all your help. I'll keep you informed about what we find."

"Uh . . . that won't be necessary. I like you guys, I really do, but this officially got too weird for me about an hour ago. Dead guys don't use computers very much. I repeat what I said before—let the police handle this from here on."

"I'll take it under advisement."

As soon as we got into her office, Katherine wrapped her arms around my neck and kissed me. She had that slight scent of flowers about her that always went straight for my libido.

"Galena said you ran off with one of my employees. What was so important?"

"Jimmy and I were chatting about the situation with Sarah and he said something that suddenly made sense to me. How'd your deposition go?"

"Never mind the deposition. *Jimmy* made sense?"

I smiled. "He's a bright kid, K.J."

"I know he's bright. That's why I hired him. Are you going to tell me what happened or do I have to beat it out of you?" she asked, grabbing the front of my shirt.

"No, ma'am. I'll talk. Just don't use the rubber hose." I gave her buttocks a squeeze for good measure, but all I got was an arched eyebrow in return. "Anyway," I continued, "our theory is that Andre set it up to *look* like Sarah fell off the cliff."

"Excuse me?"

"What if he and Sarah were trying to fake her death?"

Katherine stared at me in disbelief. "*Fake her death?* You're saying she's alive?"

"Yeah, I think it's possible."

"Well I think it's sick. Why would she do something like that? Why would anyone?"

"I don't know. Jimmy thought it might have something to do with hiding their relationship from Sarah's parents, but that doesn't play very well. It's the twenty-first century and Frank and Lucille aren't monsters. Nobody would go to those lengths to conceal the fact that they were living together. No, my money's on the file Thurman told us about."

It was probably a good time to tell Katherine about seeing Sarah at the Hyatt, so I did.

"All right," she said after a moment. "Let's come back to this in a minute. Did your outing with Jimmy produce anything else?"

I caught the tone in her voice and realized I had hurt her feelings by leaving her out. I immediately apologized.

"K.J., I'm sorry. I needed to move fast and you were stuck in that deposition. I was going mostly on instinct."

Her expression softened . . . slightly, but she pushed me away when I went to hug her.

"It's okay," she said. "Just tell me what you found. I don't want to get blindsided when we meet with Thurman later."

I explained about our examining the logs on Sarah's computer and about the missing camera. Then I told her what we found at Naresh Patel's house, leaving out the part about how we had gotten in.

"May I see the printouts?" Katherine asked.

I handed them to her and she studied the pages for nearly a minute, the crease between her eyes deepening as she read.

"I don't know what's going on here, John, but I think we should put these someplace safe. The question now is do we tell Thurman about this?"

"I guess so. Supposedly he's one of the good guys."

"Let's think like lawyers for a moment. You can't just tell him you broke into someone's home and removed evidence that might be connected to a crime. They'll lock you up and throw away the key."

I had to agree. Phil Thurman was already unhappy, and dropping this on him would be like throwing gasoline on a fire.

"All right, it's a reasonable point," I conceded. "What if we work out a deal with him first, then pass on the information, leaving out Jimmy's part?"

I'm a flexible fellow if nothing else.

THURMAN was waiting for us and we were shown into his private office as soon as we arrived. He took a small tape recorder out of his desk drawer and got down to business immediately.

"This is Phillip Thurman, senior agent in charge. Today is Monday, July nineteenth, and this conversation is being recorded. Before we go any further, I want you both to know that I'm considering charging you with obstruction of justice. Anything you say here can and will be used against you in a court—"

Katherine's face immediately morphed into her trial lawyer mode, which is always a bad sign. She stood up and said, "If this is why you asked us here, go ahead make your charges. This meeting is over."

"I said I was *considering* it, Ms. Adams. Whether I go forward or not will depend on the extent of cooperation I receive from you and Professor Delaney."

"And *I* said the meeting is over. You can take whatever action the U.S. Criminal Code says you can. If you think a crime has been committed, then do your duty—otherwise, we're leaving."

For my part, I wasn't particularly worried about any criminal charges. There was no way Thurman could make them stick. He was running a bluff, but I was curious to see where he was going with it.

I said, "Maybe we're getting off on the wrong foot—again. Frankly, I feel the same way Ms. Adams does. You want our cooperation? Fine. But it might be a good idea to quit waltzing around and tell us what's really on your mind. We both know that an obstruction charge won't fly. Ms. Adams knows it and you know that we know it. So what's the bottom line?"

Thurman glared at me and I returned his look. As I did, the image of a bull getting ready to charge came to my mind. Then he suddenly shifted gears and seemed to relax.

"Have you ever heard of a man named Joshua Silver?"

"Never met the gentleman."

"That's good, Professor, because if you had, you'd be dead. I told you you might be dealing with some very bad people. Until the other day, I had my suspicions, but I couldn't be certain. You may recall my mentioning a man named Warren Blendel. Blendel isn't your garden-variety thug. He's a crime boss with extensive resources at his command. He's also ruthless and cunning. Silver, on the other hand, is a nightmare. He works for Blendel."

"In what capacity?" I asked.

"Joshua Silver is a contract killer. He's wanted not only by Interpol, but also the CIA and the governments of five different countries. He's a complete psycho who enjoys hurting others *and* he's very good at what he does."

"What do these men have to do with us?" Katherine asked. Though the level of her voice was constant, I could see that she was gripping the edge of her chair. I had a fairly good idea why.

Thurman tapped his fingertips together and waited for several seconds before he answered. He seemed to be struggling with something.

"What I'm going to tell you is strictly confidential. May I have your words it will remain that way?"

Katherine and I both nodded.

"We found a partial fingerprint belonging to Silver on the wire hanger that was wrapped around Andre Rostov's neck. The medical examiner's report shows severe lacerations on the interior of Rostov's throat as well as in his rectum as far up as the colon. If strangulation didn't kill Mr. Rostov, he would certainly have died from an internal hemorrhage."

Katherine grimaced at the image.

"Exactly," said Thurman. "Before Rostov died he was tortured— severely tortured."

"Why would Silver torture him?" I asked.

"Because he enjoys it, for one thing. I was hoping you might shed some light on the subject . . . or possibly you, Ms. Adams."

"You think we were involved?" Katherine asked, incredulous.

"Sarah O'Connor's boyfriend turns up dead with a suicide note pointing a finger at the professor, here. So tell me, what should I be thinking?"

"But we're the ones who called you," Katherine said.

"And that's supposed to put you in the clear? It's the oldest trick in the book."

"Everything happened exactly the way we said it did. If you have any question, set up a polygraph test. I'll volunteer and so will John."

Thurman leaned back in his seat and considered me. "Is that right, Professor? You willing to take a polygraph? I'm impressed."

I held Thurman's gaze again. We were getting good at this. In the past I had a captain who liked to try and stare you down, so the technique wasn't new to me.

"He doesn't think we did it," I said to Katherine. "If he did, we wouldn't be talking now. When did you decide Sarah O'Connor didn't go over that cliff?"

Thurman laughed to himself at some private joke, then looked down at his notes.

"We confirmed your story about the DNA test on O'Connor's hair sample with Dade County's ME. That would be a strange thing for a killer to do. It doesn't clear you where Rostov is concerned, but it was certainly enough to pique my curiosity. By the way, that's another item you forgot to mention."

The pieces of the puzzle began to fall into place as Phil Thurman's point became clear.

I said, "Look, I have no idea what this Joshua Silver has to do with the case. The one thing I *am* confident of now is that Sarah O'Connor wasn't killed at Cloudland Canyon. Maybe she's alive and maybe she isn't. But if what you've told me about Blendel is true, then he probably brought Silver in for a reason. My guess is Sarah's taking the file from the U.S. Attorney's office is somehow at the bottom of this."

Thurman nodded slowly. "You're a bright man, Delaney. Assuming I'm in agreement with you—and I'm not saying I am—can you see how your meddling complicates the situation? If O'Connor *is* alive, all you've done is put Silver one step closer to her. When I told you he was a nightmare, I wasn't exaggerating. He killed his own father when he was fifteen years old and then cut the body into little pieces. The only reason we know this is because a friend ratted him out years later while trying to bargain his way out of a jail sentence. I won't bore you with the details, but the friend disappeared. Parts of him were found in a wood chipper in upstate Vermont.

"You need to let us handle the investigation from here on. I won't ask you to take a polygraph exam right now, but if I find you sticking your nose into my case again, I'll come down on you like a ton of bricks. Do you understand me?"

Katherine started to respond, but I put a hand on her forearm and leaned forward in my seat.

"Let me be just as clear. We do have a problem. I know where you're coming from, but I was retained by Sarah's family to settle her affairs. I can only do that if she's dead. According to the Superior Court, I'm the administrator of her estate until the case is either closed or dismissed. This places an ethical obligation on me, not only to the court, but to her family as well. I *have* to tell them what we've found. It's not a matter of choice."

Thurman fingertips tapped a few more times while he mulled this over.

"Could you hold off for another week?"

"Give me a reason."

"I can't, Delaney. All I can tell you is that we're at a critical stage now and any outside interference could compromise our case severely. You used to be a cop, so I don't need to spell it out. We're moving our schedule forward as fast as we can."

I glanced at Katherine and she raised her eyebrows, indicating the call was mine to make.

I said, "Let me ask you this: Do you actually know if Sarah is alive?"

"No, I don't, but we're doing our best to find out. Hopefully, if she is, I can get to her before Silver does." He let that sink in for several seconds before he asked, "Do we have a deal?"

I answered, "All right, I'll hold off notifying the family, but I want to be kept in the loop."

"I'll tell you what I can, as long as it doesn't place my people in harm's way."

With that, he pushed himself back from the desk and stood up, indicating the meeting was over. "We'll be in touch. Thank you both for coming."

TWENTY-TWO

DELANEY

KATHERINE took my hand as we walked through the lobby. Neither of us spoke until we were inside her car.

"You made a mistake back there," she said. "You can't withhold information like that from her family. They'll sue you, friend or no friend."

"I know, I know. But I needed to buy some time. Bullshit case or not, Thurman would have arrested us."

"The charges were totally bogus."

"I'm aware of that, K.J. My point is we can't afford to waste precious hours and minutes getting booked and making bond. Something he said struck a chord with me."

"What was it?"

"That printout we took off Andre's computer shows when he contacted a variety of different Web sites. I want to see it again, because a lightbulb went on a moment ago."

"I don't understand."

"A pattern. I didn't see it before, but when Thurman used the word *schedule*, it finally hit me. I'll show you as soon as we get to your office."

Katherine glanced at her watch and frowned. "We'll have to do it quickly. You still have a plane to catch."

I didn't answer because I was trying to recall what the printout said. It was a second before I realized she was waiting for my response.

"Huh?"

"I said, your flight is at six o'clock tonight and you still have to pack."

"How would you feel about putting up with me for another day or two?"

"I'd love it," she said with a smile.

As soon as we got to her office, Katherine retrieved the printout from her safe and spread it on the conference room table. She watched over my shoulder while I studied it.

The page was arranged in four separate columns. The first row contained the names of the Web sites Andre had visited. The second showed his logon and logoff times, the third was just a series of numbers indicating the bytes and bits that were transmitted, and the fourth listed the dates and times.

I ran my finger across to the last column and placed a check mark next to the final entry—the one made *after* Andre was dead. Whoever had tried to access the site had done so at 3:47 a.m. Presumably they got the same error message Jimmy and I had about the link not being active, because the session ended five seconds later.

I found an entry for the same Web site again farther up the column and placed another check next to it. Each time it appeared I marked it. When I was finished there were twenty in all. The first one appeared two days after Sarah O'Connor had supposedly been killed. It read 9:00 p.m.

I asked Katherine. "Do you have a ruler?"

"Sure."

She disappeared down the hall and returned a minute later.

I proceeded to underline each of the entries I had marked. The second one was made at 10:00 p.m. the following day. The next one skipped a day completely. Give or take a minute or two, the contacts began again at 8:00 a.m. two days later and continued like that for five days in a row, moving up by one hour each time. Once again, on the sixth day, no entry appeared. But just as before, the strange schedule resumed after a day's gap. The missing day showed up once more seven days later and again on the seventeenth day. Hoping to get a better handle on the problem, I wrote all the dates and times down on a sheet of paper.

My brain was telling me a pattern was emerging, but the missing days and ten-hour gaps made no sense. I sat there drumming a rhythm on the table with my forefinger. I don't know how much time passed before the answer struck me.

When I finally looked up, I saw that Katherine had been watching me.

I asked, "Do you have a big calendar and something I can use to prop it up with?"

"Give me a minute."

This time she returned with her secretary, Galena Olivares, who was helping her carry a large easel. Katherine hung a three-foot laminated calendar from the hooks at the top and set it up next to the conference table.

"We use this for trials," she explained.

"Great, can you get a black marker and write nine p.m. under Friday, June eighteenth, honey?"

Katherine's hand paused and a look passed between her and Galena. I assumed it was in response to my use of the word *honey*. I didn't think about it when I said it. It just came out. By rights, I should have followed the endearment up with something more romantic than, "Now put ten p.m. in the box next to it."

Katherine sighed and wrote in the time as requested.

When we were through, part of the mystery was solved. What wasn't apparent before suddenly became clear once the numbers were arranged on the calendar. For some reason Andre and Sarah didn't communicate with each other on Sundays, at least not by computer. Why, I didn't know, but there was no question about it. The second part was more difficult. Try as I might, I couldn't understand what the ten-hour gaps signified. The more I stared at the chart, the more annoyed I became. Finally, I banged my hand down on the table in frustration, causing Katherine and Galena to jump.

I apologized. "Sorry. It's right in front of me and I can't see it."

"Can't see what?" Galena asked, as she and Katherine leaned forward to study the calendar together.

Friday	Saturday	Sunday	Monday	Tuesday	Wednesday
June 18	June 19	June 20	June 21	June 22	June 23
2103	2202		0806	0904	1002

Thursday	Friday	Saturday	Sunday	Monday	Tuesday
June 21	June 22	June 23	June 24	June 25	June 26
1103	1201	0103		0203	0301

Wednesday	Thursday	Friday	Saturday	Sunday	Monday
June 27	June 28	June 29	June 30	July 1	July 2
0402	0503	0605	0702		0804

"What do the numbers mean?" Galena asked.

"The computer's clock uses using military time . . . oh-eight-hundred is eight a.m. and so on."

Galena stared at the chart some more and then shook her head. "Beats me," she said. Then turning to Katherine she asked, "Is it okay if I close up shop and head home? Sorry I couldn't help."

I went back to studying at the chart again before it hit me. I got up so abruptly I nearly knocked my chair over in the process.

"What did you say?"

Galena stopped in midstride on her way to the door. "I said I'm sorry I didn't help."

"No, before that."

"I asked if it was okay for me to close up—"

"*Shop.* You said *shop*, right?"

"Uh, yeah, I guess," Galena said, giving Katherine a puzzled look.

I snapped my fingers. "That's it."

"What's it? What'd I do?" Galena asked, looking from Katherine to me.

"Don't you see? That's the answer. Sarah was using a retail business of some kind and they closed for the night. When they reopened *ten hours later*, she and Andre resumed their communications. The one hour differences were so she wouldn't be there at a predictable times."

"That's why there's no eleven o'clock entry on the third day," Katherine said. "The store, or whatever it is, was already closed."

We threw our arms around each other and hugged. Then I pulled a startled Galena to me and kissed her on the forehead.

"Thank you, thank you, thank you. That was brilliant," I said, hugging her.

"You're welcome . . . I think. I'm going home now 'cause you people scare me."

She muttered something under her breath in Spanish and waved to us over her shoulder on the way out.

"You *are* a scary man, John Delaney," Katherine observed.

I consulted the calendar again and checked my watch. If my theory was correct the next contact would come at 9 p.m. that very night . . . assuming Sarah didn't know Andre was dead. The time was less than four hours away.

TWENTY-THREE

BLENDEL

WARREN Blendel and his wife both glanced up when a servant entered the room. Blendel was in the process of reviewing Hans Schiller's latest report with her. Because of the various wiretaps that had been placed on his house over the years, both legal and illegal, he no longer trusted telephone communications. As a result, he had his property swept by electronic experts once a week. It was important to keep up with the Joneses, or in this case, the feds. In addition to his regular security people, he employed two men who were experts in wireless technology. Their job was to stay abreast of the latest developments in the field. Neither man knew about the other, so neither could share any information they obtained while on the job. According to Linda Blendel, the arrangement balanced out perfectly.

The latest "toy" they had found was something called a "sleeper," a listening device that remained inactive and gave off no electronic signal . . . until a call came through. When that happened, the sleeper woke up and began transmitting. Once the call was over, it promptly went back into hibernation, making it virtually undetectable. His people had discovered three similar devices in the last two years. It was an enormous expense keeping such men on retainer, but as the Blendels viewed it, it was part of the cost of doing business.

"Excuse me sir, but Mr. Schiller is on the line," the servant told them. "He says it's important that he speak with you."

Blendel frowned and glanced at his wife. This was specifically against their instructions. He dismissed the servant, then put the phone on loudspeaker.

Linda answered the call. "Hello, Hans. This is an unexpected surprise. Are you enjoying your vacation?"

"Very much, madam," Schiller replied, deferential as always, in case her husband was listening. "If you have a moment, I would like to ask some advice about places to eat and perhaps a night spot to visit down here."

"Of course. Is this just for you and your companion?"

"Actually, someone else may be joining us—an old friend we thought was gone. We would enjoy showing her the good time, as you Americans say."

Linda took a moment to digest that. At first she wasn't sure she'd heard Schiller correctly. He seemed to be implying the O'Connor girl was alive, but that was impossible. Her mind worked quickly to assess the situation. It was important to remain clam and think clearly. She glanced at Warren and saw that his face had gone pale.

"Yes, that's uh . . . perfectly understandable," she said. "Why don't you give me a little time to think it over? Warren and I were about to head to the office. Call me back in say . . . two hours. And Hans, you might want to pick up a new cell phone. Your reception is breaking up a bit."

"I will, madam. I shall talk with you later. Please give my regards to Herr Blendel."

Linda waited for several seconds for her husband to say something, but he just sat there staring blankly at the phone.

"Was he referring to the girl?" she asked when they disconnected.

Blendel nodded slowly and didn't reply.

"I'd better go and change clothes," she said.

"No dear, I'll handle it. You have that luncheon to attend later."

"Warren, are you sure you're up to this?"

Blendel came around the desk and touched her face gently. The smile she gave him was practiced and automatic. He reached for the intercom.

"Joseph, this is Warren. Would you bring my car around, please? I need to run to the office for a while. Also, place a call to Martin Freeman and ask him to meet me there in an hour."

Blendel was nearly to the door when Linda said, "Make me proud of you, Warren."

He hesitated for a moment, then kept on walking.

TWENTY-FOUR

SCHILLER

Hans Schiller could just imagine what his employers were thinking. He was aware they were both in the room, and his reference about "giving his regards to Herr Blendel" was strictly for show. Linda would know what to do—she always did. He also knew the phone call was a breach of protocol, but that couldn't be helped. Sarah O'Connor was definitely alive. He had been prepared for a number of possibilities, but not that. In the end, young Rostov had talked—been glad to talk, just to stop the pain. He doubted if anyone could have stood up to what Joshua was doing. The recollection still made him cringe, and he was not a man who cringed lightly.

The plastic sheet they had brought with them took care of the blood and bits of flesh. Forensics would eventually see through that if they did the right tests, but by the time the police finished their examination he and Joshua would be long gone. If everything went as planned, the FBI would follow their standard procedure and come down on Delaney and the woman. None of it would stick, of course, but sidetracking them for a sufficient period of time would produce the same result.

Schiller was seated at a table in the corner of a crowded diner waiting for their food to arrive. There was a glass of beer in front of him. Joshua stood waiting at the takeout counter. He was pretending to examine the songs in a little jukebox. There were five others like it along the bar. Schiller observed his companion for a moment and shook his head. He knew why Joshua was there. The man was watching the cook prepare their food. This odd behavior did not surprise him. He'd seen Joshua do it a dozen times. It was a way to control the situation, at least in the albino's view. It was too easy for someone to slip poison into a meal unobserved. While being poisoned by a random cook in a

random restaurant didn't make a great deal of sense, Schiller was willing to concede Joshua's paranoia had its uses. He downed the rest of
his beer, tossed a few dollars on the table, and motioned with his head
for Joshua to join him outside once the food came.

The girl had played them all for fools. Sighting Delaney and the
woman lawyer talking to Rostov had been pure luck. That's how it
went sometimes. If Joshua had only held off a little longer, they might
have obtained O'Connor's exact location, but the albino was enjoying
himself too much. By the time he stopped him, it was too late. In his
own way Joshua was just as far gone, lost in the ecstasy of the moment, his eyes rolled upward and his breathing rapid.

Whether Rostov had died of shock, loss of blood, or strangulation
really didn't matter. They would find the girl. Hopefully they would
complete their business quickly. He didn't care for Atlanta's humidity and he missed the cooler air of Bavaria, where he had grown up.

"Madam Blendel wants me to pick up another cell phone,"
Schiller told Joshua as he entered the car.

Joshua simply nodded and put the bag of food on the seat between them.

"We are to speak to them again in two hours," he added.

Another nod.

With the afternoon sunlight illuminating half his face, Joshua
looked more like a ghost than a person, Schiller thought.

"Have you come up with any more on her location?"

"Not yet," Joshua said, removing a sandwich and taking a bite of
it. "I think she's moving around. That would explain the computer
contacts at all those different hours."

He returned his attention to the printout they had made from
Rostov's computer and studied it.

"It would have been better if you hadn't killed him," Schiller said.
"You said you were just going to scare him."

Joshua stopped chewing and turned to face him. "Didn't he look
scared?"

Schiller muttered something to himself in German and started
the car.

A SHORT while later, they located a strip shopping mall and went in to buy a new cell phone along with five hours of prepaid air time. The albino waited in the car while Schiller completed the transaction. He wore an Atlanta Braves baseball cap. When Schiller returned, he found Joshua reading the file on Katherine Adams again. There were a variety of photos of her spread out on the seat. One showed Katherine as an eighteen-year-old just after she had entered Ohio State University. Another, taken by an unscrupulous newspaper photographer, showed her lying in a hospital bed after Jenks's attack. She had been in a coma for three days. The photograph had received national attention in the media. Its caption read, OHIO CO-ED SURVIVES NIGHTMARE WITH MADMAN. The most recent picture he recognized as one they had taken outside the sheriff's office several days earlier.

Schiller asked, "May I ask what you find so interesting?"

"She really hasn't changed much since she was a young girl."

"So?"

"If you look closely, you can see where Jenks cut her finger off."

Schiller leaned over and studied the photograph. It was a newspaper shot of Katherine taken a year ago, after the *Ocean Majestic* had gone down.

"Yah . . . a beautiful woman. So what does this have to do with the girl?"

"She interests me, that's all," Joshua said, putting the pictures back in the file. He turned to stare out the passenger-side window. "She just interests me."

For a moment, Schiller considered asking what was so interesting, but decided against it. He didn't want to know. He started the car's engine and drove to a nearby park to call his employer.

TWENTY-FIVE

BLENDEL

Warren Blendel was waiting for the phone call, as was Martin Freeman, who had just gone through the office checking for electronic bugs.

"Hold please," Blendel said as soon as he answered. He glanced at Freeman, who had a meter attached to the phone wire. Freeman nodded. Blendel slid an envelope across his desk toward the young man. Freeman picked it up and stuffed it in his back pocket, then turned on his iPod, stuck a small pair of headphones in his ears, and left the room with a cheerful wave.

Blendel waited until the door was closed and punched a button on his computer console. The screen promptly split into four separate views showing the outer lobby of his office and the front of the building. Freeman appeared a minute later, his head bobbing to whatever music he was listening to. He walked past the security guard and went to his car.

"I'm sorry, Hans," Blendel said. He picked up a tangerine he had brought with him from the house and started peeling it. "I wanted to check the office before we spoke. Linda is at a luncheon, so you're stuck with me. Did I understand you correctly earlier—the girl is alive?"

"Yah, this is what we think. Her death was a ruse. She and Rostov were working together. They used the Internet to communicate. Joshua is trying to pin down the location now."

"This is a very serious situation. Do you need more help?"

"Conceivably, but I think the fewer people involved the better."

"You said she and Rostov *were* working together."

"I did. Rostov is dead. We made it look like he committed suicide, but this will not fool the police for very long."

Blendel peeled some more of the tangerine's skin and popped a section in his mouth.

"I see. And how did this happen?"

"The details would only upset you. Suffice to say, he died while Joshua was questioning him."

"Then I take it you got all the information you needed?"

Schiller expelled a long breath through his nostrils. "We learned only that the O'Connor girl is still alive and how they were communicating with each other."

"So we don't know where she is?" Blendel asked, savoring the tangerine's tartness. He chewed slowly while he thought.

"Regretfully not."

"That's very disappointing, Hans. How did you conclude Rostov had betrayed us?"

"When we didn't find the file among her possessions we decided to check with him again to see if perhaps Ms. O'Connor had left any property with him. At the school campus we saw him talking to Delaney and the Adams woman. It was pure luck, nothing more."

Blendel stopped chewing. "It seems Mr. Delaney is a very persistent man. Do you have any idea what they were talking about?"

"I do not, but the fact that they *were* talking was enough to pique our interest. Earlier in the day we trailed Delaney and another man to the home where Rostov was living. The second man is a lawyer who works for Adams. You will be interested to know they broke into the house. They only stayed for a while and came out empty-handed."

"They broke in? Why?"

"Perhaps to search for evidence; or perhaps to examine Rostov's computer, as we did. This is Joshua's opinion. On this point I agree with him. We also examined the house, but could only stay a short time due to an unexpected complication."

Blendel flicked a piece of lint off his sleeve. "And what complication would that be?"

"Apparently an FBI agent had been assigned to keep watch on Rostov. He surprised us while we were inside."

"And?"

"And Joshua was forced to take care of him. We got rid of the body in a remote wooded area."

"You killed a federal agent?"

"There was little choice under the circumstances." Schiller glanced at Joshua, who was seated in the car studying photos of Katherine Adams again; he lowered his voice. "Joshua may be insane, but he's really quite efficient with that knife of his."

Blendel leaned back in his chair and looked up at the ceiling. This was not good. In his business, killing a cop, any kind of cop, was to be avoided if at all possible. The last time he had been forced into that position, it caused all kind of problems. He didn't need more at this stage in his life. The killing part didn't bother him so much as the complications that were sure to follow. Competent or not, Joshua had just raised the stakes considerably.

He was still forming his reply when two men appeared on his security monitor. He watched them walk across the parking lot. One was familiar; one was not. They passed out of the first camera's field of view, entered the lobby, and began speaking with the guard on duty. Blendel's heart rate began to increase. Out of instinct his eyes drifted to the back door of his office. It would be so easy to get in his car and keep driving, away from all the madness.

No, he thought. *You play it out.*

"Hans, I have to ring off right now. Why don't we chat later tonight, say at around eight? I have some company I need to deal with at the moment. Do whatever you have to, but *find* that girl."

Schiller was about to reply when the line went dead.

PHILLIP Thurman and a man who was obviously another federal agent were shown into Blendel's office by a secretary. No one offered to shake hands.

"Ah, Phillip," Blendel said, "it's been a long time. This is an unexpected visit after all these years. Back from your Southern exile?"

"This is Special Agent Carl Sanchez," Thurman replied

Blendel nodded by way of acknowledgment. "A pleasure. I would invite you both to sit, but I don't think you'll be staying very long. Was there something you wanted?"

"One of my men in Atlanta is missing," Thurman said. "His name is Arthur Wolheim."

"And is that supposed to mean something to me?"

"It should. He was assigned to watch a young man named Andre Rostov, a friend of Sarah O'Connor."

Blendel didn't react to Sarah O'Connor's name other than to raise his eyebrows and turn his palms up.

Thurman asked, "Are you saying you don't recognize these names?"

"I'm afraid not, Phillip. It's been lovely talking to you again. You can show yourselves out."

Thurman, however, made no move to leave. Instead, he rested his knuckles on Blendel's desk and leaned forward.

"Sarah O'Connor was a law student and formerly an intern with the U.S. Attorney's office. She stole a file from them, Blendel . . . a file that had your name in it."

"Then I trust you'll bring her to justice. That doesn't seem like an appropriate thing for a law student to do, though heaven knows the standards in that profession have been slipping for years."

"Cute," said Thurman. "We're reconstructing the file, Blendel, so it's just a matter of time. And when it's complete we're going to nail you."

"Thank you for the advance warning, Phillip. Good day, gentlemen."

"If anything has happened to Art Wolheim you won't be going down just for racketeering or distributing porn. It'll be for murder. I'll see to that."

"A man's reach should always exceed his grasp."

Still, Thurman did not back off. "Are you aware that Sarah O'Connor was killed several weeks ago while camping in Georgia?"

"No, I was not. I don't know any Sarah O'Connor. But I'm told camping can be a strenuous pastime."

"You're just a barrel of laughs. I've been waiting for this a long while, Warren. They don't have linen suits in prison."

"You've always been very perceptive," said Blendel. "I hope Agent Sanchez is taking notes. This sounds like first-rate police work to me."

Thurman ended the conversation by saying, "We'll be seeing you around."

After they left, Blendel pulled another section of the tangerine apart and placed it in his mouth. His hands were shaking and he gripped the edge of his desk until his knuckles showed white. Thurman had been fishing; that much was clear. They had nothing on him—yet.

The visit was probably meant to rattle him and it had done just that. He took several deep breaths and waited until his breathing slowed. Then he took a pill from the bottle on the credenza and popped it into his mouth. Fifteen years ago he would have let something like this roll off his back. Still, one had to adapt to change; that was the key to survival. Eight o'clock was the time he had told Schiller.

He asked himself if calling sooner might be interpreted as a sign of weakness. Unlikely. He picked up the receiver and dialed. When the call was over, he placed another to Nick O'Connor.

TWENTY-SIX

DELANEY

THE next five hours seemed to crawl. Katherine and I caught a quick bite at a local restaurant then stopped at a computer store to buy one of those Internet cameras before returning home. According to my calculations, Sarah's next contact would come at nine o'clock that evening. Our only hope was that she hadn't heard about Andre's death yet. If she had, there was a good chance she would go underground and disappear. The sky was lead gray and it was starting to drizzle by the time we arrived.

I went into Katherine's den, spent a few minutes figuring out how to connect the camera, then turned on her computer. The software split the screen into two parts. On the lower half you could see yourself, and on the upper one you could see whoever you were talking to.

I was about to try the Web site again when I realized I had left the printouts from Andre's computer on the backseat of Katherine's car. The clock on her mantel read seven thirty.

Katherine's property is quite large and her home sits well off the main road. In other words, it can't be seen from the street. There's a motor court at the rear of the house where she and the kids park when they're in residence. I let myself out through the side door and stopped short at the sight of a man peering through the back window of her car. He was a big guy dressed in casual slacks, a golf shirt, and a sport jacket. His hair was white, somewhat long, and had a goatee. It was hard to tell any more about his face because he was wearing sunglasses.

"Something I can do for you?" I asked.

My voice startled him and he straightened up and turned toward me.

"Jesus Christ, you scared the hell out of me," he said. "I'm Ed

Marger, Katherine's neighbor. I was just admiring K.J.'s new car. My wife's been after me to get her a Lexus for months. I don't think we've met before." He held out his hand.

"John Delaney."

Marger's hand was thick and calloused. Despite his age, which I placed somewhere in his late fifties, I was immediately conscious of the strength there. He was built like a linebacker and at least six inches taller than me.

He said, "Sorry for popping in unannounced. We're having a homeowners' meeting about the road expansion the county's been trying to push through and I thought I'd better stop by and let K.J. know what's happening."

"I'm sure she'll be glad to talk to you. She's taking a bath at the moment. Why don't you come inside and wait?"

"Listen, if I've come at a bad time—"

"No, no," I insisted. "By the way, how did you get over the fence, Ed? I thought I shut the gate when we came down the driveway."

"It doesn't go completely around the property," Marger explained as we started to walk. "You sure I'm not imposing?"

"Not at all. Can I get you a drink?"

I never got an answer to my question, because I suddenly found myself flat on my face from a heavy blow to the base of my neck. Colored lights exploded in my head. A second blow from Marger's shoe caught me in the ribs, driving the air out of my lungs. It was followed by what felt like a sledgehammer to the side of my jaw.

Dazed, I struggled to my knees and tried to focus my vision. I had been out for several seconds. My first breath told me my ribs were broken. Somewhere behind me the sound of glass breaking pulled my attention around. The horn on Katherine's car began to blare. Marger was in the process of reaching into the backseat. To this day, I can't tell you how I got to my feet. I took one stumbling step toward him followed by another.

I hit Marger with a full-speed shoulder block, slamming him into the side of the door. He grunted in surprise and cursed in German. I drove my shoulder into his back twice more, then kicked the back of his right knee, buckling it. Then with all my strength I landed the hardest punch I could to his kidney. Marger screamed and struck backwards at my head with his elbow as he tried to spin around.

I ducked under the blow, and hit him in the gut. But before I could land another punch, something stopped me. A second man came out of nowhere, snaked what felt like a rubber hose around my neck, and yanked me backwards. Suddenly my air was cut off and I panicked. My arms flailed as I tried to reach behind me. Whoever it was rammed a knee into my spine and forced me to the ground. All at once the colored lights were back, but only briefly. This time a curtain of black settled over my eyes.

I awoke to the sight of Katherine's face hovering above me. An elderly man I didn't know was standing next to her. He put a hand on my shoulder when I tried to sit up.

"Easy there, son. You've had a pretty rough time of it."

"Who the hell are you?" I asked, pushing his hand away.

"Well, for one thing, I'm a doctor. The name's Edwin Marger," he responded in an offended tone.

"John, don't move until Ed finishes examining you," Katherine instructed.

I let them push me back down. I found that I was lying on the driveway near the garage. Katherine's car with its shattered window was about fifteen feet away. She was holding a gun, a .357 Magnum. From the smell, I knew it had been fired recently. Katherine grabbed a cushion off one of her lawn chairs and placed it under my head. Nearby, her cat, Peeka, sat silently on his haunches watching the scene. There was a green garden hose lying on the ground next to him.

The present incarnation of Ed Marger was a good bit older than the first one and about half his size. He was somewhere in his early seventies. He had clear blue eyes and a mustache that was mostly gray with a little brown mixed in. I winced when his fingers probed my side.

He said, "Can't tell without an X-ray, but I'd say at least two ribs are cracked." He produced a tiny penlight attached to his key chain and shined it in my eyes. "Probable concussion, too," he added. "What in the world happened here?"

"Jehovah's Witnesses," I said. "They're pushy bastards."

Marger stared at me for a moment. "All right, I suppose it's none of my business. I'm just trying to help. I'd like to call an ambulance and get you to a hospital for a proper examination. My training is in nephrology."

I had a vague notion that nephrologists were kidney doctors, but I was in no mood to ask about it.

"I'll be okay," I said, sitting up. This time they let me. "There's nothing you can do for ribs except tape them, right?"

"Well, yes, but an X-ray is still a good idea," Marger insisted.

"I don't mean to appear ungrateful, Doc, but if you could just fix me up, I'd really appreciate it. I'll stop at the emergency room later and let them give me the once-over. We'll also notify the police. At the moment, there are things I need to do."

Marger glanced from me to Katherine then back again before he made up his mind. He was clearly uneasy with the situation. I got the impression, though, he was on good terms with Katherine and willing to go out on a limb.

He said, "All right. I'm just a few houses away. If you feel strong enough to make it, I've got enough supplies there to patch you up."

"No problem."

Katherine and Marger helped me to my feet and we all piled into her car, after brushing away as much broken glass out as we could.

Along the way I learned the real Ed Marger was indeed a kidney doctor who owned three dialysis clinics in North Atlanta. Despite suffering from Parkinson's disease, he had come through the woods that separated their homes when he heard shots fired. He and Katherine tended to look out for one another. Marger picked up on my silent question and supplemented his explanation, adding that it wasn't unusual for neighbors to do that. Score another one for the South.

I'm not saying New Yorkers are callous, but I've seen them step around people lying on the street because they don't want to interrupt their cell phone conversations. Hell, I've done it myself. I thought about this as we pulled into his driveway and decided to give the next person in need a helping hand if I was able.

Inside Marger's office I sat on his desk while he applied tape to my ribs. His right hand shook continuously at rest, but seemed to work fine once he moved it.

"That's the Parkinson's," he explained, following my glance. "It's known as a resting tremor."

I recognized the symptoms from my mother who had been suffering from the same disease for the last ten years. When he finished, I found it a little easier to breathe. Next, he gently checked the base of my skull.

"You've already got a good-sized knot forming," he said. "I don't think anything's broken. Too hard-headed I suspect."

"You don't know the half of it," Katherine responded.

I laughed, but it hurt. "Thanks, Doc," I said.

"No problem. I can give you something for the pain if you like."

"I'll just stick with aspirin."

"All right. I suppose you have your reasons, but you really should take it easy for a few days."

"I'll try," I said, shaking his hand. "What do I owe you?"

"Nothing. Just take care of yourself and see that you stay away from those Jehovah's Witnesses. You owe this little lady a lot more than you do me."

I glanced at Katherine and only got an enigmatic smile in return. It didn't take a genius to figure out she had scared off the bad guys and probably saved my life in the process, but this wasn't the time or place to discuss it. The clock was ticking. When we got back to her car she watched me ease myself into the passenger seat with a look of concern on her face.

"John, are you really okay?"

"I'll live. We have to get to your office before nine. They took the printouts, K.J. I need that copy in your safe. It has the Web site's address."

"I really think we should take you to a hospital. You heard what Ed—"

"How quick can you get us there?"

Katherine searched my face for a few seconds, then took a deep breath and let it out through her nostrils. "Put on your seat belt, big boy."

Over the next few minutes I acquired a new respect for women drivers. Katherine drove like a man, negotiating curves smoothly and accelerating into the turns when she had to. We arrived at her office just before nine. She raced down the hall to her safe, retrieved the printouts, and brought them back. Fortunately, her computer had a video camera already installed. I turned it on and punched in the Web site's address.

Seconds crawled by as the progress bar at the bottom of the screen began to move. The same message Jimmy and I had seen appeared again:

PAGE CANNOT BE DISPLAYED

"Damn," Katherine muttered under her breath. "She's not going to show."

I drummed my fingers on the table in annoyance, and checked the clock at the bottom of the screen. If something was going to happen it should have done so already.

"Let's give it a few minutes."

We watched the time without speaking. It was 8:55.

The phone's ring caused us both to jump. Katherine started to answer it and then changed her mind. Her service picked up after a minute. When I glanced at the clock at the bottom of the screen, it now read 8:58:50 p.m.

My hand moved to the mouse and I clicked the GO button next to the address once more. The progress bar appeared again and began moving, only much slower this time. Something was definitely happening. A moment later a blue window appeared on the monitor, and little by little a picture began to form. We were looking at a live video feed. Beneath the picture was a dialogue box where you could type in a message to whoever was on the other end.

8:59:20 p.m.

I felt Katherine's fingers tighten on my shoulder as the words HI, BABE materialized letter by letter in the dialogue box. In the picture frame above it the top part of a girl's head had formed the eyebrows.

My hands moved to the keyboard and I sent the following message:

SARAH, THIS IS JOHN DELANEY. YOUR LIFE IS IN DANGER.
GET OUT OF THERE IMMEDIATELY!

There was a pause before her reply appeared.

WHERE IS ANDRE?

The face was almost complete now and I could see the fear in her eyes. Her hair was shorter than I remembered, but I was definitely looking at Sarah O'Connor.

ANDRE IS DEAD. YOU MUST GET OUT OF THERE NOW.
PEOPLE ARE LOOKING FOR YOU. I'M HERE TO HELP. SEND
ME A TEXT MESSAGE ON MY CELL PHONE AT 212-555-3450
AND TELL ME WHERE TO CONTACT YOU.

We stared at each other for several seconds, her eyes searching mine. People were moving in the background behind her. There was another emotion present that I couldn't identify. Then slowly, almost imperceptibly, Sarah shook her head.

IT'S NO GOOD. GOOD-BYE PROFESSOR. THANK YOU
FOR TRYING.

Katherine's hands shot to the keyboard a second before the screen went dark, hitting the CONTROL and PRINT SCREEN keys simultaneously. Then the connection was broken.

I sat there staring at the monitor, stunned. I was so certain that Sarah would turn to me, but she didn't. All I had done was drive her away—maybe for good.

"Got it," Katherine said.

"Got what?"

She explained, "I just saved a copy of the picture. Maybe we can figure out where she was broadcasting from."

"What good will that do? She's gone."

"We'll see. Move over."

I let Katherine sit down and she began typing. A few seconds later she brought up the image of Sarah she had just saved. I looked at it for several seconds but couldn't see what good it would do. Katherine then used the mouse to crop off a section of the picture to Sarah's left.

"There," she said, pointing. "I think that's a sign in the background."

"It might be, but you can't make anything out."

Katherine swung around to face me. "I had a divorce case a few years ago where we used video surveillance on a doctor who was cheating on his wife. Our investigator, Dave Maxwell, followed the man to a parking garage but lost him when he snuck out the back. Dave did some poking around and found a hotel across the street that had a security camera on the roof. I won't go into any details, but we managed to get a copy of the tape and brought it to a fellow at Georgia Tech who enhanced the images for us. He got a good picture of the defendant and his girlfriend kissing in his car. We might be able to do the same here."

"I don't know, K.J. It's a long shot. I think I screwed up."

"You didn't screw anything up," she said. "You had to warn her that she was in danger. I think it's worth a try."

I still wasn't convinced. My mind was in turmoil. There was a good chance I had just led the people who murdered Andre right to Sarah's doorstep, exactly as Thurman had predicted.

"I don't know . . . maybe," I replied. "And speaking of shots, do you want to tell me what happened earlier?"

Katherine reached forward and affectionately brushed a lock of hair off my forehead. "Peeka and I saved your life."

"Excuse me?"

"I said, Peeka and I—"

"I heard what you said. How did the cat get involved?"

"When I heard my car alarm go off, I figured you had opened the door and didn't know how to stop it, so I came out to help. The last thing I expected to see was you fighting with anyone, but there you were. Suddenly another man came out of nowhere, grabbed my garden hose, and looped it around your neck. I couldn't tell anything about him, except he looked like a ghost."

"And?"

"And I ran for my gun. Neither of them saw me. The pale man

had his knee in your back and was still pulling on the hose. His friend, the man you were fighting, grabbed a shovel near the garage and started toward you. I was sure he was going to brain you, but suddenly he tripped and fell. That's when I fired. They both took off running."

"You *shot* him?"

"I shot *at* him. He went down before I hit him."

Confused, I turned my palms up, trying to visualize the sequence of events. "K.J., that doesn't make sense."

"Don't you understand? *He tripped over the cat.* Peeka saved your life!" she said brightly. "Are you sure you're okay?" She leaned forward and examined the knot on my head.

I opened my mouth, then closed it again. There were probably any number of suitable replies, but for the life of me I couldn't think of a single one.

On the way home that night I asked Katherine to pull into the local supermarket. She gave me a puzzled look and waited in the car while I jumped out. I told her I would be right back. Five minutes later I returned with a box of catnip.

TWENTY-SEVEN

NICK O'CONNOR

THE building was located in Hunts Point, a seamy, run-down area even the locals tended to avoid. In recent years the city has made significant efforts to clean up the neighborhood, but it still has a long way to go. Grimy and industrial, Hunts Point is home to half a dozen gangs. Two blocks away on Spofford Avenue is P.S. 226, a middle school that houses three thousand students, most of them black and Hispanic. The schoolyard has a fifteen-foot-high chain link fence that's torn in at least four places, leaving openings wide enough for a person to walk through.

Near the school is a produce market where trucks come and go. In the past year, four people had been murdered within a block of the market, their bodies dumped in the Bronx River. It's an area largely devoid of people once the sun goes down. Police patrol the surrounding neighborhood and do what they can with the man-power available, which is usually in short supply. They tend to look the other way at prostitutes who ply their trade to passing motorists and in darkened corners of the schoolyard against graffiti-covered walls.

Through a window that opened out onto Halleck Street, Warren Blendel watched Nick O'Connor park his car, an unmarked police cruiser. Cautious as always, O'Connor checked the street to make sure he wasn't being watched, then walked across and knocked on the door.

Constructed in the early 1930s, the building was owned by Blendel and contained a warehouse and a shipping office. Behind it was a parking lot where trucks loaded fruits and vegetables for delivery to restaurants throughout the city. His drivers collected money from their customers on a weekly basis. The payments were not only for the produce, though. There was an additional premium for protection against *unexpected* damage to the businesses. The owners paid these without complaint. It was the way life worked in the city.

Blendel's front office contained a desk, a chair, and a faded burgundy couch that was so old, its color was nearly back in vogue. A man O'Connor had never seen before was waiting for him. He was large and rough-looking, the type you generally see down by the docks.

It was O'Connor's night off. He was dressed in gray slacks, loafers, and a yellow golf shirt. Under normal circumstances he would have waited until the following day to meet with Blendel, but his employer was insistent, so he told his wife he had to go to the station to check on a case.

The man at the desk nodded to him by way of a greeting, stood up, and knocked on the door to the inner office. Another of Blendel's employees opened it and moved aside, allowing him to enter. The room was a direct contradiction to the shabbiness of the one outside. It was carpeted and smelled of lemon furniture polish. An expensive walnut desk dominated the center. On a credenza behind it were several pieces of African art, a baseball bat signed by the entire 1963 Yankees, and a photo of Linda Blendel from a magazine ad twelve years earlier. A chair rail that matched the desk's wood ran around the perimeter of the room.

"Nick, thank you for coming," said Blendel, stepping forward to shake his hand. "I apologize for the inconvenience. Have a seat—we need to talk."

O'Connor settled into a comfortable wingback chair in front of the desk. "No problem, Mr. B. What's up?"

"A situation has arisen, a particularly disturbing one. It seems your niece is alive."

"That's impossible," O'Connor said, sitting upright. "I identified Sarah's body myself."

"Yes . . . you did. That's what confuses me. Unfortunately, there's no question about it. The medical examiner is conducting DNA tests at John Delaney's request, but I suspect they'll only confirm what we already know. I was hoping you might be able to shed some light on the subject, because it's rather upsetting, as you can imagine."

"Someone's pulling your leg. I'm telling you, I went down there and saw her body myself."

"I'm not saying you have anything to do with this, but we know for a fact that your niece is alive."

The door opened again and the man in the lobby came in, closing it behind him. O'Connor glanced at him then returned his attention to Blendel. Before he spoke, O'Connor thought about what he'd seen the day he flew down to Georgia to identify his niece's body. Her face had been damaged beyond recognition, but everything else matched up, right down to her driver's license and the necklace she had worn since her sixteenth birthday. He recalled meeting her boyfriend at the morgue and his pointing out the tattoo on Sarah's ankle. He confirmed the identifying mark to the sheriff without giving it much thought. Of course, an ID of her body had been only part of the reason for his trip. He wanted to search Sarah's house. More important, Blendel wanted the house searched.

"I don't get it," O'Connor said. "How do you know she's alive?"

"When you didn't find the file, I sent Hans and Joshua to Atlanta to see if they could locate it. They learned about Sarah quite by accident. You can appreciate my reaction when they shared this news with me."

O'Connor took a deep breath and leaned back in his seat, shaking his head. "Someone's fucking with us."

"Yes . . . that was my thought, too."

"Well, it's not me," O'Connor said indignantly. "I want you to know I had nothing to do with this. Whoever set it up jerked me around, too. I'm as much in the dark as you are."

"Of course. Still . . ." Blendel spread his hands.

"I'm serious, Mr. B. I'll jump on this right away."

"That's very kind, Nick. I would really like to get to the bottom of this situation as soon as possible," Blendel said. "There's something else I'd like to ask you. What made you pick John Delaney to help with the legal matters?"

The question surprised O'Connor. "Delaney? Nothing. Like I told you a couple of days ago, it was Frankie's idea. One of our people at the Forty-third Precinct recommended him. We could have picked anyone."

"But you didn't."

"So what? What's the big deal with John Delaney? He's a friend of the family and he's doing it for free."

Blendel smiled and put his fingertips together. "His father and your brother were partners, I believe."

"And?"

"Nothing. It just struck me as strange."

"Fine, it struck you as strange," O'Connor fired back.

"Do you suppose there's any way you can convince your brother to transfer the case to someone else . . . another lawyer, say?"

"Not without raising a red flag. Frankie's no fool. Explain."

"I really don't want to get into details at this time. Let's just say that John Delaney is quite possibly the last person I want associated with this case."

Perplexed, O'Connor shook his head. "I'll need something to go back to my brother with. It would be a helluva lot easier if you simply level with me about the goddamn file. What's in it that's got you so spooked? We went through all this trouble getting Sarah out of town. Now you're saying Delaney is a problem, too?"

"Yes, Nick. That's what I'm saying. I'd like him off the case as soon as possible."

The drift of the conversation was becoming clear to O'Connor. He understood why Blendel wanted his niece isolated. If everything had gone as expected, she would have eventually broken down and turned over the file. Suddenly telling John Delaney that he was fired didn't make sense, plus it was dangerous. Blendel might wear expensive clothes and live in a big house, but when you came right down to it, he was still a hood who wanted to control everybody and everything. He had dealt with hoods all his life and knew the type.

O'Connor got to his feet.

"Look, if this on the level—and I seriously doubt it—we'll have to handle the situation carefully, particularly where my brother Frank is concerned. We can't just kick Delaney off the case without a reasonable explanation. It'll raise too many questions."

"I see your point."

"So how do you want me to play it?"

"Do your best to convince your brother to change lawyers. Tell him you think you need a specialist. If he won't go along with that, I need to know what Delaney knows. You're close with him, so it shouldn't be a problem. If your niece surfaces again, it could spell major trouble—for all of us."

"You want me to fly down to Atlanta and find someone local?"

Blendel shook his head. "No, that would only look suspicious. Handle the matter by telephone. Tell Delaney you're just checking on his progress for the family. That's a reasonable thing for an uncle to do.

"On a related subject, I also got a visit today from a man named Phillip Thurman, a senior agent with Atlanta's FBI field office. They've apparently entered the investigation now, so we'll need to keep tabs on what they're up to. I don't want any more surprises, Nick. Am I making myself clear? We need to keep the situation stable."

O'Connor was about to tell Blendel to go fuck himself, when he suddenly realized that for all the man's attempt to appear nonchalant and in charge, what he was seeing was an act. Blendel's hands were clenching and unclenching and there were beads of perspiration on his forehead. O'Connor wasn't sure what to make of it and he wasn't about to take any action, one way or the other, until he knew what was really going on.

All he said was, "Sure, clear enough, Mr. B. I'll talk to Frankie and get back with you."

TWENTY-EIGHT

DELANEY

THE following morning Katherine placed a call to a man named Howard Epps, who, after some pushing on her part, agreed to meet with us later that day. Epps lived on a farm in a small town called New Georgia, about forty miles west of Atlanta.

"New Georgia, Georgia," I said, reading a road sign on State Highway 61. "They're not long on creativity here, are they?"

"New York, New York," Katherine replied.

I thought about that for a moment. Good point. Still, New York, New York, sounded better—at least I thought so.

When we pulled up to his home, my first thought was that we had made a mistake. The house Epps lived in was badly in need of a coat of paint and the roof shingles looked like they were about to blow off. Two cars were up on crates in the front yard; their seats sitting on the ground alongside them. We parked next to a 1966 Mustang whose engine was hanging from a portable lift and walked across a gravel path to the porch. Katherine knocked on the door.

A few seconds passed before a curtain moved slightly to one side and a man peered out at us. His eyes took Katherine in and then came to rest on me. During the ride, Katherine explained that Epps suffered from something called schizoid personality disorder, meaning he was a bit left of center, so I was prepared for some odd behavior. I hadn't heard the term *schizoid personality* since I took abnormal psychology in school and couldn't recall much about it, other than people who suffered from the illness tended to be withdrawn and often lived in a world of their own. We simply stood there looking at each other.

Epps finally spoke to us in a monotone voice. "Slip your IDs under the door."

I followed Katherine's lead, took out my wallet, and slid my driver's license through an opening at the bottom, getting a splinter in the process. From inside the house I heard the sound of footsteps retreating; they returned four minutes later and the door opened.

Howard Epps was somewhere in his late thirties. His cheeks appeared to have sunk into his face and he was unable to maintain eye contact for more than a second or two. He had a prominent Adam's apple, large bony hands, and was slender to the point of emaciated. His affect was as flat as his voice.

Katherine said, "It's good to see you again, Howard. This is my friend, John Delaney from New York."

"Pleased to meet you," I said, offering my hand to him. Though Epps took it, there was barely any response in his handshake.

"Mm-hm," he replied.

Katherine opened her briefcase and got right down to business. "As I told you on the phone, we have a photograph we'd like you to look at. We need to know if the background can be enhanced."

Epps took the photo from her and studied it for a few seconds, then handed it back, shaking his head slowly.

"Do you have the original image?" he asked. "This was printed on an inkjet and there's not much I can do with it."

"I saved a copy on this disk."

Epps stared at her for a moment, then took the disk and disappeared down a hallway, leaving us standing there. Not knowing what else to do, we followed him.

We found him in a bedroom that had been converted into an office. Unlike the rest of the house it was brightly lit and had a variety of different high-tech-looking machines scattered about the room ranging from scanners to high-speed laser printers. I counted three different computers with twenty-four-inch flat monitors. Epps's degrees were displayed on the far wall. One was a doctorate in computer science from Carnegie Mellon; another indicated he had graduated magna cum laude from Georgia Tech with a PhD in Artificial Intelligence, whatever that was.

I watched him spray the keyboard with disinfectant, then meticulously wipe it down before he started typing. Within seconds our picture of Sarah appeared on his screen. He studied it intently.

"If you look closely, there's a good bit to work with here," he said. "Will you need iterations for court?"

"Iterations?" I repeated.

"Copies," Epps explained. "I assume you want to preserve the original, so I'll make duplicates and work with the layers."

As an attorney, the necessity for keeping original evidence intact made sense to me. But I didn't understand what he meant about working with layers and said so.

"Think of a layer as a transparency that sits over the digital image. It's kind of like a sheet of plastic. Digital media is different from film. The colors you see are actually composed of thousands of little dots and each dot, or pixel, is represented on the computer by a particular number. That's how we identify them. My program looks at one section of the screen at a time and replicates those pixels on a new layer I create. It's not entirely accurate, but the end result will be a photo with far greater detail than the original."

The longer Howard Epps spoke, the more animated he was becoming. Obviously he was in his element.

"Sort of makes photographic evidence dicey in court, doesn't it?" I commented.

"Extremely, at least where digital media is concerned."

"But film is still trustworthy, right?"

"Not really," he said. "You can alter a digital photo to put Mickey Mouse in it, then take a picture using film and nobody would know the difference."

"Howard, how long do you think it will take you?" Katherine asked, interrupting us. "We're hoping to identify the location this girl was transmitting from, and time is critical."

Epps studied the monitor again. "Will I need to testify about this?"

"No. We're just trying to find her. We think her life is in danger."

His face registered nothing at Katherine's answer. No surprise, no curiosity, nothing. Whatever spark had been there a moment ago was now gone. After a few seconds he turned back to the screen and started typing.

"I'll need a couple of hours," he said over his shoulder.

KATHERINE and I stood on the front porch and looked out across Howard Epps's property. As far as I could see, the nearest neighbor was at least a quarter mile away.

"Did you know Howard used to teach at Georgia Tech?"

I glanced back into the house through the doorway. "Really?"

She nodded. "I've used him as a witness several times and he's never let me down."

"I'll bet he's a riot in front of a jury."

"Don't let his appearance fool you. Howard may not be good with people, but nobody knows more about digital imagery than he does. He's written three books on the subject. When he takes his meds he can actually come off normal . . . or at least close to normal. The problem is getting him to do it. Jimmy D had to babysit him for three days before our last trial. If his schizophrenia kicks in, life can become really interesting."

I nodded my head absently in reply.

"What's the matter?" Katherine asked.

"I'm worried about Sarah. If anything happens to her . . ."

"It won't," she said, slipping her arms around my waist. "We'll find her." She started to say something else, but changed her mind and looked up at me.

"What?"

"John, isn't it time we let Sarah's family know what's happening?"

The answer should have been obvious, except it wasn't. I spent a good portion of the night lying awake and thinking about it. I'd been a homicide detective for a lot longer than I'd been a lawyer, and the instincts I developed in that life were hard to ignore.

Too many aspects of the case didn't fit—from Sarah's bizarre disappearance to Rostov's death and the recent attack on me. And lost in the shuffle was the little question about who they really pulled out of Cloudland Canyon, since Sarah obviously wasn't dead. It was like looking into a fog. Nothing was clear, except that someone beside me had a major interest in finding Sarah O'Connor. I absolutely had to tell Frank and Lucille their daughter was alive—no question about it. By all rights I should have done so already, but I'd given my word to Thurman to hold off. I'd done so, but I couldn't stretch the situation much longer.

"I guess I'll have to," I said. "It's just that . . ."

"What?"

My words evaporated as something I had overlooked earlier clicked in my mind.

"I want to take another look at Sarah's file. Did we bring it with us?"

"Sure, it's in the car. Why?"

"I'll tell you in a second."

Katherine got the folder out of her trunk and watched over my shoulder as I located the incident report. From our previous conversations with Sheriff Sophie Clark, I knew both Andre and Nick O'Connor had identified Sarah's body. Andre did it based on the necklace she was wearing, and Nick confirmed the small tattoo on her ankle.

I flipped back to Sarah's medical records and ran my finger down the page until I got to the part that read "Identifying Marks/Scars."

The answer was NONE.

"Maybe she got the tattoo after she left home," Katherine suggested.

"Do you remember the videos we found at Sarah's house?"

"Unfortunately."

"I may be wrong, but I don't remember seeing any tattoos on her ankle."

"Assuming you were looking at her ankle."

I gave Katherine a look without responding.

"Sorry . . . that just came out," she said.

"Forget it."

"I'm confused. How could her uncle identify a tattoo if she didn't have one?"

Our eyes met and we held each other's gaze for several seconds before she got the point.

"Shit," Katherine said quietly.

EPPS said he needed a couple of hours, so we decided to make ourselves scarce. Not that we would have been missed. We drove to New Georgia's only eating establishment, a gas station with a convenience store and three gas pumps. Some hot dogs and a few brown things called corn dogs were rotating on spits inside a glass case in the store. I didn't want to guess how long they'd been there or if any of them actually contained meat, so I turned my attention to a freezer near the checkout counter. It had the usual collection of ice cream sandwiches, cones, and something called a Taco Loco.

I threw caution to the wind, bought one, and took a bite. Not bad. Katherine examined it for a moment, made a face, and selected a package of black licorice for herself from the candy rack. Her reasoning was that licorice had better carbohydrates. Whatever.

For the next hour we killed time driving around and visiting the surrounding towns, all of which turned out to be surprisingly pleasant. People nodded to you on the streets or said hello when you entered their store. Having recently been educated on the subject of Southern etiquette, I remembered to respond with a good morning back.

In the town of Dallas, we wandered along Main Street and ran into one Judge Evan Rice, an acquaintance of Katherine's. The judge was your quintessential Southern gentleman with a head of pure white hair and a seersucker suit. He informed us that he had just finished his morning court calendar and was taking a break to do some shopping for his wife. After introductions were made, I explained that I was visiting from New York.

His Honor said, "Well, we're glad to have you, son. If you stop by after lunch, I'll give you the Cooke's Tour of our courthouse."

He pointed down the street to a stately red brick building with a large clock tower that appeared to have been built around the turn of the century.

"It's a fine-looking building, Judge," I said, "but I'm afraid we'll have to take a rain check. We're meeting someone in a little while."

"Perhaps another time then. It's a shame though, because there are a lot of interesting things to see. Got our own ghost, you know. I've even seen him myself on occasion."

"Seriously?"

"Oh, yes. No one knows who he is for certain, because he doesn't stay around very long, but the popular consensus is that it's old Jonas Hardy. Jonas shot himself in the middle of a divorce trial when it came out his wife had been dallying with the stable boy."

"Divorce cases can do that," I observed. "Some of those lawyers are as mean as snakes."

The judge cast a quick glance at Katherine and started chuckling. "Well, I'm sorry you folks can't stay. Come back anytime. Our local bar association is hosting a barbecue at my house this Saturday. You're both welcome, of course. There's always plenty to go around."

"I don't know if I'll be in town then, but if we're free, we'll try to drop by."

"Fine, fine. Are you thinking of relocating to this area, m'boy, or just visiting?"

"Maybe a little of both."

I assumed the question had come up because Katherine and I were dressed casually and her arm was hooked though mine, which pretty much eliminated our being there for business reasons.

"Excellent. Katherine here may be a big-city girl, but we've been trying to get her to move out to the country for some time now. Paulding County has a great deal to offer, you know. We're not nearly as crowded as Atlanta and our attorneys tend to work with each other more than they do in the cities. We actually have a number of northerners living right here in Dallas."

"Sounds good," I said. At the same time I began searching for a polite way to extricate us from the conversation without being rude. Katherine, however, seemed to be enjoying herself.

The judge asked, "Did you happen to see the new YMCA as you drove in?"

"I think so."

"Well, sir, there's a statue of Robert E. Lee out front with his arm pointing northward in a most majestic manner." The judge illustrated by striking a pose. "Now some people think General Lee backed all the way down here and the YMCA initials stand for Yankees Might Come Again, but I assure you this is a very enlightened place to practice law and raise a family."

I smiled at his joke. "I'm sure it is, Judge. Thanks for the information. We'll certainly try to make the barbecue."

As soon as we were out of earshot, Katherine held up her hands defensively. "I had nothing to do with that."

"Naturally."

"I *didn't*," she insisted. "That meeting was purely by chance."

"Is there a sign on my forehead that says we're a couple?"

"On your forearm," she replied, giving my arm a squeeze.

She had a point.

I don't know how we wound up in front of a jewelry store, or how the subject of diamond rings came up. I also don't remember when I lost control of the situation. Looking back, I don't think that I ever had it under control. Maybe it was because Katherine's birthday was coming up and I was feeling warm and fuzzy. We started off looking at some gold bracelets in the window, then worked our way up to necklaces inside the store. At some point we made a transition to earrings.

Personally, I've always suspected some form of mystical communication exists between women where diamonds are concerned. A friendly sales clerk introduced herself as Sheila Blake and suggested a pair of gold loop earrings. When Katherine didn't react, Sheila brought out the heavy artillery—diamond studs—pricey, but still within a law professor's salary range.

I fought down a sinking feeling in my stomach, gave Sheila a weak smile, and stood there while Katherine tried them on. During the process, a mother and daughter who were in the store shopping, came over and offered their opinion that the earrings looked "simply marvelous" on Katherine.

From there, I suppose the leap to diamond rings was a no-brainer. The daughter blocked my path to the door and her mother slipped an arm though mine. She guided me to another case to show me a stone that was "almost identical her girlfriend's." To my everlasting astonishment, I found myself taking part in the conversation.

Now diamonds come in all sorts of shapes: round, square, emerald, princess cut (a new term), brilliant, marquis, and God knows what else. Once you assimilate the basics, salespeople ask you how large a stone you're looking for. I was aware the whiter and clearer it was, the higher the price, so my first inclination was to say "red," but I didn't think that would go over well with the ladies. Besides, I was outnumbered four to one.

I heard myself reply, "I really don't know. We've just started looking."

There it was. The words were out and there was no way I could take them back. Not that I wanted to. Katherine's face lit up with a smile that went right to my heart. In retrospect, I've concluded her fingers gently caressing the back of my neck might have suspended my higher brain functions. But the bottom line is that it was my idea . . . I think.

Without being obvious, I tried to read the little price tag under the stone to see what I was getting myself into. It had been a long time since I'd been engaged, and the last I checked, diamonds were going for about a thousand bucks a carat. When our saleslady casually mentioned we could get a "nice three-carat stone" for around twenty-five or thirty thousand dollars, my heart nearly stopped. I made a deliberate effort to keep the shock off my face.

The ring discussion went on for another half hour and the saving grace was that Katherine didn't like any of the settings they had to offer. Nevertheless, our friendly saleslady went through six catalogues just to be sure.

When it was over we strolled back to the car arm in arm, talking about rings and settings as if we were old pros. Surprisingly, I got the impression that Katherine was actually a bit nervous about the subject of marriage. I thought it was kind of cute.

JUST as before, the curtain on Howard Epps's door moved aside and he stared at Katherine and me through the window. Though he'd seen us only a few hours ago, we got the message and slid our licenses under the door again. They reappeared a minute later, followed by the sound of the lock turning. By the time I pushed the door open, Epps was already halfway down the hall. Katherine and I shrugged and followed him.

"The image quality is quite poor," he said without turning around, "but I think I have something for you."

Three separate pictures of Sarah were displayed on monitors around the room. Each had a different portion of the larger picture masked out.

Epps folded his arms across his chest and looked at the screen on the right. It contained an outline of Sarah's head. There was a hazy green area over her left shoulder with a white splotch next to it.

"What do you think?" he asked.

"All I can see is a green blur with some white dots," I said.

Epps frowned and looked at the image and then at me as though I were the village idiot.

"Maybe this will help," he said, clicking his mouse a few times. The image on the screen became smaller as the dots consolidated themselves into distinct shapes that looked like fragments of different lines. Still, they made no sense.

||| ∟ ||| ∪

I asked, "What's that supposed to be?"

Epps expelled a long breath. "You're not very bright for a lawyer, are you?"

"So people keep telling me. How about letting me in on the secret, Howard?"

"Try again. It's right in front of you. Katherine said you were a detective before you went into the law."

I resisted an impulse to tell him to where to go and looked at the screen again. From the black shape above the lines it was obvious something was partially obscuring whatever was there, but Epps seemed to think I could figure it out, so I stared harder and concentrated.

"Ignore the reflection on the right," Epps said. "That's just sunlight on the glass."

"Glass?" Katherine repeated.

"You told me the young lady was using a computer in a retail establishment. So my guess is that's one of the store windows, which would mean . . ." Epps trailed his words away to prompt an answer.

A few seconds passed before it finally dawned on me.

"We're looking out into a street."

"Exactly."

"And that green thing is a portion of a street sign," Katherine said. "But I can't make head or tails of it."

Still the teacher, Epps leaned back in his chair and waited as we studied the lines. His refusal to answer our questions was annoying. Then the answer presented itself.

I said, "Those first and third marks are part of the letter *M*."

Katherine grabbed a piece of paper off Epps's desk and wrote out the entire alphabet in a string across the top. It took a few more tries before we matched up the last symbol with the letter *O* and the second one with an *E*.

"MEMO?" I asked.

"Memorial Drive," Katherine replied. "It has to be."

Epps slowly clapped his hands together.

"How big a street is it?" I asked, ignoring him. "Maybe we can pin down the location."

Katherine's shoulders slumped. "It goes on for miles," she answered glumly. "We'll never find it."

Epps finally decided to break his silence. "Perhaps. We may not be able to discern the other background material, but their mass indicates buildings of some sort, so the city is where you should concentrate your search." He swung around to face the monitor on his left, becoming more animated. Almost everything on the screen was blocked out except for a small patch of white.

He continued, "This area with the shiny section above it gives us another clue. I think you're looking at a portion of one of Atlanta's buses."

"How do you know?" I asked. "I can't tell anything."

"Again, the bright area here is probably a glass reflection, but if you observe closely, it's not only above the ground, it's in the middle of a street, plus the sheer size is greater than one would expect from a car. And here you can see a number of blue, yellow, and orange dots. Those are colors that Marta buses use on their logo."

Marta is the company that runs Atlanta's mass transit system. Impressed, I stared at the screen. "You're a goddamn genius," I told him.

Epps swung around in his seat to face me and leaned forward. "I know."

Katherine gave him a kiss on the cheek. The ghost of a smile flickered across his features, but it was gone so quickly, I wasn't sure it had been there at all.

"If we can get hold of the bus schedule and figure out where they cross Memorial Drive, we might be able to zero in on Sarah's location," Katherine said.

"Easily done," Epps informed us. "Their routes are a matter of public record. We can look them up on the Internet.

With Howard's help we located the company's route map and narrowed it down to four different buses. Each crossed Memorial Drive at a different point. Not a home run, but definitely a start.

Television cop shows tend to portray detectives solving their cases through flashes of insight. It's the same way with the lawyer shows. During cross-examination a witness breaks down and shouts out, "All right, I did it. You got me. I confess."

In reality it doesn't happen that way. With the exception of Sherlock Holmes and Hercule Poirot, most crimes are solved by good old-fashioned hard work. I'll take a work horse over a show horse any day of the week.

We drove back to Atlanta, breaking several laws and most of the speed limits along the way. The adrenaline surge that used to grab my insides when a case was about to break resurfaced, gradually at first, but with increasing strength the closer we got to the city, tempered by the knowledge that Sarah's life might be hanging by a thread. I knew we needed to find her before it snapped.

TWENTY-NINE

DELANEY

KATHERINE'S description of Memorial Drive was accurate—it goes on for miles. The road begins in Atlanta and passes through such colorful neighborhoods as Cabbage Town and East Lake, eventually working its way into the city of Decatur. From there it continues on to the town of Stone Mountain. The more I studied the map Howard had printed out for us, the bleaker I thought our chances were. We highlighted each of the four intersections where the Marta buses crossed Memorial Drive and tackled them one by one.

The first was in the middle of downtown Atlanta and was surrounded by parking lots on either side. The few dilapidated buildings we saw looked like they were on the verge of collapse. The only retail establishment nearby was a barber shop that specialized in braids and something called hair weaving.

The second intersection was dominated by warehouses and vacant lots. No dice there either.

As we drove to the third intersection, I glanced at the map again. It contained a brief description of Marta's bus route, written by the company. The section below listed all the points of interest one might see while taking a leisurely bus ride. None were mentioned.

The last intersection was at least seven miles away and looked to be in the middle of a residential area. My hopes continued to dwindle until I noticed a number of businesses popping up here and there. On the corner of Hanover and Memorial sat an eight-story cream-colored building. Hanover Street had an eclectic mix of shops ranging from health food stores to a tattoo parlor that advertised, EARS PIERCED WHILE YOU WAIT.

Katherine read the sign half-aloud as we drove by and made a derisive noise. "What the hell is the alternative?"

"What are you talking about?"

She pointed. "That tattoo parlor across the street—what are you supposed to do, throw your ears in there and tell them you'll be back at five o'clock to pick them up?"

I looked at the sign again and started laughing to myself. It made my ribs hurt like hell, but the sign was so stupid, I couldn't help it. What finally stopped me was the sight of a bus going by and a coffee shop named Java & Jazz—An Internet Café.

Katherine saw my expression change and followed my gaze. "*Yes*," she said under her breath.

We parked our car four doors away and walked back to the café. It was dimly lit and contained a number of threadbare couches and chairs that looked like they had been purchased at a garage sale. I suppose they added atmosphere. A mural on the wall depicted different literary figures drinking coffee and generally hanging out. I recognized Hemingway and F. Scott Fitzgerald right away. Both were favorites of mine so it wasn't difficult. The others I had to guess at.

Several small wooden tables were situated around the room. They were occupied by students and businessmen with laptop computers. Some people had books and newspapers spread out next to their coffee cups. A long table with a row of eight computers ran along one side of the café. Opposite the computers was a large picture window. I walked to the middle of it and stared out at the street. On the corner I could clearly make out a lamppost with a sign that said, Memorial Drive. Katherine took a seat at a table in the corner to wait for me.

"This is the place," I told her when I returned.

She nodded and glanced around the cafe. So did I. Of course, Sarah wasn't there. I was the one who told her to run, which is probably what she did.

"What's next?" Katherine asked.

"Let's start with the manager and the waiters. They might be able to give us a lead."

Katherine put her hand on my arm and gently tugged until I sat down.

"I think we should go slowly," she said. "If they get it into their heads we're cops, or even lawyers, they'll probably clam up."

"You don't look like a cop." I pointed out.

Katherine raised her eyebrows and stared at me until I got the message.

"Right. Well, there's not much I can do about that now."

Katherine produced a little elastic band from her purse and pulled her hair back into a ponytail, then undid the top button of her blouse. It gave her a more casual appearance, but I wasn't sure what good the transformation would do.

A twenty-something blond waitress with multiple ear piercings finally noticed we were sitting there and came over to take our order. She was dressed in black spandex and had a silver stud through the corner of her right eyebrow that looked incredibly painful. I figured it was either for artistic purposes or magnetic balance. Take your pick.

"Hi, I'm Jenny. What can I get for you?" She had an accent I couldn't place immediately.

Katherine said, "I'll have a Diet Coke and the grilled chicken salad."

I squinted at a menu across the room. It was written on the wall in blue and white chalk. "Are your sandwiches any good?"

"Everyone likes them. We have a watercress and alfalfa sandwich with shredded carrots. And we also have dolphin-safe tuna. The chef puts onions and apples in it. I think we still have the hummus sandwich, but I'll have to check. If you want it, it comes with seasoned pita chips."

Big wow. "I'll try the tuna and a cup of black coffee."

"Cool. Can I bring you any appetizers?"

"No, thanks," said Katherine.

Jenny returned with our drinks along with a plate of hummus and those pita chips she had mentioned.

"Compliments of the house."

Time dragged and I grew edgier as we waited for the food to arrive. We needed to find Sarah and we needed to do it quickly. Every minute was critical. My instincts kept pushing me to get up, take her photograph out, and start asking questions, but K.J. was right. It would only spook the employees, who all looked like card-carrying members of Greenpeace. So I sat there and ate my dolphin-safe tuna. Truth is, it wasn't bad and the apples were a nice touch.

The third time Jenny stopped by to refill our glasses, Katherine finally broke the ice.

"Do you mind if I ask you a question?"

"Sure."

"We're looking for a girl whose been coming in here lately. She probably uses one of the computers. This is a picture of her."

The change of expression on Jenny's face was barely noticeable. She tried to hide it with a throwaway gesture by scratching her cheek, but there was no question. People who are trying to deceive often do this. She barely glanced at the photo before shaking her head.

"No idea. Sorry."

"Are you sure?" I asked. "Take another look."

"I don't have to. I don't know her and I've never seen her before. Do either of you want dessert?"

We told her we didn't and she returned to the counter.

I remarked. "That went rather well, wouldn't you say?"

"She's lying."

"I know."

At the end of the counter, Jenny was speaking in low tones to another waitress and a large disagreeable-looking fellow who had come over to join them. He had been working the register when we came in and there was no doubt we were the subject of their conversation. The big guy scowled at us, then disappeared into the kitchen. Through the window where the food comes out I saw him go to a wall phone, pick up the receiver, and punch in a number. He said a few words to whoever answered and then hung up. Meanwhile, Jenny and her companions were staring at us like they'd just found out we had a social disease.

I stood up. "This just gets better and better."

"What are you going to do?"

"I don't know—something."

As soon as the girls saw me coming they made a beeline for the kitchen. I quickened my pace and blocked Jenny before she could go in.

"Listen, we're not cops and we're not here to cause problems for anyone. We're friends of Sarah's. She's the girl in the picture and she's in trouble. I think her life may be in danger."

Jenny didn't say anything. She eyed me warily and took a step backwards, her street instincts kicking in.

I continued. "The lady with me is Katherine Adams. She's an attorney and she's helping me. My name is John Delaney. I'm a lawyer, too. It's imperative that we find Sarah as quickly as possible. I assure you we're friends."

"I already told you I don't know anything."

"I think you do."

I never heard the big guy coming. Katherine's warning shout came too late. One second I was standing there and the next I found myself lifted off the ground in bear hug. The pain in my injured ribs shot though my body like fire and I snapped my head backwards out of reflex. It was a move I'd learned growing up in the Bronx. I felt his nose break on impact and his grip lessen. As soon as it did, I brought the heel of my shoe down across his instep. Then I spun around and grabbed a metal napkin holder off the countertop. I discovered early on that street fights aren't conducted according to the Marquess of Queensbury rules. Winning on points isn't the goal. You either hurt the other guy fast or you're the one who gets hurt.

I swung the napkin holder as hard as I could, flattening it against the side of his skull. He grunted and went down like an ox. Jenny and several other women in the café screamed. A few people rose to their feet, but no one moved to interfere. One or two already had cell phones out and were probably calling the police.

I stepped over the big man toward Jenny. I had to give her credit— the girl had guts. She grabbed a knife off the counter and held it in front of her.

"I'm not afraid to use this."

"Good for you. And I told you we're not here to cause trouble. I'm not going to hurt you. Now unless you plan on buttering a piece of toast, why don't you do us both a favor and put the knife down?"

"Go to hell."

"Jenny, he's telling the truth," Katherine said, coming over to join us. "We're here to help Sarah. Her life *is* in danger. If you know anything at all, please tell us."

The trapped-animal look on Jenny's face stayed where it was and she shifted the knife between Katherine and me. I could have taken it away, but that wouldn't have helped the situation. What I didn't want was to spend the next hour explaining our story to the police. To my mind there didn't seem much point in hanging around any longer. A groan from the floor told me Jenny's ugly friend was beginning to stir. I'll admit that it might have been a trifle petty on my part, but my ribs were hurting like hell and I wasn't in the best of moods. The heel of my shoe caught him solidly behind the ear and put him out again.

THIRTY

DELANEY

Through the window of Katherine's car we watched the police arrive. They stayed for about twenty minutes, took statements, and left. An hour later, Jenny also left the restaurant in the company of the fellow I had knocked out. Her reaction hadn't been normal and we were both certain she was hiding something. Jenny and her friend walked to a parking lot at the back of the café, got into a beat-up old Chevy Malibu, and took off down Memorial Drive.

I wasn't crazy about following them for a couple of reasons: First, a single car is fairly easy to spot, and second, Katherine was with me. She has more guts than most women I know, but I would have felt a lot better if she were someplace else at that moment in case things got rough.

The first problem turned out to be minor, thanks to a bus that was heading in the same direction. We used it as a shield. Fortunately, it was also rush hour and starting to drizzle. This would make visibility difficult should Jenny check to see if anyone was following her. No one on Memorial Drive was moving very fast, because of the congestion, so we were able keep their car in sight without a problem.

After thirty minutes of stop and go, the traffic began to thin, so we drifted farther back to put some space between us. Twenty minutes later we found ourselves approaching the town of Stone Mountain, Georgia.

Stone Mountain is a dome-shaped granite monolith that rises up out of a valley to the east of Atlanta. At the base of the mountain sits a neat little town of the same name. To New Yorkers, any place with less than a hundred thousand people constitutes a town.

The Malibu pulled into a low-rise apartment complex called The Meadows, where Jenny and her companion got out. We watched them hurry across the parking lot and up a flight of stairs to a land-ing before they disappeared into one of the corner units.

Katherine flicked off the windshield wipers and killed the engine. "What do we do now?"

"I'll be back in a minute. Wait here for me. I want to check out their address and unit number."

"John—"

"I'll be fine. Just wait."

I ignored her response, which was probably just as well. Using the balcony for cover, I moved to the end of the walkway and looked up. At the corner of the building was a large number eleven indicating its position in the complex. Their door had a letter *G* on it. Next, I jotted down the license number of their car. Simple.

"Do you know anyone who can run a license plate?" I asked when I got back.

"Why?"

"All we have is Jenny's first name. If we can find out who owns the car we might be able to identify the apartment's owner."

Katherine thought for a second. "I have an idea. If it doesn't work, I'll call Dave Maxwell—he's our firm investigator."

"What do you have in mind?"

"You'll see."

Katherine fished around in her purse and came up with a pen and a piece of paper. She squinted through the passenger window at a sign that read MANAGEMENT OFFICE. Next to it was another sign that declared the apartments were OWNED AND OPERATED BY RIVERIA PROPERTIES, A GEORGIA LIMITED PARTNERSHIP. It provided a phone number to call in the event of an emergency.

Intrigued, I watched Ms. Adams dial it. She put the call on speaker-phone so I could listen.

"Good afternoon," Katherine said in a nasal twang. "This is Lois Maxwell with the Fulton County Tax Assessors Office."

"Clint Shaffer here," a voice answered. "Y'all are working kind of late, aren't you?"

Katherine's eyes darted to her watch and she mouthed a silent curse under her breath. "Yes, sir, we are. Commissioner Redfern wants us to try and catch up on our paperwork."

"I know the feeling. What can I do for you, ma'am?"

"We were just checking our records, Mr. Shaffer, and I don't see where your company filed their property return either last year or this one."

"That's odd. I'm sure we filed it," Shaffer replied. "Bob Connelly is our managing partner and he's pretty good at keeping up with those things."

"Then perhaps I should speak with Mr. Connelly. Unless you have copies you can fax me."

"I honestly wouldn't know where to look for them," Shaffer said. "You caught me here by myself. I'm with the company's acquisition department. Would it be all right if I have Bob call you back in the morning?"

"That would be fine. Give me a second while I put a note in your record. I'll be off tomorrow, but I'll ask one of my coworkers to follow up."

Katherine's next call was to the management office for the apartment complex. I still didn't know where she was going with this, but I had to admit it was creative. Someone answered on the second ring.

Katherine said, "Hi, this is Marlene, with Bob Connelly's office. Who am I speaking with?"

"Lamar Weston, the property manager."

"Oh, hey Lamar. Mr. Connelly wanted me to give you a call about a check we have here. It's only signed with a first name—'Jenny,' or maybe it's 'Jennifer' . . . I can't make out which and I don't know how to apply it."

"Jenny . . . Jenny," Lamar repeated to himself as he tried to place the name. "Is there an apartment listed?"

"Just a second." Katherine crumpled the paper she was holding near the earpiece for effect. "Uh-huh, it's Eleven-G."

"Eleven-G would be the Pechorins—Jennifer and Karel. They just got married a month or two ago. Do you want me to give them a call?"

"No, it's late. I'll phone them tomorrow. Do you have their number handy?"

To my surprise, Lamar, who was now on a first-name basis with "Marlene," furnished the number without hesitation.

"Anything else you need?" he asked.

"No, just have a good night," Katherine said. "Thanks for your help."

I shook my head when she ended the call and gave her a kiss on the cheek. "You're amazing."

"As I keep telling you," she replied with a sweet smile.

"Pechorin," I repeated. "What kind of name is that?"

"I don't know—foreign sounding. Why?"

"Something just occurred to me . . . Karel Pechorin. It sounds Russian, doesn't it?"

"A little. Why?"

"Andre's last name was Rostov. There might be a connection."

"John, there are a lot of Russians around."

"In Atlanta, Georgia?"

A few seconds passed while Katherine mulled over the possibilities; then she twisted around in her seat and stared at the building Jenny and her friend had gone into.

"I think I'll give Dave Maxwell a call now."

Fifteen minutes later we had the name of the Chevy Malibu's owner—it was Jennifer Rostov. When the call ended, Katherine said, "Okay, I have absolutely no idea what's going on here. Maybe this would be a good time to call in—"

She broke off what she was saying in midsentence when the door to apartment 11-G opened and Karel Pechorin stepped out. He trotted down the steps, got into his car, and drove off. I took some satisfaction in noting that one of his eyes was swollen shut.

I said, "I think it's time to have another talk with Jenny."

I WASN'T sure what to expect when I knocked on the door. Out of caution I instructed Katherine to wait off to one side in case our waitress owned a gun.

"What did you forget now?" Jenny asked as she opened the door.

Her expression turned to shock when she saw it wasn't her husband standing there. She immediately threw her weight against the door trying to slam it shut, but I wedged my foot inside. It didn't take much effort to push it open. To add to the other felonies I'd committed in the last forty-eight hours, I was now guilty of breaking and entering. It's a great way to run a law practice.

All the curtains in the apartment were drawn, but there was enough light to see the other person in the room clearly.

"Hello, Sarah," I said.

"Hello, Professor Delaney," she replied quietly.

THIRTY-ONE

SCHILLER

FIFTEEN hundred miles away, Hans Schiller sat in a restaurant across from his boss. His plane had gotten in an hour earlier and he wanted a shower. It was obvious that Blendel was upset. After studying him for a moment, he decided *distracted* was be a better word. The old man kept arranging and rearranging the food on his plate. Over the years Schiller had learned not to push where Blendel was concerned. He would talk when he was ready and not before.

"Did you know I had a visit from the FBI the other day, Hans?"

Schiller's fork paused halfway to his mouth. "Indeed?"

"Are you familiar with a man named Phillip Thurman?"

"Yah, he's one of their senior agents. He used to be stationed here in New York, but he stuck his neck out with the press over the Sobreski case. He promised everyone they would find the people who killed his men. When he failed to deliver, he was reassigned to Atlanta."

"Correct."

"I take it you also know him?"

"I do."

"And there is no love lost between you?"

"Also true."

Schiller nodded slowly. "May I ask the reason for his visit, *mein herr?*"

"Joshua's execution of the federal agent in Atlanta has given Thurman a reason to enter the case, which is most unfortunate. We really need to find that file quickly, Hans. I'm placing a great deal of reliance on you."

Schiller thought before he responded. "Have you considered the possibility that we may not be able to find it? I am a competent man, but we're playing catch-up as you Americans call it. What about try-ing to get this Delaney on our side—divert him, so to speak?"

One of Blendel's eyebrows went up. "How?"

"Everyone has a price. Suppose you were to offer him employ-ment with one of your companies, say in the legal department?"

Blendel stared at Schiller for several seconds. "Somehow, I don't think that will work with Mr. Delaney."

"But it might be worth a try," Schiller insisted. He looked around to make sure no one was within earshot and lowered his voice. "Killing him or the woman will only escalate matters, particularly if the FBI is now watching. But if we can get him to cooperate . . ."

Blendel stared absently out the window for a space of time.

"The street can be a scary place, don't you think?" he eventually asked.

"What are you talking about?"

"I scratched and fought my way out of it forty years ago and I don't want to go back. I'm too old to start again. I'd never survive prison."

"No one has said anything about prison, man. It's simply wise to have a backup strategy."

Blendel drew a deep breath into his lungs and let it out. In the candlelight he suddenly seemed older and more fragile. The skin on his forehead looked stretched and there was a vague translucent quality to it.

"I don't know, Hans . . ."

"Madam Blendel can handle this matter if you wish."

"Is that right? Just like that?" Blendel asked, snapping his fingers.

Before Schiller could respond, the waiter appeared to refill their glasses. The man asked if they needed anything else, but got no re-sponse from Blendel.

"Everything is fine," Schiller told him. "Leave us, please." He waited until the man was gone and then asked, "Perhaps it's time you told me what's so important about this file."

Blendel studied the wine in his glass and swirled it around before replying. "Part of it actually involves you."

"I beg your pardon?"

"Coincidence is a funny thing, Hans. Approximately fifteen years ago, most of our operations were located in the city. The Internet wasn't as big then as it is now. A significant portion of our income came from the businesses we conducted there—girls, drugs, protection. Most of this is done electronically today. It's a wonderful world we live in, very modern . . . very high tech."

Schiller folded his arms across his chest and said nothing.

"I had a man working for me at the time named Tony Gagnato. He ran our protection interests in the Bronx and Manhattan. Most of the clients simply paid their bills without involving the police. This turned out not to be the case with Mr. Kim Joong, a gentleman of Korean extraction. He and his wife owned a grocery in Riverdale and were paying Gagnato a hundred dollars a week."

"For what?"

Blendel shrugged. "Insurance against unexpected damage to their property. At any rate, Gagnato got greedy. Without telling me, he raised prices and kept the difference for himself. The result was that Mrs. Kim contacted the authorities. The case was assigned to Frank O'Connor and his partner . . . *William* Delaney."

"Ah," Schiller said. "William Delaney? He is related to the professor?"

"Precisely—William Delaney was John Delaney's father."

"I understand, but I still don't see how it involves—"

"When I found out what Gagnato was doing I was forced to curtail his activities. You had just come to work for me at the time. Once Mr. Gagnato was out of the way, we were left with the problem of the Kims, plus our friends on the police force who were now involved in the case.

Blendel took a sip of his wine, made a face, and put the glass back down.

"I really don't care for this chardonnay," he said. "At any rate, for the first time in a very long while I was forced to get personally involved to clear up the mess Gagnato had left me with. I made a personal visit to the Kims. They turned out to be very reasonable people."

"They relented?"

Blendel's smile never touched his eyes. "Not exactly. Mrs. Kim met with an unfortunate accident. She lost three of her toes and

changed her mind about testifying. The police, however, were another matter. Something different had to be arranged where they
were concerned. That is where you came in. Do you recall a man
named William Rosetti?"

Schiller searched his memory. "Vaguely."

"An automobile accident," Blendel prompted.

"Yah, yah, an automobile accident. You gave the orders." Schiller
nodded slowly in confirmation. "I remember now. It was a long time
ago. Rosetti was to run his truck into another car, kill the driver, and
then disappear. You never told me why. But how does this tie in with
the file the girl took?"

"Rosetti did not simply *disappear*. We arranged for it to look like
he was killed in a street mugging after the accident. It was the only
way to prevent the police from looking for him."

Schiller stuck out his lower lip and nodded. "A reasonable plan."

"Reasonable, *if* Rosetti had gone along with it. He surfaced two
years later and tried to shake Frank O'Connor down for money."

"I don't understand. You're saying Frank O'Connor was also involved?"

"No. The fool managed to get the O'Connor brothers mixed up.
Rosetti was a crackhead. He was lucky he could tie his shoes correctly. It was our friend Nick who tipped us off to William Delaney's
route home. He obtained the information from his brother. Rosetti
was with me when he phoned it in."

Blendel let that sink in for a second before continuing.

"Somehow, the police department's internal affairs unit got wind
of the situation and began asking questions. Nick headed off the investigation and Rosetti vanished before we could get to him."

Schiller shook his head. "So where is the elusive Mr. Rosetti
now?"

"We don't know. I can't afford to have him show up again and tie
me to the killing of a police officer. If someone should make the
connection, particularly John Delaney . . ."

"Yah, there would be many problems."

For a moment Schiller considered telling Blendel the whole situation could have been avoided had he not been so paranoid and let
him in on the plan from the beginning, but he decided against it.

Pressuring Blendel would only bring on one of his panic attacks and he needed him to remain functional. The important thing now was to limit their exposure—particularly his own. He was not angry at being left out. That was Blendel's style. Everything was on a need-to-know basis. "So, what is it you wish me to do?"

Blendel went back to staring out the window. "I really don't know. I need to give this matter some thought. If Delaney does see that file, we need to consider permanently removing him from the scene."

"Or anyone else," Schiller added.

"Or anyone else," Blendel agreed.

ON the drive to his town house in Westchester County, Schiller reviewed his discussion with Blendel. The man was running scared and that made him nervous. Perhaps age was finally catching up with them both. If it wasn't for that miserable cat, they could have finished Delaney off in Atlanta and the police would have thought it was a robbery gone wrong. Everything would have ended cleanly. But the girlfriend came out of her house with a handgun the size of a howitzer and started firing. The whole situation had a dark cloud hanging over it.

Typically, Blendel was worthless. *Can you take care of this for me, Hans?*

Easier said than done. All he had to do now was find a man who had disappeared fifteen years ago and recover the missing file before anyone put two and two together. He needed to discuss the situation with Linda.

Last year was difficult, he thought morosely. The next would probably be worse.

THIRTY-TWO

DELANEY

I CLOSED the door to Jenny Pechorin's apartment behind me and introduced Sarah to Katherine.

"Ms. Adams is a friend," I said. "She and Jenny have already met. Maybe you'd like to tell me what's going on now?"

Sarah didn't respond immediately and neither did Jenny, who continued to glare at us with unconcealed hostility.

I went on. "We already know Jenny is Andre's sister. And I also know the gentleman who just here left is her husband. What I *don't* know is why you're involved in this charade or why your father decided to drag me into it."

"My father had nothing to do with this."

"Does that include your Uncle Nick, too?"

There was a pause.

Sarah's face was drawn and her expression flat. Her eyes looked like marbles that had been shattered from the inside. She slumped down into a chair, leaned forward, and hugged her knees to her chest. Jenny walked over and put a protective arm around her shoulders while Katherine and I waited.

When Sarah did begin to speak, the words came out slowly.

"Last summer I was working for the U.S. Attorney's office in New York as a law clerk. Part of my job was to consolidate their old case files. They're scanning them all onto a new mainframe. My job was to write up case summaries for the computer index.

"I loved my coworkers and I loved being there. It was exactly what I wanted. For two months everything went fine, until I came across a file with my father's name on it."

"Frank's name was in a criminal file?"

"The case was old and they had closed it years ago, but I couldn't help reading what was in there. It mentioned my dad by name and said he was the target in an investigation—an FBI sting."

She said the last part in a whisper and her eyes grew red.

"Go on, Sarah," Katherine prompted.

"According to the report, several high-ranking NYPD officers were suspected of taking bribes and being on the payroll of a man named Warren Blendel.

"At first I didn't tell anyone because I couldn't believe it, but the longer I thought about what they said, the more it ate at me. I didn't know what to do. I've always looked up to my father. In the end, I convinced myself he would never have anything to do with taking bribes."

"So you stole the file?" I said.

"No. I went to my Uncle Nick first and told him what I had found. He thought the whole thing was funny. He said Internal Affairs investigates police officers all the time. It's their job."

"He was right. Every so often allegations come up when you're a cop, particularly if someone has an axe to grind. If were legitimate the charges, IA or the Bureau would have acted on them. This is all very interesting, but it doesn't explain your disappearing act."

Sarah took a deep breath, and revealed more of the story.

"A little over a week later, Uncle Nick told me he had quietly asked around about the investigation and was shocked to find it was still active. He said there was a good chance my dad was going to be arrested any day. We were both floored. Neither of us knew what to do. Somewhere around that time he mentioned Emory's scholarship to me."

Another piece of the puzzle suddenly clicked into place.

"*Nick* was the one who told you about the scholarship?" I asked.

Sarah nodded. "I decided to apply for it."

"All right."

"I met Uncle Nick at an Italian restaurant after class one day. He was still upset about the investigation. At the time I thought it was because he and my father were brothers and all. He kept saying if the file never existed . . ."

"I understand."

"Two weeks later, I got word from Emory that I'd won the scholarship. I didn't want to leave New York. All my friends were there, not to mention my family, but I couldn't turn down an offer like that. My parents had spent so much on my education already. I told them about it at dinner that night."

"And when did you come up with the idea of taking the file?"

"I'm getting to that. Uncle Nick, Aunt Stella, and their boys came to dinner at our home that Sunday. Uncle Nick could barely eat. Of course, I knew what was bothering him. He and my dad are really close. Before they left I pulled him aside and told him not to worry— that everything would be taken care of." Sarah paused for a long moment, then added, "I've really made a mess of things."

"To put it mildly," Katherine said.

"Andre's dead, my career is over before its ever began, and my father will probably be arrested now. I couldn't have screwed things up more if I tried."

I leaned forward in my seat. "Sarah, I understand the part about trying to protect your dad. But I'm still in the dark as to how Andre fits into this. Plus there's the little stunt you pulled at the Hyatt Regency. That was you, wasn't it?"

She nodded.

Katherine asked. "What in the world were you thinking and how did you know we would be there?"

"Because I followed you. I knew Professor Delaney was looking for me and I wanted to warn him to stay away."

"Stay away?" I repeated.

"I've gotten involved with some very bad people. I don't think they would hesitate to hurt him if they thought they needed to," Sarah told us. "When I saw you get up from the table at the restaurant I started to go to you, but I lost my nerve. I thought I saw one of the men in the restaurant, so I ran."

"And what did Andre have to do with all of this? And who was the woman they found at Cloudland Canyon?"

Sarah stared at her feet. "It's a long story."

I stretched out my legs and crossed my ankles. "Try me."

THE woman was already dead when she went over the cliff—that's what Sarah told us. According to Andre, she was a cocaine addict who had died from an overdose and had no family. The police had brought her to the medical examiner's office for an autopsy. Andre was working there as part of his training. Piece by piece, the plan they concocted was grew clearer.

After switching toe-tags with another corpse, Andre moved the unfortunate woman to a different refrigeration unit, then altered the ME's records to show that it was empty. Two nights later, with Karel Pechorin's help, they smuggled her body out of the morgue. The rest of the details we already knew.

"Sarah, why would Andre stick his neck out like that?" Katherine asked.

"Because he was in love with me."

Katherine considered that for a moment, then replied. "I don't mean to be insulting, but this whole fairy tale is a little hard to swallow. John and I saw the tapes at your house and it didn't look like love to me. It looked more like he was trying to screw you while you were half-conscious."

The silence that followed was leaden. It was punctuated by the sound of water dripping from a faucet in the kitchen. Outside the rain had turned into a blowing mist, fogging the windows of the room. Seconds ticked by.

"That's the way it started," Sarah said. "I met Andre at a party and woke up the next morning to find myself in his bed, naked. Only it wasn't the next morning, it was three days later. You're right about the drug part. They used something called roofies on me; they make you compliant. Their original plan was to use the tape for leverage and force me to turn over the file."

I interrupted. "*They?*"

"I don't know their names, but over the course of a week two different men came to Andre's apartment. One of them had a German accent. That's all I remember. They forced me to sit on the couch and watch the first tape. One of them told me he would sell me to a man in Argentina if I didn't give them what they wanted. His partner threatened to put the pictures on the Internet."

"But you didn't give them the file?" Katherine said.

"No. I stalled for time. I told them a friend in Birmingham, Alabama, was holding it for me and that he was in Europe for the next two weeks. I said I was the only one who could get it. Eventually, I convinced Andre to help me. He wasn't like the others."

"Oh, obviously," Katherine replied.

Sarah ignored her sarcasm. "Andre told me he was working for a very powerful man in New York who wanted the file. This is the same man who has been helping Jenny and Karel get their green cards. That's how Andre came to know him."

I glanced at Jenny, but only got a blank stare back in return.

I asked. "Did anyone ever say why they wanted the file?"

Sarah shook her head. "Andre only said the man wouldn't hesitate to ruin me if I didn't hand it over."

"Then why didn't you?"

"Because I was positive they would kill me the second I gave them what they wanted. My plan to stall them failed."

"How so?" I asked.

"The German man returned the following day and said he had spoken with his boss. He said perhaps they had come on too strong and if I made another film as a gesture of good faith, they would work with me. All I managed to do was trap myself and take the situation from bad to worse."

"And so you faked your death and went underground."

"Until you showed up, Professor."

An interesting way to deal with the problem. Some of what she was saying I thought was true; the rest had a theatrical quality to it. To begin with, Sarah was a cop's daughter and she was studying the law. I'm not saying it didn't go down that way, but I had a feeling we were only hearing part of the story. From Katherine's expression, I gathered we on the same page. I gave her a slight shake of the head, indicating not to push.

"I may not have done you any favors, Sarah. Your parents hired me to probate your will. That's what I was doing that when Ms. Adams noticed a discrepancy on the autopsy report. Your height and weight didn't match up with your school's medical records."

On impulse I held back telling her that it was Uncle Nick who had identified her body based on the tattoo. When I mentioned the recent attack on me, I could tell she was shaken by it, genuinely so. There was real fear in her eyes.

"I'm so sorry. I didn't mean to involve you in any of this. That's why I said you couldn't help me."

"Maybe I can't. Where is the file now? I'd like to know what's so important in it to have caused such a mess."

A silent communication passed between Jenny and Sarah, before Sarah got up and went to the bedroom. She returned a moment later.

What she handed me was a dog-eared legal folder containing an investigator's report. It was a grand total of three pages. According to the investigator, an anonymous tip named Frank O'Connor as one of three cops who had been taking bribes. In reading through the narrative, I was struck by how little there was in the way of substance. There was no corroborating evidence I could see that would substantiate the charges. More surprising was that anyone would have taken them seriously or made an arrest based on what was there.

The second page was of more interest.

I scanned it and located Warren Blendel's name along with a reference to his extorting money from a family named Kim in the Bronx. I still didn't see what Frank's connection was until I came to the part about the informant having given reliable information to the police in the past regarding Blendel's operations.

At the bottom of the page were four other names I'd never seen before:

> Mickey Fraser
> William Rosetti
> Dan Stueben
> Patrick Walker

You have to read between the lines in such matters. My guess was that the snitch had done business with each of these men at some point in the past. Furnishing background information is standard in police reports, particularly where an informant is involved. When the matter reaches the district attorney or federal prosecutor, one of the first things they ask is whether your confidential source has given reliable information before. Assuming the answer is yes, it passes the probable cause test and a warrant is issued. "Confidential source," for those not familiar with the term, is just another way to say spineless.

The third page yielded no clues. It was just the investigator's game plan about how he wanted to handle the situation. Nothing appeared after that, no entries, no supplemental notes, no interviews—nothing. It was as though the case had simply been left hanging before being dead docketed.

I asked Sarah. "Do you have any idea what's in here that's so important someone had to die over it?"

"I wish I did. The only reason I took it was to protect my dad."

"I understand that. I don't see how anyone ever took these allegations seriously. To begin with the file is almost two decades old and the case has been closed."

"But my uncle Nick told me they had reopened—"

"I know what your uncle Nick said, and it's horseshit. Nobody was in the process of resurrecting this file. Would you mind standing up for a moment?"

"Excuse me?"

"I'd like you to stand up and lift your right pant leg up."

"Fuck you," Jenny said. "She doesn't have to do anything. I want you both to leave or I'm calling the police."

I took my cell phone out and tossed it to her. "Go ahead. And while you're at it, ask them to get in touch with a man named Phillip Thurman. He's with the FBI and they're just dying to talk to Sarah."

Sarah hesitated, then stood up. She placed a protective hand on Jenny's shoulder. "It's all right. I've known Professor Delaney since I was a little girl. He's not going to hurt me. Are you, Professor?"

"No . . . I'm not going to hurt you."

She complied by lifting up her pants as I had asked. There was no tattoo, but then I didn't expect to see one.

"Why did you want to see my leg?"

"Because, according to the sheriff in Dade County, your uncle

Nick flew down and identified your body based on a tattoo on your ankle."

Sarah looked from me to Katherine and back again as the implications began to settle in. She was a sharp kid and I didn't have to draw a picture for her.

THIRTY-THREE

DELANEY

We left the Pechorins' apartment an hour later with a plan of our own, most of it made up on the fly. When Karel came home and found us there, he wanted to take up where we left off in the restaurant. Fortunately, round two never got under way. Sarah and Jenny had the good sense to intervene, which was probably better for me than it was for him. He was a big guy and looked to be in pretty good shape. On the ride, I learned that he had been a hammer thrower on his college track team in Russia. Like Andre, he tried to get into medical school, but he didn't have the grades, so he took the café job to make ends meet. That was where he and Jenny had met.

Both of them were in the United States illegally. Big surprise. The politically correct term our president and the newspapers have been hyping lately is "out of status," but it comes down to the same thing. According to Karel, Andre's employer, the gentleman from New York, had connections with the INS and had agreed to help them establish permanent residency here. I guessed this was the elusive Warren Blendel, a fellow I now wanted very much to meet. Many of the loose ends floating around seemed to stop at his doorstep. I also wanted to speak with Frank O'Connor and get his side of the story. When my father was alive, he told me Frank was a man you could trust. I hoped that was still the case. There was a good chance he could supply information that didn't appear in the file. The big problem was Nick. You don't simply walk up to a man and tell him his brother is dirty.

Families talk. It's as simple as that. I had no illusions Sarah's return from the dead could be kept a secret for very long. However we handled it, Nick had a lot of explaining to do. For reasons unknown, he had made a positive ID of his niece based upon a tattoo she never had. According to Sarah, she never even considered getting one, a fact both her friends and family all knew. Then there was the scholarship problem. Shortly after Sarah dropped the news about her father to him, Uncle Nick conveniently came up with a scholarship getting both her and the file out of New York.

Coincidence always made me leery when I was a cop and it was the same now. Whatever the outcome, it was clear Atlanta was no longer a safe place for Sarah O'Connor. This was the reason we found ourselves sitting in the International House of Pancakes. Our plan was for Katherine to drive Sarah and Jenny to her condo in Miami until I could get a better handle on the situation. By driving instead of flying, they would avoid the use of credit cards and plane tickets. Katherine's condo is located on a private island and has more security than the Vatican. You need a blood test just to get past the front gate.

These and a host of other thoughts were all competing for attention in my mind as I looked over the menu. I finally settled on the IHOP's daily special, a Tex-Mex salsa omelet that came with a side order of chocolate chip pancakes. Katherine took one look at a picture of it on the menu and promptly ordered a salad with light dressing on the side. Jenny and Sarah also went for the salads. Karel, a man after my own heart, wanted a steak.

While we were waiting for the food, we discussed whether to call Phillip Thurman and let him know what we had discovered. Katherine was in favor of it. Sarah was opposed. She was still concerned with protecting her family.

Katherine turned to her and asked, "I'm curious about the scholarship you won. We spoke with Ben Chambers and he told us it was the first time Emory had offered it. I forget the name."

"The Hoch-Halpern Endowment," Sarah said.

"Right, Hoch-Halpern. Is that your understanding as well?"

"I never really asked how long it'd been in existence. I was just happy to get the money."

"Understood. Exactly what did you receive from them?"

"Full tuition with room and board, an allowance for living expenses, plus a stipend for my law books. It came to a little over forty-three thousand dollars a year. I figured it out once."

Katherine let out a low whistle and leaned back in her chair. "Did your uncle ever mention how he knew about it?"

"He told me a lawyer friend had mentioned it to him and he thought of me. Why do you both keep asking about Uncle Nick? He could have made an honest mistake about my having a tattoo. He was under a lot of pressure, you know."

Katherine met her eyes. "Do you really believe that?"

"I don't know what to believe anymore," Sarah replied, her shoulders slumping.

I said, "Well, there's one way to find out. When I get to New York, I'll ask him directly. Then I'll meet with your father and mother. They have a right to know their daughter is still alive, wouldn't you agree?"

When Sarah hesitated, I knew what she was thinking.

"I destroyed the tapes," I told her. "No one will ever hear about them from me."

"They said they were going to put them on the Internet," she whispered.

"Your father doesn't strike me as someone who cruises the Net. If I remember correctly, he has trouble figuring out how to use a computer mouse. Your mom's not much better."

That finally produced a smile—the first I had seen.

Jenny spoke. "Mr. Delaney, can I ask you a question?"

"Sure."

"My brother did many bad things. I know this. But he was trying to help Karel and me to stay in America. It doesn't make what he did right, but do you think this man in New York was really trying to get green cards for us? We paid him four thousand dollars. It was all of our savings."

I put my fork down. "It's possible. You hear a lot about people who have connections and work outside the system. Personally, I've always found it's best to play things straight."

Jenny looked at me, then at Katherine in turn, who gave her a slight smile and nodded in agreement. Karel put an arm around his wife's shoulders and drew her to him.

"In my country," he said, "people have to find ways around the government because it is so corrupt. This is a way of life. We would like to live here, to make a life here. Do you understand?"

"I think so."

"We helped Sarah because Andre was family, but if the man he worked for lied to him, there is nothing we can do now, because we are not American citizens. Is this correct?"

"Not really," I said. "Our law still affords you protection from predators, citizens or not."

"But we will go to jail if we bring him to court, yes?"

"I don't know, Karel. I don't think so. But the fact is, unless the INS agrees to reconsider your case, you can be picked up and deported at any time. That's no way to live. There's a man at my school who teaches immigration law. I'll talk to him if you like."

Karel nodded. "I do not have much money, but I will pay you what I can."

"Let's worry about that later."

I don't know whether this satisfied the Pechorins or not. They were suspicious and frightened, and trust isn't something that can be turned on and off like a light switch. Katherine squeezed my hand under the table.

I wasn't crazy about her driving to Miami, even with that cannon of a gun along for protection, but there weren't many options open to us at the moment. After some more discussion, it was agreed that Karel would remain behind at the Java & Jazz Café, in case anyone else showed up looking for Sarah.

I didn't speak much on the ride to the airport and Katherine picked up on my mood. Women are more intuitive than men where emotions are concerned. She held my hand until I got out at the curb. It didn't help very much.

My gut was telling me it was a mistake not to bring the FBI in. Their resources exceed anything I could muster. The problem was, I wasn't entirely sure about Phil Thurman either. He had definitely held back on us, and until I knew why, it was better to keep the situation contained. Someone had set Sarah up, killed Andre Rostov, and had nearly done the same for me. It was time for the home team to take the field.

THIRTY-FOUR

DELANEY

As soon as I got off the plane in New York, I phoned Katherine to check on her progress. They were somewhere in South Georgia and cell phone reception was lousy. The call dropped three times before I finally gave up and left a message on her voice mail asking that she call me when she arrived in Miami. That wouldn't be for at least four hours.

When I arrived at my apartment, I fixed a cup of coffee and went through my mail, then took out Sarah's file and started reading through it again. A nagging feeling I had missed something simply wouldn't go away. The name of William Rosetti was vaguely familiar, but I couldn't place where I'd heard it before. A half hour passed before I gave up. I went into my laundry room, moved the dryer aside, and disconnected the aluminum exhaust duct at the back, then stuck the file in it for safe keeping. I didn't think anyone would look there, pros or otherwise. Someone had killed for the information on those pages and there was no point in taking chances.

After a quick shower, I listened to my phone messages. Most of them were routine. One call was from Babs Ramsey's secretary asking when I was going to turn in my final grades. Babs is the dean of our law school and is generally a good egg. I made a note to call her back in the morning. I already felt guilty enough about the test papers. The next call was from Nick O'Connor and I played his message twice. There was nothing suspicious or urgent in his tone; he simply asked me in touch once I was back in town. I glanced at my grandfather clock and saw it was nearly one thirty in the morning. Whatever Nick wanted would keep for a few hours. Before climbing into bed I thought about calling Katherine again and decided against it. She was probably as exhausted as I was. Five minutes later I was asleep.

I AWOKE just after six, shaved, then jumped in my car and headed for the Forty-third Precinct, a place where I had spent twelve years of my life. Since my retirement, I'd only been an infrequent visitor there.

From what I could see, not much had changed. The air-conditioning still didn't work and most of the uniforms and plainclothes people were still across the street at Bigelow's with their morning coffee. The precinct has a coffee vending machine, but whatever concoction it dispenses always smells like diesel fuel to me. I decided to check the restaurant first.

Mike Franklin was at his usual place in the corner reading his newspaper. Mike and I had been partners for five years before I left the force. He was so intent on what he was reading, he didn't see me when I walked through the door. Quietly, I slid up behind him and peeked over his shoulder.

"ERECTILE DYSFUNCTION," I said, reading the advertisement.

Mike jumped, nearly knocking over his orange juice in the process. He quickly flipped the newspaper over.

"Jesus H. Christ, they're letting anybody in this fucking place," he said. Then a smile creased his big face; he got up and we hugged. "What the hell are you doing down here with us common folk? You're supposed to be a bigshot lawyer. They didn't fire you, did they?"

"Not yet. Whatcha reading?"

"Ah, just some article."

I lifted a corner of the newspaper and looked at the ad again. MEN, DO YOU SUFFER FROM PREMATURE EJACULATION?

Mike yanked the paper away and motioned for me to sit. "You know anything about this stuff?" he asked, dropping his voice.

"It's happened once or twice, but I don't think I ever suffered."

My friend laughed to himself and shook his head. "Same old De-laney. How 'bout some breakfast?"

"I'm good. You have a few minutes?"

"Always. What's up?"

"Is it okay to talk in here?"

"That depends what you want to talk about. Is everything all right?"

"Maybe."

Mike's brow lifted slightly when he realized the conversation would be serious. "Okay, shoot."

"You ever run into a guy named Harry Batchelder?"

"Batchelder? Yeah, he used to work internal affairs. He was a real prick. He got emphysema and retired a couple of years ago. Why?"

"I'll tell you in a minute. Do you have any idea where he lives now?"

"Somewhere up in Connecticut, the last I heard. You gonna tell me what this is all about, or do we play twenty questions?"

"You remember that case you referred to me a week ago?"

"If you mean the O'Connor brothers, sure. Losing Sarah that way had to be rough on them. Rough on anybody, for that matter."

"Absolutely."

"So what do they have to do with that asshole Batchelder?"

"I don't know yet. Maybe nothing. That's why I'm here."

My former partner's smile slowly disappeared. It didn't take much for him to figure out my visit wasn't just social. He slid his chair back from the table and stood up.

"Let's take a walk. It's a little stuffy in here."

A few people finally recognized me and said hello or waved on the way out. They were the old guard, the hangers-on, the ones that would stick it out to the end and retire at 80 percent of their salary with benefits. At one time I thought that would be me.

I filled Mike in on the situation with Sarah, the missing file, and the investigation regarding Frank. He was someone I could trust with no reservations. When I reached the part about Nick O'Connor having identified her body based on a nonexistent tattoo, he stopped walking.

"It could have been a legitimate mistake, John. It's only natural to be upset at a time like that."

"No argument, except that everyone in the family knew she hated tattoos. He was also the one who brought the scholarship to Sarah's attention."

"Okay. But that still doesn't prove anything."

"What do you know about a man named Warren Blendel?"

"Not a whole lot. I've heard the name around. Why?"

"From what the FBI told me, he used to operate here in the Bronx. Several years ago he moved his entire organization out to Long Island."

"So?"

"So, I'm curious about how he managed to stay so clean all those years."

Mike asked, "You trying to connect him to Nick?"

"Let's just say I'm curious."

He glanced around before he spoke, keeping his voice low. "Listen, you're not dealing with a fuckin' meter maid. Nick O'Connor's a goddamn deputy chief with the department."

"I know what he is. There was a message on my answering machine from him when I got home last night asking me to call him. He said he wanted to pass along a good opportunity."

Mike folded his arms across his chest and leaned against a parked car. "So what? He could be trying to return a favor. You know . . . for what you're doing for his family and all."

It's definitely possible," I said. "I hope I'm being paranoid."

"Me, too. So what are you gonna do?"

"Return the call and see what the big opportunity is. Then maybe have a talk with Batchelder. I'd like to see if he remembers anything about the case with Frank."

"And what do you want from me?"

"I'd like you to check the closed files—quietly—and see what sort of situations Blendel was into and who in the department worked them."

I got a long hard look before Mike made up his mind.

"Okay, but if this turns out to be a dead end, you're going to owe me big-time. It's better if I handle Batchelder, though. I'm still with the department and he's more likely to talk to me."

We shook hands and parted. As I walked to the car, I tried Katherine again at her condo and still didn't get an answer. From past experience, I knew the drive from Atlanta to Miami was a long one, so I assumed they had probably stopped for the night. The call had just ended when the cell phone rang in my hand.

Nick said. "Welcome back, buddy. How're you doing?"

I respond in an equally upbeat manner. "Fine Nick. It's good to hear from you. You were next on my list to call this morning. I got your message last night, but I didn't get in until after eleven p.m."

"Not to worry. You free for lunch later? I have something that might be of interest."

"Like what?"

"A lawyer friend of mine mentioned that he has a client who's been looking for someone to consult with their company. Naturally, I thought of you. I told him you were a hotshot professor and he said he'd love to talk with you."

"No kidding? What sort of consulting?"

"Something legal, I suppose. I don't know much other than the client does construction all over the metro area."

"It sounds interesting, Nick. Unfortunately, I don't do construction law. I can pass along the names of a few good people, if your friend is interested."

"I think the work is mostly contracts," he said a little too quickly. "Like a lot of big companies, they get involved in lawsuits from time to time, and the way Jerry explained it . . . that's my friend, by the way, they're looking for a third party to review any potential cases and help them decide whether to settle or take them to court. The term he used was 'risk management,' if that makes sense."

"Sure."

"Jerry's their in-house lawyer and he doesn't handle that sort of stuff. He's strictly a paper guy. You've supposed to tell them what evidence can be used in a courtroom and what can't. Understand?"

"I don't know, Nick. I'm pretty tied up with my classes."

"Listen, don't be a schmuck. These guys are loaded. According to Jerry they're willing to pay seven hundred bucks an hour for the right guy."

I whistled through my teeth. "Jeez, that's a lot of money, still . . ."

"Johnny, at least talk to them. You owe it to yourself."

It was painfully obvious the more I hesitated, the more insistent he was getting. I say "painful," because that's exactly what it was to me. I couldn't believe, didn't want to believe, the thoughts that were circulating in my head about Nick O'Connor, a man who was supposed to be a friend. Part made me sad; the other part made me angry as hell. We'd known each other forever.

"I guess it wouldn't hurt to talk."

"Exactly. How about if I set up a meeting between you and Jerry for later today? I lied and told him you were a great guy. By the way, how did everything go in Atlanta? I probably should have asked about that first."

"Everything went fine. The papers are all filed and we put Sarah's property in storage. I spoke with Frank about going over the inventory, but I haven't heard anything back yet. At some point I'll have to meet with him and Lucille to find out whether they want to sell her stuff or keep it."

"I understand. I'll mention it to them tonight. Is there anything I can do?"

"Maybe a gentle push to help get the process started. I know this is tough on the family, Nick, but it's got to be done."

"Sure, sure, no problem. Why don't you give me the list? I'll sit down with my brother and go over it. If you'll be seeing Jerry later, I could meet you in front of his building and pick it up."

"Sounds like a deal. Where's he located?"

Nick gave me the address then spent the next five minutes telling me about Legacy Construction, Jerry Barnwell, and how much money they made. I was depressed when I hung up.

It was possible he was just trying to help, but my instincts were telling me different now. Maybe it was because I'd traveled to Atlanta to attend to Sarah's affairs and he spent all of thirty seconds asking about them, and maybe I was reading too many things into an innocent situation.

When I got to the law school, I phoned Babs Ramsey and told her assistant that I'd be finished with the test papers by the end of the week. She said that would be fine and informed me my secretary wouldn't be in until after lunch due to a doctor's appointment. Irwin's office was fielding my calls until then. There were no message lights flashing, so I got out the remainder of the exams and went to work.

An hour later, I was interrupted by a call from the aforementioned, Jerry Barnwell. Just as Nick had said, he was happy to meet me, anxious in fact, and suggested I drop by his office after lunch. Then he passed along Nick's regrets about not being able to be there. Apparently, Deputy Chief O'Connor had gotten tied up on police business and asked Jerry to relay the message.

When the call ended, I swiveled around to my computer and punched in the name Legacy Construction. It took a few minutes to learn they had been in business for twenty-six years. Different newspaper articles mentioned some of the properties they had acquired and one or two carried accounts of lawsuits they had been involved in. There weren't many.

All of the online information was pretty boilerplate and I began to relax. So maybe the meeting was legit. Then, out of curiosity, I decided to check the corporations division at New York's Secretary of State's office. I wanted to see who Legacy's corporate officers were. None of the names were familiar and I was about to log off until an entry at the bottom of the screen caught my eye. The registered agent for the company was listed as Linda Blendel.

I felt the bottom drop out of my stomach.

Linda could have been Blendel's wife, his sister, or even his mother, for all I knew, but there was no way to write off the coincidence. On the wall was a photo of my dad and Frank O'Connor taken many years ago. Their arms were around each other's shoulders. Next to it was another photo of graduation day at the Academy. Nick was there in the third row. My father and Frank were standing next to him. I stared at the photos for a long time. Nick was playing me just as he had played his niece.

But to what end?

The answer was obvious. He and Blendel were in bed together. After a minute, I found I had been squeezing the edge of my desk so hard, my hands hurt. I printed out a copy of Legacy's corporate registration from the screen, circled Linda Blendel's name, then scrawled a note in the margin for Mike Franklin to check it out if anything happened to me. I locked it away in my desk drawer. I tried Katherine again and got her voice mail. It was the same at the condo.

When you care about someone, your mind can start playing tricks on you. You begin to imagine all sorts of reasons why they haven't called. For every one that's rational, seven aren't.

In light of recent events, though, I didn't think I was overreacting. I simply wanted to assure myself everyone was all right. I decided to give it an hour and try again. Frustrated, I went back to the test paper I'd been grading. After staring blankly at it for nearly a minute, I pushed it away. Between Katherine's not answering and Nick O'Connor I simply couldn't stay focused. Eventually, my thoughts turned to why Nick was trying so hard to put me together with Jerry Barnwell. It was flattering to think it was because of my legal expertise. Unfortunately, I knew better. There were plenty of attorneys with more experience than me. Obviously Blendel wanted something—that is, Sarah, the file, or both. And since he didn't have her and I now controlled her personal property, I was the logical place to start. That would explain the seven-hundred-dollar-an-hour carrot being dangled in front of my face. Money buys everything—or so some people think.

The sword, however, cut both ways. If I said yes, they could keep tabs on me, but I'd be that much closer to them.

THIRTY-FIVE

KATHERINE

KATHERINE knew they were in trouble. All the restaurants had closed for the night and the only things open at the service plaza were the bathrooms and vending machines. Fortunately, a number of cars were in the parking lot. The Florida Turnpike might well be one of the most boring roads in the United States, but it's a heavily traveled one. What concerned her now was a black Audi A8 sedan parked off to the side in the shadows. Both sun visors were lowered and there were two men sitting in it. It was impossible to see who they were, but she didn't have to. She'd seen the car twice in the last three hours. The first time was when she and the girls stopped to get a snack. The Audi simply kept on going then, but it reentered the highway once they passed the next exit. By itself that might mean nothing. A lot of people traveled this route. The black sedan reappeared a short while later, maintaining a constant pace a few cars behind hers. That was when Katherine started to take notice.

When she slowed, they slowed. And when she accelerated to nearly ninety miles per hour, so did they, always keeping a car or two cars between them as a buffer. She wasn't into cloak-and-dagger games, but John had told her to be careful and that was exactly what she was going to do.

Her sudden decision to veer off the highway after the Ocala exit startled Sarah and Jenny, who were both were sleeping at the time. Not wanting to alarm them, she explained that she was just looking for a gas station. The road they turned onto was unlit and grew increasingly dark after a few miles. It was obvious they weren't going to find an open station there. Not that Katherine wanted one. Her maneuver was simply to see whether the Audi would follow. It did.

In the fleeting seconds when the two cars passed each other, going in opposite directions, she caught a glimpse of the driver's face. It was so pale, it reminded her of a ghost. The image caused her heart to skip a beat. Katherine Adams didn't believe in ghosts. She believed in her own powers of observation and ability to assess a situation. She had seen that face before. The man had been wearing an Atlanta Braves baseball cap at the time and he had a garden hose looped around John Delaney's throat. He moved quickly when she fired her gun at him—so quickly, it startled her. She kicked herself for not taking a second shot, but she'd panicked because she thought John was dead. The ghost and his companion took off across her property at a dead run.

Once they were back on the turnpike she reached for her cell phone and cursed under her breath when NO SERVICE appeared on the screen. A green road sign with luminescent white letters told her the next service plaza was fifty miles away. The Audi was back again, still keeping its distance. She continued to check the phone as they drove through the night. Its signal strength hovered around one bar. Minutes crawled by.

Not enough to make a call.

Gradually, the little indicators increased to two and then to three bars. The service plaza was now only a mile or so ahead. Concluding they would be safer with people around, Katherine pulled into it and waited outside while Jenny and Sarah went to the ladies' room. As soon as they were gone, she pulled Phillip Thurman's business card out of her purse and dialed his number. There was a delay as the call was forwarded.

"Thurman."

"This is Katherine Adams. I may need your help."

There was only a slight hesitation before he responded, "Where are you, Ms. Adams?"

"I'm at a rest stop on the Florida Turnpike a little south of Kissimmee. I have Sarah O'Connor and a young lady named Jennifer Pechorin with me. Jennifer is Andre Rostov's sister. There are two men following us in a black Audi."

Thurman went silent as he digested that. "Are you certain you're being followed?"

Katherine noted that he didn't seem surprised to learn Sarah was alive.

"Positive. I don't know who they are, but I think they're the same ones who tried to break into my car the other day. John Delaney surprised them in the act and they got into a fight."

"Really?"

"Yes."

"It might have been better if you shared this with me, but I don't suppose there's much we can do about that now. Can you describe the men?"

"Only one. All I can tell you is he's seriously in need of a tan. I caught a glimpse of him when they passed us a little while ago. At the moment he and another man are sitting in the shadows at the far end of the parking lot."

Another pause.

"Shit," Thurman said under his breath. "Now listen carefully—I know who you're talking about and you're in grave danger. This is the man I mentioned in my office . . . Joshua Silver. I want you to leave there at once and drive to the nearest police station. It'll will take me a while to get help to you. How far are you from a major town or city?"

"I don't know. It's probably Osceola."

"Hold on a second."

Katherine heard the sound of a keyboard clacking in the background.

"All right, that won't work," Thurman told her. "It's too small and we don't have a field office there. You'll need to reverse direction and head for Orlando. There's a state building at 550 East Robinson. You'll see a security entrance on the side of it. Go directly there and don't stop for anything. Do you think you can find it?"

"I'll find it."

"Great. I'll have my people waiting for you. What are you driving?"

"A white Lexus 430LS with a broken window on the passenger side."

"That shouldn't be too hard to miss. In the meantime, I'll try to have the local sheriff's office or the State Highway Patrol intercept you along the route. Are there any people where you are right now?"

"A few."

"Good. I doubt that Silver will make a move if there's a crowd around."

As soon as they hung up, Katherine left her car and went to get Sarah and Jenny. She told them what was happening.

"Don't look," Katherine warned when Sarah started to turn. "So far they've only been following us. We don't want to push them into anything foolish."

Jenny asked, "What should we do?"

"Walk calmly to my car and get in as if nothing is wrong. We're heading back to Orlando. The FBI is trying to have someone meet us along the way and escort us to their building."

Sarah's eyes flicked toward the parking lot and back to her again. Katherine could see it was taking an effort to hold herself together.

"Is it safe?" she asked

"I've got a gun in my purse," Katherine replied, trying to keep the fear out of her own voice. "Now let's start moving before they . . ."

Katherine's words trailed away when she realized Sarah was no longer looking at her, but at a point over her shoulder. She turned to see two men get out of the Audi at the end of lot. Both started walking toward them.

THIRTY-SIX

DELANEY

A T half past twelve I found myself standing across the street from a sixty-story granite skyscraper at the corner of Lexington and Fifty-first Street. I was trying to identify which windows belonged to Legacy Construction. As I stared up at the building, I gradually became aware of a large heavyset man standing next to me. He was dressed like a construction worker, complete with hard-hat, and was also staring up at the building.

"Whatcha lookin' at?" he asked.

"Nothing."

"Yeah?" The man's eyebrows came together and a puzzled expression clouded his features. He glanced at the building again and then back at me. "How come you're lookin' at nothin'?"

For a moment I actually considered answering him. That was the way my day was going. I left my friend to ponder the mystery and crossed the street.

According to the building's directory, the offices of Legacy Construction were located on the twenty-third floor. An elevator let me off directly into their lobby. A pretty young receptionist in her early twenties gave me a friendly smile and asked if she could help.

"My name is John Delaney. I have an appointment with Jerry Barnwell."

"I'll let Mr. Barnwell know you're here, sir. May I offer you something to drink?"

"A Coke would be nice, thanks. Uh . . . better make that a Diet Coke," I added, remembering my doctor had told me it wouldn't hurt to lose five pounds.

Despite the advertising hype, the drinks do *not* taste the same. Diet Coke is one of those small sacrifices you make when you're past forty and dating someone who has a dancer's body—Katherine's, not mine.

If Jerry Barnwell had ever sacrificed anything, it wasn't obvious. His face was florid, jowly, and he probably weighed three hundred pounds. He was dressed in a white shirt with rolled-up sleeves and a tie that had a stain on it. It wasn't warm in the lobby, but judging by the sweat stains under his arms, his respiratory system appeared to be working overtime.

"Mr. Delaney," he said, extending a meaty hand to me, "I've heard a lot of good things about you from Nick O'Connor."

"You can't believe everything Nick says," I joked.

A chuckle rippled through his body. "Let's go to my office. It's a little cooler in there and we can talk privately."

The receptionist, who happened to be wearing a sweater, rolled her eyes, a gesture only I was meant to see, and handed me a Diet Coke. I thanked her and followed Barnwell down the hall. At the end of the corridor I could see a small library. Shelves of books covered an entire wall. In front of them was a cream-colored marble conference table.

"That's our company's law library," Jerry said, noticing my glance. "Of course, it's not as big as a your law school's, but everything is up to date. If there's a text you need, just let Wanda know—that's the girl at the front desk—and she'll order it for you."

"Wonderful."

"I've pulled out a couple of files that I'd like to go over with you."

It occurred to me that we were certainly moving along pretty well for a first meeting, particularly since I hadn't been hired yet.

"Maybe we should discuss what you want me to do for your company first."

Jerry chuckled again. "It's not my company. I just work here—as little as possible." He seemed to think that was funny and laughed some more.

I smiled out of courtesy.

"Seriously, John—may I call you John?"

"Sure, Jerry."

"Most of the time we have it pretty easy—except when a lawsuit is filed. Then all hell breaks loose. The bosses call meetings and try to figure out who's to blame and how they can be proactive the next time. *Proactive* . . . they love that word. Everything is proactive these days."

"I see."

"That's where you'll come in. Your job will be to take the heat off me when someone pops out of the woodwork and sues us for a million bucks. Whether we settle or go to court, we still take a hit because our *Errors and Omissions* policy is self-funded. You understand?"

"I think so. So I'll be working with you?"

"Some. Mostly you'll report directly to the higher-ups."

"And they would be?"

He rattled off a few names, but the only one that caught my ear was that of Linda Blendel. I did my best to keep any reaction off my face.

As we sat there getting to know each another, I concluded this was conceivably the fastest job interview I'd ever been on. Eventually, Jerry got around to discussing such mundane topics as salary and the hours I was expected to keep, but they were thrown in more as an afterthought. His manner was easygoing, affable, and he made Legacy's offer sound believable—almost.

The catch was that it was too simple. When an incident occurred, all I had to do was to review the supervisor's report and any witness statements, with the clock ticking at seven hundred dollars an hour. Not bad. I wasn't expected to prepare memos or even investigate. My skepticism may have been downright dumb. Everyone's heard the expression about not looking gift horses in the mouth, but I'd also heard the one that says there ain't no free lunch.

"Do you think this is something you can handle?" Jerry asked, interrupting my thoughts.

"I imagine so. When would you like me to start?"

"How about right now? After the big buildup Nick O'Connor gave you, I mentioned you might be stopping by to one of our principals and she'd like to meet you. Risk management is pretty much Linda's bailiwick."

"Linda?"

"Linda Blendel. She and her husband own a large chunk of the company. She keeps her finger on all the legal expenses."

I fought down a wave of guilt as an image of a pile of test papers languishing on my desk flashed into my mind and said I'd love to meet her, too. After giving Jerry my home address and contact information, I followed his ample backside down the hall.

Linda Blendel's office was roughly twice the size of his and looked like something out of *Architectural Digest*. Everything was perfect, right down to the silk Bokhara rugs and the exquisite Meissen sculptures on her bookshelves. No harsh fluorescent lights here, just incandescent ones set into the ceiling to give the room a warm, comfortable glow. There were a number of paintings of museum quality on the walls, only these might have been better. The frames alone looked like they would set me back two months' salary.

Linda Blendel was elegantly dressed in a designer suit and several inches taller than the man standing near the window holding a book he had been reading. Sitting in a wing chair in front of Mrs. Blendel was a large gentleman with a deep chest and broad shoulders. Despite the fact that he was dressed in a blue blazer and gray slacks, he reminded me of a linebacker.

"Mr. Delaney," Linda said, extending a hand to me, "Warren and I are so pleased to meet you. Or should we call you Professor?"

"John will be fine," I said.

Mrs. Blendel possessed a trim athletic figure and moved with a runway model's grace. Her suit went well with the room's décor, I thought.

"We're very happy you've decided to join us," she said. "This is my husband, Warren. And this is Hans Schiller, our head of security."

I shook hands with them. When I gripped Schiller's hand, it felt like grasping a block of wood. His accent was noticeably German. It occurred to me that either the Blendels were psychic or my joining their little group was a foregone conclusion. As far as I could tell, Jerry hadn't communicated my acceptance to them yet.

"Jerry said you wanted me to start right away."

Mr. Blendel opened his mouth to reply, but it was his wife who answered. "Yes, we do. We have a situation with a man on one of our construction crews. He fell off a roof at an apartment complex in Yonkers."

"He's from Honduras," Jerry added, giving me a knowing look. "Unfortunately, he broke both legs in the fall, fractured his shoulder, and wound up with a concussion. Some asshole of a personal injury lawyer got a hold of him and sent him to a doctor friend. They've provided us with a thermography report that claims he has brain damage."

"Thermography?"

"It's a pseudo technique that's supposed to show different regions in a person's head in color," Schiller explained. "His lawyer just sent us a settlement demand for one million dollars."

I asked, "Have we had the man examined by our own doctors yet?"

Jerry, Linda, and Schiller all looked at each other as if they'd heard this suggestion for the first time.

"John, that's an excellent idea," Jerry said, patting me on the shoulder.

Linda smiled and nodded in agreement, equally pleased at my revelation. Warren Blendel merely gave me a tight-lipped smile from the window.

"I think we made the right choice," Linda announced.

Our meeting lasted for another hour, during which time I impressed one and all with my brilliance. Partway through, Schiller excused himself with curt nod in my direction and left the room. Jerry took copious notes, or pretended to; I wasn't sure which. The insights I was giving, by the way, were the same ones most second-year law students could make.

Warren Blendel said very little during our meeting. Mostly he watched and listened. Of the two, I decided he was more subtle than his wife, whose eyes bored into you. Blendel simply sat back, content to let her take the lead. In the end, they thanked me for my time and Jerry reminded me to send a bill for my services.

The only real surprise from our little conference was an invitation to attend a charity function the Blendels were throwing at their summer house on Martha's Vineyard two days later. I told them if I could finish grading my exams in time, I'd be happy to attend.

I didn't find out why I was such a popular fellow until I returned home.

PRIOR to my leaving the house, I took a few cautionary measures to ensure that everything would remain secure. Call it paranoia, but I figured the people who killed Andre Rostov and the man who had tried to strangle me might not be Atlanta residents.

The two hairs that I had placed across the doorjamb were now gone, as was the sewing needle I'd propped up against the inside of the front door. The needle trick only works if your fingers aren't too big and there's enough space at the bottom of the doorjamb. I found the needle three feet into the room, dragged there when someone opened my door. I gently probed the lock with my forefinger and detected a fine powdery black substance—graphite. There was no question someone had been in my apartment. Around the same time, it occurred to me my visitors might still be there and my gun was twenty feet away in the desk drawer.

I listened for any sound inside. Hearing none, I flicked on the light switch using my elbow. Nothing seemed out of place and the only thing I could hear was the ticking of my grandfather clock. When the telephone rang, I jumped and muttered something under my breath I wouldn't want repeated in mixed company. I stayed put and let it ring until the answering machine came on.

"Professor Delaney, this is Phil Thurman. Give me a call as soon as you get this message. We have an urgent situation I need to make you—"

I crossed the room in three steps.

"Delaney here," I said, picking up the receiver.

"Jeez, thank goodness. I need to talk to you about an urgent—"

"Not now and not on this phone," I said, cutting him off. "There's a good chance someone's been in my apartment. I just walked in and haven't had a chance to check the rooms yet."

"Understood. We're on the way. Don't do anything stupid, Delaney."

THIRTY-SEVEN

DELANEY

THURMAN and two men in gray suits, standard FBI issue, knocked on my door less than twenty minutes later. All three entered with guns drawn, probably making a great impression on my neighbors.

"It's clear," I told them.

Thurman relaxed, holstered his weapon, and nodded to his men. They separated and began searching the apartment. One of them took an electronic device from a briefcase he was carrying and extended an antenna. I watched as he took a reading at the base of my telephone. Once he was finished, he moved to each of the room's light switches and electric receptacles. Thurman motioned for me to remain quiet by holding one finger over his lips. The gadget man disappeared into the kitchen and eventually made his way to the den and bedrooms. He returned several minutes later.

"Clean," he said to Thurman.

His partner joined him, giving us a thumbs-up sign.

I turned to Thurman. "You were about to leave a message on my answering machine about an urgent situation."

Thurman took a deep breath before he began. "Ms. Adams, Sarah O'Connor, and Jennifer Pechorin are missing."

A sick feeling took hold of my insides and my legs suddenly felt like I had just climbed six flights of steps.

"What are you talking about?"

"Do I have to paint a picture? You decided to play lone wolf and it's backfired. Katherine Adams called me last night from a service plaza in central Florida and said that a car was following her. I told her to meet me in Orlando and arranged for the State Highway Patrol to intercept them along the way. Unfortunately, they never found her. What they did find was her car on the side of the road."

I dropped down into the nearest armchair. "Oh, Jesus. Were there any signs of a struggle?"

"We found traces of blood on the front passenger seat near the floorboard. It's being analyzed now. The car also had a broken side window, but Ms. Adams told me that happened at her home, another little fact you forgot to mention."

I suppose I had this coming, but I was in no mood for a lecture just then. Katherine and the girls were my first concern.

"Anything else?"

"Yes," Thurman said. He reached into the inside pocket of his sports jacket, pulled out a cell phone, and tossed it to me. "I believe this is registered to your girlfriend. We found it thirty feet from her car. Maybe you'd like to level with me now? You've already broken a half dozen laws. Don't add obstructing justice to the mix."

"Who was the first person on the scene?" I asked, forcing myself to think.

"A cop from the State Highway Patrol. He reported the engine on the Lexus was still warm but the car was abandoned. There was no sign of anyone in the area."

"Is that it?"

When he hesitated, I knew he was holding back. "Come on, Thurman, give," I prompted, rising to my feet.

The other agents started forward as soon as I did, but stopped when he held up his hand.

"All right. There *was* one other item, but we don't know what to make of it yet. A patrolman remembered speaking with a trucker around the time Ms. Adams disappeared. The man mentioned seeing an unmarked police cruiser pull another vehicle off the road onto the shoulder. The time fits because it was just after I got her phone call. He couldn't describe the first vehicle as anything other than a black sedan, but he definitely claims he saw a cop on the scene and blue lights."

"So?"

"The trucker asked the trooper when the State Patrol had started using unmarked cars and the officer mentioned it to his boss. Unfortunately, they have no record of a stop at that location. They're checking now with any off-duty personnel. What the hell were you people doing with Sarah O'Connor and this Jennifer Pechorin? And before you answer, I promise, if you're not straight with me this time, you're going to jail."

I gave Thurman the details about how we had found Sarah O'Connor, the attack on me, and our subsequent decision to get her out of Atlanta.

"Why couldn't you trust me with this? Jesus Christ, Delaney, what the fuck is wrong with you?"

"Katherine and I both thought you were holding out on us. Tell me I'm wrong."

There was a pause. After several seconds Thurman turned to the men with him. "Wait for me in the lobby, please."

Neither had bothered to introduce themselves and I never found out their names.

After the door closed he asked, "You have anything to drink here?"

"I can make some coffee?"

"I said *drink*."

I looked at him for a moment, then went to the china cabinet and returned with a bottle of scotch and two glasses. I poured a double for each of us. Thurman took a sip, then sat down on the couch, and nodded his thanks. He glanced around the room.

"Nice place. You rent or own?"

"Own. I inherited it from my aunt fifteen years ago."

He lifted his glass in a toast.

"Fifteen years ago I was senior agent in charge of our New York office. At the time, two of my men were working an extortion case in conjunction with Treasury. After sixteen months we finally caught a break and found someone willing to talk with us. We took the information to the U.S. Attorney and were about to lay a whole raft of charges on Warren Blendel's doorstep when our witness mysteriously disappeared. He was found dead at the base of the Palisades in Jersey with his head bashed in. Two days later the men doing surveillance on Warren Blendel also vanished. One was never heard from again; the other was found near Fort Tryon Park with his throat cut."

I nodded. I was in law school at the time, but I recalled hearing about the case. It was a media circus. "Gangland killings" the papers had called it.

Thurman continued, "I won't bore you with the details, but the murdered agent was my brother-in-law. My wife blamed me for his death because I had put him into the situation. Things were never quite the same between us afterward and eventually our marriage fell apart. A few months later, the Bureau transferred me out of New York and reassigned me to Atlanta."

"And that's why you want Blendel so badly," I said. "I think I understand now."

"You don't understand shit, Delaney," Thurman answered. He set his glass down on the coffee table, spilling some scotch over the side. "Marriages end for all kinds of reasons. And it's not because I got booted out of New York. Blendel is a disease. He's the kind of scum that skulks in the dark and preys on innocent people. He doesn't care who gets hurt if it suits his own ends. The fact is he doesn't even need the money; he's set for life. According to our forensics shrinks, he operates on autopilot, because it's all he knows how to do. His kind is everything I was meant to fight."

This I didn't expect. I considered the man in front of me for several seconds before I made up my mind.

"Wait here," I said.

It took a little effort to move the dryer aside and get the exhaust duct open again. I returned with Sarah's file and tossed it onto his lap. He spent about the same amount of time reading it as I had, and judging from the look on his face, he was equally as lost.

"I don't get it. What's so important about—"

"There's something there," I told him. "We're just not seeing it. What are you doing about Katherine, Sarah, and Jenny Pechorin?"

"We're treating the situation as a kidnapping, which gives us jurisdiction. The local sheriff's office is assisting. We have a team on the ground scouring the area. Like I told you, only one car was found on the scene—the Lexus, so for the time being we're operating on the theory the women were abducted."

For the time being meant, *until they found the bodies*. Thurman didn't have to spell it out. Another wave of fear rolled through me. This couldn't be happening. A little voice in my head whispered, *Panic now, they're as good as dead.*

My next thought was clearer and better reasoned. Sarah no longer had the file in her possession, so there was nothing for Blendel's people to find. This left me as the logical candidate. If Blendel wanted it, he would have to come out in the open and contact me directly *and he would need something to bargain with.* His bogus employment offer was just a preliminary step in the negotiations.

The telephone's ring snapped me back to the present. I snatched the receiver off the hook. It was Mike Franklin.

"You sitting down?" he asked.

"Actually, I'm standing here with a fellow named Phillip Thurman. He's a regional director with the FBI."

"That's just peachy, John. The feds are involved now?"

"They are."

"Then maybe I'd better not say anything else."

"Mike, Katherine and two other women disappeared last night. They called Agent Thurman for help. Katherine told him they were being followed. Unfortunately, his people couldn't get to them in time. One of the women is Sarah O'Connor. . . ."

"What the fuck are you talking about?"

"I said one of the women is Sarah O'Connor, Frank's daughter—"

"I know whose fuckin' daughter she is. Look, if this is some kind of a joke—"

"Sarah isn't dead, Mike. I've seen her and I've talked to her. I don't have time to go into the details with you, but I need whatever you've got."

I could hear him breathing on the other end of the line.

"Is this shit really on the level?"

"I swear to God."

Several more seconds passed before he reached a decision.

"All right . . . I don't know how any of this ties in, but here you go. In the last ten years there have been four investigations involving Warren Blendel. All of them are closed cases. Three list him as a principal. The fourth mentions him as having ties to a guy named

Louis Benedetto, a small-time hood out of Queens. In each instance the supervising officer who shut down the investigation was Nick O'Connor."

"It figures. Anything else?"

"Yeah. In the for-what-it's-worth category, the name of a former Interpol agent named Hans Schiller crops up in the two most recent files."

"I've met him. Thanks, buddy. I owe you," I said.

"You sure as hell do."

After we hung up, Thurman raised his eyebrows in a silent question.

I said, "Earlier today I asked a friend to check out whether there was any connection between Blendel and anyone in the NYPD."

"And he came up with Frank O'Connor," Thurman said, slapping the back of the file with his hand.

"Wrong. He came up with *Nick* O'Connor."

"His brother? I don't get it. What does he have to do with this?"

"At this point, all I have are pieces of a puzzle, but I'll tell you what I know."

I went on to explain about Nick O'Connor's misidentification of Sarah's body, the scholarship offer that got her out of New York, and the sudden opportunity that he passed my way regarding Legacy Construction.

The crease between Thurman's eyes gradually deepened as I spoke. "All that can be rationalized away," he said when I finished.

I added, "Two of the principals of Legacy Construction are Warren and Linda Blendel."

Thurman leaned back in his chair and took another sip of his scotch. "Is that so?"

"The fellow who was just on the phone also told me that Nick O'Connor was the supervising officer who signed off closing four cases in which Blendel was under investigation. And to cap matters off, while I was conveniently out of the house today for my meeting, someone rifled my apartment. I presume to search for that," I said, pointing to the file on Thurman's lap.

Thurman was silent for a long time.

"I'll need to run each of these names," he said. "But I agree with you, we're missing something—something so important, Warren Blendel is willing to kill for it. Can I count on you to work with us, or do you still want to go it alone?"

"I'll work with you," I told him. "I've been invited to the Blendel's summer cottage on Martha's Vineyard the day after tomorrow for a charity luncheon. Someplace called West Tisbury."

"Interesting."

"It seems I'm a very popular fellow of late. Do you know anything about a man named Hans Schiller? He was at the meeting this morning, too, and I'm told his name shows up in two of the cases that Nick O'Connor shut down."

"Schiller? He's the head of Blendel's security. From what I've heard, he services both the company and Mrs. Blendel, but that's only rumor. If you're going to Massachusetts, you'll need to keep your eye on him. He's a real SOB. What's the reason for this trip?"

"On the surface, it's to discuss more legal work for Legacy, but I think we both know that's bullshit. The way I see it, they didn't find the file here, and they didn't get it from Katherine or Sarah, so I'm the next stop on their list. The women were taken as bargaining chips."

Thurman thought about this for several seconds and then slowly nodded. "I think you're right. The question is how to handle this situation. Normally, I'd ask you to wear a wire, but we've never been able to get anything on Blendel. He has experts who sweep his house on a regular basis. How about if I send two of my men with you?"

I shook my head in the negative. "They'll stand out like sore thumbs and I won't do anything to jeopardize Katherine or the others."

Thurman remained insistent. "You can't go up there by yourself, Delaney. If you suddenly drop off the face of the earth, it leaves me with nothing. These are very dangerous people you're dealing with."

"Gee, I'm touched by your concern, Phil."

He ignored the comment.

"I've got a man and woman who work for me. They can act like they're on vacation together. We'll put them up in one of the hotels in Edgartown, which is about fifteen minutes from Blendel's place."

I started to protest again, but Thurman cut me off.

"Look, it's either that or you're not going at all," he said. "I can't risk any more lives."

His words made the muscles in my jaw clench. He was talking as if Katherine, Sarah, and Jenny were already gone. Unfortunately, I didn't have much choice in the matter. I turned around, pulled open the top drawer of my desk, and took my gun out.

"What's that for?" Thurman asked.

"Nothing, I'm just a cautious person by nature."

THIRTY-EIGHT

KATHERINE

KATHERINE squinted into the glare of the police cruiser's spotlight as two officers approached her vehicle. In accordance with standard procedure, they separated and went to opposites sides of her car. She opened the door and started to get out.

"Please stay in your car, ma'am," one of the officers instructed her.

She closed the door.

When the blue lights suddenly appeared in her rearview mirror it had startled her, but Thurman said that he would have someone meet them along the way, so she pulled onto the shoulder. Even if it wasn't Thurman's people, she reasoned having a police escort was a good idea. In the background, she could hear the crackle of a two-way radio.

Sarah twisted around in her seat and held a hand up in front of her eyes, shielding them from the light.

"I can't see anything."

"Neither can I," Jenny echoed.

Both officers stopped at the rear of the car.

"Are you Katherine Adams?" the one on her side asked.

"That's right."

The officer moved forward. "May I see some identification, ma'am?" He was holding a large flashlight in one hand and kept it trained on her face.

"Of course," Katherine replied, shifting her head away from the glare.

"Who are the other people in the car with you?" the officer asked.

"Sarah O'Connor and Jennifer Pechorin."

"I'll need to see IDs from everyone, please."

"Fine. Would you mind taking that light out of my eyes?"

"No problem, ma'am. Sorry."

The light promptly flicked off and Katherine reached into the backseat to retrieve her purse. That was when she caught a glimpse of the second officer in her sideview mirror. While he was behind the steering wheel, all she had been able to see was his chest. He was clearly wearing a uniform, but it was difficult to make out any other details in the darkness. The turnpike was lit only by headlights from passing motorists that flashed by and disappeared into the night. Suddenly, a truck traveling in the opposite direction illuminated the man's face.

THIRTY-NINE

JOSHUA

THE last thing Joshua Silver expected was a pistol flash from the car's interior. A deafening bang followed it a millisecond later. The shot caught him just above the sternum and exited through his right collarbone, shattering it in the process and knocking him backwards. That he was already twisting his body sideways when he heard the gun's hammer cock probably saved his life.

Joshua's years of martial arts training kicked in. He completed his turn and came up behind Katherine, seizing the pressure points at the back of her neck. A second shot went wide as his fingers dug into her flesh. Inside the car someone screamed. Time seemed to slow as Joshua's fingers tightened. It would take less than twenty seconds for the woman to lose consciousness.

He leaned forward until his lips were close to Katherine's ear and whispered, "There's no escape this time—nowhere to run, little girl." They were the same words Richard Jenks had whispered to her so many years ago in the basement of his home. He could feel Katherine stiffen as soon as she heard them, but her struggles were growing weaker and weaker.

Perhaps adding "Whistle a Happy Tune," from *The King and I,* would be a nice touch, he thought.

After studying newspaper accounts of how Jenks had played mind games with his victims, he'd been unable to get the stupid song out of his head. It was a shame he never knew the man. *Human heads mounted on the walls? Body parts in jars as trophies? Creative!*

Joshua breathed in Katherine's scent through his nostrils and began to whistle softly in her ear.

FORTY

SCHILLER

ON the opposite side of the vehicle, Hans Schiller was in the process of bringing his sawed-off shotgun to bear when the Lexus's engine suddenly roared into life. Tires squealed as Katherine floored the accelerator. The rear end of the car fishtailed outward, smashing into his hip and sending gravel flying everywhere. He could smell burning rubber. The impact knocked him to the ground as the car surged forward, clawing the pavement for traction.

Out of the corner of his eye he saw Joshua drop to one knee, draw his semiautomatic, and fire three shots in rapid succession. For a moment he thought the shots had no effect, but then the car suddenly veered and left the road, careening down a small embankment.

Schiller touched his fingers to his forehead and winced. He was bleeding. Nearby, Joshua was breathing heavily, his face deathly pale in the cold moonlight. Schiller slowly got up and went to him. He put a hand under Joshua's arm and helped him to his feet. Joshua responded by yanking his arm away. He began walking unsteadily toward Katherine's vehicle, weaving as if he were drunk, all the while talking to himself.

"We must leave," Schiller said.

Joshua stopped and looked back at him, fury etched across his features.

"You require medical attention." Schiller said calmly.

Joshua turned and continued toward the car.

"Imbecile," Schiller muttered.

He trotted back to their car and shut the flashing blue lights. The lights, along with security uniforms, had been purchased from a supply company earlier that day after his return flight from New York. They were close enough to the real thing to pass a casual glance.

Joshua was walking with a pronounced limp by the time he pulled their car alongside him. Schiller rolled down the window.

"Get in, my friend," he said. "We're too exposed out here and you need see a doctor."

"It's unprofessional to leave a job half finished, Hans."

"Listen to me. Twenty people have probably seen us by now. We need to vacate this area."

"You vacate. There's a truck stop at the next exit. Leave the car in the parking lot for me. I'll meet you at the airport in the morning."

"And how am I supposed to get back to Atlanta?"

"Call a cab," Joshua said over his shoulder.

Schiller watched him for several seconds. The situation had become a mess and the Blendels would not be happy. But as the Americans said, if you want to make an omelet, you must break a few eggs. He wasn't sure if the expression actually applied to this situation. It was just something he had heard. He watched Joshua continue to limp toward the Adams woman's car.

Perhaps it's just as well to get this over now. They still had a little time. Linda wanted him back in New York for the meeting with Delaney.

He accelerated around his companion and brought the car to a stop above the ditch where the Lexus had come to a rest. At first he couldn't believe his eyes—it was empty. In disbelief, he got out and checked the passenger compartment to be sure.

Joshua arrived a second later and stared at the scene, incredulous. Then he did something completely out of character for him—he threw back his head and screamed. It made him look like a banshee. Schiller took a step backwards, his hand edging closer to the gun in his holster. His companion was quite insane, of course, and the last thing he needed then was a howling lunatic on his hands. But what of the women? He scanned the surrounding area for them and spotted an orange grove a hundred yards away. Row after row of trees stretched into the blackness all the way to the top of a hill.

Schiller cursed under his breath in German.

When Joshua finally regained control of himself, he also focused on the orange grove.

Reading his thoughts, Schiller said, "We'll never find them in there. Let's go. We'll get more help and come back later."

If Joshua heard him, he gave no indication of it. Instead, he limped back to their car, retrieved a high-powered rifle from the trunk, and started down the embankment toward the trees.

FORTY-ONE

KATHERINE

KATHERINE moved back into the shadows and watched the police car disappear over a rise. One of the men, the albino, had remained behind, presumably to finish the job. Her mouth was dry and her heart was pounding so loudly, she was certain he could hear it. The back of her neck hurt like hell from where he had grabbed her. She checked her gun again. There were only two bullets left.

Unbeknownst to Joshua, he had done her a favor. Just as a dark curtain had begun to settle over her eyes, she heard him whistling. It was so much like the monster she had fought years ago, the image of Richard Jenks burst into her consciousness. Richard Jenks who had whistled the same tune to her as he cut her finger off. Memories long buried, memories that surfaced in nightmares and in her flashbacks, flooded to the surface and galvanized her into action. The scene of a basement smelling of formaldehyde and rotting flesh became so real, she could almost touch them. Minutes earlier, they had exploded in her mind, just as they were trying to do now. It took all of Katherine's willpower to shove them away. Like a black leopard, they retreated into the shadows, waiting. She could almost feel the large green eyes watching her.

A few feet away, Sarah and Jenny also waited, hidden behind another tree. Using hand signals, Katherine indicated for them to stay put. They were all in trouble—serious trouble. Her first thought was to call Phillip Thurman for help, but her cell phone was still in the car. Sarah didn't have one and Jenny's battery was dead.

This just gets better and better, she thought.

Another thought now began to take hold of her; the urge to run, to get away and save herself. To make matters worse her medicine was also locked in the trunk of the car. The leopard inched closer as long-buried memories crawled from their dark hiding places. She wasn't surprised, for they had been constant companions since she was eighteen. The strength with which she fought them now would have surprised Joshua. Somehow Katherine willed herself to remain clam and catalogue their options. If she allowed the flashbacks to take over, it could mean the difference between paralysis and functioning. The rational part of her mind knew the albino was not Richard Jenks. Jenks was dead, burned to death in his cabin outside Columbus, Ohio, by his own hand. Jenks, the religious zealot who had murdered six coeds in the most gruesome ways imaginable. The albino must have read the newspaper accounts and was playing some sick game.

Katherine glanced down at her left hand and stared at the place where her finger had been. Sometimes she could still feel it there. Phantom limb syndrome, the doctors called it. They needed to put as much distance between themselves and the man stalking them as quickly as possible. For a moment she considered the highway and signaling a passing motorist for help, but rejected the idea. The man's partner could be waiting for them just over the hill. From her hiding place she watched Joshua sweep his flashlight back and forth against the trees, searching.

That he was going about the task methodically despite his wound made him even more dangerous. He was too far away to risk a shot and Katherine didn't think she would get a second chance if she did. This had to be the Joshua Silver Thurman had told her about. Wounded or not, he was fast—incredibly fast, and apparently determined. A minute ticked away and then another as they waited. All the while the albino continued to move his light along the rows of trees. Twice it passed close to her.

Maybe he'll give up.

Just when she began to think that might actually happen, one of the girls stepped on a branch. Joshua's light immediately swung in their direction and he started limping toward them.

"*Run,*" Katherine hissed.

She didn't know which of them had done it and it didn't matter now. The only thing that did matter was to get them out of there. With Jenny and Sarah in front, she started down the nearest row of trees, constantly checking over her shoulder. Behind her she could sense that Joshua was closing. Occasionally she caught glimpses of his flashlight through the branches. On their side was the fact that he was hurt and didn't know where they were. Katherine was certain her first shot had hit him. It was unbelievable he could still be on his feet, but he was.

The orchard seemed to go on forever. Branches flashed by her face. Twice Sarah stumbled and fell. The second time she hit the ground heavily, knocking the air from her lungs. Katherine reached down, grabbed her by the elbow and pulled her up.

"We've got to keep moving."

"I twisted my ankle," Sarah whispered.

"Can you walk?"

"I think so."

Her first step produced a gasp, as did the second. Katherine checked over her shoulder again and her heart sank. Despite his injuries, the albino was gaining ground.

"There's a house on the other side of the field," Jenny said. "If it has a phone, we can call for help."

"Right. Let's go."

Supporting Sarah between them, they started off. The ground was uneven and the going difficult. Worse, they were now making enough noise to wake the dead. After less than a minute, Katherine found that she was breathing heavily. Her eyes met Sarah's. The girl's fear was giving way to resignation.

"I still have my gun," she said, trying to bolster her.

A grimace passed over Sarah's face. To her credit, she nodded and kept moving.

Katherine had no idea where they were and no doubt the man following intended to kill them. With Sarah hobbling along as best she could, they made for the end of the trees and an open field. The house was now a silhouette against a moonlit landscape.

Suddenly the flashlight went out. It was followed by two sharp cracks. The first bullet stuck the ground near Jenny's feet, kicking up a puff of dirt. The other smashed into a tree trunk, sending splinters of wood flying everywhere. Jenny screamed. Katherine searched the area for anything they could use for cover and found nothing. The field stretching before them was at least two hundred yards long. Three more bullets hit the trees ahead and to the right of the women forcing them to turn.

FORTY-TWO

JOSHUA

A FAINT smile appeared at the corners of Joshua's mouth as he
worked the bolt on his rifle. He watched through the night scope
and took careful aim. A branch exploded just above Katherine's
head. When she ducked out of reflex, he giggled to himself. Despite
the pain in his collarbone, which was getting worse by the minute,
this was going to be fun.

Not that it mattered. The mind controls everything. He had
learned that growing up in his father's home in order to survive the
beatings and worse. The Army's Special Forces training reinforced
it. Joshua concentrated harder, shutting the pain out. Schiller was
right. He needed medical attention; unfortunately, it would have to
wait until his work was done.

His fingers drifted to the photographs in his shirt pocket. Earlier
that day, he had selected two from his collection he thought Katherine
would like. Not his best work of course, but they were . . . *representative*. He took them out and examined them in the dim moonlight.
He had liked both women. Tall professional types were his favorites,
the ones who had it all together. They were so cool, so calm . . . until
he started cutting. He wondered how Katherine would look without
ears. Maybe not so cool and calm then.

Ever since Schiller had handed him the file on her, he had been
fascinated, not only by Katherine, but by Jenks himself. The pressure building inside needed to be released and it would . . . soon. He
asked himself what kind of girl could survive for three days in the
woods without training or resources. What kind of man was Jenks? It
was a shame they never met. From the newspaper accounts he read,
Jenks was described as brilliant but disturbed. Joshua knew better.
The simple fact was that Jenks had been sloppy. He made mistakes.

A true genius wouldn't have done that. No, Joshua concluded, Jenks was a good example of what not to do. Still, there was no denying the subtle beauty in his work.

If he were given to mystic mumbo-jumbo, he might have said a cosmic connection existed between himself and Richard Jenks, a link, if you would. He could see the man's face clearly in his mind. And those eyes! They were pale blue just as his were. The newspapers said Jenks loved classical music. So did he. He didn't mention these similarities to Schiller, because the man was incapable of understanding such things. Schiller was strictly business. Boring.

He touched his collarbone again and winced. The bitches would pay for what they did to him. All women were bitches when you came right down to it. He had seen the way they looked at him from the time he was little—like he was some kind of freak. And he had seen the way they looked when they knew they were going to die—acknowledging his power and his supremacy, a man in absolute control. Just once it would have been nice to wake up in the morning next to a woman who didn't want money, who wanted him for himself. That wasn't going to happen—ever. He knew that now. He shook his head sadly and took a deep breath. The next few hours would be . . . his masterpiece.

FORTY-THREE

DELANEY

SLEEP didn't come easily that night and when it did, it was accompanied by a nightmare. I awoke at three with my face bathed in sweat. Visions of Katherine's body lying in the woods filled my mind's eye until I forced them away and switched on the television. There was no proof she was dead yet and I clung to that thought.

For the next two hours I watched infomercials that hawked everything from ThighMasters to an electronic gadget that toned the abdominal muscles while you sat in your chair. Pitchmen told me how to earn a million dollars in real estate with no money down, and one shopping channel offered its viewers genuine *antique* gold rings from Italy (only two hundred and counting). The seller must have stumbled across a shitload of antiques.

I did my best to keep calm and work the situation out in my mind. No good; I was too agitated. I kept looking at the phone, willing it to ring. Nothing happened, of course; it simply sat there looking back at me. I knew Katherine would call if she were able to, which only made matters worse. For the third time that night I checked the clip on my gun, making sure it was full and the spring action was working properly. Other than my single meeting with Warren Blendel, I didn't know him from a hole in the ground. If it turned out he was responsible for harming Katherine, Sarah, or Jenny, I promised myself he would never harm anyone again.

I gave up on the infomercials around eight in the morning and put on a T-shirt, shorts, and running shoes. Physical exercise always helps when I'm upset. It gives me time to think. Maybe it's those endorphins doctors are always talking about.

The building I live in sits along Central Park's west side. Some years earlier all the apartments had gone condo. Most are passed from generation to generation, as mine was to me. It's like being in a club and owners guard their units fiercely. They don't want the "wrong type" moving in. To this day I'm not sure how I got past the Fitness Committee. George, our doorman, glanced at my outfit with a look of unconcealed disapproval and promptly turned the other way as I passed through the courtyard.

I ran for nearly a half hour with no particular destination in mind. I just ran. I worked my way down to Central Park South. The real name is Sixtieth Street, though no self-respecting New Yorker ever calls it that. A U-turn brought me to the Guggenheim Museum on the opposite side of the park, where I came to a halt, having sprinted the last two hundred yards.

My chest was heaving and sweat was running freely down my back and arms. I bent over, put my hands on my knees and waited for my breath to return. Katherine, Sarah, and Jenny's faces kept drifting in and out of my thoughts along with the pages from the file Sarah had taken. Frustration built to the point where I felt like screaming, but even in New York that's not a good thing to do. With nothing left to do but wait, I started back toward the house. It was nearly nine o'clock.

When my cell phone went off, I grabbed it out of my pocket so quickly, the ring barely had time to die away.

"Delaney."

"Hey John, it's Lissa. Remember me? Your sister?"

"Fuck," I muttered under my breath.

"Thanks, it's nice to hear from you, too."

"Sorry, I was expecting someone else."

"Obviously."

"I'm sorry, Lis. I'm a little distracted at the moment. How are you doing?"

"Better, now that I know you're alive. Why haven't you returned my calls or Mom's? She called me last night. She's afraid you were hit by a truck."

I shook my head. Both messages were still sitting on my answering machine. I apologized again and explained that I had been out of town, hoping she wouldn't ask questions. Both my mother and sister have a sixth sense when something is wrong. Don't ask how—

they just do. To make matters worse, they can always tell when I'm lying if I deny anything is.

"How come you were out of town?"

"Just business."

That seemed to satisfy her.

"Are you free for lunch today? I have some photos I need to drop off at the gallery and I thought we might get together."

"I'd love to, but this is probably not a good day. I have to head up to Massachusetts later."

"Really? What's going on in Massachusetts?"

"A charity luncheon on Martha's Vineyard with a client."

"Fancy," she said, drawing out the word. "I did a photo shoot there with a model who lives in Edgartown. You should give her a call. She's a real knockout."

"The last model you fixed me up with was a lesbian; besides, I'm seeing someone."

"You're so narrow minded."

I stopped to wait for a light across from my building. "I'm sure she's nice, but like I said—"

"You're seeing someone—Katherine, right?"

"Right."

"That's okay. I like her. So how's it going between you two?"

"Pretty well," I said, trying to sound offhand.

"All right, I understand about today. When can we get together?"

"Is something wrong?"

"Not really. It's just that Brenda and I were discussing prenuptial agreements and we wanted your advice before we do anything."

Brenda has been my sister's "life partner" for the last five years. These days the politically correct term plays better than *lesbian lover.* Though I've never been comfortable discussing the subject with her, I've done an about face on the topic of gays in recent years. The fact that Lissa is gay probably has something to do with this. My philosophy now is live and let live. You're either born that way or you're not. If the lifestyle works for you, fine. I don't judge.

"You have to be married to have a prenuptial agreement," I explained.

"We were thinking of taking a vacation in San Francisco next month. Gay marriages are legal there now."

"I see."

She asked, "Are you driving or taking the train to Massachusetts?"

"Driving. Why?"

"I was thinking . . . if we get together around eleven thirty, you could be up there by four o'clock, couldn't you?"

"Sure, but why all the rush?"

"I also want to talk to you about Mom. I really think her Parkinson's is getting worse and I can't convince her to make an appointment with the doctor."

I took a deep breath. There was no way of getting out of this.

"All right, where do you want to meet?"

"Are you sure?"

"Yeah, I'm sure. Where do you want to meet?"

"Because if it's not convenient, we could do it another—"

"*Lissa.*"

"Okay, okay, how about at Enrico's? It's halfway between the gallery and your place and you can jump right on the West Side Highway from there."

"No problem. I'll see you at eleven thirty."

"Is it okay if Brenda comes along?"

"Of course."

When I got home I showered and tried Katherine again. I didn't really expect an answer, but I tried anyway. My next call was to Phil Thurman, who told me they had added another team of agents to the search, along with a helicopter. He also let me know that his people were already in place at Martha's Vineyard. They were registered at the Collingworth Inn under the names of David and Sherri Watson and were posing as tourists.

I wasn't sure what good their presence would do, since Blendel's place was supposedly crawling with security. According to Thurman, no one could get within a mile of the house, but I thanked him anyway. He promised to let me know the moment he had any news on Katherine and I promised to call as soon as the meeting was over.

If my assumption about Blendel was correct, I was going to need a bargaining chip and the only one I had was Sarah's file. Since Thurman now had the original, I removed my copy from its hiding place and started reading through it again. I was definitely missing something. That much was certain, but it was like trying to grasp smoke. For the better part of an hour I stared at the names and dates on the pages before giving up. As a cautionary measure against the information "disappearing," I scanned each page into my computer, then e-mailed copies to myself, Katherine, and Mike Franklin.

It was nearly ten thirty and I needed to get moving. In the past, my exposure to charity affairs has been minimal and I had no clue what to wear to Blendel's party, so I placed a call to Jerry Barnwell.

"Finished with those test papers already?" he asked.

"Almost, Jerry," I said, eyeing the untouched stack on the corner of my desk.

"Wonderful. Linda and Warren really took a liking to you. They'll be thrilled to hear you're coming. From what I understand, the luncheon's nothing formal . . . just jacket and tie. The Vineyard is a pretty laid-back place. I'm glad you phoned."

"Why is that?"

"I'm thinking now since you're coming up tonight, there's another case we can go over together. Warren says you're welcome to stay at his guest house."

"Well, I wouldn't want to impose."

"No imposition at all. When the Blendels like someone, they treat them like part of the family. That's the kind of people they are."

Yeah, the Galliano crime family. Before I had a chance to respond, I heard the sound of a buzzer in the background.

"Excuse me for a second," Jerry said.

The line went silent and he came back a moment later.

"John, that was Warren. I told him you'll be there tonight. He's going to call you in a few minutes. We'll talk later."

IN precisely five minutes the phone rang and Warren Blendel came on the line.

"John, I'm so glad you can attend the party. We really appreciated your input yesterday."

"Glad to help, Mr. Blendel."

"To be perfectly honest, there's another matter that's been causing us quite a bit of concern lately."

"Yes, Jerry mentioned another case to me."

"Oh, this isn't about a case. It's a different problem entirely."

"Such as?"

"It has to do with a file . . . a particularly important file. You
know about files, don't you, John? And missing people?"

A hand of ice closed around my heart.

"Are you still there?" Blendel asked.

"I'm here, Warren."

"Excellent. I was hoping we can spend some time alone and discuss the matter before it gets out of hand."

"And you think I can help?"

"I have every confidence you can. You're a clever and resourceful
man, and you have clever and resourceful friends—close friends,
from what I understand."

"Is that so?"

"Yes, it is. I feel it would be better if you talk to them before my
employees do. The result might not be pleasant and people tend to
listen to someone they know. I'll have a lot of guests at my home this
weekend, but I'll see you're given ample opportunity."

"Listen, you smug son of a bitch. If anything—"

"Now, now, I can tell you're upset. There's no need to worry. Your
friends are quite safe . . . *for the time being.* We'll go over all the details
when you arrive. You seem like a reasonable fellow and I'm hopeful an
accommodation can be reached that suits everyone. You'll get what
you want and I'll get what I want. In the meantime, I'll trust in your
discretion to treat this matter confidentially."

The line went dead before I could reply.

FORTY-FOUR

BLENDEL

I'M so proud of you, Warren," Linda Blendel said as her husband placed the receiver back on its hook. "I knew you could do it."

Blendel closed his eyes and took several deep breaths as the doctor had instructed him.

"It's insanity asking him to come here. Of all people. . . ."

"Take one of your pills, Warren. You'll feel better."

Blendel reached for a bottle of Ativan and began fumbling with the cap until Linda got up and took it from him. She opened the bottle, tipped out a single pill, then poured a glass of water from a silver pitcher on the corner of the desk.

"Drink," she said.

Blendel drank.

"This situation is completely out of hand," Blendel said.

"Everything is under control, Warren. Hans told me Joshua is tidying up the loose ends in Florida."

"Then why haven't we heard from him?"

Linda shrugged. "Joshua's a bit odd. You know that."

"But—"

"But nothing, dear. We simply need Mr. Delaney to *believe* his friends are alive and that we have them. He'll be happy, if not eager, to turn the file over to us."

Blendel's fingers beat a nervous rhythm on his desk with his pen.

"Stop that," Linda said. "It makes it difficult to think."

The pen tapping stopped.

"And then what?" Blendel asked.

"And then nothing. We'll have the file. The women will be dead and there'll be no witnesses. That will be the end of it."

"What if he made copies? It's not the file; it's what's in it."

"If Mr. Delaney made any copies, I'm sure Hans can find a creative way to deal with him. But you make a good point. We really do have to know, don't we? Hans is quite good at that sort of thing."

Blendel's laugh was rueful. "Hans. I saw you coming out of his room last night."

Linda's only response was to examine the polish on one of her nails. "We were discussing business, Warren."

"Is that what you call it? Do you think I'm a fool?"

"I'd rather not have a scene right now, dear. I have a million things to do before the party. Why don't you go out on the patio and read for a while?"

Blendel did not get up. He leaned back in his seat and looked at her. "You think I'll take anything, don't you?"

"I know you will."

"Goddamnit, this is still my home."

"*Our* home," she corrected, checking another fingernail.

"You told me there wouldn't be any more of . . . that."

"Hans is very important to us. He does your job, Warren. The one you're too scared to do."

"You're a bitch."

"And you're a coward. I'm simply too tired to argue now. We can argue later if you like."

When Blendel didn't respond, his wife got up and left the room. He stared at the door for a moment then picked up the phone and placed a call.

FORTY-FIVE

DELANEY

MY conversation with Warren Blendel encouraged rather than depressed me. It meant Katherine and the others were alive. When push comes to shove, there's not a great deal of difference between the way terrorists and thugs work. Both want you to believe they're all-powerful and control everything. The moment you buy into their bullshit you develop a bunker mentality. Decisions get made out of fear—fear of what might happen. Blendel could be playing me for a fool, but if he wanted the file, he would have to prove the women were alive and healthy.

I dialed Phil Thurman's number.

"Thurman."

"This is John Delaney. I thought you might like to know I just had a conversation with Warren Blendel about a missing file."

"Blendel called you directly? That doesn't sound like him."

"You'd know better than I would. The important thing is that he made a number of veiled references to Katherine, Sarah, and Jenny Pechorin, implying he has them."

"Damnit. That's not good, Delaney. Tell me what he said."

"It was nothing specific. Just a lot of crap about all the guests who will be at his party this weekend. He wanted me to talk to Katherine before his employees did. Then he asked if I knew about missing files and missing people. The message was clear enough."

"That's not enough for a search warrant, even if we believe—"

"I think he's bluffing; otherwise, he would have put one of them on the line for verification. He didn't. He just said if he got what he wanted, I'd get what I wanted."

Thurman was quiet for several seconds. "I need to give this some thought and maybe run it by a few other people before we decide how to respond."

"There's nothing to decide. I'll be on Martha's Vineyard tonight. Is there any news from Florida yet?"

"None so far. Our forensics team is going over the car now. We found some blood on the ground near where it went into the ditch. We also came up with a set of tire tracks belonging to another vehicle. This was probably the car that pulled them over."

"Is that it?"

"No, there's more. According to the techs, there was a noticeable smell of cordite inside the Lexus, indicated someone fired a gun. Hopefully, it was your girlfriend. One of our men spotted three sets of footprints leading away from the car toward an orange grove. Based on what you just told me, that's probably where Blendel grabbed them. I've called in more people to help, but . . ."

Two scenarios occurred to me. One was that there was a fight and Katherine and the other women had been forced from their car. The other was that they were running. The question now was did Blendel really have them or not?

Thurman's voice pulled me back to the conversation. "Delaney?"

"What?"

"If you won't wear a wire, we need to establish some kind of communication protocol."

"Negative to the wire. You said Blendel has experts who check for that and I won't do anything to jeopardize their lives, assuming he's actually holding them."

"But—"

"I'm not wearing one. We can use my cell phone to communicate. I'll set your number up on speed dial. If I need help, I'll press the button and you can send in the cavalry."

Thurman wasn't happy with the arrangement, but short of arresting me, there was nothing he could do. We agreed that his team in Florida would continue their search for the women in the hope they were still alive and on foot. At least until we learned otherwise. We also agreed I would phone every hour to confirm I was still in one piece. If I failed to check in, that would be his signal.

ENRICO'S is a hole in the wall on Eighth Avenue. It had been in the same location for as long as I could remember. In the past, after a Knicks game, my dad and I would catch a late dinner there on our way home. The food is always good and the atmosphere is comfortable. I kept the practice up with my son.

The only concession Enrico has made to the changing times has been to put four tables on the sidewalk in front of the restaurant, café style. They have brightly colored red-and-white checkered tablecloths and green umbrellas. Whether this attracts a more upscale crowd, I don't know. To me it looked like the same people were still eating there.

The moment I came in, the headwaiter, a man named Mario, saw me and his face lit up in a big smile.

"Hello, John," he said, giving my cheek an affectionate pat. "Your sister and her friend are in the back. Go sit. I'll bring you a nice tomato salad."

Mario knew all of his customers by name and could quote their favorite dishes from memory: Anderson—veal parmigiana; Mr. Hooks—shrimp scampi; Mrs. Hooks—a salad and part of Mr. Hook's scampi. Mine was the tomato salad. One day, I promised myself I'd order something different just to see his reaction. No point in being predictable.

Lissa and Brenda were waiting for me at a corner table. On the wall behind them were a series of photographs showing Enrico and Mario with various celebrities who had eaten there over the years. Frank Sinatra, Dean Martin, and Sammy Davis, Jr. were the most notable along with several others I couldn't name. My favorite is a photo of Kirk Douglas with his arm around Sophia Loren's shoulder. It was taken at a Hollywood party of some sort. Kirk's eyes are clearly looking down at Sophia's cleavage rather than at the camera. Understandable.

Lissa took my face in her hands and kissed me. I got the same greeting from Brenda. We Delaneys are a very touchy-feely family.

Brenda said, "If I ever leave your sister, you're the first person I'm calling."

"I'll be waiting."

"Ah, that's what they all say," she said with a dismissive gesture with her hand.

Brenda is an attractive brunette in her late thirties, the owner of two art galleries. One is in SoHo; the other is in Midtown. She was carrying a Judith Leiber purse that probably cost three thousand dollars. Her business suit was a designer model and its burgundy color matched the intricate beadwork Leiber is famous for. My education on women's fashion comes almost entirely from Katherine, who owns several of these purses, though God only knows why. At best a woman *might* be able to squeeze a small compact, a credit card, and maybe a cell phone into the largest model, assuming she pushes real hard. Katherine displays her purses in the bedroom like artwork and only brings them out for special occasions. I have a basketball signed by the '83 Knicks and a pair of Oscar De La Hoya's boxing shorts.

Brenda's marriage had fallen apart five years earlier when she decided that she liked women more than men. She and my sister became a couple shortly afterwards. She's protective of Lissa and fiercely loyal, qualities I hold in high regard.

While we were catching up on family news, Mario showed up with a basket of garlic bread, my tomato salad, and cappuccinos for everyone.

"He always brings us cappuccinos," Lissa said, watching him walk away. "I've been off them for three months but haven't had the heart to tell him."

"How come?"

"Low carbs. That's what the South Beach Diet recommends. I'm trying to lose six pounds."

Brenda rolled her eyes. Lissa worked out four days a week and had recently run in two marathons. She's been trying to lose the same six pounds since middle school. I considered telling her that she didn't need to drop any more weight, but it would only go in one ear and out the other.

"So what's up?" I asked

Brenda reached out and took Lissa's hand. "We want to make our relationship permanent. Lissa told me you said gay marriages aren't legal everywhere yet, but we want to know if there's anything else we can do."

"At the moment, the question is up in the air. From what I understand, a year or two ago the Massachusetts Supreme Court ruled same sex couples have the right to marry. They told their legislature to rewrite the law."

"So can't we just drive to Boston and get married there?" Brenda asked.

"It's not as simple as that. I'll have to check, but I imagine you'd need to establish residency first and then even if you did, I'm not sure New York recognizes the legality yet."

I went on to explain about full faith and credit and other constitutional intricacies that lawyers care about. The longer I talked, the more crestfallen they looked. I felt bad, but figured the best policy was to give it to them straight. You should pardon the expression.

Once the subject was exhausted, Lissa shifted topics to my mother's health. After listening to her for a minute it became apparent the situation wasn't nearly so serious as she had made out on the phone; nevertheless, I agreed to call my mom and urge her to make an appointment with her doctor for a checkup. She's one of the main reasons I still live in New York. Family is family, and you don't run out on them.

By way of history, my mother has been living in the same house in Queens for the past thirty years. We tried to get her to move after my dad's death, but she wouldn't hear of it. We tried it again after the doctors diagnosed her with Parkinson's and got the same response. The news came as a shock to everyone in the family because my mother has always been active and healthy as a horse. I read everything I could on the disease and found most of the symptoms can be controlled through medication. Lissa, however, is our family alarmist. She downloaded articles from the Internet, went to the library, and came up with a host of new treatments she wanted my mother to try. They ranged from traditional medicine to holistic crap that involved drinking a mixture of five special juices a day. It was all well-intentioned, and we took it in stride, my mother better than most.

Whenever I come down with a cold, I usually keep the news as far away from Lissa as possible. If not, I'm sure to be bombarded by a host of exotic cures. She once suggested numerology as a way to deal with allergies.

Over the years I've gotten used to my sister's peculiarities. The bottom line is that she has a good heart and I love her to death. This time, though, I was annoyed at the interruption in my day because of the situation with Katherine. Lissa was taking up the one thing I could least afford to waste just then—time.

"John?"

"What?"

"Are you listening to me?"

"Sure. Say it again."

A long-suffering sigh followed. "You're in another world. What are you doodling on that napkin?"

"Nothing. I'm working on a case and this date has been sticking in my mind for some reason."

Brenda asked, "What kind of case is it—something juicy?"

There was no point in worrying them, so I made up a story that was close to the truth.

Lissa frowned and tilted her head sideways to get a better look at the napkin. Then she glanced at Brenda and shook her head.

"My brother, the absent-minded professor," she said, motioning to me with her thumb. "Don't you know why that date looks familiar, silly?"

"No, but you're about to tell me."

"That's the date Dad was killed."

The moment she said it, time froze. I stared at the napkin in shock. It was fifteen years ago and I was still with police department when the call had come in. My captain buzzed me on the intercom and asked me to come to his office.

"You want both of us?" Mike Franklin called out to the speaker box.

"No, Mike, just Delaney."

My partner continued typing up the report he was working on. "What'd you do now?" he asked without looking up.

I shrugged. "No idea," then I pushed my chair back and got up. "I'll let you know in a minute."

I could still see the orange-and-black Halloween decorations hanging across the hallway as I walked to the captain's office. When he gave me the news, it felt like someone had yanked the rug out from under me. My father and three other people had been killed on the Cross Bronx Expressway. He was on his way home from work.

Even now, memories of riding to the scene with Mike Franklin are vivid. They've remained etched forever in my mind. Neither of us spoke. Uniform cops and ambulances were already on site by the time we arrived. It was the single worst moment of my life, almost as bad as when I had to break the news to my mother and the rest of our family. I remembered looking at my father's body on a stretcher and only half-believing my own eyes. Someone had put a sheet over him. I kept thinking, *Where did his life go? How could this happen?*

Over the years the thump in my stomach that comes when someone asks about my dad has retreated to a dull ache. But the sharper pain is still there—it always will be.

Brenda noticed my expression and placed a comforting hand over mine.

"I'm fine," I said, giving her a smile.

The visions dissolved into a haze and I looked back at the napkin. Until a second ago the date was just a disconnected fact in Sarah's odyssey. Then without warning the clouds parted. I now knew what was bothering me. I never got to eat my tomato salad. Instead, I grabbed my briefcase and pulled out Sarah's file. My eyes slid down the page until they came to rest on the third name there. The garlic rolls I consumed earlier suddenly felt like rocks in my stomach.

"What's wrong, John?" Lissa asked.

"I need to leave."

FORTY-SIX

KATHERINE

KATHERINE couldn't remember how long they had been running. Her sense of time had become muddled. The adrenaline rush that was sustaining her had long since worn off. It was replaced by a steely determination to keep everyone alive. Mixed with this was anger. The man stalking them was playing some kind of sick game. She knew Thurman and the local police had to be searching for them by now. The question was whether they would find them in time.

The albino seemed to know what she was thinking. Every time they tried to circle around him, he placed a series of shots at their heads or near their feet. During the last hour, the pattern had finally dawned on her. They were being herded deeper into the swamp. She needed to find a way out before he grew tired of the cat-and-mouse game.

A half hour earlier they crossed back under the highway using an old construction tunnel. Water trickled across its gravel bottom. The moment they slowed to catch their breath, two bullets hit the ground six feet away. Another struck the tunnel wall, splintering cement. A chip caught Sarah below her right eye and she began to bleed. To her credit she gasped but didn't cry out. All of them were wet, miserable, and on the verge of exhaustion.

Katherine motioned for the others to stop and crouched behind a tree, waiting for her heartbeat to slow. Jenny and Sarah were ten feet to her right. Both of them looked like hell. She probably did, too.

She could almost feel the albino out there, watching—biding his time. He could have killed them already, but for some reason he hadn't. His misses were no accidents; she was positive about that. Twice during the night he had deliberately shown himself against the moonlit landscape trying to draw her out. His purpose, she decided, was to instill panic and force her to waste her remaining bullets. Her mind worked rapidly, assessing their options, all of which were depressingly bleak. There was nothing but swamp in every direction.

Katherine peered into the darkness. Somewhere in the distance a fox barked. Closer, an owl's hoot drifted back on the wind. There were other things in the swamp—things she didn't want to think about.

Try as she might, she couldn't stop the old images from forming in her mind. Richard Jenks's face appeared as the flashbacks tried to break through the surface of her will. Along with Jenks came the faces of the five girls he had mutilated. Sometimes they would enter her sleep and sometimes they would come in broad daylight. They were so vivid, often they took her breath away and left her paralyzed.

In the hospital room where she lay recovering from the ordeal, her mother had once tried to make sense of what happened.

"There are monsters in the world, K.J. They feed on fear. If you give in and let the fear destroy you, they win. It's as simple as that. You fought him and I'm proud of you for that, so proud."

The flashbacks started soon after the hospital released her. They continued to plague her through the years. Medicine held them in check and allowed her to lead a normal life, but the pills were in the car and there was no way to reach them. She would have to do the best she could.

Delaney was aware of her history and had seen the attacks first-hand early in their relationship. He took them in stride the way he seemed to do with everything. In spite of this, their love had continued to grow. He was an anchor in a world of turmoil—solid and unshakable. That thought helped steady her. Katherine took a deep breath, letting it out slowly. The two girls with her were frightened and drained, not unlike the girls Richard Jenks had murdered. Somewhere in the stillness she could hear the albino whistling Jenks's tune. Sick bastard. Of course, it was no coincidence. He obviously knew about her past and was playing on it. Perhaps her mother was right: There were monsters in the world.

I won't make it easy for you. If you want us, you'll have to come and get us.

With an effort she shoved the fear backwards and gathered herself for the coming fight. She was so tired.

Better to dwell on other things.

Katherine thought of her children and of John Delaney. She'd been in love with him for over a year and was sure he felt the same way. He was so funny in the jewelry store that day they looked at engagement rings, trying to appear nonchalant when the saleslady told him how much a three-karat stone cost. *Thirty thousand dollars!* She would never have let him spend that much money. But his expression was priceless.

When he said, "We've just started looking," her heart had leapt. The possibility of getting married again had occurred to her more than once over the past year and she was pulled in two directions by it. A bitter divorce had left her shaken and disillusioned. No one needed that kind of pain. Marriage could be really hard if things didn't work out. It was hard even when they did. She didn't want to be hurt again. Letting down your defenses and trusting your heart to someone involved risk. Was she really ready for that now? Excellent question, Counselor. The urge was there—no denying it. She came up with a dozen arguments against marrying. But wasn't there a certain comfort in the familiar? In brushing up against your partner's leg in bed and just knowing he was there? And all those sounds that fill a house with two people in it. "Couple sounds," a girlfriend had once called them. She supposed there was a word for it. Oh, that's right—life.

Keep your mind on business, K.J. You can't get married if you're dead.

From her hiding place she scanned the landscape once again.

Nothing. The albino was too good, too patient.

She made eye contact with Sarah and Jenny and held a finger to her lips. Minutes passed. Though the temperature had dropped during the night, the air was still heavy with humidity. It hung about their faces like a damp cloth. When something crawled across the back of her ankle, Katherine jumped and barely stifled an involuntary gasp. There was water all around them. It percolated out of the ground, black and fetid. A slight movement in the reeds caught her attention and she saw an orange-and-black tail slither away.

Her grandfather had collected snakes and kept specimens in jars

filled with alcohol in his basement. When she was a young girl playing hide and seek with her cousins, she accidentally knocked two of the
jars over, sending them crashing to the ground. They shattered into a
thousand pieces, spilling their contents out. The cold dead eyes of two
snakes stared up at her and she began to scream. She still dreamt of
that from time to time.

After her grandfather died and his house was sold, her father
burned the jars in a trash can in the backyard. She could still remember hearing them explode in the fire's heat. Fighting down a
wave of revulsion she forced her mind back to their present situation. Above the tree line to the east the sky was beginning to lighten.
That was good and bad. They would be able to see better, but so
could he.

"Katherine," Jenny whispered. "Look over there. Can you see the
power lines?"

Katherine squinted into the dark toward the outline of a metal
tower rising up against the sky. It was perhaps two hundred yards
away.

"There's a shed at the bottom of the tower and a road of some
sort," Jenny said quietly. "I can just make them out."

Katherine cupped her hands around her eyes and looked harder.
A moment later, she left her hiding place and moved closer to the
girls.

"Maybe there's a phone we can use to call for help," Sarah whispered.

It was obvious they couldn't stay where they were much longer
because the mosquitoes and flies were eating them alive.

"Let's go," she said.

FORTY-SEVEN

JOSHUA

A SMILE appeared on Joshua's face when the three women began to move. He knew exactly where they were going.

"Run all you want, little girls," he chortled, repeating Jenks's words. "There's nowhere to hide . . . nowhere to hide."

Soon the circle would be complete. Women had run from him all his life. They were shallow bitches who were blind to his power. Perhaps he would take the two younger ones first and make Katherine watch, their screams filling her ears. It would give her a taste of what was to come. She shot him, and for that she had to pay—slowly, very, very slowly. With any luck, she might last two hours. Most didn't, but he would take his time with her.

The pain from his shattered collarbone laced through his shoulder when he adjusted his position. That didn't matter. He welcomed the pain and made it his ally. It would help keep his mind sharp. This was to be a special night. A slight sensation on the back of his hand caused him to look down and he saw that a blackfly had landed on his wrist and was feeding on him.

Quick as lightning he seized the fly between his thumb and forefinger. Joshua brought the struggling insect up to his face and stared at it. Then his fingers began to close. His own blood spurted from the fly's body as he crushed the life out of it.

Silently, he got to his feet and started toward the shed.

THERE was no lock on the door because there was no need for one. Neither was there a phone as the women had hoped. The only items inside the shed were a desk, a chair, and some tools employees of Florida's Central Power and Light Company used during their infrequent visits. A maintenance ledger sat on the desk. Its last entry had been made three months earlier. The building was a squat cinder block structure, perhaps twelve feet square. It contained no windows and the only way out was through the front door.

Sarah knew it was a wrong move the moment they entered. "We need to get out of here," she said.

"But why?" a voice behind her whispered. "I was hoping we could all get to know each other a little better."

Sarah spun around, flattening herself against the wall. Framed against the lightening sky was the silhouette of a man.

"We haven't done anything to you," Jenny said, raising Katherine's pistol. "I've got a gun. Leave us alone."

The only reply from the man was high-pitched laughter.

Jenny fired, missed, and fired again as Joshua darted sideways, avoiding the bullets. In the little room the explosions were deafening. Several clicks followed indicating the gun was now empty. It was all so simple.

Still smiling, Joshua slid his knife out of its sheath and stepped into the room. "Time to say good-bye, ladies. . . ."

The rest of his words trailed off and his expression gradually melted into one of confusion. In disbelief he looked down at the prongs of a pitchfork sticking out of his chest. This couldn't be happening. Not to him. He had planned every detail so carefully, so meticulously. Each contingency had been accounted for. He was a genius. Without warning, an image of Richard Jenks's face came into his mind. Was that a smirk on Jenks's face? His mouth opened and closed twice, but no sound came out. A second later, his knees collapsed and he fell face forward to the ground. The wooden handle of a pitchfork embedded in his back stood straight up, pointing at the ceiling.

"Good-bye," said Katherine.

FORTY-EIGHT

DELANEY

I T took less than fifteen minutes to fight my way through New York's Midtown traffic to my condo. I left the Jag at the entrance and told the doorman to watch it. Without waiting to hear his reply I headed for our basement and found the box I was looking for in my storage bin. Inside was an envelope faded with age.

I hadn't seen my father's death certificate in years. Behind that was the accident report made the day he was killed. My hands were shaking as I read the narrative.

Driver of Vehicle One, Detective Lt. William T. Delaney was found dead on the scene of a two-car accident by the undersigned officer. Responding to a call from central dispatch at 3:49 p.m., Patrolman Patrick Hayes and I arrived at approximately 4:05 p.m. In accordance with standard procedure we cordoned off the area and called for an ambulance along with the traffic fatality unit.

According to statements taken from witnesses, it appears the driver of Vehicle Two lost control of his utility truck and crossed into the lane striking Vehicle One and sending it into a cement divider.

Witnesses stated that Vehicle One burst into flames on impact. They pulled the driver to safety, but could find no pulse. Officer Hayes and I administered CPR to victim until EMS arrived without success.

The report went on for a full page and contained a diagram of the accident along with measurements taken by the officers of the skid marks and point of impact. Although my copy didn't contain them, the narrative stated that photographs had been made. I'd seen them once years ago and was happy not to relive the process. What I did want to see was the second page of the report.

In the section listed as VEHICLE TWO, William T. Rosetti was listed as the driver of the utility truck. Another piece of the puzzle clicked into place and that left me light-headed. *Rosetti* was the third name in Sarah's file. This would have been unsettling enough had my eye not come to rest on the section marked, WITNESSES. I read the last entry half out loud—*Hans Schiller,* and began to hyperventilate.

"When the Blendels take an interest in you, they treat you like part of the family." Jerry Barnwell's words came back to me again. *Part of the family.*

A red haze filled my vision and I lashed out with my fist, hitting the door to the storage bin. It sent a shock up my arm. The door banged closed and I was alone in the musty basement, my chest heaving. So many thoughts were going around in my head, it was impossible to separate them all . . . Katherine, my father, Blendel, Schiller. Amidst a rising tide of anger, two things were now clear: My father's death had been no accident and Warren Blendel was somehow connected with it. Why, I couldn't begin to guess.

That Blendel had chosen to involve me in Sarah's case made the least sense of all. I was the one person he'd want to keep as far away from her and the file as possible. Whatever the answer, it wasn't going to appear in the basement. I put the envelope away, stood up, and leaned my head against the locker, closing my eyes.

I had to learn who William T. Rosetti was and how he fit into the picture. Several scenarios ranging from conspiracy to coincidence occurred to me and each lasted less than thirty seconds. One chance occurrence I could write off—three were impossible. It was a little after noon by the time I got back on the road.

MIKE Franklin answered his phone right away. "Franklin speaking."

"Have I used up my share of favors yet?"

"Hey, buddy. How are you doing?"

"Have I used up my share of favors yet?" I repeated.

A brief pause followed. "Does this have something to do with what we were discussing yesterday?"

"It does."

My former partner swore under his breath. "Okay, John, what's up?"

"Do you recall the day my father was killed?"

"Your father?" he said, genuinely surprised. "Of course I do. How do you forget something like that? We were both there when the call came in. Why?"

"Because the driver of the truck that killed him was a fellow named William Rosetti. He was working for a company called Metro Sanitation in Brooklyn at the time."

"Yeah, your family filed suit against them and you settled out of court, right?"

"I'd like to see what you can find out about Rosetti and Metro Sanitation."

Mike's tone shifted into cop mode. "Why all the interest now? I thought Rosetti was killed in a street mugging a few months after the accident."

"He was. The lawyer we hired didn't investigate too deeply because he didn't have to. The case was a slam dunk. Metro's insurance company contacted us and admitted they were liable, so we went with the settlement."

"Then I don't get it," Mike said. "How does this tie into our earlier conversation?"

"Let's say I'm curious."

"Bullshit, John. This is me you're talking to. Either you explain why you're opening this can of worms again or I'm out. You never used to hide things. Besides, your mom's got Parkinson's now, doesn't she? Why go through all the aggravation?"

"This has nothing to do with my mother."

"Then I'm waiting."

"Are you where you can talk freely?"

"We're fine. Now, what the fuck is going on?"

"Do you remember I told you the reason Sarah O'Connor left town was because Uncle Nick had set her up with a scholarship? What I didn't say was that Sarah was working for the U.S. Attorney's office at the time. She came across a closed file with her father's name on it that contained allegations of bribe-taking."

"I don't believe it. I know Frank O'Connor and so do you."

"I'm not saying I buy it either. For a little while, Sarah kept what she found to herself, but eventually it got too much and she went to Nick. He told her to keep the information quiet until he could check it out. A few days later he gets back to her and tells her there's a good chance the feds are about to open the case against Frank again. Then he drops a suggestion that if the file were to disappear, it might fix everything up. You follow?"

"I'm with you," Mike said. "Keep going."

"Within a week, Uncle Nick pops up again. This time he tells Sarah he knows about a scholarship to Emory University which conveniently get her out of town."

"I see."

"So Sarah and the file go south. The plan was for Nick and his people to grab it in Atlanta, but Sarah threw a monkey wrench in the works by faking her own death."

"Jesus. Why would she do that?"

"I can't get into the details now, but she had a good reason for it. You'll just have to trust me with this. I gave her my word."

"All right. Keep going."

I continued, "Here comes the interesting part. She showed me the file a couple of days ago and I read something in it that bothered me, only I couldn't figure out what. It was like an itch you can't scratch. Until a half hour ago I was still in the dark . . . until I saw the accident report on my dad again."

The line was silent as Mike digested this. "All right, Rosetti's name shows up in the missing file and on the accident report as the guy who killed your father. Let's say I believe you. What do you want me to do?"

"I want you to check out Rosetti—anything you can find on him. The report also lists a man named Hans Schiller among the witnesses."

"And?"

"I met Mr. Schiller yesterday at Warren Blendel's office. He's a former Interpol agent who now heads their security team."

"What?"

"I swear to God."

"I'll be a motherfucker."

This time the silence that followed was so thick you could cut it with a knife.

"All right, I'm on it," Mike said. "I liked your old man, John. He was a decent guy, a real decent guy. If the O'Connors had anything to do with his death, I'll personally take them down. You have my word on it."

"At this point, I'm positive that Nick is dirty. I just don't know about Frank yet."

"You leave that to me. Any news on your lady friend?"

"Not so far."

Mike let out a long breath. "What's the best way to get in touch with you?"

"By cell. I'm on the way to Martha's Vineyard to meet with Blendel."

"Are you nuts?"

"No choice, partner. Phil Thurman and I talked it over and he'll have two agents in the area if I need help."

"*If you need help?* Blendel will drop you in the ocean ten seconds after he gets his hands on that file."

"There's no other way to handle it if I want to see Katherine and the others again. I'm the only chance they have. Blendel invited me because he thinks I have the file. We're supposed to negotiate."

"Oh, that's just fuckin' wonderful," Mike said. "Give me Thurman's number. Maybe we can run this together."

"That won't work. If someone else suddenly enters the picture, it might spook Blendel."

"Shit. Is there any way I can talk you out of this?"

"None."

There was a long pause on the other end of the line.

"Do you mind if I ask you something?"

"Go ahead."

"What do you plan to do when you come face-to-face with Blendel, given what you just told me?"

I had been asking myself the same question for the past hour and found that my hand was resting on the 9 mm Sig in my hip holster.

FORTY-NINE

KATHERINE

THE service road only took them deeper into the swamp. After walking for three hours, Katherine knew they were going in the wrong direction. The "road" was little more than a dirt track. Any hope of reaching civilization gave way to anxiety as the sun rose higher in the sky. With it came the humidity. Sweat was rolling freely down her back and arms. Out of the corner of her eye she glanced at Jenny and Sarah and wished that she were twenty-four again. Both seemed to be tolerating the heat better than she was.

They left Joshua Silver where he fell, but took his gun for protection in case any of his friends decided to come looking for him. Katherine had never killed a man before, though the thought had crossed her mind once or twice during her divorce. Doing it, though, was far different from thinking about it. She needed to know who Joshua really was. Obviously, he was not a police officer. He had no identification and almost nothing on him besides his gun, some folding money, and a cell phone. She supposed the police would determine his identity in time.

No feelings at his death touched her. In fact, she felt nothing at all, except that she was tired, hungry, and scared. Their immediate concern now was survival. The swamp seemed endless.

She tried placing a call on Joshua's phone but found the keypad had been locked. As quickly as hope soared, it returned to the reality of their situation. A little earlier, they had come across a canal and stopped to rest. The dirt track simply ended there. A discussion ensued among the women as to whether they should follow the canal or backtrack. Sarah thought the canal would lead them to civilization. Jenny wasn't certain.

The argument was settled when Katherine noticed a long snout and wide-set pair of eyes silently watching them in the water twenty feet away. Slowly, she raised the rifle to her shoulder.

"Jenny, I want you to move away from the bank."

The expression on Jenny's face turned to shock. "Katherine, what are you—"

Three sharp cracks rang out in rapid succession as the alligator launched itself out of the water with a roar. A split second later its head exploded. The creature fell dead five feet from where the girls were standing. Jenny screamed and Sarah lost her footing, fell, and went scrambling backwards on her hands and heels, putting as much distance between herself and the gator as she could.

"Sorry. I didn't have time to warn you."

Sarah's eyes were as wide as saucers and she seemed unable to move. "Maybe following the canal isn't such a good idea after all," she said to Katherine. She looked nervously at the water. "Do you suppose he has any relatives around?"

Jenny reached out and helped her friend to her feet. "We don't have alligators in Russia, only bears and KGB."

Katherine glanced at their surroundings. "I don't think we'll find any KGB here. I'm not so sure about the bears, though."

"You don't know KGB," Jenny said.

Katherine smiled and patted the rifle. "We'll be okay as long as I have Ol' Betsy."

"Ol' Betsy?"

"The name of Davy Crockett's rifle," Katherine explained.

"Ah . . . I never saw *Jaws*."

Katherine opened her mouth to reply and closed it again. Instead she turned to Sarah. "I'd like to ask you something, if you don't mind."

"Sure."

"I understand why you took the file and about Cloudland Canyon. But exactly what did you plan to do, once you were officially dead, I mean?"

"Andre told me he knew how to obtain a false identity. I thought could start over someplace new."

"And do what? Getting a new identity is one thing; it's another coming up with a whole set of college grades and SAT scores. How did you plan on managing that? Or did you just give up on becoming a lawyer?"

"I don't know. I guess I wasn't thinking that far ahead. I just wanted to get away from them."

Katherine nodded. "Yes, you mentioned 'them' at Jenny's apartment—the men who came to see you. If I'm remembering correctly, you made one film with Andre because he drugged you and a second one for 'them' as insurance that you were acting in good faith."

"That right."

"But there were *four* films, Sarah, not two. I've risked my life for you and so has John Delaney. Maybe it's time you told me the truth. I think I'm entitled to it."

Sarah stared down at her feet for a long moment. "Each time I made an excuse for not turning over the file, I only made the situation worse—*my* situation, that is. I thought if the films were ever revealed, I could say they weren't me, that they were made with trick photography or something. I also thought it was possible the men who came to me might be from our own government and were trying to trick me so they could arrest my father. Remember, my uncle told me the case had been reopened. I needed to be sure.

"When everything is collapsing around you, you don't think clearly, but it was the best I could do the. Each time I stalled, they asked me to make another movie to show I was *sincere*. I was trying to be clever, but all I did was paint myself into a corner. You can't imagine what it was like."

"No, I can't," Katherine said quietly. At least this version of the story made a little more sense. Technically, Sarah might look like a woman, but she was barely twenty-three. Not very long to learn about all the manipulators and bullies in the world. It was a pity. One tragedy had compounded another. She couldn't wait to meet Warren Blendel, who seemed to be at the center of the web.

"We'd better get moving," she said.

FIFTY

SCHILLER

A THOUSAND miles away, Warren Blendel sat on the balcony of his summer home eating breakfast. Hans Schiller was with him. Schiller was dressed in a pair of loose-fitting khaki pants and a shirt of the same color.

"Any word from Joshua yet?" Blendel asked.

"No, but I'm not worried. He's probably unwinding."

Blendel grimaced. He had seen examples of the way Joshua unwound. "He knows to contact us, doesn't he?"

"Yah, but once this affair is over, I think we must separate ourselves from Mr. Silver. The man is quite insane. You understand that, don't you?"

"One problem at a time," Blendel replied.

"May I ask a question?"

Blendel's first reaction was to say no, because questions made him uncomfortable. Instead, he said, "Of course."

"Why have you kept Joshua around this long? I know you two read together, but surely that can't be the only—"

Blendel held up a hand to forestall the rest of the inquiry. "Joshua has been useful to me in the past. As to what he reads, knowing a person's taste in books can tell you a great deal about them. Information is always helpful."

"I see."

"What if he doesn't get them, Hans?"

Schiller seemed unconcerned. "If he doesn't, the swamp certainly will. The file was not in the car when I searched it, so our Professor Delaney is the only one who can have it. If he wants to see his lady friend again, he'll cooperate. To do this, we must make him believe she is our guest."

"This is such a goddamn mess," Blendel said in disgust, pushing his plate of grapefruit away.

"Yah, coincidence can be strange," Schiller agreed. "Who knew Frank O'Connor would pick Delaney to help with the girl's estate? It's odd the way things work out, no?"

"Very. Unfortunately, it's my ass on the line. And your ass, too, if Delaney ever makes the connection."

"Unlikely," Schiller replied. "To remember the name of a witness thirteen years after the accident would be quite remarkable."

"You know what I'm talking about, Hans. That's only one facet of the problem."

A pair of cold blue machine gunner's eyes regarded Warren Blendel for a moment; then Schiller took the 9 mm Kurz out from his shoulder holster, opened the chamber, and looked down the barrel.

"We'll deal with it if the subject comes up. In the meantime, you need to pull yourself together. You'll be the one talking with Mr. Delaney and you must be convincing."

"I'm always the one," Blendel muttered. He shifted in his seat and stared across the marshland at the ocean.

"Your wife has been giving you a hard time again?"

Blendel gave him a sour look. "It's nice that you're so concerned."

Schiller ignored the comment. "Anyone can panic under the right circumstances. Why don't you get rid of her and pull yourself together, man? She's a complete bitch. Surely, you know this."

Blendel knew exactly what Schiller was referring to. It had been five years since the first panic attack had struck him and it had come at the worst possible time. They had just caught one their employees skimming the weekly numbers take and Blendel had decided to make an example of the man in case any of his coworkers had similar aspirations. They arranged to meet him at their Bronx office and Linda insisted on coming along. Her curiosity in such matters had always been morbid.

After the man confessed his sins, Blendel picked up a baseball bat from his desk and was about to bring it down on the man's head when he froze. At the time, it felt like he was having a heart attack. Schiller finished the job with a single gunshot. He could still remember the look on Linda's face, a mixture of fascination, contempt, and shame for her husband.

A doctor was sent for and after a brief examination declared that there was nothing wrong with Blendel *physically*. He prescribed medication for a panic attack and went back to his home in Suffolk County. Shortly after the incident a change also took place in Linda Blendel who began to grow more and more distant from her husband. If Schiller dined with them at breakfast, her eyes were constantly on him, appraising and measuring. Her glances, subtle at first, became bolder as the days went on.

"Has anyone ever told you you have big shoulders, Hans?" she asked one morning, right in front of her husband.

Schiller smiled and turned his palms up, attempting to play the comment off. "Perhaps . . . I don't recall."

"And you have a very strong jawline. That signifies strength, you know."

"Oh, yah, this is me," Schiller replied, feigning indifference to what she was doing.

At first Blendel ignored, or pretended to ignore, the exchanges. Schiller was a physically imposing man who had had more than his share of women, but he would have been the first to admit he was no matinee idol. Madam Blendel was merely amusing herself, turning the knife in the wound.

Blendel suffered his wife's comments with a mixture of mounting anger and shame. They spoke about it, quarreled about it, and relations between them were never quite the same again. For a while he thought she might lose interest in her game. She didn't. And in the years that followed, his panic attacks increased in frequency. The medicines he took were ineffective to control them and he lived a life consumed by fear. Fear that his enemies would learn of his ailment and fear his own associates would find out and take advantage of it. If only the past would let him go. But it was not to be. The inexorable march toward an end he very much wanted to escape continued unchecked.

Blendel shook away the depressing thoughts and asked, "Have you and Linda worked everything out regarding John Delaney?"

"She talked to me earlier about the possibility of other copies. At some point I'll have to get him alone and ask. Hopefully, he made none and just wants the women back. If this is the case, either Linda or I can discuss a trade with him, but it would be better coming from you," Schiller said, patting Blendel on the shoulder. "You're quite good with people. Why don't we go down to the lake and do a little bird shooting? Nothing like that to get the blood pumping, eh? What do you say?"

"We could go shooting," Blendel replied. "It might be a good—"

He didn't finish his sentence. Linda Blendel had just walked out onto the terrace. She was wearing a pair of skintight black pants, gold high-heeled shoes, and a gold silk blouse that wrapped in the front. The blouse was cut very low to reveal her cleavage.

"Good morning everyone," she said in a cheery voice.

"Good morning," both men answered.

She gave her husband a perfunctory peck on the cheek and deliberately trailed her fingers across the back of Schiller's neck before taking a seat.

"Maybe we'll do it another day," Blendel said to Schiller.

"What were you boys talking about?" Linda asked.

"I was just asking Herr Blendel if he would like to do a little shooting before our guest arrives."

"Wonderful, I'll come, too. I'd love to see Warren shoot something."

"There's no need of that," Blendel said.

"I wouldn't miss it for the world. I could bring my own gun for a backup."

Blendel glowered at her. "We won't need a backup. It's just bird shooting."

"Oh, that's right," Linda said, pouring herself a cup of coffee. "Birds don't shoot back, do they?"

Blendel pushed his chair away from the table and got up. "If you'll excuse me, I have work to do."

"Don't forget to take your medicine, dear," Linda called after him.

Schiller listened to the exchange and said nothing.

"What?" Linda asked when she saw him staring at her.

"Was that really necessary?"

"I guess not," she said with a sigh. "It would be just as well if

Warren stays out of the picture once Mr. Delaney arrives. He'll only mess things up."

"Your husband is a very intelligent man and he knows people. It's we who should remain in the background."

"Don't tell me you're frightened, too?"

Schiller's cold gaze fixed on her. "Fear has nothing to do with it. We're trying to achieve a result, not play a game. This is business."

"What do you think will happen if Professor Delaney makes the connection that you were one of the witnesses to his father's death?"

"I really don't know."

"But does it bother you, Hans? Warren is positively beside himself. He barely slept a wink last night."

Schiller was silent for a long moment. "No, it doesn't bother me. If Delaney finds out about Rosetti and connects him to us, the situation could become sticky. For the moment, I'm only a witness and the world is full of strange occurrences. I suppose we will cross that bridge once we come to it."

"Then let's hope he never finds out. It would be a shame to lose someone with your talents."

"I can always find employment elsewhere. The question is, what would you do? I don't believe they're hiring models your age anymore."

A faint smile touched the corners of Linda Blendel's mouth. She reached out and ran the back of her hand across Schiller's cheek. "Rough," she observed. "You should get a new razor. I believe I'll handle the negotiations. As you say, we don't want things becoming . . . unraveled."

"Once again, it is more appropriate to leave this to your husband."

"Why? Because he's a man? I know every aspect of Warren's businesses and I'm not likely to fall apart at the last moment. Between the two of us, we can certainly handle one law professor."

Schiller had thought about this, too. Ever since that fool Frank O'Connor insisted on asking his dead partner's son to help with the girl's estate, he had been studying Delaney. This was one reason he had kept alive as long as he had. Never underestimate an opponent.

John Delaney was tough, intelligent, *and* he had a personal interest in getting the Adams woman back.

"Perhaps," he said.

Linda laced her fingers together and watched him over the top of them. "You seem a bit distracted this morning."

"Distracted? No. I'm merely thinking."

Linda sighed, pushed her chair back from the table and got up. "Well, don't think too hard, my dear. It's not your strong point. I'll see you later."

"Before you go, I'd like to ask you something. I posed this question to your husband a while ago and his answer was, shall we say, a trifle evasive."

"Concerning what?"

"Our friend Joshua. I asked Herr Blendel why he keeps such a man around. He's volatile and mentally, well . . ." Schiller made a see-saw motion with his hand to illustrate.

"Joshua and Warren have a special relationship."

"Yes, I know. This is what Herr Blendel said. I also know they were both abused as children and Herr Blendel's son died in a car crash. Perhaps he sees Joshua as a substitute."

Linda's face reflected her surprise. "Warren told you that?"

"No, I learned this from my talks with Joshua."

Linda's brows came together and she turned to look at the door her husband had just gone through.

"He's really quite despicable," she said.

"Explain."

"To begin with, Warren's father was a hardware salesman. He died of a stroke when Warren was fifteen. I've never heard him mention anything about abuse. And as for his *son* being killed in a car crash, that would be somewhat difficult, since Warren's only child is a daughter. She lives in Switzerland and hasn't spoken with him in years. They're estranged."

Schiller blinked and stared at Linda for several seconds as her words settled in. Then he began to chuckle to himself.

"What's so funny?"

"Your husband is quite a fascinating man. Did you know that?"

"I thought so once, but he's just a shell at this point. If he didn't have us here to run everything for him, his entire operation would fall apart. Warren is pathetic."

"You underrate Herr Blendel. He is a great deal more complex than you, or I for that matter, have given him credit for."

Linda responded with a dismissive hand gesture. "What are you talking about?"

"Just this. Everything about Joshua comes down to control. He *needs* to control others. If he can't, it's almost physically painful to him."

"So?"

"All this time I have thought it was Joshua who was taking advantage of Herr Blendel's generosity. But I think now it may be the other way around. All your husband would tell me was that Joshua has been very useful to him. Ironic, is it not?"

"What's ironic, Hans?"

"The master of control is the one being manipulated—fascinating."

"Warren isn't that smart," Linda replied. She stood up and carefully smoothed her blouse, then removed a compact from her purse and examined her reflection in the mirror. "He's just a scared little man, trying to hang on to what he's got left. It's up to you and me now. I'll see you for dinner."

Schiller watched Linda walk back to the house and disappear through the patio door. Perhaps she was right, but his instincts were telling him different. No, he decided. He had missed something with Warren Blendel, a quality he should have seen earlier. A comment his father once made surfaced in his mind.

People are like an onion. They have layers. Some are obvious and some are hidden. A wise man will remember this. When you deal with them you'll find even the dullest has more than one side. Disregard this at your peril.

FIFTY-ONE

DELANEY

THE drive to New England took longer than I expected. In the New York area you never really break free of the city's traffic pattern, which seems to extend as far up as Massachusetts. I printed directions to Martha's Vineyard off the computer and read them over with a grimace. It looked like something Ferdinand Magellan had put together after a long night drinking. As a result, I decided to do things the old-fashioned way. I hauled out my map and plotted the course. It probably saved me an hour's driving . . . maybe more.

I pulled in to the town of New Bedford at around 5 p.m. and spotted a street sign near the highway exit that read VISITOR INFORMATION CENTER. Six more signs and an equal number of turns finally brought me to an old red brick building near the wharf. A plaque outside declared the center had once been the home of the OLD FISH AUCTION HOUSE and was constructed during the Roosevelt administration's Works Project. It looked it.

Three friendly women greeted me in chorus as I walked through the door, all asking if they could help at the same time. Maybe people here do everything in stereo, I thought. I picked the nearest lady because she reminded me of my third-grade teacher, Ms. Starr.

"Can you tell me the best way to get to Martha's Vineyard?"

"Why, the ferry, of course," she replied. The other two nodded in agreement.

"Great. How do I find it?"

She pulled out a map and used a green Magic Marker to highlight the route for me. "Just leave your car in the parking lot and take the shuttle bus. Which boat do you want?"

"Uh . . . the one that floats the best, I suppose."

No smile . . . nothing. Just three puzzled looks in return.

"Charlotte means you have a choice," the woman on the left said. "We have a slow ferry and a fast ferry—that's what people around here call them. I have schedules for both."

"Yes, we have schedules for both," the woman on the right echoed.

"What's the difference?"

"About twelve dollars and one hour," Charlotte answered.

I smiled. "Then I guess I'll take the fast one."

All three exchanged glances. Then, for some reason, they went into a huddle over the schedule, studying it while I waited, bemused. After some whispering back and forth, Charlotte turned to me.

"You just missed it," she said. "The last one left twenty minutes ago."

I counted to five mentally. "Fine, then guess I'll take the slow ferry. Is that still running?"

"Oh my, yes," said Charlotte.

"Definitely," said the second woman.

Another schedule materialized from beneath the counter and they all consulted it again.

"It leaves in thirty minutes," the woman on the left told me. "You can still make it. The ticket booth is right there on the wharf."

I LEFT my Jag in the parking lot with a high school attendant who looked up from an algebra book he was studying and said, "Whoa, cool wheels, dude. Is this like a Maserati or something?"

"No, it's like a Jaguar XK-150."

"Awesome. How old is it, man?"

"1961."

"No way."

"Way. Is there any chance it'll still be here when I get back?"

"Oh, definitely. I'll tell Shaun to keep a special eye on it. He comes on after me. He's really into cars, too. That's mine over there in the corner."

I followed his glance to a late-model black Honda Civic sitting by the fence. It had the largest air spoiler attached to the trunk and the brightest chrome rims I had ever seen.

"Those are spinner rims, dude. They set me back almost five hundred bucks."

"Awesome."

Thanks to the shuttle I arrived on the pier five minutes later and located the ticket booth. The "slow ferry" had a sign next to it that read:

STOP AND SMELL THE ROSES
IT ONLY TAKES AN HOUR MORE
SLOW FERRY–$24 FAST FERRY–$34
COMPARE AND SAVE

Not a brilliant advertising strategy, but honest. And since I had no other choice, I bought a ticket and walked up the gangplank with twenty other people, two dogs, and three teenagers who were carrying their bikes.

The ferry was an ungainly-looking affair in need of a fresh coat of paint. Two inside decks had booths and tables. There was also something they called a "sun deck" where I supposed I could relax and smell the roses, if there were any. What I really wanted, though, was time to think. I'd done plenty of that on the drive up and hadn't been able to get Katherine and the other women off my mind. Frankly, I was worried sick about them and ready to hand the file over to Blendel if he would show me they were all safe and unharmed. At some point during the trip I also reached the conclusion that not only Nick but his brother Frank had been involved in my father's death. Frank was one of a few people who knew my dad's route home and the time he left the office that day. I didn't know how they had managed it or why, but I intended to find out.

I leaned back against a wooden bench and stared across the water as the town of New Bedford fell away. Gulls soared above the harbor, and ships with black-and-white masts moved gently on the current. We crawled past large vessels with rusted hulls and a small stone lighthouse that looked like it had been built around the turn of the century. Factory smokestacks and a Ferris wheel stood out against the sky on the far shore. Once we cleared the headland the wind kicked up and the ferry began to pitch and bounce over the whitecaps. Houses and commercial development appeared and disappeared as spray broke across the ship's bow. It splashed the ferry's windows and soaked a few of the more adventurous passengers who were hanging out on the catwalk. The locals, I noted, were staying inside with their crossword puzzles and newspapers. I went in to join them.

After a few minutes, the captain came on over the loudspeaker and told us where to find lifejackets in the "unlikely event of an emergency." No one appeared to be listening. I found an empty seat near the bow and watched the ferry slide past a number of forlorn strips of land. There were only a few houses and one or two of the islands had lighthouses on them. Had the circumstances been different, I might have enjoyed the ride, but I was too preoccupied with trying to fit all the pieces of the puzzle together. I finally gave up, took a photo out of my wallet, and studied at it. It was taken in Portofino shortly after Katherine and I had met. We had others and there was nothing very special about this one. She was simply standing behind me with her arms around my chest and I was looking back at her. We were both smiling at a joke I couldn't remember just then. I don't know why I decided to carry this particular one in my wallet. I suppose I like it because it's natural and doesn't seem posed. I traced my finger along Katherine's jawline and closed my eyes.

The sound of another person taking a seat behind me pulled me back to the present.

"Please don't turn around, Professor. There's a newspaper on the seat next to you. Why don't you pick it up and pretend to read it?"

"And you would be?"

"A friend. My name is Stanley Curtain. I'm an FBI agent. Phil Thurman asked me to touch base with you."

I started to turn to see who I was talking to.

"Uh-uh," he cautioned. "Keep facing forward. We don't know who else is on this tub. By the way, this is my fourth trip today. I'm here with another agent, Marcia Mazurski—she's in the ladies' room at the moment, probably throwing up. Apparently, shipboard travel doesn't agree with her either."

"Sorry."

"Part of the job risks," Curtain replied. "Now, how about picking up that paper?"

I picked it up. "If you wanted to get in touch with me, why didn't you just call? Thurman has my cell phone number."

"We didn't want to risk it, particularly since your apartment was searched. Blendel employs a lot of very sharp people and it's possible your cell phone might not be safe. Our guys forgot to check it when they were there."

"Great. Before we go any further, let's see some proof that you're from the Bureau."

"Fair enough," said Curtain. "I'd rather not pass my ID back and forth, this being out in the open and all. Maybe this'll help. A couple of hours earlier you called your former partner and asked him to check on a man named William Rosetti. You also spoke with Senior Agent Thurman at your home last night and asked him to let you know as soon as he heard anything about Katherine Adams, Sarah O'Connor, and Jennifer Pechorin."

My chest constricted at the mention of Katherine's name and I braced myself for the bad news.

"And you're here to tell me, aren't you?"

"I am, and some other things as well."

"Go on."

"We picked up Ms. Adams and the other two women about four hours ago. They're all right, except for some dehydration, bug bites, and a few minor scratches. They're in protective custody in Orlando."

I squeezed my eyes shut as relief washed over me. "I want to speak to her."

"Understandable. Unfortunately, there's no cell phone service on this boat. At least my phone doesn't work. I don't know about yours, but I imagine it's the same. If you'll stay calm for a few minutes and hear me out, I have a few important tidbits to pass along to you. Afterwards, I'll see if we can arrange that phone call. Deal?"

"Deal. What do you have?"

"A bad fuckin' headache and an upset stomach from the food here," Curtain replied. "Apart from that, Mike Franklin and Agent Thurman have located a gentleman named William Rosetti."

"Located?" I said, twisting around in my seat. "If you mean his grave, I don't know what good that will—"

"Please face forward, Professor. William Rosetti is very much alive. At least the reports of his death have been greatly exaggerated."

My mouth fell open and I stared at him for several seconds before I turned back around. It felt like my head was spinning. "What the hell are you talking about? Rosetti was killed—"

"I'm saying Mr. Rosetti's death was faked—at least that's our theory. But I'm getting a little ahead of myself. Turns out he was arrested nine months ago in Philadelphia on a possession charge. He made bond and is presently awaiting trial. We've asked the Philadelphia PD to pick him up. They may even have him already."

For several seconds I had the sensation of being in free fall. My world had just been turned upside down. Of all the things I expected to hear—prepared myself to hear—this was positively the last. My joy at learning that Katherine and the others were alive gradually was replaced by something bordering on rage. Rosetti had driven the truck that killed my father and he did it on Warren Blendel's orders.

"Oh, God," I whispered to myself as a long-closed wound in my heart opened again.

"Look, I know how you feel, and we're going to nail Rosetti's ass to the wall. That you can make book on. The FBI doesn't like cop killers any more than the NYPD does. What's important now is that we tie Blendel into it."

I spun around to face him. "At the risk of offending you, Mr. Curtain, you don't have the slightest idea how I feel. This changes—"

"Jesus, Delaney, they said you were a smart guy. Turn the fuck around and start acting like one or you're going to blow our cover."

I got to my feet. "I don't give a goddamn about your cover and I'm through playing spy games."

A pale-looking middle-aged woman dressed in jeans and a yellow pullover was coming up the steps. She had salt-and-pepper hair and was about twenty pounds overweight. We made eye contact. The pleasant expression on her face promptly evaporated the moment she saw us speaking. She glanced around to see if there were any passengers nearby. This, I presumed, was Agent Marcia Mazurski.

At the stern of the ship four teenagers were watching a foam trail the ferry was leaving on the water. They were laughing and talking and didn't seem concerned with our conversation. Curtain noticed his partner standing there and shook his head.

"John Delaney, meet Marcia Mazurski."

"Pleased to meet you," I said.

"I'd say the same," she replied, "but you're putting our lives at risk. My kids won't appreciate that." She walked directly past me to the ship's rail and looked at an island we were passing, then took out one of those tiny digital cameras from her purse and began taking photos. For all I knew she might have been doing just that.

"All right, I get the picture," I said, sitting back down. "But you just dropped a bomb on me." I picked the newspaper up and pretended to read it.

"Sorry to have upset you," Curtain said. "And believe me, I *do* know how you feel and what a shock this must be. The question now is how are you going to handle it?"

Several seconds passed before I reined my emotions in. "What do you want me to do?"

"Obviously, we need to build a case against Blendel and Schiller. We'd like you to meet with Blendel as planned and see how far he'll go to get the file back. You understand where I'm coming from?"

"I think so."

It was now obvious why Warren Blendel was so anxious to get his hands on Sarah's file. William Rosetti was the link that could tie him to the death of a cop. After the accident they counted on Rosetti to disappear, but something had gone wrong.

"Let's say I keep my meeting with Blendel. Thurman told me his home is constantly monitored for electronic surveillance. That knocks out using a wire."

"Right," Marcia said from the rail, "but we have something you can use. She held up a Panerai watch with a black face. "This not only tells time, it's a microrecorder. Not very high tech, but it will get the job done. If you can maneuver Blendel into talking about the kidnappings, we'll nail him. You understand making a recording like this has to come from you as a private citizen. Officially, we're not involved."

"Got it. I can also testify if he tells me anything of substance," I said.

"Except that you have a personal interest in the case," Marcia pointed out. "At the moment we're on pretty thin ice. We don't have enough to tie Blendel to the death of your father, Andre Rostov, or the attacks on Ms. Adams and her companions. He's always one step back."

"What if you pick up Nick O'Connor up and sweat him? The man's definitely dirty."

"It's unlikely Deputy Chief O'Connor will talk," Curtain said. "Whatever he is, he's not stupid. Our only hope is getting Rosetti to crack or what you can finesse out of Blendel."

I held Marcia's eyes for several seconds before she looked away. Her story about recording my conversation with Blendel was pure bullshit. Without a warrant it was illegal as hell. The best they could hope for was an exception in the rules of evidence that says if a private individual makes a recording of another, the government can use it at trial, *provided* they weren't involved in fostering an illegal act. All I had to do was keep my mouth shut—and expose myself to a criminal charge in the process.

I didn't have to give the matter a lot of thought. I wanted Blendel— wanted him so much I was willing to take the risk.

FIFTY-TWO

DELANEY

JERRY Barnwell was waiting for me in a black Hummer. He gave me a cheery wave. I waved back. Ten minutes earlier I had stepped into the ferry's restroom and placed a call to Katherine using Stan Curtain's cell phone.

Life is often defined by special moments. Some are good—some are bad. This was one of the good ones, though not completely. The moment I heard Katherine's voice a wave of relief washed over me. She told me what happened in the swamp and it amazed me once again at just how tough and resourceful she could be. I shouldn't have been surprised, because I'd caught glimpses of that side of her a year earlier. Jenny and Sarah were unhurt except for some nicks and dings. Katherine told me she had declined Thurman's offer of protection and would be flying to New York the following morning. We had no time for a lengthy talk, but it was enough to let her know what our plan was for Messrs. Blendel, Schiller, and the O'Connor brothers. She was adamantly opposed to my getting anywhere near them, let alone recording a private conversation. The phone call ended with us both upset. It was the first time we had fought in a long while.

Barnwell and I shook hands. He took my briefcase from me and tossed it on the backseat.

"Good to see you again, John."

"You, too. Just one big happy family, right?"

"Huh? Oh, sure."

"Tell me, Jerry, are you in on this, too?"

Barnwell started the engine, put the car in gear, and pulled out into the street. "What are you talking about?"

I noticed he was sweating again.

"It's a simple question. I asked if you're in on this, too. Is that confusing?"

Jerry gave a nervous laugh. "Clarification   se, Counselor."

"All right, I'll make it simple, so listen c   .ıy. If I find that one hair on Katherine Adams's head has been hurt, I'll find you and I'll do a lot worse."

"Who's Katherine Adams? And what the hell are you talking about? I do legal work for the Blendels, nothing more."

"I hope you're telling the truth, Jerry. I really do. Kidnapping, extortion, and murder are serious charges. And when they involve my friends, I tend to take it personally."

Jerry's face turned a deeper shade of red and he pulled his car onto the shoulder of the road. "Look, I do legal work for Warren, period. My job is to keep him straight and I'm good at it. That's why he pays me what he does. I wasn't born last night and I know he's into some shady stuff, but I keep my nose clean."

His speech sounded nearly as convincing as the act I was putting on. If we were hooked to lie detectors, the needles would have jumped off the chart. I had no doubt everything I was saying would get back to Warren Blendel, which was precisely what I wanted.

"If I were you, I'd have a long talk with my boss—real soon. Then I'd get as far away from him as I could. Like I said, if anything's happened to Katherine Adams, I'm coming after him and anyone else who gets in my way."

The rest of the ride passed in silence. My speech wasn't much of a stretch because I *was* livid. I had no illusions about my acting ability, but this was the plan Stan Curtain, Marcia Mazurski, and I had cooked up. My job was to play the part of a distraught lover and make them believe I really thought Katherine was their prisoner.

We finally pulled up to Blendel's summer home, a sprawling ranch-type mansion set well off the main road. I caught Barnwell's slight shake of the head to Schiller as he approached the vehicle.

"Herr Professor," he said, extending his hand. "We're glad you could make it."

I didn't accept his handshake. "Fuck you, Schiller. I'm not here to socialize. Let's get this over."

The smile faded from his face but it returned again a moment later. "Yah, perhaps this is best," Schiller said. "I could see you were the bottom-line man the moment I met you. Honesty is better between friends."

I said nothing.

"Good. I can tell you agree," Schiller continued. "Would you mind?"

I raised my hands and let him pat me down. It took all of two seconds for him to find my gun.

"This won't be necessary for your negotiations."

I remained silent, watching him.

"Do not worry, I will keep it safe for you until the meeting is over. Herr Blendel is very particular about people carrying guns in his presence." He also removed the cell phone from my pocket. "You will not need this either. If you wish to make a call, feel free to use any of the house phones."

Schiller pointed to my briefcase, indicating he wanted me to open it for his inspection. Except for the file, it was empty. He didn't so much as blink when he saw it.

"So . . . everything is good," he said, closing the case. "You'll find Herr Blendel waiting for you on the verandah."

I walked toward the back of the house, turning on the tape recorder as I went. Herr Blendel looked like he had just come from a Yale–Princeton polo match. He had on a pair of white linen pants, Gucci loafers, and a pink shirt. The sleeves were rolled up precisely two turns and tucked under rather than over. Very chic. On his wrist was a Brueguet chronograph watch that probably cost as much as a small sports car. When he saw me he smiled, displaying a set of white, even teeth.

"Ah, Professor Delaney, there you are. We've been expecting you."

He held out his hand but I didn't take it.

"Come, come," he said. "There's no need to pout. This is business, nothing more."

"Business? Is that what you call it?"

"Oh, don't be tedious. You have something I need, and I have something you want. Three somethings to be exact. Therefore, I propose a trade. This way no one gets hurt and we all go our separate ways. And if it will make the arrangement more palatable, you may continue to do consulting work with our company. I understand they don't pay very much where you teach."

"Just like that, huh? How do I know you'll keep your word?"

Blendel smiled. "Oh, I've given you no word to keep. In my view you simply have no choice. You turn over the file, and I turn over what you're looking for. I understand your skepticism—lawyers are like that. Perhaps this will help."

Blendel reached under the table and produced two wallets. One belonged to Katherine and the other belonged to Sarah O'Connor.

I said, "These don't mean a damn thing. For all I know one of your thugs could have stolen them. I need proof Katherine, Sarah, and Jenny are alive before we go any further."

"Jenny? Oh, I see. She's the third girl. Sorry, I didn't know her name until just now. And who said anything about people not being alive? I'm just trying to return a pair of wallets one of my employees found. I was hoping we might make a trade."

"For this?" I asked, opening my briefcase. I showed him the file.

Blendel, however, made no move to touch it. "I'm afraid that looks like a copy, Mr. Delaney. I need the original *and* I need to know there are no other copies floating around."

"You're an observant man. You're also right about this being a copy. Unfortunately, a fellow named Phil Thurman has the original and he's not likely to return it. I believe you know each other."

Blendel's face lost most of its pleasant aspect. "*That* is unfortunate."

"Let me ask you something, Warren. What's so important about this file you're willing to kill for it?"

"Kill? My goodness, you've been watching too many gangster movies, John. You don't mind if I call you John, do you? I'm a businessman—a successful businessman. Over the years I've made enemies. I don't deny that. The police amuse themselves by trying to pin various offenses on me. None of them have ever stuck.

"All I'm interested in is making sure the *file*, as you refer to it, doesn't fall into the wrong hands, such as the media or newspapers. It comes down to protecting one's reputation. Surely you can understand that."

The cold smile returned again. He picked up his cup of coffee and took a sip. He was really very good at this kind of game—very smooth.

"Who's William Rosetti?" I asked.

The coffee cup paused halfway to his lips and a drop of sweat slid down his face. "Ros . . . Rosetti? I'm sorry I—"

"You remember William Rosetti, don't you, Warren? He was the one driving the car that killed my father fifteen years ago. Supposedly, he died in a street mugging following the accident."

I picked up Katherine and Sarah's wallets. "Tell you what I am going to do. I came out here with the intention of breaking your neck, but a little while ago I decided there's another way to handle this. It took five years of night school for me to become a lawyer. My father would have been proud of that. He was a man who went strictly by the book when it came to the law, and killing you isn't the best way to honor his memory. As far as I'm concerned, you can spend the rest of your life rotting behind bars. They tell me time moves very slowly when you're in prison. There don't have manicures or designer suits . . . just days and weeks to look forward to. I'm going to bring you down, pal. You have my word on it."

What happened next surprised me.

Blendel began to gasp for breath and grabbed his chest. His eyes bulged. He started to rise, but his legs gave out and he collapsed to the ground. I couldn't tell whether this was an act or not, but if it was, it was a good one.

I stood there impassively watching him as Schiller and Linda Blendel came running. A servant carrying a portable oxygen tank and a breathing mask was close behind them. I guessed Linda had been listening from the doorway.

It took several minutes to stabilize Blendel. Two other servants showed up and carried him back into the house.

Linda watched them for a moment, then turned to me. "I'm sorry, John. Warren is not in good health. Were you boys able to conclude your business?"

"Not really."

"Then perhaps I can be of some help."

"Perhaps. Your husband was interested in a file I have. He was in the process of making me an offer for it."

"Warren is a very generous man. I'm sure whatever you and he work out will be more than fair."

"Yes, he offered me two wallets in return for it," I said, patting the briefcase. "Along with continued employment with your company."

"And I take it that's not enough?"

I shook my head slowly.

"I see. Am I correct in assuming you'd like proof that Katherine Adams, Sarah O'Connor, and Jennifer Pechorin are still alive?"

Linda Blendel had just made a mistake. I could see it from the way Schiller's expression changed. He hadn't been expecting her to use their names; nevertheless, he covered his surprise well. Linda, however, was determined to play the game out.

"Sometimes negotiations require a leap of faith," she said, slipping her arm through mine. "Let's go in the house where we can discuss this in detail."

I gently disengaged my arm from hers. "I don't think there's much more to say. If you'll pardon me."

"John, we really were hoping you'd be more reasonable. What's to stop Hans here from taking the file?"

"Nothing, except for that fellow with a high-powered rifle trained at his head. I suspect he's about a hundred yards away, but I'm thinking he can make the shot." I put a hand over my eyes to shield them from the sun and squinted toward the tree line. A brief reflection from Stanley Curtain's sniper scope told me he was still there.

Schiller followed the direction of my gaze and saw the same thing. He nodded to himself and then slowly clapped his hands. "Well played, Professor."

"Save it, Adolf. You want the file so much? Here you go." I opened my briefcase and tossed it to him. "See you in court, pal."

The phrase was a cliché, like "Follow that cab," or "I'll be back," but I've always wanted to say it. I turned and walked down the driveway. The tape recorder was still running.

PART II

THE TRIAL

FIFTY-THREE

DELANEY

SAINT Joan's Cemetery is located in the borough of Queens. You can see it from Grand Central Parkway just before you hit the LaGuardia Airport exit, and it's one of the most depressing places I know. This was where my father was buried. I've only been there a few times since he died. I know that sounds lousy, but it's not due to any lack of respect or love. I just don't like cemeteries, particularly this one.

A long time ago . . . I don't remember when . . . I saw a photograph of New York's skyline taken from Saint Joan's and it made an impression on me. The time of year looked like winter and the photographer must have had an extraordinary eye. In the foreground were rows of tombstones and juxtaposed behind them was Manhattan's skyline. The similarities were remarkable.

I've never understood what possessed my father to buy a plot here. Maybe it was the cost back then. Or maybe it was the location, because our family was living in Kew Gardens at the time, but every time I visit I leave feeling rotten.

The last time I visited was with my sister. She insisted we go together and I didn't want to cause an argument. So we trekked out from Manhattan, lit candles in the chapel, and placed small stones on the grave to mark the occasion. Lissa wasn't with me now—Katherine was.

She was wearing a conservative charcoal gray suit and black pumps. Where she had gotten them I didn't know. Earlier that morning when I told her I wanted to visit my dad's grave, she didn't bat an eye.

"What time do we need to leave?" was all she asked. Typical Katherine.

On the ride out we didn't speak much. The image of my father trapped in a burning car still weighed on my chest like an anvil. I wasn't sure why I suddenly felt the need to see him. Maybe it was to put his soul to rest . . . or mine. When I became a cop we had an understanding that if one of us bought it, the other would find whoever was responsible. Recent events had crystallized that obligation in my mind.

Katherine is one of those rare women who are comfortable with silences. She knows when to leave me alone and doesn't talk just to fill in the spaces. We left our car in the parking lot and walked down the path together to my father's grave, her hand in mine.

William T. Delaney is buried alongside his father and mother. His younger brother, Ernest, who died in Vietnam, is near them. In recent years it's become vogue to display photographs of the deceased in their tombstone. Lissa and I once discussed this, but our mother was against the idea. She thought, and I agreed, it was a morbid practice.

I looked at the tiny cherry laurel hedge we paid the cemetery to plant at the foot of my father's grave. It needed trimming. The stones Lissa and I had left on our last visit were still there, along with another I noticed for the first time.

After a minute or two of silence, I said, "Dad, this is Katherine. I love her very much . . . more than anything. We're going to be married."

She responded by giving my arm a squeeze; then she dropped down on one knee and brushed some leaves off the grave.

"Pleased to meet you, Bill," she said softly. "I want you to know that I love your son, too. He's a wonderful, decent man and he would have made you proud. I promise to take good care of him."

She looked up at me and we smiled at each other. New York was fine. It was the Big Apple. Maybe everything else was just camping out, but it didn't matter. If you're lucky—and I mean really lucky—someone like Katherine comes along once in your lifetime.

It was mid-fall in the city and there was a bite in the air. For most of the day it had been gray and overcast. As a rule, I'm not big on mysterious signs or mumbo-jumbo where religion is concerned, but the clouds chose that moment to part and the sun shone through, bathing the area in a warm red glow. When I thought about that a moment later, and I did many times, the look of love on Katherine's face became etched in my mind forever, a crystal point of light in a world that was sometimes dark and forbidding.

The sound of a snapping branch pulled me back to the present. I turned to see Frank O'Connor standing there.

"Hello, Johnny."

"Frank."

"I haven't had a chance to meet your lady friend yet."

I stopped the words that were forming in my throat and simply introduced them. "This is Katherine Adams . . . Katherine . . . Frank O'Connor."

"The lady from the boat, right?" Frank asked, shaking her hand.

"That's one way to put it. Nice to meet you, Detective."

"I hope so," Frank said. "I hear good things about you. You and Johnny are a nice-looking couple."

Katherine smiled but didn't respond. He smiled back. Frank looked tired and a lot older than the last time I had seen him. It was like he had shrunken in on himself.

"I'll give you and John some privacy," Katherine said. "I'm sure you have a lot to talk about."

Frank held up his hand. "That won't be necessary. I can say what I have to right here." Then he turned to me. "Johnny, your dad and I were partners for a long time and I loved him like a brother. But I need to tell you that I'm partly responsible for his death."

I couldn't believe the words. Over the last two days this unpleasant thought had occurred to me several times. But its ramifications were so far-reaching, I shoved them away, feeling guilty and embarrassed for having thought it at all. Frank was a friend, and friends don't do that. I forced myself to stand there and hear the rest.

"How so?"

Frank took a deep breath and expelled it slowly. "Fifteen years ago I found out that my brother was on the take. It was the same with a number of guys in the department."

I opened my mouth to speak, but he cut me off before I could.

"Your dad wasn't one of them, Johnny. He was too much of a straight shooter."

I closed my eyes for a long moment and then opened them. Like I said, the possibility that Nick hadn't acted alone had already crossed my mind. The thought didn't make me proud, but I was trained as a cop, and the man lying in the ground next to me would have done the same.

Frank went on. "The problem is, I wasn't straight. I never went as far as the others, but being just a little dirty doesn't make it right. It started with free tickets to ball games and maybe a meal or two here and there. Then there were the gifts—merchandise that fell off the back of Blendel's trucks and made its way to us. Stuff like that. Nicky fronted for me, but it came down to the same thing."

"Jesus, Frank." I turned and looked across the river at Manhattan, unable to keep eye contact with him any longer.

"Your dad found out what was going on and tore into me. That was the only fight we had in our eight years together. He wouldn't have any part of it and told me I needed to clean up my act or we were through as partners.

"So I went to Nick and let him know I was out. He was worried that your father would go to Internal Affairs. I told him Bill could already have done that if he wanted to. I remember the look on Nicky's face. He was scared, but it was mixed with something else. I told him to relax, that everything was cool. Your old man wasn't the kind of guy to rat out his friends.

"The next day Nick came to the station and said he was going to talk with Bill and straighten everything out. That was the last time I saw your father alive."

I looked at Katherine and then back at him. "I don't get it, Frank."

"Don't you see? I was the one who told my brother your dad was leaving early that day and where he was heading. I didn't know how he would use the information, Johnny. I swear to God."

"So why are you telling me this now?"

"Internal Affairs came to see me yesterday. They issued an arrest warrant for Nick two days ago. Did you know that?"

"No, I didn't."

"They laid everything out for me. About Blendel, about my Sarah, the murders, about what you and the lady have done, the feds' investigation. Everything.

"I didn't expect to find you here today. I came out because I wanted to have a word with your dad—to apologize, because I let him down. Partners don't do that."

"I understand."

"When I saw you both here, I knew I had to tell you what really happened. I couldn't have you thinking your old man was on the take. Understand?"

"So, what are you going to do now?"

Frank shook his head slowly. "I don't know. My brother's a fugitive. My little girl can't look me in the face anymore. Everything is pretty messed up."

We spoke for a while longer, but nothing was resolved. I could tell that he was in pain. He had lost his daughter for the second time in as many months, a hard thing for any man to take. Strangely, it was Katherine who provided the answer.

"When I was with Sarah in the swamp I learned a little bit about her," she said. "She's a lot tougher than you give her credit for. She didn't take that file for herself; she took it because she loves you and was trying to protect you. Unfortunately, they don't hand out instruction manuals when we have children. I think if you go to her and tell her the truth, she'll listen. She has a strong sense of right and wrong."

Frank held her gaze for several moments before he looked away and smiled.

"You've got quite a lady here, Johnny."

That was all he said before he headed back toward his car.

FIFTY-FOUR

DELANEY

WILLIAM Rosetti aka Billy Rose, aka Bill Ross, was a weasel, plain and simple—five feet ten inches of skin and bone with an Adam's apple that bobbed up and down when he spoke. I'd seen junkies before and he fit the image to a T.

The Philadelphia police found him at a methadone clinic, where he was trying to kick a two-hundred-dollar-a-day habit. They questioned him, but he clammed up and demanded to see a lawyer. Mr. Rosetti was apparently no stranger to the criminal justice system. Phil Thornton, Stan Curtain, Marcia Mazurski, and I arrived in Philadelphia early the following morning and went straight to the police station.

From my conversations with Thurman I learned that Jenny and Karel Pechorin were now in a witness protection program along with Sarah O'Connor. All of them were being kept at undisclosed locations pending an upcoming criminal trial against the Blendels. Not surprisingly, Katherine continued to refuse Thurman's offer of protection. She opted to stay at my place instead, saying it was easier to do her research there. She handled most of her business via telephone and e-mails. God bless technology.

The Thirtieth Street Police Station is a modern-looking building. It's shaped like a circle and nothing inside it quite lines up correctly. Despite this architectural anomaly, the City of Brotherly Love is proud of it and schedules photo ops there whenever possible. I've never been able to figure out why.

One of the cops brought Rosetti into an interrogation room, nodded to us, and closed the door behind him.

"Mr. Rosetti, I'm Phillip Thurman, Senior Agent with the FBI. This is Professor John Delaney of John Jay College of Criminal Justice in New York, and these are Agents Curtain and Mazurski with my office."

Rosetti's glance passed over all of us. There wasn't the slightest flicker of recognition when he heard my name. It meant nothing to him.

"I already told you people, I want to see a lawyer. You got no right to question me without one here. I know my rights."

"Sure you do," Thurman said. "We just want to have a friendly chat—nothing formal."

"I want my lawyer," Rosetti repeated.

"We're not interested in the drug charges, Rosetti," Thurman said. "As a matter of fact, we might even be of some help to you. We're here about something entirely unrelated to them—a man named Warren Blendel. Ever hear of him?"

"I don't know any Warren Blendel."

"Right," said Thurman. "You look thirsty. Maybe you want a drink or a sandwich? We could get you one."

"What I want is a fucking lawyer. Listen, I've been clean for nine months and I didn't do nothing wrong. You had no right to pick me up."

"Like I said, we're not interested in your drug problems. You could do yourself a lot of good by helping us out. The DA works closely with our office."

"I never met anyone named Blendel and you talking to the DA won't do me any good if I'm dead."

"Witness Protection can set you up someplace far away from here where you'd be safe."

Rosetti shook his head. "There ain't no place I'd be safe. You don't know what you're dealing with."

"Well, let's talk about it," Thurman said, taking out a pack of cigarettes. He offered one to Rosetti, who accepted it and pulled a long drag into his lungs. Thurman then placed the pack and the lighter on the table.

Rosetti blew out a stream of smoke. "It's no good. I've got nothing to say. Put me back inside."

"If that's the way you want it. But how long do you think you'll last? Blendel and his people went to a great deal of trouble to make you disappear. They know you're alive now and my guess is they'll correct that situation before too long. You see what I'm getting at?"

Rosetti shook his head again.

"I'd like to ask him a few questions," I interrupted.

Thurman nodded and pushed his chair back. I came around the table and sat on the edge directly in front of Rosetti.

"Mr. Rosetti, I'm not with the FBI and I don't work for the government, so I'm only going to ask this once. Fifteen years ago you were driving a truck on the Cross Bronx Expressway. You hit a car forcing it into the median where it burst into flames. The driver was killed. Six weeks later you and some other people faked your death. Does any of this ring a bell?"

Rosetti's eyes got a little wider and he swallowed; his Adam's apple moved up and down. "Look, I didn't—"

I moved so suddenly he had no time to react. One second he was sitting in his chair and the next he was on the floor. I grabbed Thurman's cigarette lighter off the table and yanked his head back, bringing it close to his left eye.

"The man you killed was my father," I said, bringing my face inches from his.

In the meantime, Thurman, Mazurski, and Curtain all looked the other way. I mean literally. They turned and stared out the window at the parking lot.

I flicked the lighter open and lit it.

"You can't do this," Rosetti yelled, trying to pull away. "This is police brutality."

I drove my knee hard into his lower abdomen. "I just told you I'm not the police, you little maggot, and I don't have the patience they do. I'm going to start with your left eye and then I'll move on to your right eye."

When a single drop of lighter fluid fell onto Rosetti's cheek, he lost it. A few strangled sounds escaped from his throat but they could hardly be said to qualify as speech. I didn't plan the lighter fluid, but it was a nice touch.

I said, "Good-bye, Rosetti. I don't think we'll be seeing each other again." I supplemented it by putting what I hoped was the most insane look I could imagine on my face.

"For the love of God," he begged.

"Talk," I hissed, putting more weight on his stomach.

"It was Schiller, man. I swear to Jesus, he made me do it. He was the one who set everything up." The words all came out in a rush.

I moved the flame closer, singeing the hair on his forehead. "What about Blendel?"

"I never met Blendel—I swear on my mother's life. You gotta believe me."

I didn't give Billy Rosetti's mother much chance after that, but I did believe him. I snapped the lighter closed and jerked him back into his seat. He had wet himself and was looking at me like I'd just fallen out of a tree.

"Get him the fuck away from me!" he shouted at Thurman.

"Hmm?" Thurman asked, turning around. "Did you say something, Mr. Rosetti? I was just admiring that new 350Z in the parking lot. Those Japs really know how to make a car, don't they? I heard they're fast as hell."

"Are you crazy?" Rosetti squealed. "The son of a bitch just tried to kill me."

"Crazy?" Thurman repeated. He stuck out his lower lip and considered that for a moment. "Gee . . . I don't think so. Harming a prisoner would be illegal. Did you see anything, Agent Curtain?"

"No, sir."

"What about you, Agent Mazurski?"

Marcia Mazurski was in the process of freshening her lipstick and looked over the top of her compact. "See what?" she asked.

"You people are all nuts," Rosetti whined.

"I can tell you and Professor Delaney have a lot to talk about, so we'll just leave you alone," Thurman told him.

"No!" Rosetti screamed.

"We're willing to offer you protective custody," Thurman said, "but the U.S. Attorney has been getting really tight with the program lately. I'll need a sworn statement to convince him you're cooperating."

Rosetti looked at Thurman for several seconds before his shoulders slumped. He nodded his head.

FIFTY-FIVE

DELANEY

News about the civil trial began to leak out slowly. Shortly after Katherine and I filed our civil suit against Warren Blendel and his companies, my secretary put a call through to my office. It turned out to be from a reporter on the *Times* asking for more information about the case.

"Mr. Delaney, this is Bonnie Cochran with the *New York Times*. I was looking over the court docket and noticed you're listed as one of the attorneys in a civil case that was filed last month. Can you tell me a little about it?"

"Sure," I said. "It just so happens I'm sitting here with two of the plaintiffs' lawyers."

Jimmy d'Taglia and Katherine each looked up from their notes as I scribbled "N.Y. Times" on a piece of paper and pushed it toward them.

"Be careful," Katherine mouthed.

Jimmy echoed her warning with a hand gesture to go slowly.

Ms. Cochran said, "It looks like you're suing for an enormous sum of money. When I first read the complaint, I thought it might be an error."

"What does it say?" I asked.

"Well, they have you listed as seeking a hundred million dollars in damages."

"Sounds about right. Of course, that excludes the punitive-damage claim."

The interest level in Ms. Cochran's voice ticked up a notch. "What kind of case did you say this was?"

"I didn't, but since you ask, it's a suit for wrongful death, with separate counts for extortion, false imprisonment, and assault, amounting to attempted murder. There are a few other charges, but I won't bore you with them right now."

The sound of her taking notes could be heard in the background and I winked at Jimmy, who was watching me with closely. He didn't look happy.

"And the defendant is Warren Blendel?"

"Yep."

"The billionaire?" she asked, incredulous.

"I don't know the extent of Mr. Blendel's assets, but I've heard he's well off. Whether he is or isn't is beside the point. We're also suing his corporation, an entity wholly controlled by him."

"Wholly controlled by him," Bonnie repeated to herself as she clacked away on her keyboard. "Okay," she continued, "I noticed the estate of William T. Delaney is listed as one of the plaintiffs in the case—any relation to you?"

"William T. Delaney was my father."

Several seconds passed. "Wow. Can you tell me who the other plaintiffs are?"

"Sure . . . one of them is Katherine Adams. She's one of the lawyers I mentioned a moment ago. The others are Sarah O'Connor, daughter of Detective Lieutenant Frank O'Connor with the NYPD, and Jennifer Pechorin, the sister of Andre Rostov, a young medical student who was murdered in Atlanta, Georgia, recently."

"Wait, you just said *murdered*?"

"I believe so."

There was a silence.

"Professor, you just threw me a major league curve. I thought this was an automobile case."

"No . . . it's a little more than that."

Her typing became even more frenzied. "Are you available for an interview? I'd like to meet you face-to-face and get some background on you and the other attorneys."

She was hooked. "I suppose that could be arranged," I said, letting a note of hesitation creep into my voice. "I'd have to be careful about what I say, though. Technically, it's unethical for a lawyer to seek publicity to gain advantage in civil proceedings."

"Understood. Look, I'm not out to sensationalize anything. I only want to report the facts and make sure I get my story straight." She didn't wait for my answer and continued. "Let me ask you this, if people were murdered, as you say, why isn't the DA going after the defendants criminally?"

"He is. So is the U.S. Attorney. In fact, indictments are being presented to the grand jury now. Criminal cases take some time, as you might imagine. We didn't want to wait, so we're proceeding on our own."

Bonnie asked a few more questions and I fed her just enough information to keep her interested, passing along some facts and hinting at others. Katherine and Jimmy didn't look happy at what I was doing for a number of reasons. I was telling the truth when I said a lawyer is prohibited from using publicity as a weapon. There are attorneys who routinely ignore this, as you might imagine. Others, like Katherine and Jimmy, play by the book. I was fully aware of approaching the line. While I wanted to bury Blendel and his whole corrupt crew, I'd also taken the same oath they had and I wasn't about to violate it. This didn't mean I couldn't push the envelope a little.

AFTER we hung up, Katherine folded her arms across her chest and gave me a look.

"What?" I asked.

"What was that all about?"

"I was just passing along some facts about case to the press."

"Mm-hmm," she said.

I turned to Jimmy for support and found none.

"Listen, I agreed to come up here and represent you," he said. "You have plenty of reason to hate those guys, but I don't want to get myself disbarred over this and neither do you. That would only compound the tragedy of your father's death and hand Blendel another victory."

"All right, all right," I said, holding my hands up in surrender.

"I'm serious, John. I can't have any more of that stuff. It's crazy that you and K.J. are listed as counsel at all—you're parties and you shouldn't be acting as your own lawyers. You're too close to the forest."

"I know that, Jimmy. This is something I have to do. I want to see the look on that son of a bitch's face when the jury comes back. Afterward, the feds can put him away for good."

Jimmy turned to Katherine. "Same here," she added.

He asked, "Is there anything I can say to change your minds?"

Neither of us responded, but we didn't have to. The answer was written on our faces.

THERE'S an old legal expression that says, "He who represents himself has a fool for a client." That's probably true. When I explained my plan to Katherine, she pretty much voiced the same concerns to me, but to her credit she never once tried to back out. If anything, once she learned that Blendel was behind trying to have her killed, she became equally committed to bringing him down. From personal experience, I knew just how tough she could be when she put her mind to something, and over the next few weeks I got to see that firsthand.

BONNIE Cochran turned out to be a redhead, dyed I thought. She was medium height and somewhere in her late forties. She had intelligent brown eyes and a no-nonsense manner. Her business suit was at least ten years out of style. We met at a coffee shop a few blocks from my law school. After everyone was introduced we took a table near the window. Bonnie and Katherine ordered cappuccinos; Jimmy and I went for regular coffee.

"I've been reading up on your claim since we spoke, Mr. Delaney, or would you prefer Professor?"

"John will do," I replied.

"All right . . . John. You're an interesting fellow. A former detective with the NYPD, wounded in the line of duty and twice decorated for bravery. You went to law school at night while you were convalescing and were hired by City College Law before they changed the name to John Jay. Your colleagues say you're tenacious and one of the best people in the country at reconstituting a crime scene."

"My colleagues talk too much."

"And you, Ms. Adams, are at least as interesting in your own way.

You head a law firm in Atlanta. Before that you were an assistant U.S. Attorney. Most notably you were responsible for identifying the people who sank the *Ocean Majestic* last year."

"This cappuccino is really excellent," Katherine said, taking a sip.

Bonnie smiled at her and Katherine smiled back.

"I couldn't find much about you," Bonnie said, turning to Jimmy, "other than you graduated at the top of your class from Fordham Law School three years ago."

"I'm also sensitive and I like dogs and long moonlit walks on the beach," Jimmy replied.

"So do I. Unfortunately you're too young for me. Cute ass, though."

"Yeah?" Jimmy twisted around and studied his reflection in the mirror. "My girl says the same thing."

"She's right. So what's the deal with you people? Apparently you're suing Warren Blendel and his companies for a hundred million dollars, and alleging that he . . . let me see if I have this right," Bonnie said, referring to her notes, ". . . *that he orchestrated the death of John's father, William T. Delaney, a member of the New York Police Force*—"

"That he attempted to murder Ms. Adams, Sarah O'Connor, and Jennifer Pechorin. And that he did murder, or ordered the murder of, an individual named Andre Rostov in Atlanta, Georgia," Jimmy said, finishing the sentence for her.

"I was speaking to Ms. Adams," Bonnie said.

"I know. And now you're speaking to me," Jimmy told her.

They held each other's eyes for a few moments before Bonnie closed her pad. "C'mon, guys. What's really going on? Are you just looking to make a bunch of money off Blendel or what?"

"The pleadings are self-explanatory," Jimmy replied.

"Okay . . . off the record, why don't you tell me what this suit is really about? When I called, you could have told me to piss up a rope, but you didn't. Now we're all sitting here like old friends, having coffee. This cappuccino is really good, by the way. Is this complaint on the level or just a publicity stunt?"

Jimmy started to respond, but I did it for him.

"I don't mind if it's on the record," I told her. "The lawsuit is totally legit and we can prove everything we're saying. As far as Katherine and I making a bundle off the case, any proceeds Ms. Adams receives will be donated to the Goodrich Shelter for Battered Women in Atlanta. Mine will be split between the Police Benevolent Fund and John Jay College for a scholarship to be set up in my father's name."

"Sarah O'Connor and Jennifer Pechorin aren't part of that arrangement," Jimmy added. "Ms. Pechorin is Andre Rostov's sister and represents his estate. What she and Ms. O'Connor decide to do with any money they receive will be totally up to them."

"And you're their lawyer?"

"That I am," Jimmy told her.

Bonnie sat back in her chair and looked from him to Katherine. "Well, this should make a hell of a story. And you're in for a hell of a fight. Joe Spencer of King, Sanders, and Elmore just filed a fifty-page answer and counterclaim against you on Warren Blendel's behalf this morning."

To emphasize her point, she took out an inch-thick packet of papers and dropped them on the table.

FIFTY-SIX

DELANEY

Joseph A. Spencer has been a fixture on the New York legal scene for over thirty years. Flamboyant, aggressive, and outspoken, he's been associated in one form or another with a dozen cases that have attracted national, if not international, attention. Where some lawyers see litigation as a chess match or adopt a conciliatory attitude and try to settle, Spencer's view is that litigation is a battlefield. When he gets involved in a trial, his office is referred to as the "war room" within the confines of his law firm. King, Sanders, and Elmore is one of New York's oldest firms. They have over three hundred lawyers and their clientele reads like a who's who list. People come to them because they want results and are willing to pay for them. The last time I checked, their billable rate was hovering around seven hundred dollars an hour, with Spencer's topping out at a thousand. My last case resulted in an award of six hundred dollars the court granted me as legal fees.

Never one to let the grass grow under his feet, Spencer wasted no time in firing the first shot by holding an "impromptu" press conference on the courthouse steps. Mr. Spencer didn't shun publicity; he courted it and used the press to his advantage whenever possible. Thus, the tenor of the trial was set from the beginning.

Jimmy d'Taglia turned out to be a pleasant surprise. I'd known all along that he was a bright kid, but this case brought out the best in him and he flourished in the limelight. He presented himself intelligently and was deadly serious about the claims his clients were making. Spencer's daily quotes were quickly countered by Jimmy's own press releases, which he sent to the media via e-mail. After some internal squabbling, it was decided that Katherine and I would remain in the background and let Jimmy run with the ball. He did.

After months of motions and countermotions, the case was finally called to trial in the Supreme Court of the State of New York on November 18. The Supreme Court is New York's highest court of general jurisdiction. Other states sometimes refer to them as superior courts or circuit courts, but it comes down to the same thing.

On the day of trial we arrived at the courthouse early and found Joe Spencer already there, looking resplendent in his blue pinstripe suit. He was in the process of addressing the press and television people.

"Let me be perfectly clear," he announced in a rich stentorian voice. "This case is about money, pure and simple. The *real* victim here is Warren Blendel, a man who has given this city millions in charitable donations."

I made eye contact with Bonnie Cochran, among the throng of reporters, and nodded a greeting to her.

"Mr. Spencer, do you have any comment about John Delaney and Katherine Adams donating any proceeds they might recover to charity?" she called out.

The question only stopped Spencer for a moment. "Bonnie, I've heard that rumor, too. Normally, I don't like to cast aspersions on my fellow lawyers, but it's clear to me they're motivated by a pathetic desire to seek glory. If they can destroy a man like Warren Blendel, they can parlay that into a lot of future cases."

It was a good thing Joe Spencer didn't want to cast aspersions. *Pathetic* was definitely the operative word here. If nothing else, the man was flexible in his views. There was no point in hanging around for the rest of his speech, so we continued up the steps, snaking our way through the crowd. The atmosphere was already circuslike.

New York's Supreme Court is located on Centre Street in downtown Manhattan, only a few blocks from where the World Trade Center used to be. Looking up at the columned structure evokes images of Rome, or maybe it's Greece—I can never tell which. The overall effect is meant to intimidate. Inside, the building is a mixture of dark wood paneling, granite floors, and worn marble. Over the years, the place has acquired a somewhat musty smell.

Judge Davis Murray's courtroom was already filled to capacity when we entered. Seated at the defendants' table was Warren Blendel. Hans Schiller and Linda Blendel were in the audience directly behind him. The moment Linda saw us, she shot a look of pure hatred in our direction. Her husband never moved; he simply stared straight ahead. Seated across the aisle were Sarah O'Connor and Jennifer Pechorin. Karel, Phil Thurman, and Horace Womack were also there. They acknowledged us with nods. I picked out four federal cops in the audience, who probably were there for security purposes. We made eye contact, but I got no reaction from them. Frank and Lucille O'Connor were several rows behind Thurman. Of his brother Nick there was no sign at all. No one had seen or heard of him since the arrest warrant had been issued.

After months of legal preliminaries, Judge Murray finally decided he'd had enough of reporters calling his office and abruptly set the case down for trial. His ruling caught everyone by surprise and prevented us from taking the depositions of Blendel's final two witnesses, a Dr. Harlan Skinner and one Ellen Guinn, PhD. Joe Spencer had added their names to his witness list the night before we were notified of the judge's order. We received it via fax.

Jimmy promptly requested a continuance and his request was turned down just as quickly. This was an odd thing for a judge to do, particularly since both Skinner and Guinn were supposedly out of town and not expected back until that evening. Later that day we began to understand why—we were dealing with a stacked deck. Thanks to some legwork by my friend Irwin Zeller and two law students, who had volunteered their services, we discovered one of Blendel's companies had donated fifty thousand dollars to Judge Murray's reelection campaign.

The second blow came out of left field when the Assistant District Attorney in charge of Warren Blendel's criminal file called to say that his boss had directed him to hold off presenting the case to the grand jury that month. Apparently it was an election year, and Bernard Wheaton, New York's DA, felt there wasn't enough evidence to gain an indictment. I spoke with him three different times laying out the facts, but he remained adamant. He was unwilling to risk a "no bill" against someone as powerful as Blendel.

Following a hunch, I asked our team to do some more digging

and they unearthed campaign contributions to Wheaton totaling nearly twice the amount His Honor had received. Blendel was consistent if nothing else. We got the news on Katherine's cell phone as we were walking to the courthouse. It was going to be a long day.

"YOUR honor, may counsel approach the bench?" Jimmy asked.

Murray nodded and motioned for us to come forward. "What is it?"

"I have two matters I'd like to discuss in chambers." Jimmy said.

"What are they, Mr. d'Taglia?"

"One has to do with the motion I filed on Friday morning asking for a continuance."

"The court has already denied that, Judge," Spencer said.

"Yes, that was denied, Counsel," Murray echoed. "If you're asking that I reconsider, I'll save you the trouble. This case has dragged on far too long. I read the reasons in your brief and unless you have something new to add, I see no reason to change my ruling. What's the second matter?"

Jimmy, however, was not ready to concede the point. "Your Honor. We believe Mr. Spencer's addition of two witnesses at the eleventh hour constitutes unfair surprise and denies us to right to examine them in deposition. Allowing it to stand would be reversible error."

"Well, we certainly want to make sure everyone is treated equally here. And that includes Southerners," the judge added with a smile. "I'll tell you what, prior to Mr. Spencer's calling his witnesses, I'll give you a chance to *voir dire* them in one of the witnesses rooms. Will that satisfy you?"

"No, it won't," Jimmy said. "I would appreciate it if the court would note my exception for the record. And by the way, I was born and raised in New York."

"So noted," Murray responded. "I'm not trying to make things difficult, but I need to move my cases along. We've got a three-ring circus here. What was the other matter you wanted to address?"

"I really would prefer to discuss that in your chambers."

Murray glanced up at the clock on the wall and blew out a long breath. "All right, but let me caution you that you'd better not be wasting my time. I'm not going to stand for any stall tactics." He then looked out at the assembled audience and announced, "The court will be in recess for fifteen minutes."

Once we were in the judge's chambers, Murray took off his robe, hung it on a coat stand, and invited everyone to seat themselves. He was a man between fifty and fifty-five with salt-and-pepper hair that had probably been jet black in his youth. He was slender and had a prominent nose with a bad complexion.

"Your Honor, I'd like to have a court reporter present for this discussion," Jimmy said as soon as everyone was settled.

Murray leaned forward and picked up his phone. "Diane, have Larry come to my office and bring his machine."

For the next few minutes we made small talk while the court reporter set up his equipment. He nodded to the judge when he was ready.

"Proceed," Murray said to Jimmy.

"Judge, it's come to our attention that a company called Twin Tree Corporation contributed fifty thousand dollars to your reelection campaign two years ago. This company is either owned or controlled by Warren Blendel. So with all due respect to the court, I'm compelled to ask you to step aside."

Murray chuckled. "A lot of people contributed to my campaign, Mr. d'Taglia. Until just now, I can tell you that I've never heard the name Twin Tree Corporation before."

"Your Honor," Spencer said, "I understand this young man's concern and we certainly don't want a cloud hanging over these proceedings, but his information is faulty. First off, Warren Blendel no longer owns any stock in Twin Tree. He transferred that to his wife over eighteen months ago. I've personally examined the corporate books and I can assure you he also holds no elected position with that company."

Jimmy responded, "Husbands and wives transfer property and investments between each other all the time. Our position is the same with respect to Mrs. Blendel. There is a clear conflict of interest here."

"Well, it's not clear to me," Murray said. "Mrs. Blendel isn't a party to this case, and as such, I'm going to deny your motion."

"There is one other thing, Judge," Spencer added. "I was going to raise it later, but I think, given the potential for it to damage Mr. Blendel's reputation, I'd just as soon do it in here."

"All right, Counselor. What have you got?"

"During the discovery process we were informed that Mr. Delaney secretly recorded certain conversations he had with Warren Blendel and his wife while he was a guest in their home. Our position is that these recordings are illegal and we would like the court to prevent them from being introduced into evidence. We are also asking that counsel be directed not to make any mention of them during the proceedings."

"Yes, I read both of your briefs on the subject," said Murray. "Mr. d'Taglia?"

"As you indicated, Linda Blendel is not a party to this proceeding, so we don't think the rule would apply to her."

"Young man, if the recording's illegal, it's not going to come in for *any* purpose. I agree with Mr. Spencer and I'm going to grant his motion. Is there anything else?"

"No, Judge."

"Fine. Then let's get this show on the road."

This ruling was the first of several blows to our case.

JURY selection lasted most of the day. A group of sixty-four people lined the first four rows of the courtroom and listened as the judge introduced the lawyers and parties. He then made a few preliminary remarks explaining what the *voir dire* process was all about.

"Now I'm sure all of you have already seen something like this on television or in the movies. In this part of the trial the lawyers get to ask you questions about yourself and your background. Ladies and gentlemen, these questions are not meant to pry into your personal lives or to embarrass you in any way. They're all part of a time-honored system that will allow us to select twelve people who are fair and impartial for our jury. We will also pick two alternates."

While the judge was busy talking, Katherine leaned over and whispered in my ear. "See the man sitting behind Spencer?"

"Sure."

"That's Randall Fuller. He's a jury selection expert. The two women to his left are part of his staff."

"What makes him an expert?"

"He's has a Ph.D."

"In jury selection?"

"No, psychology," Katherine whispered. "I've run into him before."

"How did the case turn out?"

She looked slightly offended by my question. "I won."

"Then I'd rather hire you. You can work closely under me."

The corners of Katherine's mouth twitched, but she kept her expression neutral. "Women on top," she whispered back, rubbing my ankle with her foot.

I said, "Not much we can do about him now. We'll just have pick our people the old-fashioned way."

And we did. While Fuller and his two helpers made charts and furiously scribbled notes, passing them back and forth to Joe Spencer, Katherine, Jimmy, and I engaged in the mystical process of selecting a jury—that is to say we took our best guesses. The decision was based largely on how people looked to us, their perceived intelligence, and whether we thought their backgrounds made them good prospects. It's all very scientific. Some lawyers will tell you there's an art to picking a jury, but over the years I've come to the conclusion you can do just about as well by flipping a coin.

When we finally took a break around four thirty, Randal Fuller came over and introduced himself. He was wearing a charcoal gray pinstripe suit and looked more like an attorney than I did. We shook hands.

"I thought that went nicely," he said, handing his card to me. "I'm Randy Fuller. Katherine and I are old friends. Good to see you again."

"Good to see you, too, Randy," she replied. "You've already met John, so let me introduce our attorney, James d'Taglia."

This time it was Jimmy's turn to shake hands with the affable Mr. Fuller. He did it briefly and then excused himself before Fuller could launch into a sales pitch on the huge verdicts he had been instrumental in helping his clients win. We weren't quite as fast as Jimmy and had to suffer through his spiel all the way to the lobby.

"I think we've got a pretty solid jury, don't you?" Fuller asked. "I noticed we were in agreement on a lot of the choices."

I nodded.

"Would you mind if I asked you why you picked Mr. Scolari? He was . . . let's see, juror number seven, I believe," Fuller said, consulting his notes. "And, if you don't mind, I'd like to know what your thoughts were on Mrs. Rasmussen. She's the schoolteacher."

"Sure, I don't mind. Scolari has been a building inspector for twenty years, plus he grew up here in New York. My guess is he's heard just about all the bullshit a person can hear in that time. He struck me as a guy who could put two and two together."

"Interesting. And Mrs. Rasmussen?"

"I liked the way she smiled at us," Katherine explained.

Fuller blinked. "You liked the way she smiled? Is that it?"

"She's also a science teacher," Katherine said, "I felt she would look at the facts logically, plus she was wearing a Miriam Haskell pin. I collect them myself, so I figured she couldn't be all bad."

Fuller's jaw dropped slightly and he consulted his notes again.

"Miriam Haskell . . . Miriam Haskell," he muttered, running his finger down one of the columns.

We left him standing there to ponder the mystery. Maybe selecting a jury was an art after all. We were about to find out.

FIFTY-SEVEN

DELANEY

THE next morning Katherine and I spotted Sarah outside the courtroom talking with her father. Two FBI men were close by, watching over her, thanks to Phil Thurman. We decided not to interrupt and went inside. If anything, the room was more packed than the day before. Jimmy was already seated at the plaintiffs' table. Joe Spencer and his team were deep in discussion at theirs.

"Get a good night's sleep?" I asked Jimmy as we sat down.

"Not really. I didn't get to bed until after two. I kept going over my list of questions and rearranging the witness order."

Katherine smiled and affectionately massaged the back of his neck. "I've been doing the same since I graduated law school. Have you had a chance to talk to Spencer's mystery witnesses yet?"

Jimmy shook his head. "They're supposed to be here at ten o'clock. I talked to Spencer earlier and asked him what they're going to testify about. He told me that Skinner is a psychiatrist who works out on Long Island. Apparently, he's been treating Blendel for a panic disorder for the last fifteen years. Guinn is his therapist."

Katherine's eyebrows went up. "A panic disorder? Is that supposed to draw some kind of sympathy from the jury?"

Jimmy shrugged. "I can't tell what Spencer's going for, but I trust him about as far as I can throw him. And that goes double for the Honorable Davis Murray. I don't mind losing a fair fight, but I hate getting sandbagged."

Katherine and I had discussed the same thing in bed last night. While Murray was smooth and knew all the right things to say, it had quickly become obvious, at least to us, where his sympathies lay. Not only did he turn down our motion to recuse himself, but he also threatened to hold Jimmy in contempt if he raised the subject again in open court. I was about to reply when the door behind the judge's bench opened.

"All rise," the bailiff called out.

Davis Murray entered and took his seat. "All right, is everyone present?"

I got to my feet and announced, "Ms. O'Connor is outside, Your Honor. If the bailiff can let her know we're ready—"

"Counsel, it's your responsibility to have your clients here on time," he snapped. "Go and get her."

Fortunately the door opened and Sarah O'Connor came in just as the judge was concluding his remark. I wasn't prepared to get jumped on right out of the gate, but given Murray's earlier demeanor, I wasn't totally surprised either. Jimmy rolled his eyes at me when I sat back down, a gesture only I was meant to see.

The judge directed his next comment to Sarah, who was halfway to her seat. "Ms. O'Connor, this is not a classroom or a school social. This is a court of law and I expect you to treat it with dignity and respect. If you're late again, I'll impose sanctions. Do I make myself clear?"

The attack caught Sarah by surprise and some of the color drained out of her face. She stammered, "Y-yes, Your Honor. I'm sorry. I was just talking to my father."

The judge pursed his lips and turned to Jimmy. "I understand you're acting as lead attorney, Mr. d'Taglia. Are you ready to proceed?"

"Yes, sir."

"Counsel?" he asked, looking at Spencer.

"The defense is ready, Your Honor."

"Very well, bring the jury in."

Our jury consisted of eight men and four women. The two alternates were also women. They represented a cross section of New York: teachers, construction workers, a building inspector, store clerks, professionals, housewives, an actor, corporate mid-management, and a college student.

I studied them out of the corner of my eye and thought they were a good group—honest, decent people who had been called together to perform one of society's most underrated functions—serving the law. Maybe the concept is a little naive, given the times, but it's something I've believed for as long as I could remember.

"Ladies and gentlemen," said Murray. "We all met yesterday during the selection process. The lawyers tell me this case is likely to take between three and four days. Many of you have jobs and families and problems of your own to deal with, so we'll try to get you out of here as quickly as possible.

"This is a civil action in which one party is suing another for damages because of wrongs they claim were committed against them. It is *not* a criminal case and no one is going to jail. Cases of that type are brought by either the State or the federal government.

"Now various counts of injury are alleged in the complaint. These are allegations and *not* facts nor should they be taken as such. Under the law the plaintiffs must prove their claim and the extent of their injuries. Later in the trial, I'll issue instructions to help you reach your decision.

"In this case, John Delaney claims that Warren Blendel and Twin Tree Corporation, a company owned and controlled by Mr. Blendel, wrongfully conspired to cause the death of William T. Delaney some fifteen years ago. This, of course, is denied by the defendants.

"It is also claimed by Sarah O'Connor that Mr. Blendel and agents working for him conspired to cause her grievous bodily injury, falsely imprisoned her, attempted to extort property from her, and caused her deliberate mental anguish.

"Katherine Adams, who is also a plaintiff, and strangely, one of the attorneys trying this matter, contends the defendants trespassed upon her property in Atlanta, Georgia, caused damage to it, and also attempted to inflict bodily harm to her.

"And last, Jennifer Pechorin, a foreign national, who I believe is in the United States illegally, claims that her brother, Andre Rostov, died due to actions taken by Warren Blendel and others on his behalf."

Jimmy d'Taglia was on his feet immediately. "Your Honor, I have a motion."

Murray glanced up with a look of exaggerated surprise. "Well, that didn't take very long," he said with a smile to the jury. "We hardly got started."

"Yes, sir. If it please the court, I would like to argue this outside the presence of the jury."

Murray's smile turned into a scowl and he let out an exasperated breath. "Very well. Bailiff, please escort the jury out. My apologies, ladies and gentlemen."

The moment the door to the jury room closed, Jimmy said, "Your Honor, I move for a mistrial. The court's comments about Jennifer Pechorin's nationality and the fact that she is here legally or illegally can only taint this case. With all due respect, they were completely improper."

The judge turned to Joe Spencer, who stood up and carefully fastened the middle button on his suit jacket.

"Judge, I understand counsel's concern and we certainly don't want to take unfair advantage, neither do I want my client to go through more expense preparing for another trial. Perhaps a curative instruction to the jury might solve the problem."

Murray nodded sagely as he considered Spencer's suggestion. "Mr. d'Taglia, it was not the court's intention to taint these proceedings, as you say. Do you have any law on the subject that would be helpful to me?"

"I do, Judge. Anticipating this issue might come up, I took the liberty of making copies of two cases."

Murray's eyebrows rose and I could tell that Spencer, though he concealed it better, was also surprised.

"Fine, let me have a look at your cases. Do you also have—"

Jimmy was already in the process of handing copies to Spencer.

"Oh, I see you do," said Murray. "Very well, give your papers to the bailiff."

Jimmy was fuming as he sat down. The color of his face was at least two shades higher. I was about to tell him to relax, when Katherine pushed a note she had just written toward me. All it said was, "Setup."

I looked at her, then nudged Jimmy with my elbow. He read the same thing, opened his mouth to reply, then thought better of it. The calm manner in which Katherine was dealing with the situation communicated itself to him.

Meanwhile, Murray was pretending to read the cases Jimmy had given him. "Mr. d'Taglia, the way I see it this case says, 'that such evidence, *if left uncorrected*, may be grounds for a mistrial.' In view of this language, I'm going to accept Mr. Spencer's suggestion and instruct the jury to disregard my remark. Please bring them back, Bailiff."

As soon as the jury took their seats Murray addressed them once again.

"Ladies and gentlemen, unfortunately judges are human and I just made a mistake a moment ago by mentioning the nationality and the legal status of, Jennifer Pechorin. You are to completely disregard that remark and put it from your minds."

"Sure, y'all remember to forget now," Jimmy muttered in a mock Southern accent,

The judge continued, "Are there any among you who are incapable of doing that and carrying out your oath to render a fair and impartial verdict? If there are, please raise your hands."

I didn't expect anyone to do it, and from the derisive noise that came from Katherine's throat, neither did she.

"Very well, Mr. d'Taglia, your motion is denied. We'll take opening statements next."

JIMMY'S opening was solid and straightforward. He told the jury ours was a case for wrongful death, assault, terroristic threats, and the intentional infliction of emotional distress. He told them the weight of evidence would prove that Warren Blendel was directly responsible for orchestrating these acts. The jury listened intently while he spoke. A number of them took notes. A few, including the newspaper people and television reporters, glanced at me when he mentioned my father's name.

I sat there quietly trying not to show any reaction, which wasn't easy, because I wanted to throw Warren Blendel out the nearest window. Katherine reached for my hand under the table and tried to calm me down. I can assure you, there's a big difference between being a party in a suit and representing one.

I learned a long time ago that jurors tend to make up their minds after opening statements and usually hold that opinion throughout the course of a trial. I expected this would be the case here. Jimmy's remarks took over forty minutes, and when he finished, there was a leaden silence in the courtroom. Then it was Joe Spencer's turn.

"Ladies and gentlemen of the jury, if what Mr. d'Taglia says is true, we wouldn't be here today. We would have settled this matter a long time ago. But the sad truth is, it's not.

"Now, I want you to know we are just as sorry as we can be about the deaths of William Delaney and Andre Rostov, but my clients had nothing to do with those deaths, nor with any of the other acts Mr. d'Taglia is accusing us of. Just because Warren Blendel is a wealthy man doesn't make them true. All of you took a solemn oath to render a fair and impartial decision, and that's exactly what we're asking you to do, no matter how much sympathy you might feel for the plaintiffs.

"This case is about money and opportunism. It's that simple. William Delaney died in an automobile accident on his way home from work fifteen years ago. His son has waited all this time to come forward, claiming he now has *new evidence* the accident that killed his father was no accident at all.

"We're content to let you decide how credible this evidence is and how credible the people he expects to testify are.

"The plaintiffs would have you believe that Warren Blendel is the mastermind of a vast criminal empire. This is same Warren Blendel who personally funded the Children's Hospital and donated millions to charitable organizations throughout this city for years.

"You will learn that Mr. Blendel is a very sick man. He is also a very brave one who has taken these *scurrilous* charges stoically and with the same grace he has demonstrated all of his life. Ladies and gentlemen, I am honored to be his attorney.

"We will present expert testimony from highly respected doctors and health care professionals on the subject of Warren Blendel's health. You can judge for yourselves if what I'm saying is true or not. And I want you to hold me to this. In the end, we are going to ask you for a verdict in our favor and judgment against the plaintiffs for having brought such a frivolous lawsuit."

Whether Joe Spencer was worth a thousand bucks an hour I didn't know, but he was definitely good. Doubts about representing myself crept into my thoughts. Katherine has a steel-trap mind and could probably handle anything Spencer threw at her. She's one of the best trial lawyers I know. I wasn't so sure about myself. The bottom line was that we were talking about my father and I owed him my best effort. That's a son's duty—my duty.

In view of the District Attorney's decision not to seek an indictment until he had "more evidence," we were left with no other options. The civil suit would be our one and only chance at Warren Blendel. Jimmy's opposition to my involvement as a lawyer on the case was probably correct. I knew that as well. Katherine was standing by me out of love, so her judgment wasn't the clearest in the matter either.

A few nights earlier, my sister and I talked the situation over and she raised a similar point. So did my mother. Objectively, they all made sense, but it's hard to be objective where your father is concerned. In the end, I refused to be swayed and held to my original decision. If I failed, I failed, but one way or the other William T. Delaney's soul would be laid to rest.

When Spencer was through, I turned in my seat and looked toward the rear of the courtroom where two men were seated.

"Who are they?" Jimmy whispered.

I shrugged. "Just interested observers, I guess."

Katherine also looked. Our eyes met briefly when she turned back around. Her expression conveyed nothing.

FIFTY-EIGHT

DELANEY

JIMMY, Katherine, and I ate lunch with Lissa and Brenda at a restaurant a few blocks from the courthouse. It was a little after noon when the judge decided to take a break. He told everyone we would reconvene at one thirty. Sarah stayed behind to finish speaking with her father. Jennifer and Karel went to the cafeteria along with the two FBI agents who had been assigned to guard them.

"So, now we know where Joe Spencer is coming from," Jimmy said. "Warren Blendel is a sick man and the doctors will testify to that. Sick or not, I don't think the jury will buy it."

"I don't know," Katherine said. "There's something else going on. I just need to understand what that is."

Lissa asked, "If Blendel killed my father, what difference does it make whether he's sick or not? Murder is murder."

"Right," Brenda agreed.

Katherine shook her head. "It comes down to whether the jury accepts their story. They were listening while Spencer was talking. My guess is he's trying to set up some kind of diminished-capacity defense."

Jimmy nodded. "You understand we're not going to produce a smoking gun here. Blendel wasn't driving the truck and all we have is a junkie named William Rosetti to tie him to the accident through Hans Schiller. Not a very strong link. The accident—"

"*Murder*," Lissa corrected.

"Murder," Jimmy agreed. "The point is, we can't take this doctor business lightly. If that's Spencer's angle, I need to counter it."

"How?" I asked. "If he's got a doctor and a therapist to say that Blendel's sick, what can we do? Get one of our own and say he's not? The judge won't grant an independent medical exam at this stage."

"But they sprang the witnesses on us at the last minute. It's reversible error," Jimmy insisted.

Katherine said, "I agree with John. We'll just have to sail with the wind we've got."

Surprised, Jimmy looked at her, "But you always told me—"

"Let's drop it for now, Jimmy."

He wasn't happy—no trial lawyer is when you're tying their hands. Katherine knew it and so did I. Unfortunately, it couldn't be helped right now. If what we had in mind worked, it would put an end to Mr. Blendel one way or the other. There was still a lot preparation to be done before we got under way again, so we said good-bye to my sister and Brenda and headed back to the court.

WHEN the judge returned to the bench, I glanced around the courtroom looking for Lissa and Brenda and was a little surprised they weren't back yet. They were probably running late.

The first witness to take the stand was Sarah. She was plainly nervous, but she handled Jimmy's questions well. The jury listened carefully when she explained why she had taken the file from the U.S. Attorney's office. Some of them nodded sympathetically. Jimmy however, ran into a brick wall when he asked why she and Andre had faked her death.

"Ms. O'Connor, you've told us that you left New York for two reasons: One was to accept a scholarship to Emory University, and the other was because of the file you took."

"That's correct."

"But you didn't stay in law school, did you?"

"No, I didn't."

"And why is that?"

"I met a young man named, Andre . . . Andre Rostov. He was a third-year medical student."

"Where did you meet Mr. Rostov?"

"At a party a few weeks after I arrived in Atlanta."

"I see. What happened after your meeting?"

"I woke up the next morning in his bed. They had put something in my drink."

"Objection, Your Honor," Joe Spencer said, coming to his feet.

"Frankly, I don't care about this young lady's social life or her sexual adventures, but there's no foundation for her last statement. She used the term *they . . . they put something in my drink.* We don't know who 'they' are and I certainly can't cross-examine them. The question is clearly prejudicial to my client."

"Mr. d'Taglia?" asked the judge.

"I understand," Jimmy answered. "Let me ask the question another way. Did you have anything to drink at the party?"

"Yes."

"And did you get that drink yourself or did someone hand it to you?"

"Andre got the drink for me."

"Did you ever come to learn that your drink had been tampered with?"

"Yes, I did. It was later, but Andre told me—"

"Your Honor, I'm going to object again," said Spencer. "I don't mind Ms. O'Connor telling us what she actually knows, but the Dead Man's Rule prohibits her from introducing statements that Mr. Rostov made. He's deceased and there's no way we can refute them."

This time Judge Murray didn't bother asking for Jimmy's response. "You're quite right, Mr. Spencer. A witness may not testify as to statements a deceased person made and I will not allow it."

Jimmy continued. "All right, Sarah. What happened after you woke up in Andre's bed?"

"He showed me a tape he had made—a tape of him and me."

"Having sex?"

Sarah's nod prompted a warning from the judge.

"Ma'am, you'll need to respond with an audible yes or no so the court reporter can take down your answer."

"Yes," said Sarah.

"Proceed, Counselor," the judge instructed Jimmy.

"What occurred after you saw this tape?"

"I was in shock. I couldn't believe what was happening to me. I went home and took a bath. I wanted to tell someone, but I was so ashamed. I didn't know who to turn to."

"I understand. What happened after that?"

"Andre came to my house the next day and demanded that I

come with him. He said he would send the tape to my parents and put it on the Internet if I didn't."

Spencer started to get to his feet, but changed his mind and sat back down. He shook his head when Jimmy paused, motioning for him to continue.

"Was this the only sex tape you made, Sarah?"

"No."

"How many were there?"

"I really don't know; four, I think." Sarah's eyes darted to her father and away again.

"Sarah, did it ever occur to you to go to the police and tell them you were being blackmailed and forced into these . . . performances?"

"Yes, but I was afraid that it would get my father in trouble."

"I'm confused," Jimmy said. "How would your making sex tapes with Andre Rostov get your father into trouble?"

"A few weeks after I met Andre, two men came to my home. They wouldn't tell me who they were. They said I had something that belonged to their boss and if I didn't hand it over—"

This time Joe Spencer did object. He rose to his feet and spread his arms wide for emphasis. "Your Honor, this is not only hearsay, it's double hearsay. These men aren't in court. They're not on any witness list, and I'm never going to have an opportunity to cross-examine them. She might as well say Santa Claus came to her house and threatened her."

"Absolutely," the judge agreed. "The jury is instructed to ignore the witness's last remark. The court reporter will—"

"Your Honor," Katherine said. "There is an exception to the hearsay rule that allows statements of this kind to come in. A witness is permitted—"

Murray cut her off before she had a chance to finish her sentence. "Ms. Adams, you may be listed as co-counsel in the case, but Mr. d'Taglia is conducting this portion of the trial and as such you will not make objections."

"Sorry," Katherine said with a sweet smile. "I guess I'm not completely familiar with New York's civil procedure."

"Then I suggest you educate yourself. I will not tolerate these interruptions."

"Yes, sir. Is it all right if I hand Mr. d'Taglia the cases?" she asked, holding out a small stack of papers.

The judge took a breath through his nostrils and gave her a baleful look. "Go ahead."

Jimmy took them and addressed the court. "Your Honor, there *is* an exception to the hearsay rule, which I was about to point out. The rule in New York is that a witness *can* testify to statements that would otherwise be hearsay, *if* the statement is introduced for the *limited purpose of explaining their conduct*. I have six cases here, if you would like to see them."

The judge turned to Joe Spencer for a response. But Spencer shook his head and sat back down. A slight smile played at the corners of his mouth as he and Katherine exchanged glances. He had just made his first mistake—never object if it doesn't advance your cause. Katherine, Jimmy, and I had worked out this scenario the night before and it came off without a hitch. Instead of blocking Sarah's testimony, he had just succeeded in getting everyone in the courtroom to focus on it.

From the expression on Judge Murray's face, it was equally clear to him. He took a few minutes to read the cases before handing them back to Jimmy.

"Ladies and gentlemen, what this witness will testify to is hearsay and such statements have *no* evidentiary value. That means you should not accept them as being true. I'm permitting them for a *limited* purpose so Ms. O'Connor can explain her conduct." The judge gestured for Jimmy to continue.

"Would the court reporter please read back the last question and Ms. O'Connor's answer?"

The court reporter searched his notes for several seconds. "You said, '*I'm confused. How would making sex tapes with Andre Rostov get your father into trouble?*' The witness replied: '*A few weeks after I met Andre two men came to my house. They wouldn't tell me who they were. They said that I had something that belonged to their boss and if I didn't hand it over . . .*'"

"Right, I've got it now. All right, Sarah, please finish your answer."

"They said they were going to send the tapes to my school. They also told me they would sell me to a man in Argentina if I didn't give them the file."

Out of the corner of my eye I saw two of the women on the jury sit back in their seats and exchange looks with each other.

Jimmy asked, "What happened then?"

"I stalled for time."

"How?"

"I knew Andre had a crush on me so I went to him and told him what the men had said."

"Did you have similar feelings for Andre?"

Sarah paused before she answered. Her eyes passed over Jennifer, who was seated at the plaintiffs' table.

"I thought Andre had gotten into something over his head. He was looking for a way out, just like I was."

"That's not what I asked you, Sarah," Jimmy said in a softer tone.

"No, I didn't share the same feelings for him. But I didn't know where else to turn or what to do. I knew how he felt about me and I thought he would help if I asked him.

"I see. Tell the jury what happened next."

"We developed a plan to fake my death. Andre was a medical student and he was working with the coroner's office at the time. He smuggled a body out of the morgue at night that was about the same height and weight as I am.

"Two of our friends were going camping in north Georgia the next day, so we went with them and set it up to look like an accident . . . like I fell off the cliff.

"After that, I took some clothes and personal items from my house and went into hiding. I thought if the men believed I was dead, they would go away."

"And did they?"

"No . . . they didn't go away," Sarah said quietly.

The rest of her testimony went quickly. She explained how I had found her and about our decision to take her to Miami. She told the jury about the ordeal she, Katherine, and Jennifer underwent in the swamp and about the man who had tried to kill them.

While she spoke, I glanced across at Warren and Linda Blendel. His face gave no indication of what he was thinking. If anything, he looked somewhat sad. Linda, on the other hand, contented herself by sighing loudly and shaking her head in disbelief at the testimony.

Sarah's direct examination took nearly three hours to complete, and when it was done I expected Joe Spencer to start his cross. He didn't.

"Your Honor," Spencer said, "I don't know about the jury, but I could sure use a break. If counsel and the court have no objection, I'd just as soon begin fresh tomorrow. My cross-examination will take a while and I'd rather not have to split it in two parts."

"That's fine with me," said Murray. "Any problem with that, Mr. d'Taglia?"

"No, sir," Jimmy replied.

"Very well, we'll be in recess until ten o'clock tomorrow morning."

FIFTY-NINE

DELANEY

THE moment we stepped off the elevator I knew something was wrong. Mike Franklin and two uniform cops were standing in the lobby talking with Brenda. It looked like she was crying. Mike spotted us at the same time and started walking toward me. A cold feeling seeped into my stomach when I saw his expression. Katherine noticed as well and put a hand on my shoulder.

"It's your sister, John," Mike said as he got closer. "There's been an accident." He held up his hands in a calming gesture. "She gonna be okay, but she's been hurt."

"What? How?"

"We don't know. I was just in the process of taking a statement from that lady over there. Lissa's at NYU's Downtown Hospital right now. I was a couple of blocks away when the call came in. I didn't even know who was involved until a few minutes ago."

When Brenda finally saw us, she broke away from the officers and ran across the lobby into my arms. "Oh, John."

The officers started after her, but Mike waved them off. It took a second to recover my wits. Everything was coming at me at once.

"Tell me what happened," I said.

Brenda pulled a ragged breath into her lungs and regained her composure. Her eyes were red and her face was streaked with eyeliner.

"We just came back from lunch and Lissa wanted to use the bathroom before we went inside. I said I'd meet her in the court. When she didn't come back I decided to see if she was all right. She wasn't in the bathroom so I checked the halls, but there was no sign of her. If I had just . . . if I had . . ." Brenda dissolved into tears again.

Katherine put an arm around her shoulders. "Shh. It's okay," she said in a soothing tone. "Just tell us what happened."

A few passersby stopped to ask the police officers what was wrong. They cast sympathetic glances in our direction and kept on going. One lady from the clerk's office brought a Dixie cup filled with water for Brenda to drink.

Brenda finally got herself under control and continued. "I saw Lissa's purse on the floor near the entrance to the stairwell, so I poked my head inside." She grabbed my arm. "John, she was lying at the bottom of the stairs—there was blood everywhere. Her eye, her face . . . it was . . ."

I swallowed and hugged her again. "All right. Which hospital did you say she was at?" I asked Mike.

"NYU on William Street. C'mon. I'll give you a ride. Ma'am," he said, turning to Brenda, "I know you're upset, but it's very important that we get the rest of your statement. How about if you come with us? We can talk some more later."

Brenda nodded and we all started for the door together. Katherine kept her arm around her shoulders the entire way. There were a hundred questions going around in my head, but I didn't want to discuss what had happened yet. A few reporters shouted to us and started to approach only to be stopped by a pair of uniforms who were waiting outside. I got in the front seat with Mike and waited until we pulled away from the curb.

"Talk to me," I said.

His look was worried. "I don't have all the details. Burt Aguilar called me from the emergency room and said the docs think she'll pull through okay. From what he told me she has a severe injury to her left eye and possibly a broken leg and pelvis. I guess her face was pretty beat up from the fall."

I rested my head against the window for a moment. "Any idea how it happened?"

"I only know what the bailiff and the lady told me," he said, gesturing to Brenda with his head. "Apparently the bailiff was coming up the steps to deliver some papers when he heard her yelling for help. He radioed 911."

"Brenda, did you speak with Lissa?" Katherine asked.

Brenda shook her head. "She was barely conscious when I found her. She was lying at the bottom of the steps. It was horrible."

AN hour trudged by and then another while we sat in the hospital's waiting room. The couches and chairs were made of molded plastic and uncomfortable as hell. All the receptionist could tell us was that Lissa was in surgery. She didn't know how long it would take. I left a message with her asking for the emergency room doctor to get in touch with us as soon as possible. He showed up three hours later. At that point my mind had already conjured up a dozen scenarios regarding my sister's condition, each one worse than the next. The doctor's name was Terry Billings and he looked a little older than my son, Mark. He was dressed in jeans, a T-shirt, and had a stethoscope draped around his neck. He was sympathetic, but knew little more about Lissa's condition beyond his original assessment. He explained about the trauma to her face and eye and confirmed my sister's leg and pelvis had, indeed, been broken in the fall. This prompted him to call in several specialists: an orthopedic surgeon, an ophthalmologist, and a plastic surgeon. I thought Brenda would start crying again when he said *plastic surgeon,* but she held herself together.

Waiting is the worst part. It gives you time to think and you're helpless to do anything. Mike stayed with us the whole time, though he occasionally stepped outside to smoke. I'd quit years ago but the thought of a cigarette was sounding better and better to me as the afternoon dragged on.

It was close to six o'clock by the time they finally let us up onto the floor where Lissa had been moved. A nurse told us the doctor would speak with us in a few minutes. A short while later a heavyset man in green scrubs came through the double doors at the end of the hallway.

"Mr. Delaney?"

"I'm Delaney," I said, shaking hands.

"I'm Myron Epstein, Lissa's doctor. I take it you're her husband?"

"Her brother. This is Brenda Yamamoto, Lissa's partner." Then I introduced the others. "How's she doing?"

There was a slight hesitation as Dr. Epstein processed the implications of talking to his patient's brother and her partner. He seemed satisfied.

"Your sister's had a pretty rough time of it. We've stabilized her, so she's in no immediate danger at the moment, but she's been hurt—terribly hurt."

Katherine and Mike both moved closer to hear what he had to say. Katherine slipped her arm through mine.

I said, "Just give it to me straight, Doc."

Epstein drew a breath and paused. I could see he was trying to choose his words carefully. "We managed to save one of her eyes, but the left side of her face has been badly—"

Brenda gasped and her hand went to her mouth in shock. *"Omigod!"*

"Damaged," Epstein continued. "It's going to require several operations to correct. My colleague Steve Shackelford was called in to set her hip and leg. He had to use a number of pins and screws, but he said they got a good result. We think, in time, Lissa will make a full recovery. There have been wonderful advances in prosthetics over the last ten years."

"A fall did all that damage?" Mike said.

Epstein leveled his gaze on him. "Detective, considering the nature and extent of her injuries, I would say it's *highly* unlikely she suffered them in a fall. Lissa Delaney was attacked, viciously attacked, by someone of great strength. She was stabbed several times in the abdomen and around her kidneys with a pointed object."

The last statement hit me like a sledgehammer. Someone had attacked my sister in broad daylight in the middle of the courthouse. "Are you certain?" I asked.

"Positive. There's no question in my mind."

Mike and I exchanged glances and started down the hall together.

"Is she able to talk now? Mike asked the doctor.

"She should be. They brought her up from recovery about an hour ago. She'll be a woozy from the pain medication, but I think it will be all right for a little while. No more than a few minutes, Detective. That's all I'll allow."

Mike started to say something and decided against it. "Deal," he said, opening the door to Lissa's room.

I'd been preparing myself mentally for the way she would look; still, the sight came as a shock. Lissa was a mess, worse than any image I had conjured up. Her face was heavily bandaged and there was a cast on her right leg that went all the way to her hip. It took a good deal of effort not to let my reaction show. Brenda immediately went to her side and took her hand, stroking it gently.

Bandages covered most of my sister's face with the exception of her right eye and mouth. But even they were swollen and bruised. On a metal pole was a plastic bag with clear liquid that steadily dripped down a tube into a vein in her forearm. Alongside the bed was a machine monitoring her vital signs. A mixture of anguish for her and hatred for whoever had maimed her knotted the area between my shoulder blades.

Mike's mouth tightened when he saw Lissa and he shook his head in disbelief. It was several seconds before she opened her eye and noticed us standing there. There wasn't much she could tell us. We spoke for maybe five minutes before the doctor stepped in and called an end to it, ushering everyone out of the room. The sedatives were taking hold again and she was fading in and out of consciousness. I kissed my little sister on her cheek and was about to leave with the others when a hoarse whisper stopped me at the door.

"John."

"I'm here," I said, moving to her side.

She reached out and grabbed my sleeve. She was so weak. I put my hand on hers and patted it gently.

"It's all right. You need to sleep now. I'll be right outside. Just rest."

To my surprise, her grip tightened and she pulled harder on my arm. Her lips were moving, trying to say something. I bent closer to hear.

"He said he was going to kill you and Mom and everyone in Katherine's family," she whispered." Her voice little more than a croak.

"What? Who said that?"

"I couldn't see his face. He said the next time he's going to cut my hands off and take my other eye if you don't back off."

A chill ran up my spine. *If I don't back off.* "Lis, can you remember *anything* about him? Anything?"

Her head moved from side to side. "He said he's going to kill Mom. You can't let him, John. You can't let him do that."

"I won't, honey. I won't. I swear to God."

A tear slowly trickled out of the corner of her eye and slid down the side of her face. I wiped it away with my free hand.

"He hurt me, John. He hurt me so bad. I tried to fight him, but he was too strong."

Her voice was becoming thick and the words were slurred. I could barely make out what she was saying. The last thing I heard clearly was, "He had an accent."

SIXTY

BLENDEL

WARREN Blendel sat back in the limousine and stared out its tinted windows at New York's skyline as they crossed over the Fifty-ninth Street Bridge. Every time he passed this way it reminded him of Simon and Garfunkel's song. Across from him, Linda was speaking with Hans Schiller, ignoring him as if he wasn't there. It didn't matter.

Thus far everything had gone as planned, from getting the O'Connor girl out of town to forcing her to make those videos. Alone and without resources, she had played directly into his hands. Whatever credibility she gained with the jury was quickly offset by the porno films. It was like the madam of a brothel trying to convince people she was really a social worker at heart.

He knew any link between himself and the murders was tenuous at best. Hopefully the jury had enough sense to pick up on that. Still, it was a gamble anytime you placed your fate in the hands of others. Unfortunately that couldn't be helped now. The name of the game was damage control. Blendel reflected on the collective ignorance people tended to display in groups, like the twelve imbeciles who awarded some fool millions of dollars for spilling hot coffee in her lap and claimed she didn't know it would burn.

His old friend in the District Attorney's office had managed to kill the indictment, which also helped. But they weren't home yet. The press was having a field day, but that was all to his benefit. Refusing to take the case to the grand jury was only a temporary reprieve at best. The real hurdle would come tomorrow, or maybe the day after, when d'Taglia trotted out the resurrected Billy Rosetti, or whatever he called himself now. That was what Delaney and his crew were counting on.

Joe Spencer claimed he wasn't concerned about Rosetti's testimony because the man was a junkie who had criminal charges hanging over his head. According to their sources, Rosetti was looking to cut a deal, which wouldn't be lost on anyone in the courtroom.

He glanced at Schiller and looked away again. Linda was giving him instructions about how to answer questions if he was called as a witness. It must be wonderful to be an expert on so many things, he thought.

Schiller nodded in agreement and listened, or gave the appearance of listening. Blendel wasn't sure which. His head of security had a more pragmatic view of their situation. One day after the process server had brought out Delaney's lawsuit, Schiller quietly made arrangements to leave the country using one of his many aliases.

The fact that he hadn't done so yet meant he was biding his time. He wanted to see how the trial would turn out. As a group, Germans always demonstrated excellent survival skills. Whatever Schiller decided also wouldn't matter. He could be replaced. It was a shame about Joshua, though.

Joe Spencer was confident of a victory. The man was a supreme optimist, having rarely lost a trial in the past thirty years. Blendel wished he could be as confident. Even if they won, the residual effect on his business couldn't be underestimated. People remembered rumor and innuendo longer than they did facts. A few well-placed donations and charity functions would take care of that. His public relations firm was standing by, ready to swing into action once the trial was over.

"Warren, are you listening to me?" Linda asked, shaking him out of his musings.

"What? I'm sorry, dear. I'm just a bit preoccupied. What did you say?"

"I asked if you took your medication today."

"I don't think so," Blendel said. "Actually, I'm feeling quite well."

Linda ignored him and opened the limo's minibar. Removing a small bottle of Perrier, she poured half the contents into a glass, then took a pill from a tiny box she kept in her purse and handed it to Blendel.

"Take it now, please. I can't have you falling apart if they call you to the stand."

"But—"

"Warren."

Blendel smiled. "Perhaps you're right."

He was still smiling when he put down the glass and the pill was still in the palm of his hand.

SIXTY-ONE

DELANEY

I was livid when I left the hospital, angrier than I could ever remember being. When I told Mike what Lissa had said, he reacted the same way. We placed a conference call to Phil Thurman, who had already heard about the attack and was busy questioning people at the courthouse. Thus far he had nothing. His theory, and it made sense in light of Lissa's comment about my backing off, was that Blendel was at the bottom of it. But theories weren't enough to make an arrest. Our call ended in frustration.

Mike posted a guard at Lissa's door around the clock and stationed another man at my mother's house in Queens. Throughout our discussions I was aware that Katherine had been watching me. I could tell something was bothering her, but decided to wait until we were alone to discuss it. This didn't happen until dinner.

"We can always drop the case and refile later," she said. "The statute of limitations hasn't run yet."

"We're not dropping anything."

"Are you sure, John? If it was my family—"

"K.J., they can go after Lissa again the next time, or my mother, or your children, for that matter. It has to end. I can't live my life jumping at shadows."

Katherine stared at me for a long moment before she nodded. She got up, gave me a hug, and went into my office to do some research. The attack on Lissa had shaken me. I'd like to say that my mind launched into high gear, crystallized by that horrible episode, but it wouldn't be true. I was having trouble thinking straight. If this was what Blendel was shooting for, he got it—in spades. I was consumed with guilt at not having protected my baby sister, and as a result she had been maimed for life. Try as I might, I simply couldn't concentrate for more than a few minutes at a time . . . plus I felt like a rat for not staying at the hospital. I couldn't get the way she looked out of my head, and there were still hours of preparation I had to do before court. It was going to be a long night.

THE second day of trial began with Joe Spencer's cross-examination and he wasted no time going on the attack. Jimmy, Katherine, and I talked on the phone and agreed because of Katherine's greater trial experience she would be the one to handle this portion of the case. Jimmy was shaken by the news of Lissa's attack and echoed Katherine's suggestion about dismissing the suit. To his credit, he never wavered or brought up the subject again after I told him of my decision. I prayed it was the right one.

"All right, Ms. O'Connor," Spencer said, checking his notes, "let me see if I've got this straight. After you stole a file belonging to the U.S. government, you accepted a scholarship to an Atlanta law school, met this Andre Rostov fellow, and began making porno films with him. Yes or no?"

"Your Honor," Katherine said, rising to her feet. "The witness is not required to answer with a yes or no. She can answer any way she chooses. Mr. Spencer just asked her a compound question and she has a right to explain whatever she says."

"Let her respond first," said the judge. "Then she can explain her answer." He nodded for Sarah to continue.

"That's just part of what happened," Sarah said. "I didn't *begin* making porno films with Andre. I was blackmailed into it."

"Right, you were blackmailed. How much were you paid to do these films, Ms. O'Connor?"

"I wasn't paid anything."

"So you did these because you wanted to?"

"I just told you I was forced into it."

Spencer looked at the jury and shrugged elaborately, indicating his disbelief. It was a showy thing to do.

"Okay, have it your way. Now at some point in time, these evil men who were forcing you to make sex films came to you and asked about the stolen file, then they threatened to sell you into white slavery in Brazil if you didn't give it to them."

"It was Argentina," Sarah said.

"Sorry, Argentina."

"Yes, that's what they said."

"So you and Mr. Rostov, the same man who initially drugged you and forced you to make the films, concocted a scheme to steal a body from Atlanta's county morgue. Then damaged the face so the police couldn't recognize who it was and threw the poor woman off a cliff, all with the intention of deliberately misleading the authorities into thinking that it was you. Do I have this right so far, ma'am?"

"Yes."

"And after doing all this you went into hiding."

"Yes."

"But you came out because Mr. Delaney and Ms. Adams, your partners in this lawsuit, found you and told you Mr. Rostov had been murdered."

"Yes, but that wasn't—"

"Of course you believed them, because it was further evidence of the conspiracy, didn't you? Particularly since John Delaney was your former law professor and a friend of the family?"

"Yes, I did."

"Well, that's quite a story, ma'am," Spencer said. "I've been practicing law for thirty-five years and it's certainly the most entertaining one I've ever heard."

"Objection, Your Honor," Katherine said. "Counsel is not asking a question. He's engaging in closing argument."

"Sustained."

Spencer chuckled and held up a hand in surrender. "I'll withdraw it. Let me ask you this, Ms. O'Connor. Did Mr. Delaney ever tell you the Atlanta police found a suicide note with Andre Rostov's body saying that his death should be on Mr. Delaney's conscience?"

The surprise on Sarah's face was obvious to everyone in the courtroom. "Professor Delaney couldn't—"

"That's not what I asked you," Spencer said, cutting her off. "I asked if—"

"No, Professor Delaney never mentioned that."

"Yes, I'm sure he didn't."

Katherine was halfway to her feet again when Spencer announced, "Withdrawn." She sat back down.

"Now, Ms. O'Connor, you are or *were* a law student before all this began. And I assume that you took the classes most law students take."

"Yes."

"I'm curious—is it also a crime in Georgia to do what you did, the same as it is here in New York State?"

"Objection," Katherine said.

"Overruled," Murray said replied. "She can answer that. This young lady has a background in the law."

"Yes," Sarah said. "What I did would be a crime in both places."

"Let's see now, how many crimes would that be?" Spencer asked. "We have stealing a government file, stealing a dead body, mutilating it, then perpetrating a fraud upon the police. My math's not too good, but I make it out to be four. Does that sound about right to you?"

"Yes, it constitutes four crimes," Sarah agreed.

I spared a quick glance at the jury and didn't like what I was seeing. They wanted to believe Sarah but were finding it more and more difficult.

"Ms. O'Connor, am I correct in assuming that you and Jennifer Pechorin took off on the swamp odyssey we heard about yesterday based solely on the representations of John Delaney and Katherine Adams?"

"Ms. Adams was with us."

"All right, Ms. Adams was with you."

"Yes, we did."

"And it never once occurred to you to check out their story and see if it was true or not? You just went with a total stranger?"

"I trusted Professor Delaney and I trust Ms. Adams."

Spencer shook his head. "Now, the man you said was trying to kill you in the swamp, did he ever speak to you?"

"Not really."

"He didn't tell you he was working for Warren Blendel, did he?"

The question produced some laughter around the court, prompting the judge to rap his gavel for order.

"No, he didn't say that."

"In fact, you never laid eyes on Warren Blendel until the moment you walked into this courtroom, did you?"

"No."

"And you've never had the first conversation with him, have you, ma'am?"

"No, I haven't."

"And not one of the shadowy figures you mentioned earlier, those men who were blackmailing you . . . none of them are here today, are they?"

"No, they're not."

"Ms. O'Connor, would it be safe to say these men never spoke the name of Warren Blendel to you, did they?" Spencer asked.

"No."

"Thank you for your candor. There's one other thing I'd like to ask you. Do you understand that when you become a lawyer you take an oath to tell the truth and uphold the law?"

"Yes, I do."

Spencer stared at her for several seconds before he shook his head. "I have no further questions for this witness."

Linda Blendel flipped a triumphant smile in our direction as Sarah returned to the plaintiffs' table. As before, Warren Blendel stared straight ahead.

Jimmy took over once more and called Phillip Thurman as our next witness. Thurman told the jury he was with the FBI and went on to explain what was in Sarah's stolen file. I thought Spencer might object at that point, but he didn't. He just sat back and let Thurman summarize the file's contents for the jury. This was a strange tactic for a trial lawyer of his experience to take.

Then it was Joe Spencer's turn.

"So, Mr. Thurman, you're telling us that Warren Blendel was the object of an investigation some fifteen years ago. Is that right?"

"It is," Thurman replied.

"And can you advise the jury whether he was arrested as a result of this investigation?"

"No, he wasn't arrested."

"But surely he was indicted?"

"No, Mr. Blendel was not indicted. There wasn't sufficient—"

"No arrests *and* no indictment?"

"No."

"In fact, to this day, Warren Blendel has *never* been prosecuted for anything nor has he spent a single minute in jail, has he, Agent Thurman?"

"Not to my knowledge."

"That's exactly right. Now, I'd like to ask you a few questions about yourself if you don't mind. Are you the same Phillip Thurman who used to head the FBI's New York branch?"

Thurman shifted in his seat. "I am."

"And if I understand correctly, following your failure, or I should say the failure of your office, to solve the Sobreski case, where two agents of yours were murdered in cold blood, you were transferred out of New York and reassigned to Atlanta?"

"I was reassigned to Atlanta," Thurman agreed. "I'm not privy to the director's reasons for doing so. He sent me where I was needed the most."

"All right," said Spencer. "I can understand your reluctance to admit to the first part of my question. Would I be correct in saying, though, it's your belief that Warren Blendel was somehow involved in the Sobreski case?"

"I believed then, as I do now, that Warren Blendel ordered the murder of my agents," Thurman told him.

"But of course he was never prosecuted for those crimes, was he?"

"No, he wasn't."

"And you've harbored a grudge against Mr. Blendel all these years, haven't you?"

"To answer your question, I think he's manipulating scum, Counselor."

"That's very refreshing, Mr. Thurman. But my question was whether you have a grudge against Warren Blendel."

"I'm a federal agent, Mr. Spencer. It's my job to catch criminals. I'm not on a first-name basis with them, so grudges don't enter into the equation. I do my job."

"Of course you do. May I ask if federal agents often go to the businesses of people they're investigating and tell them they're going to 'bring them down'?" Spencer made a show of consulting his notes. "Yes, I think that was the phrase you used."

I felt Jimmy stiffen next to me as Thurman went red in the face. Phil Thurman had neglected to mention this to us.

"I did meet with Mr. Blendel as part of my investigation, but I don't recall the specifics of our conversation," Thurman answered.

Spencer shrugged. "I suppose we could get the security tapes in here to help refresh your memory, but I'm hoping that won't be necessary. Would you agree with me that you visited Warren Blendel's offices in the Bronx four months ago and confronted him with the allegations surrounding this case?"

"I just said I met with him. The reason I went to Blendel's office was because one of my men in Atlanta was missing and I wanted to know if he knew anything about it. We found the man's body a few weeks later."

"Did Mr. Blendel confess to the crime or even say he knew anything about it?"

"No, he didn't."

"But you saw fit to threaten and harass him, didn't you?" Spencer asked, leaning closer to Thurman.

"I don't remember what words were used. I was upset at the time, and yes, it probably amounted to a threat. I take it personally when someone murders my people."

"I'm sure you do, Agent."

When Thurman was through, the judge excused him, but instructed him not to leave the building in case the lawyers had more questions. He then declared a lunch recess. Blendel left, supported under his arm by Linda, who was still playing the dutiful wife. Schiller gave me a good-natured pat on the shoulder as he passed. It took all my control not to get up and punch the smug bastard in his face. Katherine and Jimmy said they'd be in the lawyers' conference room preparing for the afternoon session.

I needed to walk.

SIXTY-TWO

DELANEY

IT took five minutes to regain my composure. What happened in the court didn't surprise me. Katherine and I were prepared for it. In one form or another, we'd discussed several scenarios over the past few weeks. Ups and downs in a trial are a fact of life. Even Jimmy, who tends to be upbeat even when the circumstances are dismal, looked depressed at the close of Thurman's testimony. After fifteen minutes, I found myself standing in front of Trinity Church, one of the oldest buildings in the city. Over the years, the original brownstone had darkened with age. Next to the church was a little cemetery.

I didn't know if they still buried people there. Probably not. A lot of the graves dated back to the early 1700s and 1800s. Alexander Hamilton was interred there. When I was in middle school, the teachers took us on field trips to Wall Street. Trinity Church was a regular stop on the program. Not much had changed since I was a kid. Hemlines went up and hemlines went down with the times, but Trinity Church remained a constant, implacable and solid. A couple of blocks east of it was where the World Trade Center had once stood. The principal attraction now is a discount clothing store called Century 21. I walked past it, dodging a group of women coming out the front door, and crossed the street to "ground zero."

The site is far bigger than it looks on television. Workmen had long since cleared away the rubble and were now busy rebuilding. That's America for you. The sound of jackhammers and heavy machinery filled the air. I'd heard rumors the powers that be had decided not to try to duplicate the old skyscrapers. New plans called for a cluster of seven smaller buildings. During the planning process, people were invited to send in their ideas about what the new buildings ought to look like. I think there may have even been a contest to this effect. One of guys I teach with drafted a letter to the commission suggesting they construct at least one of them in the shape of a middle finger and point it toward the Middle East. The story made the *New York Post,* but then everything makes the *Post.*

While I stood there watching the bulldozers, I became aware a man in a black suit was standing next to me. Sal the Tailor was one of the two men who had been sitting in back of the courtroom since the trial had begun. He was middle-aged and neatly groomed. His shoes were alligator and had probably set him back fifteen hundred bucks. Neither of us acknowledged the other. Eventually, I set my briefcase down, stretched, and checked my watch. There was still enough time to grab a slice of pizza before I headed back to court. Sal picked up the briefcase and headed in the opposite direction.

I saw Jimmy enter the courthouse lobby. He spotted me, waved, and started walking in my direction. The second man who had been watching the trial with Sal said good-bye and left before he got there. We didn't shake hands.

"Who was that?" Jimmy asked.

I lifted my shoulders. "Just some guy who likes trials. He was asking how I thought we were doing. He likes your style."

"How come?"

"He thinks you have a good presence—very aggressive."

"Yeah, that's me—Mr. Personality. I hope the jury feels the same way. I saw that man talking to K.J. earlier."

"Did you?"

"Wait till he sees her in action. He doesn't know from aggressive."

"She's a handful," I agreed. "I guess this trial's bringing them out of the woodwork."

"How's Lissa doing?"

I made a seesaw motion with my hand. "Katherine and I stopped by the hospital this morning. She's holding her own, but she's in a lot of pain."

It was time to go in, so we headed toward the elevators and got on with about ten other people. Jimmy didn't speak until we reached our floor.

"What you said in the lobby about people coming out of the woodwork isn't the half of it. A little while ago some lady came up to me and asked for my autograph."

"You're kidding?"

"No, I'm serious. There's also a television reporter from Channel Two who wants to set up an interview later."

"Your fame precedes you, Mr. d'Taglia," I said, clapping him on the shoulder.

"I don't give a shit about fame," he said, lowering his voice. "What I want is to shove this case up Spencer's ass and wipe the smug expression off his face."

"What were you saying about being aggressive?"

"Never mind. Maybe things will improve this afternoon. I'm calling Rosetti as my first witness. I'll follow him with Jennifer. That will leave K.J. for last. Once she's finished testifying, she'll be free to handle Jerry Barnwell's direct. I don't think they're prepared for that. We'll also call Frank O'Connor, but I'll give you two guesses what will happen when we do."

"He'll refuse to answer because criminal charges are pending against him."

"Bingo."

I pointed out, "Don't kid yourself. A lot of that Fifth Amendment stuff is overrated. When you stand on your rights and refuse to answer twenty or thirty questions in front of a jury, they start wondering why. It's like *Jaws* or *Alien*. Once the creature jumps out and scares the shit out of you, it's not so bad the second time around."

"I don't get it," Jimmy said.

"It works this way. What the mind imagines is usually a lot worse than the reality."

"I hope so, because we're getting our asses kicked at the moment."

"You think so?"

"Yeah, John, I do. So, how come you're not worried?"

"I'm not the worrying type."

He gave me an odd look and glanced around the hallway to make sure no one was near us before he spoke again.

"Look, I know you're not blind. Our link to Blendel is hanging by a thread. The jury liked Sarah, but only one or two of them bought her story. They didn't like Thurman at all."

"Maybe we'll get lucky with Rosetti."

"We damn well better."

In response to Jimmy's questions, Rosetti admitted he had been driving the truck that killed my father. He said was ordered to do it by Hans Schiller. Then he pointed to Schiller in open court and identified him as Twin Tree Corporation's head of security, the same company that Warren Blendel was CEO of at the time.

Schiller and Linda Blendel only looked at each other and shook their heads sadly.

Rather than let Spencer surprise the jury with Rosetti's criminal background, Jimmy did the smart thing and raised the topic first. He got him to admit that he was now in a witness protection program because he feared for his life. I noticed a few more heads around the room nodding while he gave his testimony. In the end, all Spencer could do was to point out Rosetti's conflict of interest for the jury.

Frank O'Connor was one of the biggest surprises of the day. Contrary to our predictions, he did not decline to answer Jimmy's questions. Instead, he admitted that he'd been taking bribes when my father was killed. Frank identified Blendel's company as one of the contributors, and like Rosetti, he also named Schiller as his contact along with his brother, Nick.

When Jimmy turned Frank over to Spencer for cross-examination, Spencer remained in his seat for several seconds, staring at Frank over the tops of his fingertips.

"Mr. Spencer?" the judge prompted.

Spencer came out of his reverie and stood up. "So, Detective O'Connor, let me see if I understand you correctly. Fifteen years ago you, your brother, and your partner all accepted bribes from Warren Blendel. Is that true?"

"Objection, Your Honor," said Jimmy. "Counsel is mischaracterizing the evidence. Mr. O'Connor never said William Delaney accepted a bribe."

"Sustained," the judge answered. "Keep to the facts, Mr. Spencer."

"My apologies. It's just that I'm just somewhat taken aback by this witness's sudden desire to cleanse his soul after all this time."

"We don't need those kind of gratuitous comments," Jimmy countered. "The plaintiffs move to strike them from the record."

"I'll withdraw the statement," said Spencer. "All right, Detective, who else beside you and your brother took bribes from Warren Blendel?"

"If you're suggesting that Bill Delaney ever took a bribe, I can tell you this—it never happened. The only reason I knew about my brother's involvement was because he was the one who pulled me in. All the money and gifts came through him and occasionally through Mr. Schiller."

"The money and gifts came through him," Spencer repeated. "And I assume Deputy Chief O'Connor is waiting right outside this court to come in and corroborate what you've said, isn't he?"

"No . . . Nick won't be doing that."

Spencer's face was a study in contempt and distaste. "I didn't think so, Detective. I have no further—"

"My brother's body was found in the water off Rikers Island late last night. He'd been shot in the head four times, Counselor."

The murmur of conversation in the courtroom rose immediately. Notebooks and pens came out and people started writing. The two artists who had been doing sketches for the evening report since the trial began reached for their pads. Several reporters left to phone in this latest development.

Frank's testimony caught Spencer off guard.

Everyone knew Nick O'Connor had been missing for several months, but it was assumed that was because he was in hiding. Spencer, of course, knew he wasn't going to show, but had asked one question too many. When he recovered from his surprise, he made a motion to strike the last remark, which the judge granted. Big surprise there. Just as he had done before, Murray instructed the jury to disregard it. From their reactions, however, I could tell the damage was already done.

KATHERINE was the last witness to take the stand for our side. Spencer got through the preliminaries on her background quickly and went right after her.

"Ms. Adams, you're a lawyer, so I won't spoon-feed you with the preliminaries, except to say if you don't understand what I'm asking, stop me and I'll rephrase my question. If you don't, I'll assume you understand me and I'll expect you to answer, okay?"

"That's fine."

"In a notarized affidavit you filed with this court, you swore the allegations in your complaint were true, didn't you?"

"Yes, I did."

"All right, ma'am. Let me direct your attention to Count Six of your complaint. In it you state that, 'persons employed by Warren Blendel entered upon your property and attempted to do harm to John Delaney.' "

"May I read it over, before I answer?"

"Of course," Spencer said, handing his papers to her.

On the bench, Judge Murray also picked up his file and located the paragraph they were discussing. After a second or two he raised his eyebrows and tossed it back on his desk as if it were unworthy of belief. Since the start of the case he had done a number of similar things, ranging from incredulous looks during a witness's testimony to bemused head shakes. These displays, some more subtle than others, were for the jury's benefit.

For the most part, people who sit on a jury want to do a good job. They come to the process believing the playing field is level and the judge, seated high above everyone else in the courtroom, will make sure it stays that way. As a result, judges are in a position to exert a tremendous influence in a trial. The vast majority do their best to avoid this and come off as neutral, but in Davis Murray we found an exception to the rule.

Katherine, Jimmy, and I discussed what to do about him the night before. We considered moving for a mistrial, but Katherine vetoed it. "I've run into his type before," she said. "Let me handle him."

As I glanced at my fiancée now, she looked quite calm and composed, as if she and Spencer were simply discussing the weather. When she was through reading, she handed the papers back to him.

"Yes, I believe that's what I said."

"These men obviously didn't do Mr. Delaney much harm. I'm looking at him now and he seems perfectly healthy to me."

"Everyone is entitled to an opinion, Counselor."

Her statement caused Judge Murray to twist around in his seat toward her. "Ms. Adams. I won't stand for smart remarks in this court. You're to answer Mr. Spencer's questions and not fence with him, do you understand me?"

"I'll be happy to answer a question when he asks one," Katherine replied. "The last thing he said was that John Delaney looked healthy to him. He looks healthy to me, too, but that doesn't alter the fact that two men tried to kill him fifty feet from my back door. I was there when it happened."

"You watch your attitude, young lady," Murray shot back, pointing his gavel at her.

"I will, Your Honor."

After a few seconds Murray glanced at the jury and rolled his eyes upward with a slight shake of his head.

Katherine immediately saw the opening and attacked. "Did Your Honor wish to say something else to me?"

"What? No. Get on with your questions, Mr. Spencer."

"Because I noticed you just rolled your eyes at the jury," she went on. "That's the fourth time you've done it."

Murray's face darkened. "The witness will confine her comments to counsel's questions and *only* to those questions. Do I make myself clear?"

"Of course, Your Honor."

"My job is to see this trial is conducted in a fair and impartial manner. I hope you are not trying to imply this court is in any way biased."

"Well, you certainly have the right to hope, Judge."

Murray's gavel hit the bench so hard, it caused everyone in the court to jump. "You are in contempt, Ms. Adams, and I will deal with you once the trial is over. Mr. Spencer, I told you to get on with your questions."

Spencer's jaw had dropped slightly as he followed the exchange. Provoking a judge is never something any lawyer does lightly and he was taken aback by Katherine's comments.

THE next morning the lead story on page two of the *Times* read:

Blendel Trial—Attorney Won't Buckle Under to Judge's Antics.

A similar piece ran on ABC television that night.

SIXTY-THREE

DELANEY

THAT evening in bed I put my arm around Katherine's shoulders and pulled her closer. "That was a pretty risky thing you did in court today. He could put you in jail."

"We'll see," she mumbled, rubbing her face on my chest.

"The next time you get the urge to do that, let me know first, huh?"

"Mmm."

"I know you didn't like Murray's behavior, but I don't want you putting yourself at risk."

Katherine lifted her head and an expression I'd never seen before appeared on her face. "I don't like bullies and I don't like losing," she said slowly, emphasizing each word. "He won't pull that garbage again, because everyone in court will be watching for it, particularly the reporters.

"Speaking of which, I forgot to tell you I mentioned Murray's campaign contribution from the Twin Tree corporation to Bonnie Cochran before we left. She's saving it for a follow-up story on corrupt judges. It's going to be called, 'Judges for Sale.'"

I started laughing and kissed her on the forehead. "You are a woman of many talents, Ms. Adams."

"Want to see some others?"

WE had to push our way through the crowd just to get into court the next morning. Davis Murray came in stone-faced. He took the bench without his usual good morning greeting to everyone and merely said, "Proceed, Mr. Spencer." My guess was that he had read the *Times* story.

Katherine was already back on the stand. Spencer got up and automatically buttoned his suit jacket again.

"Ms. Adams, during your direct examination yesterday you testi-fied the man you saw in your courtyard was the same person who al-legedly pursued you, Ms. Pechorin, and Ms. O'Connor into a Florida swamp."

"He was, except I don't recall using the word *allegedly*."

Spencer ignored that. "And do you recall my asking how you could swear that he was working for Warren Blendel? I assume he didn't make such an admission to you."

"No, he didn't say anything like that."

"Then perhaps you'll enlighten us."

"I'd be glad to. The man's name was Joshua Silver, and he was wanted for questioning in regard to murders in five different coun-tries."

"You have personal knowledge of that, do you?" Spencer snapped, taking a step toward her.

"No, I'm relying on what Phillip Thurman told me," Katherine said evenly. "We can call him back to verify it if you like."

I spared a quick glance at the judge, expecting him to issue a warn-ing, but none was forthcoming. Spencer also paused, until he realized that Murray wasn't going to say anything.

"Thank you for your advice, ma'am. I'll bear it in mind if we de-cide to recall Agent Thurman."

Katherine inclined her head to him by way of a response.

"So . . . what you're telling us is that Agent Phillip Thurman is your source of information about the link to Warren Blendel. The same Agent Thurman who was demoted and kicked out of the bu-reau's office in New York? Phillip Thurman who has held a grudge against Warren Blendel for years? That's who you're relying on?"

By all rights, Jimmy d'Taglia should have objected at this point but he didn't. Instead, he leaned over and whispered in my ear. "Here it comes."

"Actually, no," Katherine said. "When Mr. Silver died he had a cell phone on him—"

Spencer interrupted her in his most sarcastic tone. "Yes, yes, yes, registered no doubt to Warren Blendel, right?"

"I really don't know who it's registered to, Mr. Spencer. But I do know the last two calls that were placed from it. They were in the phone records your office provided us. I have them right here: One was to Hans Schiller, the gentleman who was seated alongside Mrs. Blendel the other day. The other was to Twin Tree's corporate office here in New York."

It took Judge Murray four minutes to restore order, and that was only after he threatened to clear the court. Some people on the jury might have been listening to his instruction about disregarding Katherine's last answer, though I very much doubted it. Spencer's case had just received a body blow from a five-foot-eight, 125-pound woman.

Consistent with everything I'd heard about him over the years, Joe Spencer was unwilling to concede the battle without a fight. He moved to strike the last part of Katherine's answer and Murray granted it.

"Very good, Ms. Adams, it looks like you managed to get in some self-serving testimony after all. I suppose the jury can determine how much credibility it deserves. Before we were interrupted, I asked if your testimony was based on the information Phillip Thurman provided you. Was that your entire answer?"

Katherine turned toward Warren Blendel and looked directly at him. "Actually, it wasn't. Far from it, as a matter of fact."

Spencer was too much of a pro to fall into the same trap again. With a dismissive gesture he told the judge, "Nothing more can be gained from this witness, Your Honor. I have no further questions."

"Quite so," Murray responded. "The witness is excused."

"Uh . . . Your Honor," Jimmy said, rising to his feet. "I'd like to ask another question or two if I may."

"Mr. d'Taglia, I will not allow you to cover the same ground again. Nor will I let you to go into any matters that weren't raised during your direct."

"I understand. All I want to do is to clarify Ms. Adams's last response, particularly since Mr. Spencer just opened the door when he asked if her knowledge is based exclusively on facts that Mr. Thurman provided her."

The judge started to speak, but Jimmy went on before he could. "I have some cases directly on point if the court would care to see them."

"I'm familiar with the law, young man," Murray answered. "Proceed."

Jimmy turned to Katherine. "Now, Ms. Adams, in drafting the complaint for this case, did you acquire your knowledge of the facts from any source *other* than Agent Thurman?"

"I did, Mr. d'Taglia."

Jimmy folded his arms across his chest and sat on the edge of the plaintiffs' table. "I'm just dying to hear this. Tell us about it."

"When I began talking to Sarah O'Connor I was struck by the coincidence of her uncle coming up with a scholarship to Emory University immediately after she took the file from the U.S. Attorney's office. So I began making some inquiries.

"I found this was the first year the Hoch-Halpern Endowment, as the scholarship is called, has been offered. A few weeks ago I tried calling them to get some information on their organization. It turns out all they have is an answering service in Rego Park.

"While John—Mr. Delaney, that is, was in Philadelphia, I took a cab ride to their place of business and spoke with the office manager. I learned the monthly statements for phone service and their mailbox are addressed to a company called Wickersham Realty. When I couldn't find a listing for Wickersham in the phone book, I checked with the Secretary of State's office. According to their records, the company was incorporated about seven months ago—one week after Sarah told her uncle, Nick O'Connor, about the file.

"Interestingly, the lawyer who formed the company also serves as their registered agent. His name is Jerry Barnwell. Mr. Barnwell's other job is corporate counsel to Warren Blendel's company, the Twin Tree Corporation."

I don't know whether Joe Spencer was prepared for this or not, but he immediately moved for an adjournment to confer with his client and got it.

As soon as the courtroom emptied, I stepped out to get a drink of water, then made my way to the men's room and splashed some cold water on my face. Mike Franklin was there. He had been in court since we began that morning.

He said, "That was pretty good stuff a while ago. Your lady's a real fireball."

I smiled and nodded in agreement as we started walking. "She is that."

"So, what did Sal the Tailor want?"

"Who?"

"Salvatore Scarsa. I saw you guys talking together in the hallway yesterday, but I didn't want to interrupt."

"I didn't catch his name. I thought he was just an interested spectator."

"I'll just bet ol' Sal is interested. About as much as his buddy. That's the man sitting next to him, Carmine Mylonas. They're in the same business as Blendel. What Carmine doesn't control, the Tailor does; Carmine has most of the south side. As a matter of fact, Frank told me your old man knew Scarsa. They grew up together."

"You're kidding."

"Ask him yourself. I stopped by the hospital and saw your sister this morning. She looks like she's doing a little better."

"Yeah, Katherine and I were there earlier. Anything on who attacked her?"

Mike shook his head. "Nothing yet. But I did hear some interesting stuff on Blendel."

"In connection with Lissa?"

"No, about his health. Do you remember in the beginning of the trial when Spencer told the jury he was a sick man?"

"Sure, they're calling two witnesses to testify that he has panic attacks, which I totally don't get. How can he run an operation that size if he's so damn ill?"

Mike pulled me off to one side and lowered his voice. "The word on the street is the other bosses aren't sure what to do. I'm guessing that's why Carmine and Sal are camped out at the back of the court. They smell an opportunity, but are scared to get off the dime. Apparently with Blendel you never know if you're dealing with the real thing or walking into a trap. He's a genius at putting up smoke screens. If they had proof that he was really incapacitated, I'm told they'd move on him."

"Interesting," I said. "And his doctors' testimony won't be enough?"

Mike shrugged. "He could have bought them for the trial."

"What about . . ."

My voice trailed off when I noticed a man leaning against the wall, his arms folded across his chest. It was Hans Schiller. There was a vague Cheshire cat smile on his face. He made an exaggerated bow with his head as we approached.

"Herr Professor, how is your dear sister? I heard she was recently taken ill. You have my deepest sympathies."

I started to reply but Mike grabbed me under the arm and pulled me along. "Let's keep going, buddy."

"Perhaps you would like one of our pens," Schiller called after us, removing one from his pocket. "They don't write very well, but they are most useful for other things."

When I turned around to look at him, he tapped the pen point with his finger and his smile broadened.

In that instant I knew without question Hans Schiller was the man who had attacked Lissa. Something inside me snapped. I spun around and hit him with a looping right hook that knocked him backwards a half step. Mike grabbed my jacket to restrain me. A second later Jimmy was there, throwing his arms around my shoulders. Flash units went off in the hall and someone screamed. Oddly, Schiller made no move made to respond. Instead, he simply raised the back of his hand to his lower lip and slowly wiped the blood away. The smile never left his face.

A red haze filled my vision and I tried to go after him again. This time, Mike and Jimmy weren't having it. They forced me against the opposite wall.

"Knock it off," Mike said between clenched teeth. "This isn't the place. If he's the prick who hurt your sister, we'll nail him. I swear it."

"Are you out of your mind?" Jimmy hissed, still holding me. "We're in the middle of a goddamn courthouse. You'll get disbarred."

"What the hell's going on here?" Joe Spencer asked, coming down the hall. "You just attacked one of my witnesses, Delaney."

Two police officers were trailing right behind him.

"Officers," Schiller said. "I wish to press criminal charges. This man has attacked me without provocation."

"I'm gonna fuckin' kill you!" I yelled, lunging at Schiller again. With the help of the uniforms, Mike and Jimmy pinned me against the wall.

"Goddamnit John, get a hold of yourself," Jimmy said in my ear. "This is exactly what they want. You'll only cause a mistrial. You either stop right now or I swear to God I'm withdrawing from the case." He grabbed the sides of my face to get my attention. "I'm telling you man, knock it off *now*."

A long moment passed before I was able to gain control of my emotions. People were still shouting and flash units were still going off. When I finally calmed down, Mike relaxed his hold on me and motioned for the officers to leave. Jimmy let go as well.

Joe Spencer ushered Schiller back into the courtroom, saying something about informing the court of my actions. Before the door closed he looked at me over his shoulder and shook his head. I didn't catch rest of his words, nor do I remember when Katherine arrived on the scene, but I was glad she was there. The enormity of what I had done was just beginning to dawn on me.

"Are you all right?" Katherine asked, brushing the hair off my forehead.

I nodded and tucked my tie back into my jacket as the crowd began to disperse. "Yeah."

"What in the world happened?" she asked.

"Schiller was the one who attacked Lissa."

Katherine blinked and looked at Jimmy, then Mike, for an explanation.

"I only came in at the tail end," Jimmy said.

Mike turned his palms up. "Schiller asked how his sister was doing and John went nuts."

"That's *not* all of it," I said angrily. "The son of a bitch offered me a pen and said they were useful for other things besides writing. Don't you get it? That's where Lissa's puncture wounds came from. I took one look at his face and knew it was him."

Katherine started to respond, but the courtroom door opened and the bailiff poked his head out.

"Judge Murray wants all lawyers in his chambers immediately."

"Ah, shit," Jimmy muttered under his breath.

"Don't say anything," Katherine whispered as we walked down the aisle. "Let us handle this."

Sal the Tailor and his friend Carmine were back in their places at the rear of the courtroom. Sal tracked me with his eyes as we passed.

Joe Spencer and his assistants were waiting for us outside the judge's chambers along with Murray's secretary. As soon as she saw us, she ushered everyone inside. I noticed the court reporter was also present.

"Mr. Delaney, it's been reported to me that you attacked one of Mr. Spencer's witnesses in the hallway outside this court."

I opened my mouth to reply but he held up a hand to cut me off. "You can save whatever you have to say for the District Attorney and the State Bar. I can't begin to count the number of rules you've violated, not to mention criminal laws.

"This meeting is to inform you I am forwarding this matter to the Ethics Committee with my strong recommendation that you be barred from the practice of law in this state. I find your conduct reprehensible and I want you to know I'm considering a mistrial."

I stood there and took it because I had to.

"Your Honor," Katherine said, "there's no reason to declare a mistrial. I don't know who started the fight, but I do know Mr. Delaney, and I think as an officer of the court he should be given the benefit of the doubt. It seems to me we're jumping the gun and convicting him before he's had a trial. I can assure you if that ever occurs, we'll contest any charges vigorously."

"Perhaps if Your Honor would care to speak with the victim," Joe Spencer cut in.

"*Victim?*" Jimmy said. "I saw the other man outside and he's a full head taller than Professor Delaney and maybe fifty pounds heavier. If anything, Mr. Delaney is the victim here."

"*He attacked my witness,*" Spencer said, indignantly.

"Yeah, the same witness who was identified as orchestrating the death of William Delaney, a New York City police officer," Jimmy replied. "Not a great recommendation, Counselor."

"*This is horseshit,*" Spencer yelled, pointing at the door. "There are a half dozen people outside who'll testify that Delaney attacked Hans Schiller."

"Your Honor," Katherine said, "if charges *are* brought we'll respond to them at the proper place and time. Nothing can be accomplished here. The jury was sequestered, so they have no idea what happened. As long as that remains the case I see no reason to declare a mistrial. It would result in tremendous cost to the parties as well as to the city, *plus* the press would have a field day with such a ruling—particularly if it turns out there was no foundation to it."

The last remark finally got through. Murray laced his fingers together and rested his chin on them. Several seconds passed before he nodded. I noticed a copy of the *Times* with Bonnie Cochran's article sitting on the corner of his desk.

"She has a point, Joe," he said to Spencer. "Do you have any evidence the jury was prejudiced by this incident?"

"No," Spencer said, "but—"

"All right, I am going to refer this matter to the District Attorney and the Bar Association as I've told you. It'll be their call if they want to pursue it. I'll reserve my decision about the mistrial until I've had more time to consider it. Now let's get back out there and finish this case, people."

SIXTY-FOUR

DELANEY

M Y hands were shaking when I called Warren Blendel to the stand. I was fully aware I'd done a great deal of harm to our case, particularly with the press, who had been favorable to us up until that point. I saw it in their faces. I was disgusted with myself and still upset by what happened.

Rather than wait for Spencer's direct examination, I made an impulse decision to take Blendel on cross first. It was a risky move because Spencer would have the last word. I was prepared to deal with that.

For six months I'd waited for this moment, practicing my questions over and over again. It made no difference now. My heart was thumping so hard I was sure the nearest juror could hear it. This was something I had to do. It was the promise I made my father that day in the cemetery. I owed him that much. I owed Lissa and my family that much.

Immaculately dressed in a dark blue suit, white shirt, and a conservative maroon tie, Warren Blendel rose and took the stand. He was to be was our last witness.

I began, "Mr. Blendel, fifteen years ago you were the president and chief executive officer of Twin Tree Corporation, weren't you?"

"Yes, I was."

"According to what your lawyer has told us, at some point in the past you turned those responsibilities over to your wife, didn't you?"

"I did. Though I remained chairman emeritus, I've had no involvement with Twin Tree for many years. Linda—my wife—ran the company."

"Are you familiar with a man named Hans Schiller?"

"Yes, I know Mr. Schiller. He reported directly to my wife and was head of security for several of our companies."

I caught Blendel's use of the past tense and an uneasy feeling began to form in the pit of my stomach. It was like going up the first hill on a roller coaster. You know you're about to take the plunge, but you don't know how bad it will be.

"You said 'ran,' Mr. Blendel. Are you telling us your wife no longer runs the company, or was that just a slip of the tongue?"

Blendel looked down at his hands for several moments and smiled sadly. "I've learned a great many things since this trial began, Mr. Delaney. And by the way, I'm terribly sorry about your father's death. I know what it's like to lose a parent that way.

"One of the things I learned was that Mr. Schiller and my wife have been having an affair for the past several years. As a result, I filed for divorce two days ago and moved out of my home."

Pandemonium ensued.

Linda Blendel rose from her seat in the audience, her mouth open in shock. The sketch artists dove for their pads, scrambling to get a likeness of her, while the judge banged his gavel in an attempt to restore order to the courtroom.

This was not what I expected. I wanted to look at Katherine and Jimmy to gauge their reactions, but I knew that would have been interpreted as a sign of uncertainty on my part.

Once order was reestablished, Judge Murray asked, "Was the witness finished with his answer?"

"No, I wasn't," Blendel replied. "I'd like to respond to Mr. Delaney's question fully.

"As a result of an audit we recently conducted, I came to learn that vast sums of money have been funneled out of Twin Tree and placed in German bank accounts in the names of both Mr. Schiller and my wife. As a result, our board met in emergency session and voted unanimously to remove Linda from any further association with the company. Mr. Schiller, of course, was fired.

"I bear full responsibility for these things, but I hope and pray our stockholders will understand that my health has prevented me from devoting the time to the business I might have wished."

Linda Blendel turned on her heel and left the courtroom.

The roller-coaster sensation gripped me once again, only this time it was more like vertigo. I began to feel the case slipping away. When you're a trial lawyer conducting a cross-exam, you're out there all by yourself, as much exposed as the witness on the stand. There's nowhere to hide.

Despite my best efforts to nail Blendel, he went on to explain how he'd been struck down by a panic disorder years earlier and how this had all but destroyed his life. He told the jury about his medications and how he had trusted the people closest to him to carry on his work—people he believed were friends and family, and how he had been betrayed.

This I expected. Blendel was trying to shift blame and suspicion away from him and hide behind the panic attacks. Katherine, Jimmy, and I had already examined his medical records and we knew we couldn't out-medicine the medicine men on this subject.

Through my questions, I pointed out that Blendel still attended charity functions and engaged in a wide variety of other activities. My only hope was that the jury would see though the charade. But by time I sat down I realized I had done much of Joe Spencer's work for him. Katherine placed a comforting hand on my forearm. Jimmy wouldn't meet my eye and I generally felt like shit.

BLENDEL'S experts confirmed the story about his attacks. Both of them told the jury they considered him completely debilitated. Harlan Skinner, a doctor with a long list of credentials and publications to his credit, explained that panic attacks could masquerade as heart attacks and were often brought on by stress. He said he had been Blendel's physician for over twenty years and had done numerous tests to verify that they were real.

Jimmy got him to admit there were few physical ways to verify the existence of a panic attack, and that doctors generally relied on what their patients told them. During his testimony I cast a glance at the jury and my feeling of impending doom increased.

The case ended at around two o'clock in the afternoon and the jury was sent out to deliberate. Davis Murray announced the court would be in recess and left the bench without a word. I had no doubt the newspaper articles and television reports of his conduct throughout the trial had a great deal to do with that.

Except for the lawyers, nearly everyone filed out of the court-room, including Warren Blendel. I noticed that he made eye contact with the two men who remained seated in the last row on his way out. A flicker of recognition passed between them, but they didn't acknowledge each other. Sarah and Jenny excused themselves and said they would be in the cafeteria if we needed them. When Joe Spencer finished putting his papers into a battered old trial briefcase, he came over to shake hands.

"That was a fine job you did on closing," he said to Jimmy. "If you ever decide to relocate, give me a call. We can use someone like you in our firm."

"I'm happy where I am," Jimmy told him. "The boss is a little tough now and then, but you learn a hell of a lot." He threw a quick smile in Katherine's direction and gave her forearm an affectionate squeeze.

Spencer nodded. "It's a shame we couldn't get it on together," he said to Katherine. "I've heard a lot of good things about you from your colleagues in Atlanta. They say you're a helluva trial lawyer."

Katherine returned a cool smile. "I'll have to remember to thank them." My girlfriend never been quick to forgive or forget.

And finally he turned to me. "You did a nice job, too, Counselor, notwithstanding the boxing match outside. Trial work is a little different from teaching in a classroom, isn't it?"

"Yes, it is."

"Any bets on how long the jury will be out?" Spencer asked.

I replied, "No idea. I haven't guessed right once since I started practicing law."

"Me either. You know we could cut this matter short if you people are willing to entertain a settlement offer."

"I appreciate that," I said. "Why don't we just wait and see what happens?"

"I don't get it. You've had your day in court now. Win, lose or draw, Blendel's life will never be the same again. What are you looking for—a pound of flesh?"

When Katherine and I didn't answer, he got the message. "Okay, it's personal; I understand that. But you haven't got this case locked up by a long shot, at least not in my view. I'm giving you an honorable way out. If you settle, you both come away with enough money to retire on. You really need to look at this objectively."

I asked Spencer, "Could you do that if it was your father?"

He held my gaze for a long moment. "No . . . I don't suppose I could. I'll be in the lawyer's conference room if the jury comes back."

The jury didn't come back in the first hour nor did they come back in the second. Time dragged on as the end of their third hour of deliberations approached. At five o'clock the judge returned to the bench and told us he would wait another half hour and then dismiss everyone for dinner if they weren't close to a decision. His Honor was in the process of saying we'd pick up the following day when the light above the jury room went on.

Almost immediately, the activity level in the court seemed to increase. Word spread into the hallway and down the corridors as people hustled back to their seats. Murray motioned to the bailiff and asked him to see what the jury wanted. The bailiff knocked on the door and then disappeared inside the room. He returned a minute later and gave a small nod toward the bench, indicating that a decision had been reached.

Katherine straightened my tie as they filed back in. Over the years I've heard colleagues say if the jurors look at you it's a good sign. Not one of them glanced in my direction and I could read absolutely nothing in their faces.

"Ladies and gentlemen, have you reached a verdict?" Judge Murray asked.

A heavyset balding fellow at the end of the second row stood up. I recalled he was a firefighter.

"We have, Your Honor."

"Very well. Have you written it down on the form I gave you?"

"Yes, sir," he said, holding up a piece of paper.

"Very good. Please hand your verdict to the bailiff."

The bailiff took the paper and brought it to the judge, who read it while everyone waited. For nearly a minute the only sound in the courtroom was the ticking of a large clock over the entrance. At some point during the process Murray's eyebrows lifted and he looked directly at the foreman, who was still standing. After an imperceptible shake of his head, Murray handed the paper back to the bailiff, who returned it to the man.

"The verdict appears to be in proper form," the judge announced. "If the foreman will please read it to the court."

We all held our breath.

"We the jury, find in favor of defendant, Warren Blendel as to counts one through eight."

I couldn't believe what I'd just heard. There were gasps from all around the court. Murray's gavel pounded to restore order as I sat there in shock. When Katherine's grip on my forearm abruptly tightened I realized that the foreman was still standing. Apparently he had more to say.

"If there is one more outburst like that," Murray warned, "I'll have this room cleared." He gestured for the foreman to continue.

"The rest of these aren't exactly in order, Judge."

"That'll be fine, just read your verdict to the court."

"Okay, uh . . . for Count Ten, Jennifer Pechorin's claim for the wrongful death of her brother Andre Rostov, as representative of his estate, we find in favor of the plaintiff and against defendant Twin Tree Corporation in the amount of twenty million dollars.

"As to Counts Six, Seven, Eight, and Nine . . . Sarah O'Connor's claims of false imprisonment, assault, battery, and intentional infliction of emotional distress, we find in favor of the plaintiff and against Twin Tree Corporation in the amount of one hundred thousand dollars in compensatory damages and five million dollars in punitive damages.

"As to Counts Two, Three, Four, and Five, Katherine Adams's claims of assault, battery, criminal trespass and intentional infliction of emotional distress, we find in favor of the plaintiff and against Twin Tree Corporation in the amount of fifty thousand dollars in compensatory damages and one million dollars in punitive damages.

"As to Count One, the claim of John Delaney as representative of the Estate of William T. Delaney, for his father's wrongful death, we find in favor of the plaintiff and against the defendant Twin Tree Corporation in the amount of twenty million dollars in compensatory damages."

People began applauding. And with a rap of judge's gavel and a curt, "Case dismissed," it was over.

A LOT of the details about that day have become muddled in my mind, but one still stands out clearly. When the dust settled, Warren Blendel showed no reaction to the verdict whatsoever. He simply stood up, straightened his tie, and turned to leave. Before he did, however, he looked directly at me. The barest hint of a smile touched the corners of his mouth, and then he winked.

SIXTY-FIVE

DELANEY

A COLD wind blew down the street, whipping trash and debris around in circles. Earlier that day it had started snowing. Large flakes stuck to the sidewalks covering the grime in the vast expanse of concrete that was the Hunts Point Terminal Market. Tractor trailers came and went during the daytime, but their loads were now stacked in rows for the night, safe behind steel fences and razor wire. On the opposite side of the street from where I was standing was an old brick building. Behind it the black waters of the Bronx River flowed swiftly past the market into Flushing Bay. A series of railroad tracks ran along the east end of the terminal. Their side spurs jutted off and ended at warehouses where the cars were offloaded. Each spur now was lined with boxcars and flatbeds stacked high with crates. Elsewhere on the yard were four giant cranes holding metal cargo containers suspended high above the ground. In the morning the containers would be loaded onto barges and sent downriver.

From the shadows of a doorway fifty yards from Warren Blendel's office I pulled my coat tighter shutting out the chill. I'd been there for over two hours and my toes were numb. In my pocket was a Smith & Wesson .38 revolver that once belonged to my father. My fingers touched its cold metal surface.

The trial had been over for three days and most of the excitement had died down. I slept very little during this time. There was an empty feeling in my stomach that wouldn't go away. I fielded the reporters' questions over the phone as best I could and agreed to an interview with Bonnie Cochran later that week. For the most part Jimmy continued to act as our spokesman, letting Katherine and me slip away from the commotion unnoticed. The kid had fought his heart out for us.

For the first time since we knew each other, Katherine and I had a major argument. And that's saying it mildly. She wanted an end to the nightmare and to put it behind us. I wasn't ready. Earlier that day while getting dressed, I caught a glimpse of myself in the mirror. There were dark circles under my eyes. I stared at my face for a long time as doubt began to creep in again. I'd made a promise to my father. The question now was did I have the guts to keep it?

I moved backwards a half step as a stretch limo crept silently down the street. It stopped in front of Blendel's office. He and another man got out and went inside. The lights came on a second later. I waited a few more minutes before I left the doorway and walked to the end of the block. The terminal's yard was sealed off from the public by a fifteen-foot-high chain-link fence. Earlier that night, I examined the lock at the employee's entrance. It took me less than a minute to open it.

The rear of Blendel's building was about seventy yards away. It was framed by two parallel lines of railroad spurs that formed a corridor leading directly up to it. What I had to do would be done quickly and quietly. Using the cars for cover I started toward Blendel's door, my hand on the gun.

The first blow snapped my head back, knocking me into the side of a boxcar. For a moment I didn't know what had hit me.

"Where are you going, *Herr Professor*?" Schiller asked as he climbed down off a flatbed. "You are a long way from your school."

Without warning his leg lashed out and caught me squarely in the middle of my back, knocking the wind out of my lungs. He grabbed my shoulder, spun me around, and backhanded me across the face. Colored lights exploded in my head.

"You are a brave man to come all by yourself. Brave, but stupid— very stupid." He drove his fist into my stomach and I doubled over. "No funny comments this time? Perhaps the cat has taken your tongue?"

"The cat's *got* your tongue, asshole," I gasped. I launched myself at his legs in an attempt to tackle him to the ground, but it felt like grabbing a pair of tree trunks.

Schiller's response was to pick me up bodily and fling me into the door of another boxcar. The son of a bitch was as strong as an ox. I bounced off it trying to get to my feet. Instinctively, I blocked a punch he aimed at my head, but never saw his right leg coming. The edge of his shoe caught me alongside my jaw and my mouth filled with blood.

"I watch you out there for hours, little man," Schiller said, spreading his arms wide. "And you don't go away."

Another punch to the side of my head drove me to the ground. In desperation, I tried to crawl under the nearest boxcar to buy myself some time, but he grabbed my ankle and pulled me back. Once again I found myself flying through the air like a rag doll. I hit the ground hard.

Schiller walked toward me in no particular hurry as I struggled to get my father's gun free. I had my hand on it for all of a second before he kicked it away. The gun landed in the snow with a thud. He made no effort to get it.

"Professor, you have caused me a great deal of trouble. That is about to end. As you Americans say, payback is rich."

"A bitch—payback is a bitch, shithead."

I tried getting to my feet, but only made it halfway. This time another blow caught me in the side, probably breaking my ribs again. All I could do was roll over weakly. That's when I saw a rusty screwdriver someone had left lying alongside the tracks. My fingers closed around the handle.

Schiller stuck out his lower lip and nodded. "Payback is a bitch, yah. I will remember that."

When he reached down to grab the front of my coat, I struck out with all the strength I had left. A howl of pain exploded from him as the blade buried itself in his upper thigh. Before he could recover, I rolled under the boxcar and crawled to the opposite side of the tracks. One look told me my situation had gone from bad to worse. All I had done was to corner myself in a section of the yard surrounded by crates on three sides. The only way out was along an eight-foot opening at the back and that was partially blocked by a forklift. I looked for anything to defend myself with and spotted a heavy steel chain. No good either—it was attached to an iron ring-bolt in the ground. The other end ran up at an angle to the nearest crane, where a thirty-foot-long metal container hung suspended above the ground.

Slowly, painfully, I got to my feet and staggered toward the forklift. One eye was nearly shut and the middle of my back felt like a truck had hit me. I made it perhaps twenty feet and stopped as Hans Schiller emerged from under the next boxcar, blocking my means of escape. The side of his leg was red with blood and he was holding the screwdriver.

"So, Professor, now we end it, yah? I'm going to beat you to death with my bare hands." He started limping toward me.

"I always heard you Interpol pricks were tough—except for the Germans. I never met one of you Nazi bastards who was worth shit when the chips were down."

A small tic appeared under his left eye, but he didn't reply. I retreated several steps, putting some distance between us and backed into a stack of crates. The only way out was through Schiller. The moment he changed his grip on the screwdriver, I knew he was going to bring it down overhand rather than use it as a thrusting weapon.

This was my chance.

As Schiller raised his arm I launched myself off the crate at him, coming in under his blow. I landed two punches to his bad leg. They produced a curse in German I didn't understand. My uppercut caught him on the chin and he grunted. A hard right hand to the base of his earlobe caused him to drop the screwdriver.

A knee to my stomach drove me backwards several feet. All I had done was piss him off. He glanced around for another weapon. Resting against one of the crates was a five-foot-long steel pry bar. We both went for it at the same time, only I got there first.

I swung backwards without looking and connected with his upper arm, spinning him sideways. The next blow landed across the flat of his back. A blind rage seized me and I swung the bar at him again and again, battering him to the ground. The last time he rose on all fours, I hit him as hard as I could and he stayed down. I was barely able to stand myself.

For some bizarre reason, Schiller started laughing. Blood foamed at the corners of his mouth.

"It was business, nothing more," he rasped.

I had to lean against the pry bar to keep from falling. "Business. Tell me something, Hans. Was all that bullshit in court about Blendel's panic attacks part of his plan?"

He coughed up some blood before he answered. "Herr Blendel is a clever man—more clever than I gave him credit for. The attacks may have been real once. Now? Who knows? Either way it makes no difference. You will never touch him."

"We'll see about that."

I turned and started walking down the corridor of boxcars.

"You cannot win, Delaney," he called out. "It's over. What will you do? Arrest us all by yourself?"

"No . . . I'm not going to arrest you."

The release mechanism holding the cargo container was hanging from a post. My pry bar came around in an arc and hit the green button squarely. Chain shot through the crane's metal frame gaining speed with every foot as the container started to fall. Schiller realized what was happening too late. His scream stopped abruptly when the container landed on top of him.

FIVE men were waiting at the back door to Blendel's office. Three of them I didn't know; two were the same ones who had watched the trial from the back of the courtroom. Through the open door leading to the inner room I could see Warren Blendel seated at his desk. There were two more men with shotguns standing on either side of him. It might have been the fluorescent lights but Blendel seemed pale in spite of his tan.

Sal the Tailor looked me up and down shook his head. "Jesus, Delaney, you look like shit."

"Thank you for noticing."

He opened his mouth to say something but changed his mind. Shaking his head, he handed my briefcase back to me. Warren Blendel's medical reports were still inside it.

"Interesting reading," he said. "This may be a little late, but I'm sorry about your old man. He was one tough son of a bitch, but he was a decent guy. You always knew where you stood with him. Pass my condolences along to your mother, okay?"

I nodded to him and glanced at the other two men. Neither displayed any reaction. It didn't matter. I looked past them at Warren Blendel and caught his eye. We held each other's gaze for several seconds. Then I winked and turned away.

SIXTY-SIX

DELANEY

THE snow was coming down heavily by the time I reached the car. I must have looked pretty bad because Katherine gasped as soon as I opened the door. She immediately pulled me to her and hugged me.

"Oh my God, John, are you—"

"I'm okay. It's over."

She started the engine. "I'm taking you to a doctor."

I put my hand over hers before she could put the car in gear. "I'm okay, honey. I swear."

"But—"

"All I need is to be home in bed with you." I glanced at my face in the passenger mirror and added, "After a hot shower."

Katherine's look was worried, but she didn't argue further. We pulled into the street. A white layer of snow covered the asphalt and old cobblestones. Out on the river I could see a barge creeping slowly along. Someone had decorated it with a few strands of colored Christmas lights. On the far bank in the borough of Queens were cookie cutter rows of small private homes. I remembered playing on those streets with my friends when we were growing up. Funny how some memories never leave you. It seemed like a thousand years ago now.

I rested my head against the window and Katherine held my hand as she drove. Neither of us spoke or needed to. The snow continued to fall, shutting out the ugliness of our surroundings. Somehow all that white made the world seem fresh. I wasn't sure if it snowed in Atlanta.

I STOPPED at a newsstand in LaGuardia Airport and picked up a copy of the *Times*. Halfway down the front page was a story by Bonnie Cochran. I read it quickly and showed it to Katherine. She studied it for a moment then lifted her shoulders slightly and selected a copy of *Architectural Digest* from the magazine rack. The headline read:

Warren Blendel Found Shot to Death

Police had little comment about the incident other than the killing was probably gang related.

Blendel's name had recently been tied to several organized crime families in the New York area. In a spectacular trial held recently, one of his companies, Twin Tree Corporation, was found guilty of causing the deaths of William T. Delaney, a New York police detective, and Andre Rostov, a medical student who resided in Atlanta, Georgia.

Twin Tree filed for bankruptcy yesterday in federal court. Officers of the company could not be reached for comment. Their attorney said a statement would be forthcoming later in the week.

A source at the FBI, speaking to this reporter under a guarantee of anonymity, speculated that after news of Blendel's panic attacks leaked out, his opponents thought the time was ripe for them to move in on him.

"There's really not much honor among thieves," the source said.

Jimmy d'Taglia was waiting for us at the gate. "Did you hear the news about Blendel?" he asked me.

"Sure did."

"Too bad. He was such an upstanding guy. It didn't take long for the wolves to smell blood, did it?"

"Nope."

"You understand with the corporation filing bankruptcy we probably won't get a cent from the judgment."

Katherine sighed, "Oh, well. Easy come, easy go."

The crease between Jimmy's eyebrows deepened as he looked from her to me. "By any chance, did either of you happen to come across those missing medical records on Blendel? I haven't been able to find them."

"I imagine they'll turn up," Katherine said. "I wouldn't worry about it, Jimmy."

I lifted my shoulders in an I-don't-know gesture.

Several seconds passed before a degree of understanding crept over his face and he began to nod slowly. "Right," he said, drawing out the word.

"Do you think you're going to like teaching law in Atlanta, John?"

I glanced at Katherine and got one of her smiles. It went straight to my heart as it always did. There was still my sister and mother to consider, and leaving was out of the question, at least for the time being. Perhaps reading my thoughts, Katherine smiled to herself and exhaled a long breath; then she turned to look out the window at a plane that was slowly rolling up to the gate. I smiled back at her, but I don't think she saw it.